Acclaim for Elin Hild ✄

The Castaways

"*The Castaways* is a sensitive portrayal of the complexities of friendship. Hilderbrand's characters illustrate the alliances, insecurities, and joys that color adult relationships. . . . When it's done well, as it is here, reading about other people's problems is ever so satisfying."　　　　　—Kristi Lanier, *Washington Post*

"Hilderbrand captivates with a racy narrative, topical references, and characters who are both familiar and memorable."
　　　　　　　　　　　　　　　　—Joanna Powell, *People*

"Hilderbrand's stories really capture island life and all the intrigue that occurs when people live so closely together, surrounded by water. And her characters are so real—you will love them, curse them, but most important, recognize them."
　　　　　　　　　—Caroline Campion, Glamour.com

"Hilderbrand has a master's touch at characterization, making the novel's players seem so familiar that the revelation of their secrets is irresistible. Great fun, and with a few poignant moments, too."
　　　　　　　　　　　　　　　　　—*Kirkus Reviews*

"Hilderbrand's writing is smart and engaging, and locals will love the authentic Nantucket details peppered throughout."
　　　　　　　　　　　　　—Marissa Grey, *Boston Common*

"A tale of knotty relationships set against the lovely Nantucket backdrop. . . . Hilderbrand goes deep into each of the surviving Castaways' hearts, revealing old affairs and new entanglements."
　　　　　　　　　　　　　　　　　—*Publishers Weekly*

"An entertaining summer read. . . . Hilderbrand cleverly adds a layer of suspense and intrigue."
　　　　　　　　　　—Bronwyn Miller, Bookreporter.com

The
Castaways

The
Castaways

A Novel

Elin Hilderbrand

BACK BAY BOOKS

Little, Brown and Company

NEW YORK   BOSTON   LONDON

Copyright © 2009 by Elin Hilderbrand
Reading group guide copyright © 2010 by Elin Hilderbrand and Little, Brown and Company
Excerpt from *Swan Song* copyright © 2024 by Elin Hilderbrand

Back Bay Books / Little, Brown and Company
Hachette Book Group
1290 Avenue of the Americas, New York, NY 10104
littlebrown.com

Originally published in hardcover by Little, Brown and Company, July 2009
First Back Bay paperback edition, June 2010
Back Bay paperback reissue, April 2024

Back Bay Books is an imprint of Little, Brown and Company, a division of Hachette Book Group, Inc. The Back Bay Books name and logo are trademarks of Hachette Book Group, Inc.

The Hachette Speakers Bureau provides a wide range of authors for speaking events. To find out more, go to hachettespeakersbureau.com or email hachettespeakers@hbgusa.com.

Little, Brown and Company books may be purchased in bulk for business, educational, or promotional use. For information, please contact your local bookseller or the Hachette Book Group Special Markets Department at special.markets@hbgusa.com.

The author is grateful for permission to reprint the following: "Sixtieth Birthday Dinner" by Michael Ryan, which first appeared in *The New Yorker*. All rights reserved. Used by permission.

Library of Congress Cataloging-in-Publication Data
Hilderbrand, Elin.
    The castaways : a novel / Elin Hilderbrand. — 1st ed.
        p. cm.
    ISBN 9780316043892 (hc) / 9780316043908 (pb) / 9780316578547 (pb reissue)
    1. Friends—Fiction. 2. Nantucket Island (Mass.)—Fiction. 3. Family secrets—Fiction. 4. Psychological fiction. I. Title.
    PS3558.I384355C37 2009
    813'.54—dc22   2009006621

Printing 1, 2024

LSC-C

Printed in the United States of America

For my twin brother, Eric Hilderbrand,
my oldest and truest friend

The
Castaways

THE CHIEF

Because the accident occurred out on the water and not on the land that fell under his jurisdiction, it was unusual that the Chief was the first one to find out. But that was the benefit of an official position: he was a lightning rod for information, a conduit. Everything went through him first.

Dickson, his best sergeant, came into the office without his usual peppermint breeze of self-confidence. Was he sick? His skin was the color of frostbite, even though it was the first day of summer. In the seconds immediately before Dickson shuffled in, the Chief had been thinking of Greg with envy. The wind was strong; you couldn't ask for a better day to sail. Greg planned to go all the way to the Vineyard, and if he caught the gusts, he would be there in five minutes. Tess would hate it; she would be clinging to the mast or down below in the cramped head, her face as green as a bowl of pea soup.

"What's up?" the Chief said. Dickson, who had the broadest shoulders the Chief had ever seen on a human being, was hunched over. He looked like he was going to upchuck right there on the Chief's desk. He had gotten a haircut that morning, too, his summer buzz, which made his head seem square and strange, his scalp vulnerable.

"The Coast Guard just called," Dickson said. "There's been an accident on the water."

"Hmmm," the Chief said. This was the stuff of his days: accidents, crime, people fucking up in big ways and small. Mostly small, he had come to realize after seventeen years on the force.

"Chief?" Dickson said. "The MacAvoys are dead."

The Chief would have called himself impossible to faze. Even on an island as privileged and idyllic as Nantucket, he had seen it all: an eight-year-old boy shot in the face by his father's hunting rifle, a woman stabbed fifty-one times by a jealous ex-boyfriend, heroin overdoses, a Bulgarian prostitution ring, cocaine, ecstasy, moonshine, high school kids stealing diamond rings from beach cabanas, gangs, and a host of domestic disputes, including a man who broke a chair over his wife's head. As it turned out, the Chief was right, he was impossible to faze, because when Dickson said, *The MacAvoys are dead*—the MacAvoys being Tess, Andrea's cousin, and Greg, the closest thing to a brother or a best friend the Chief had ever had—the Chief coughed dryly into his hand. That was the extent of his initial reaction—one raspy cough.

"What?" the Chief said. His voice was barely a whisper. *What? What are you telling me?* His hands were cold and numb, and he stared at his phone. It was not reasonable, at this point, to panic, because there might have been a mistake. So many times there were mistakes, messages got crossed, people jumped to conclusions; so many times things weren't as bad as they seemed. He could not call Andrea until he spoke to the Coast Guard and found out exactly what had happened. It was four-thirty now. Andrea would be . . . where? At the beach still, he supposed. The kids, finally, both had summer jobs, and by Memorial Day weekend Andrea had embarked on what she called "the Summer of Me." She had been good to her word, too, doing her power walking every morning and spending the afternoons on the south shore, swimming like the Olympic Trials qualifier that she was. She was getting fit, getting tan, and exercising her mind by reading all those thought-provoking novels. She tried to talk to the Chief about the novels when they climbed into bed at night, but the Chief's life was its own novel and he didn't have room in his mind for any more characters. Just yesterday he had heard Andrea on the phone with Tess, talking about her book. He had overheard words like *ambivalence* and *disenchantment*, words he had no use for.

The Chief could not raise his eyes to Dickson's about-to-puke face. He could not call his wife and drop the bomb that would destroy the landscape of her life. Her first cousin, her closest friend—a person Andrea held dearer, possibly, than himself—Tess MacAvoy, was dead.

Maybe.

"I don't know what happened," Dickson said. The Chief couldn't look at him or the haircut so short it looked painful. "They just called to say there was an accident. And the MacAvoys are dead."

ADDISON

Addison Wheeler was having cocktails at the Galley with clients. It was a celebration, and Addison had ordered a bottle of Cristal. A purchase-and-sale agreement had just been signed for a $9.2 million waterfront home on Polpis Harbor. But even as Addison was sipping champagne, even as he was mentally spending his whopping commission, his eyes scanned the whitecaps that frosted Nantucket Sound. The restaurant had plastic siding to protect diners from the wind, which was driving out of the north. There were boats out on the water, a lot of boats, despite the six- to eight-foot seas. Was one of them Greg and Tess? They would have made it to the Vineyard by one or two, and now would be returning home. Unless, of course, they had decided to spend the night. Addison would have said he was beyond this kind of jealousy, this kind of obsession, but he was feeling both things, jealousy and a panicky obsession. If Tess and Greg stayed on the Vineyard, in a room at the Charlotte Inn, would they make love? Addison sipped his champagne. Of course they would. Today was their twelfth anniversary.

He had tried to call her no fewer than five times before she left, but she didn't answer.

There were many indications that the day was special. They were taking champagne and a picnic that Andrea had prepared for them as a gift. Greg was bringing his guitar. He had stopped by Addison's office that morning on his way to the dock.

"Your guitar?" Addison said.

"I'm a better singer than I am a sailor," Greg said. He shook his head to get his floppy bangs out of his face, a gesture that made Addison shudder. "I wrote her a song."

Wrote her a song. He would play the troubadour, try to win Tess back. After all that had happened last fall, Greg needed to make Tess trust him again.

"Good luck with that," Addison said.

The final time Addison called Tess, he left a message. *Are you going to tell him? Are you going to tell him you love me?* The question was met with electronic silence.

The maître d' caught his eye. Addison tilted his head. His clients were talking between themselves now, awkwardly, about the quality of the champagne, and about the water, the impressive wind. It would sweep Greg and Tess to the Vineyard, but they would have to come back in the teeth of it. Would they risk it? If they spent the night at the Charlotte Inn, Addison would lose his mind. The place was too romantic, with its pencil post bed, white grand piano, towel warmer, silver buckets filled with blooming roses. Addison had stayed at the Charlotte Inn with his first wife twenty years ago, and he remembered that the hotel had had the magical power to improve their relationship, for the nights they stayed there, certainly, and for several days afterward. Addison did not want Greg and Tess to stay there, because what if they experienced the same balm? He reached into his pocket to touch the heart Tess had given him on his birthday. She had cut the heart out of red felt, using child's scissors. Addison treated it like a talisman, though he was far too old and reasonable to believe in such things. He fingered the heart—now grotty and pilled and dangerously close to ripping—and wondered if Tess was thinking about him. Would she have the courage to tell Greg? Addison could hope all he wanted, but he knew the answer was no. Never in a million years.

The wife of the client couple asked Addison a question, but he didn't hear it. He was dropping the ball conversationally; he had to get back into the game, $9.2 million, and his office had the listing as well as the buyer. This was the biggest deal of the year so far. But something was going on at the front of the restaurant. Was the maître d' signaling him? He wanted Addison's attention?

"Excuse me," Addison said. He stood up, forced a smile. "I'll be right back."

Phoebe was in the parking lot. It *was* Phoebe, right? There was her car, the red Triumph Spitfire, and there was a woman Phoebe's shape and size with the shining blond hair—but her face was pink and crumpled like a dropped handkerchief, her cheeks were streaked with makeup, she was keening, hiccupping, *freaking out.* Losing her shit, here in public! This was not his wife. His wife, Phoebe Wheeler, rarely cracked a smile or shed a tear. Addison grabbed her by the shoulders. Was it really her? Yes, those eyes, blue fire. She was emotionally absent, a woman made of ice, steel, chalk, plastic, stone, rubber, clay, straw, but her eyes revealed a spark, and that was one reason Addison hung in there. He was convinced she would return to him one day.

"Phoebe?" he said.

She pushed him away. She was making noises like an animal; her beautiful hair fell into her face. She was trying to speak, but she could not form any coherent words. Well, there was one word, over and over again, like a hiss: *Tess.*

"Tess?" Addison said. Did Phoebe know, then? She'd found out? This was impossible, because no one knew and there was not one scrap of evidence that would betray them. The cell phone bill, maybe, but only if Phoebe had gone through it with a fine-tooth comb and seen the calls that Addison had made to Tess while he was visiting his daughter two weeks ago in California. Yes, that must be it. Addison's heart cracked and sizzled like an egg on the hot griddle of the parking lot. He could explain away the phone calls; he and Tess were, after all, friends. He could come up with a plausible reason for the calls.

"Honey, you have to get ahold of yourself," Addison said. He could not believe his marriage was going to explode here, now, when he was completely unprepared—but a part of him was intrigued by Phoebe's unbridled reaction. She was hysterical. He couldn't believe it. He would have said that when Phoebe found out about Tess, she would do nothing more than roll over and sneeze.

Just like that, her meds kicked in. She reined in the horses that were running away with her. She stopped crying; she sniffed. Addison had seen her crumble like this only one other time— September 11. Her twin brother, Reed, had worked on the hundred and first floor of the second tower. He had jumped.

"Tess," Phoebe said. "And Greg. Tess and Greg are dead."

JEFFREY

The third week of June had a smell, and that smell was strawberries. Strawberry season normally only lasted about five minutes, but this year the spring had been warm, punctuated by just enough steady, soaking rain, and voilà! The strawberries responded. Jeffrey flew the strawberry flag at the beginning of the week, and people came in droves for pick-your-own, seven dollars a quart. These strawberries were red and juicy all the way through, the sweetest things you ever tasted, tiny bits of heaven pulled off the vine. The air over Seascape Farm practically shimmered pink. They were living in a miasma of strawberries.

At the end of the day, Jeffrey was getting the tractor back to the shed after fertilizing his cash crops—the corn, the herbs, the flowers, the beets, cucumbers, and summer squash—when he spied his wife's silver Rubicon in the parking lot. Delilah had brought the kids up to pick berries.

He and Delilah had started the day off on the wrong foot. Delilah had stayed late at the Begonia and had had "a few drinks" with Thom and Faith, the owners, and Greg, who had been playing guitar last night. "A few drinks" with those three was nearly always a slasher film. Thom and Faith were professional vodka drinkers and Greg was a certified booze bully, ordering up shots of tequila and Jim Beam for everyone, especially when Thom and Faith were footing the bill. Then, as if to soften the treachery of the drinks, Greg would pull out his guitar and play "Sunshine, Go Away Today," and "Carolina on My Mind," and everyone would sing along in slurred tones. When Delilah would look at the clock and see it was three in the morning, she couldn't believe it.

Delilah had stumbled home just as the sun was coming up, which was when Jeffrey usually rose for the day. He liked to have the watering finished by six, and the market opened for business at seven.

He and Delilah had crossed paths in the bathroom. She was on her knees, retching into the toilet.

"Good morning," he whispered. He tried to keep his voice light and playful, because Delilah's recurring complaint was that he was stern and judgmental, he was no fun, he acted more like her father than her husband.

And I ran away from my father, she said.

It was true that Jeffrey did not approve of her staying out until all hours; he did not approve of the restaurant life in general—there was drug use and drinking—and even though Delilah promised him she steered clear of everything except a postshift glass of wine, enough to clear her head while she rested her feet, he didn't believe her. Two or three nights a week she came home absurdly late, smelling of marijuana smoke, and ended up like this: head in the toilet, vomiting.

What are the boys going to think? Jeffrey would ask her.

I make them a hot breakfast, Delilah would snap back. *I get them to school in clean clothes, on time. I pack them healthy lunches. I engage with them more than you do.*

She was correct: no matter how late she came in, no matter how many postshift drinks she indulged in, she was up with the kids, flipping pancakes, pouring juice, checking homework. He couldn't give her parenting anything less than his full endorsement.

You want me to be a farmer's wife, Delilah said. *You want me in braids and an apron.*

Their arguments were all the same, so alike that it was as if they simply rewound the tape and pushed Play.

You should be glad I'm independent, I have my own life, a job, friends, a supplementary income. The kids understand this, they respect it.

Jeffrey did not begrudge his wife her own life—he just wished it coincided more neatly with his life as a farmer. He got out of bed at five; he liked to be in bed at nine, and many times he fell asleep reading to the kids. What he craved was time in front of the fire, just the four of them, he did want a roast with potatoes and carrots cooking in the oven. But Delilah needed a crowd. Always she invited the group over—Greg and Tess and their twins, the Chief and Andrea, Addison and Phoebe—and she mixed martinis and pressed sandwiches and opened chips and turned on the Patriots or pulled out the Parcheesi or badgered Greg into playing every Cat Stevens song he knew. There was no downtime with Delilah. It was always a party, and it was exhausting.

This morning she had been in a particularly foul mood, despite his chummy, nonjudgmental *Good morning!* She was retching and crying. He couldn't decide whether or not to ask her what was wrong. Sometimes when he asked she told him to mind his own business, but if he didn't ask, she accused him of not caring. If he were to be very honest with himself, he would admit that he didn't always care what was troubling Delilah. She had dramas constantly spooling around and out, and Jeffrey couldn't keep track. That was why she had Phoebe. God, Phoebe could listen for hours.

As Jeffrey was buttoning his shirt, Delilah approached him, sniffling.

"It's Greg and Tess's anniversary," she said.

"Is it?" he said. Then he remembered. It had been strawberry season when they got married. He had attended that wedding alone. Andrea had been the matron of honor; she had looked shockingly beautiful. Many times in the years since they'd split, he'd been filled with regret, but on the day Greg and Tess got married, the pangs had been unbearable. Andrea wore a dusty pink satin dress that showed off her shoulders; her hair was in a sleek twist, her smile lit up the church. At the reception, he had asked her to dance, and she'd said yes, and as they danced, she talked about how happy she was for Greg and Tess, while Jeffrey tried not to notice the Chief eyeing them from his post at the bar.

Delilah said, "So I'm taking the twins today. Greg and Tess are sailing to the Vineyard."

"That's nice," Jeffrey said.

"It is nice," Delilah said. "They're taking a picnic." She burst into tears.

See? He just didn't get it.

"What's wrong?" he asked.

"We never do things like that!" she said.

Now Jeffrey went to hunt down his wife in the strawberry fields. She was the kind of mother who was always *doing* things with the boys. Today, he knew, had started off with a nature walk; then they had picked up sandwiches in town and gone fishing on the south side of the pond, out of the wind, with Delilah tirelessly hooking and rehooking their lures. Often the day would end with an ice cream or a movie, but today it was strawberry-picking. The boys were eight and six; they both had energy like Delilah's—they never stopped, they never tired. Their life was one long adventure with their mother, punctuated by treats. She rarely said no to them. But four evenings a week, when she left for the restaurant, Jeffrey took over and reality closed in. He made them eat vegetables, he made them bathe, he made them rest. He wasn't as exciting as their mother, but they needed him.

He spotted Delilah right away in a white flowing sundress and a wide-brimmed straw hat that she wore every year when she went strawberry-picking. Because of the wind, her skirt kept flying up and her hat was threatening to blow off down the rows. Jeffrey smiled in spite of himself. Delilah was a beautiful woman, and the four kids—their own sons, Drew and Barney, and Tess and Greg's twins, Chloe and Finn—were happy and laughing, alternately dropping strawberries into the green quart baskets and stuffing them in their mouths.

"Hey," Jeffrey said.

Delilah looked up, but she was not happy to see him. Was she still miffed about this morning? If he understood her, she was upset because it was Greg and Tess's anniversary and they were sailing to the Vineyard. Jeffrey had spent the better part of the day trying to dream up something—an excursion, a surprise—that would match this in Delilah's mind. *We never do things like that!* Jeffrey couldn't argue with her there. They were slaves to the insanity of their schedule: Jeffrey worked all day, Delilah worked four nights a week. Tonight she was home, though. They could get a sitter and go out for dinner. Would that be exotic enough? It was too windy to eat at the beach, but they could pick up sandwiches and a bottle of wine and spread a blanket between the corn rows. The corn was waist-high already; no one would see them. They could make love in the fields. They used to do this before they were married, before they had a home together, before kids—but now the fields, and Jeffrey's absurdly long hours tending them, were a sore spot, and it was hard to imagine them feeling romantic about the farm the way they used to.

It was a full moon tonight. The wind was due to die down; it would be clear and beautiful. He would suggest a picnic in the fields and see what she said.

At that second, there was a buzzing in his pocket. His phone. He checked the display. It was the Chief.

"Okay," Delilah said, smoothing down her skirt and straightening her hat. "We have enough berries to last us the rest of our lives. Let's go home and make jam."

"Jam!" the kids cried.

Jeffrey opened his phone. "Hello?" he said.

Jeffrey was a farmer's farmer. He was methodical and straitlaced; he was sober, Delilah said, even when he was drunk. He had the posture of a minister—upright, straight, broad. He believed in process, he believed in cycles—the moon, the tides, the seasons. He respected the many complexities of nature, from a spiderweb to a bolt of lightning. He, Jeffrey Drake, could handle anything—blight, hurricane, famine, the apocalypse. Or so he thought.

Jeffrey and the Chief were friends, but there had always been something blocking the path between them, and that something was Andrea. Andrea had been Jeffrey's girlfriend first. They had dated for seven months, and then they had lived together in the tiny cottage on the farm property for another year and a half. That Andrea was now married to the Chief and had been for years, that they were all part of the same tight-knit group of eight, was weird and uncomfortable, but probably only for Jeffrey. It didn't seem to bother Andrea or the Chief at all; they treated him like a member of their family.

The Chief did not bother with hello. He never did. "Does Delilah have the twins?" he asked.

Strange question. The Chief was so humorless, he made Jeffrey feel like Jay Leno.

"Affirmative," Jeffrey said. He considered making some staticky walkie-talkie noise, but he wasn't funny enough to pull it off. No wonder Delilah found him tiresome. "Yes, Chief, she does. They are here at the farm as we speak, absconding with five quarts of strawberries."

"They're headed home?"

"Yes, sir. Home to make jam."

"Okay," the Chief said. "Keep them there. I'll be over in . . . God, I don't know. A little while. See that they sit tight, okay?"

"Roger Dodger," Jeffrey said. This mock-cop shtick was the best way to negotiate small talk with the Chief, but today it seemed to be falling flat. "Is something going on?"

The Chief took a breath and then made some indistinguishable noise. A laugh? A guffaw? (It was safe to say the Chief had never guffawed in all his life.) A sob?

"I don't know how to say this. God, I just can't say it."

Now Jeffrey was worried. "What?" he said. But no sooner had the word left his mouth than he knew. "Jesus, don't tell me."

"They're dead," the Chief said. "They drowned."

Jeffrey and the Chief were cut from the same cloth. Everyone said so. Jeffrey had never been able to decide if he was flattered by this or bothered by it. They were both serious and steady. Jeffrey knew the Chief expected him to take this news like a man. They were to figure things out, make a plan. But Jeffrey found himself gutted. He had been shot once, by a hunter's stray bullet; he had caught buckshot in the side that felled him from his plow. Receiving this news—*They're dead. They drowned*—was like that, but worse. He was breathless. He could not respond.

The Chief said, "I know it's hard."

Jeffrey almost said, *Fuck you, don't patronize me. Let me wrap my mind around it, let me draw a breath, Ed, for Chrissakes.* Suddenly Jeffrey wanted to sock the Chief in the mouth. He realized with those words—*I know it's hard*—that he'd wanted to sock Ed Kapenash in the mouth for twenty years.

He was saved from a grossly inappropriate response by the sight of the twins, Chloe and Finn, proudly carrying their quart containers. Their mouths were smeared with red and Chloe's white blouse had red stains on it that looked like blood. *Your parents are dead,* Jeffrey thought. They were happy kids, seven years old; they were well behaved, the closest friends of his own kids; the four of them were like siblings. The twins called him Uncle Jeff and they called Delilah Auntie Dee. He could not tell them their parents were dead; he could not tell Delilah either. The Chief served people up with horrible news every day; it was his occupational hazard. But it was not Jeffrey's.

He realized he still hadn't said anything.

"We'll come to your house . . . in a little while," the Chief said.

"Okay," Jeffrey said. And then he thought, *Andrea.* "Does Andrea know?"

The Chief cleared his throat. "Not yet. I'm going to find her. Tell her in person."

Jeffrey and Delilah had been friends with the Chief and Andrea—and Tess and Greg and Phoebe and Addison—for years and years. They hung out every weekend, they checked in, they helped out, lending a hand with the everyday stuff— *Would you drop me off at Nantucket Auto Body so I can get my car? Can I borrow your deep fryer?* They had taken six vacations as a group, but only rarely did Jeffrey's old feelings for Andrea resurface as they did this second. He thought, *I will go tell her. I will tell her in person.* Jeffrey had known Tess since she was fifteen years old. When Andrea and Jeffrey started dating, Tess was still in high school in Boston. But the Chief was the Chief. It was hard to argue with his authority or his sense of ownership in situations like this one. Andrea was his wife.

"Okay," Jeffrey said. Delilah and the kids were walking toward the car. He had to follow them home. He would tell Delilah first, and they would wait for the Chief and Andrea before they told the kids. Andrea—what would she do? Tess was her pet, her doll, her treasure. When Jeffrey and Andrea lived together and Tess came to visit, Andrea and Tess slept in the bed side by side while Jeffrey took the couch. And then there was that weird week this past fall when Tess and Greg had separated. Tess had taken the kids and moved in with Andrea and the Chief. For Andrea, losing Tess would be like losing a sister. Like losing a child.

Jeffrey was sweaty and grimy and his side hurt. He was heavy with the news, impossibly burdened with the prospect of sharing it.

He hung up with the Chief and hurried to catch Delilah. He tapped on her window. She turned, put down the window. The radio was blaring, as always; the kids were bobbing their heads and mouthing the words to a rock song Jeffrey had never heard before. The whole car smelled like strawberries.

Jeffrey looked at Chloe and Finn. The twins were carefree

now; they would be carefree for another hour or so. The thought was hideous to him.

"I'm going to follow you home," Jeffrey said.

"What?" Delilah said. "Why?"

"I'll meet you there," he said.

ANDREA

The Summer of Me: it was a joke, but not really. Andrea Kapenash had been a parent for sixteen years, which meant that for sixteen years her summers had consisted of wading pools, plastic beach toys, juice boxes, swim diapers, playgrounds, boogie boards, skim boards, surfboards, baseball camp, football camp, gymnastics camp, lacrosse camp, tennis lessons, golf lessons, sleepovers, tents set up in the backyard, thousands of packed lunches, thousands of pick-ups and drop-offs, mosquito bites, missing flip-flops, and the constant application of sunscreen. Andrea loved her children, but she could never have predicted the joy she would feel at watching them spread their own wings. Her daughter, Kacy, scooped ice cream at the Juice Bar, a job she loved because she was always busy. The line was always out the door and Kacy felt she was in the center of things. Although it wasn't exactly brain surgery, she was, in a small way, bringing happiness to people. When Kacy passed a hot fudge sundae across the counter, people smiled, they thanked her, they tipped her. Andrea's son, Eric, worked two doors down at Young's Bicycle Shop, setting people up with rental bikes, writing rental agreements, and when the shop wasn't busy, he was in the back, doing repairs. The job played to his strengths: his easy, natural charm, his attention to detail, his love of tinkering with a machine. Eric had been born with the uncanny ability to fix anything, which had served him well, since the Chief was not handy at all, and furthermore was never home.

Andrea's summer now fell into the pleasant routine of seeing the kids off to work and going about her day. She was free to do as she liked—go to lunch with Tess, Phoebe, or Delilah, go to the beach and swim to her heart's content, read half a novel without interruption. She had time to walk into town to go shopping, she had time to linger at the farm truck, picking through vegetables, she had time to stop by the station and see her husband or surreptitiously check on her children working. The Summer of Me: she was an adult again, doing adult things.

She had the time now for simple kindnesses. For example, she had made the world's most delicious picnic lunch for Tess and Greg's sail to Martha's Vineyard: chilled gazpacho with chunks of creamy avocado, lobster salad sandwiches on challah bread, potato salad with bacon and blue cheese, a fruit salad of strawberries, raspberries, mango, and mint, and chewy coconut macaroons. The picnic was an anniversary gift—though as a rule, they did not exchange gifts among their group—because this anniversary was special. It wasn't the twelve-year milestone that was remarkable; it was the fact that Tess and Greg had managed to stay married through everything that had happened in the past nine months. Greg had been accused of committing a transgression last autumn with one of his students, and whether it had happened or not, the tempest surrounding the accusation would have been enough to topple the strongest fortress; it was the story that would not go away, the rumor that would not die. Everywhere Tess went, she said, she heard whispers. Every time Greg left the house, she harbored suspicions. They screamed, they yelled, they cried, they went into counseling, they gave up counseling, they separated for a week. And yet they hung in there. They stayed married. The anniversary should be celebrated.

Call me when you get home! Andrea said when she dropped off the picnic basket at Tess's house that morning.

Okay, I will! Tess said. She was wearing a red bikini and jean shorts, and a pair of red sunglasses with white polka dots. In a lower, more serious voice, she said, *Thank you for the picnic. You didn't have to go to all this trouble.*

I know I didn't, Andrea said. *But I wanted to.*

Andrea and Tess were first cousins. Their fathers were brothers, the mighty and formidable DiRosa brothers, both narcotics detectives for the Boston Police Department. Andrea had three younger brothers and Tess had three older brothers, so in addition to being cousins, they were sisters, the only DiRosa girls. Andrea was nine years older than Tess, so in addition to being cousins and sisters, they were mother and daughter.

In all of Andrea's memories of childhood, she was wet. She was diving into the community pool at the YMCA, she was swimming fifty yards off the shore of Thompson Island, sluicing through the green water of Boston Harbor; she was a mermaid, the water was her natural habitat, it was hers and hers alone. Her brothers fooled around in the waves at the beach, but they didn't swim the way Andrea did.

Andrea's natural ability in the water gave her authority. Because she was so gifted at something, adults trusted her, they treated her like she was older; from the time she was twelve years old, she was allowed to baby-sit for Tess; she was allowed to take Tess for long walks in her stroller. When Andrea was fifteen and received her junior lifesaving certificate, she was allowed to lead beach excursions for her brothers and her cousins—eight DiRosa children, with Andrea in charge. Andrea swam butterfly for the Boston Latin swim team, and in her senior year she won the city championships in the 100-meter and 200-meter. That same year she pulled a grown man who had had a heart attack while swimming laps out of the middle of the pool at the Y. She was awarded a medal by the city council; her picture was in the *Globe*.

When Andrea was eighteen, she got a job as a lifeguard at L Street Beach. She wore a red tank suit and zinc oxide on her nose. She had Ray-Ban aviator sunglasses and a whistle on the end of a braided cord that she spun around her fingers, first this way, then that way. When Tess came to the beach, she sat, quite literally, in Andrea's shadow, on the first rung of the lifeguard stand, sucking on cherry Popsicles. In Andrea's memory, it seemed like Tess was there every day. Andrea would look down and see the straight white part in Tess's dark hair. Tess would swim, and Andrea would watch her. Tess would attempt the butterfly, but she flailed and humped. Andrea tried to teach her the movement, but Tess's shoulders weren't strong enough yet, and Andrea was busy working. There were hundreds of kids to watch.

It was at the end of the summer, the week before Andrea started her freshman year at Boston College, that Tess nearly drowned. Andrea was spinning her whistle, scanning the sand and the shallow water, dreaming about finally living away. After months of battling, her parents had agreed to allow her to board, although she easily could have commuted. In the end Andrea's winning argument was that she was attending BC on a partial swimming scholarship and the team practices were at dawn. *You don't want me riding the T to Brookline at four in the morning, do you?*

In truth, Andrea wanted to separate herself from her family. The DiRosa clan was too close-knit, too loud, too steeped in the politics of the BPD, too Italian, with their garlic and ricotta and veal involtini, their heavy gold crosses and crucifixes everywhere she turned. Andrea wanted to experience a life that was quieter, more reserved, more refined, a collegiate life, an intellectual life. (*Lord help you!* her grandmother said. *You're going to the Jesuits!*) The fact that Andrea had not been able to escape the city of her birth discouraged her a little, but there had been no avoiding a Catholic education if her father was to pay for it. Andrea had gotten into Notre Dame as well, but South Bend was deemed too far away.

Andrea was thinking these things, she was twirling her whistle and scanning the shallow water, she was listening to Van Halen on someone's boom box, she was enjoying the sun on her shoulders, when the feeling struck her: a panic like a sickness. It was as though she had looked down and noticed the lifeguard stand was gone, she was sitting on thin air, about to fall. It was *Tess* who was gone. This was not unusual—Tess swam and played and visited the snack bar and the restroom just like everybody else. Andrea saw Tess's Popsicle stick, stained pink, sticking out of the sand. This wasn't unusual either; Tess, at age nine, was a habitual litterbug.

Lifeguarding was a job that required assiduousness rather than instinct, but it was instinct that kicked in. Andrea scanned the water out past where any other nine-year-old would be swimming, and there she saw a hand. Or what she thought was a hand. A hand!

Andrea blew her whistle—three short blasts, an emergency! She jumped recklessly from the top of the stand and nearly broke both her knees. She grabbed her board, dashed into the water, and started paddling. Andrea spied a flash of someone's face—yes, it was Tess! Tess was out way over her head. What was she doing out there? The face disappeared, the hand slapped the water. Andrea abandoned her board; it was slowing her down. She was the fastest flyer in the city—she could get there quicker on her own. She swam to the spot where the hand and face had been and dove down and pulled Tess up off the bottom. The effort of this, of getting sixty pounds of deadweight to the surface, nearly killed her. Tess was waterlogged. But not dead, right? Andrea could not let herself worry about anything except textbook lifesaving. Get the swimmer under the chin and paddle with her to the board, secure the board under Tess, and swim for shore. There were lifeguards coming toward her, three of the big lunks Andrea worked with, whom she had thought completely useless until this moment. One of them, Hugo, took Tess and the board and powered her to shore. The other two guards, Roxbury and Toxic Moxie (these were their nicknames; Andrea had no idea what their real names were), laid Tess out on a towel and pumped her chest and gave her mouth-to-mouth while Andrea stood at Tess's feet and shivered and said the Hail Mary and promised God that if Tess lived, Andrea would repay him by becoming a nun.

An ambulance arrived. There was a crowd around Tess's gray, limp body, including Roxbury, Toxic Moxie, and Andrea, who was praying and standing as still as a statue of the Virgin Mary. The paramedics sliced through the bystanders, and as they did, Toxic Moxie put the breath into Tess that saved her. He blew death out. Tess coughed up harbor water, spewing out a whole stream in a projectile vomit, and then she pinkened. The crowd sighed, and Andrea wept as Tess opened her eyes. Andrea thought, *I will become a nun.*

She was forty-four years old now and swimming once again. She hadn't swum in sixteen years; she had been too busy building sandcastles, and later watching her kids boogie board, pacing back and forth on the shore while they battled the pounding waves. But she was back at it religiously, half a mile of freestyle out past the breakers. God, it felt good! She wore goggles now, showing her age; her eyes couldn't take the salt anymore. She swam and swam and swam—all the way down to Surfside—and then she swam back. When she climbed out of the water, her legs were shaky and weak from the workout. She was reminded of the superstar she used to be, the fastest swimmer in high school, and then in college. She had been named to the First Team All-American; she had broken four Big East fly records; she had made it to the Olympic Trials in Mission Viejo, where she missed placing in the 200-meter by three one-hundredths of a second.

During the years that her children had been small, Andrea had rarely looked upon her trophies or thought about her name on the record board that hung at the Boston College pool. But when she did, she wondered, was that swimmer really the same person as the one who was now mixing rice cereal with baby food? This summer, swimming as strongly as ever, the answer was yes. (She pictured herself flipping at the wall, or shaking her muscles loose on the blocks before tensing for the gun . . .)

Andrea DiRosa!

It was impossible to see with her goggles on—it was like looking through a windshield in a downpour. But when she emerged from the water, she thought she saw the Chief sitting on her towel. She removed her goggles. It was the Chief, Ed Kapenash, Eddie, her husband of eighteen years, sitting on her beach towel in his uniform. His cruiser was parked up on the bluff. From out of nowhere the feeling returned, the sick, panicked suspicion that she was sitting on air and was about to fall. It was five-thirty. The kids got off work at six and the Chief normally knocked off around seven, if there were no emergencies.

Was there an emergency now, or a lack of emergencies? Had he shown up to surprise her, to be romantic? The Chief had only one facial expression and that was stoic, but at this moment the stoic looked different, though Andrea couldn't say how.

"Is everything okay?" Andrea said.

He patted the spot beside him on the towel. "Sit down."

"Is it one of the kids?"

"No."

She sat, dried her face, ran her fingers through her hair. Her book was there, *The English Patient,* open facedown. She had seen the movie but had not read the book, though she'd always meant to. And that was another treat of the Summer of Me—she was actually doing things she'd meant to do for years. The book, as it turned out, was sumptuous and textured, it was a feast for her mind. She had a college education, after all; she had majored in comparative literature, she had read Kafka and Saul Bellow and E. M. Forster, but the ideas and images that had been ignited by those books so many years ago were gone.

Reading again was a luxury and a delight. Until this second, seeing her paperback copy of *The English Patient* had made her feel privileged, intelligent, worthy. But now she got the strange feeling that she would never finish it.

"It's Tess," the Chief said. "And Greg."

"They're dead?" Andrea said. She said this only to eliminate it as a possibility.

"Yes," he said.

When Tess was nine years old, when she nearly drowned on L Street Beach, the paramedics had, as a precaution, taken her to Children's Hospital, and it was there that Andrea faced the rest of her family: her parents, Mikey and Rose; Tess's parents, Giancarlo and Vivian; her grandmother; her aunts; Father Francis, the parish priest; and Sister Maria José, the nun from Guatemala who lived in a room in Mikey and Rose's basement. Half the family thought Andrea was a hero—again, a hero!—for saving Tess, who had ventured out over her head. But there was a certain faction of the family—Aunt Agropina, who was not actually Andrea's aunt but rather Vivian's aunt, as well as maybe Giancarlo and Vivian themselves—who wondered how long Tess had been swimming before Andrea noticed her. Tess was not just any swimmer on L Street Beach, she was Andrea's beloved younger cousin. *Practically sisters, the two of them! Why wasn't she watching? It's family!* Tess's older brother Anthony had been on the beach as well, and he reported that he had seen Tess swim out, doing the butterfly. Andrea saw the imperceptible head shakes, she heard the soft clucking. Not only had Andrea not been watching, but she had not been watching as poor Tess struggled to swim the butterfly like her older cousin. Tess had been trying to impress Andrea, and she had nearly died.

Andrea was filled with regret and guilt and shame. She sat with Sister Maria José, who wore a starched white blouse, blue A-line skirt, and black and white wimple, and thought, *I will become a nun*.

When Andrea heard the Chief say that Tess and Greg were dead, she pitched forward, coming face-to-face with her own weary legs. She emitted a long, guttural moan, the kind of moan she had not uttered since childbirth. She felt the Chief's arms close around her.

"I've got you," he said. "It's okay. I've got you."

She howled. Tess. *They're dead? Yes.* Andrea thought of the picnic. It had been the picnic of a lifetime. She had pureed all the vegetables for the gazpacho; she had ripened the avocado in a paper bag for three days; she had made the lobster salad herself, boiling the buggers, cracking them open, pulling out the precious meat. She had risen at 6 A.M. to snatch a loaf of challah from Daily Breads, hot out of the oven. At the last minute, she had tucked in a bag of chocolate-covered cranberries for Greg, a peace offering. He was crazy for them. Andrea thought about Tess, wearing the red sunglasses with white polka dots. A person did not die while wearing such sunglasses. She remembered the near-drowning in its entirety, Tess in a heap on the sandy bottom of Dorchester Bay. Tess might have died twenty-six years ago, but Andrea had saved her. Andrea had not, however, been true to her word: she had not become a nun. She had married Edward Kapenash and had two children. She had brought Tess to Nantucket, where Tess met Greg, who became her husband. Several times during the anguish of the past nine months, Andrea had blamed herself for bringing Tess to Nantucket. Andrea felt as responsible for Tess as she did for her own children—more so, maybe, because she had known Tess her entire life. She had nearly let Tess drown, she had not been watching, she had been absorbed in her own thoughts, and she had not become a nun.

Tess was dead. Andrea picked up her book and tore at its pages senselessly; then she flung the book into the sand a few feet away, but not as far or as furiously as she wanted to, because of the arms constraining her. *I've got you.* Andrea moaned. She would never finish the book. She was giving birth to her own grief.

JEFFREY

The kids were outside at the picnic table with butter knives, cutting the stems off the strawberries. It looked like a crime scene; everything was stained red and pink—the wood of the picnic table, their hands, their faces. It was nearly six and still as bright as midday. The children happily hacked away at the fruit of Jeffrey's labor. He watched them for a few seconds, but did not say anything.

Delilah was in the kitchen, rummaging through the cabinets for a pot.

"I have to talk to you," Jeffrey said. He was glad the children were occupied. He would tell Delilah first, and she would help him figure out what to do. They would either tell the children together, or they would wait for someone else to show up—the Chief and Andrea, Addison and Phoebe. They would gather here, as they always did.

"I want to make jam," Delilah said. "I promised the kids, and I'd like to get it bubbling before I start dinner." She looked at him. Her good mood and cheerful resolve were wearing down; she had had only an hour or two of sleep. "Do you think I should make it in the pressure cooker?"

"Come with me into the bedroom," Jeffrey said.

Her brow folded; she glanced at the kids. "You're kidding me," she said. She thought he wanted sex. And as wrong as she was, she was also right: a part of him wanted to defy the terrifying news of Tess and Greg's death by loving his wife, by lifting her skirt and taking her up against the wall.

"I have something to tell you," he said.

She huffed as she followed him down the hall to their bedroom; he heard her muttering. "My mother made jam, but I don't know how she did it. She never used a recipe. Strawberries, sugar, and something to make it gel."

Pectin, he thought. But he said nothing.

She said, "What is going on?" She was standing in front of their closet door, which was open, revealing his Carhartts, her hostessing dresses, his navy suit (he would wear it to the funeral, he supposed), her camisole tops, her high heels. He should advise her to sit down, that was best when delivering bad news, but it felt like simply another delay, he had to tell her *now!* Just tell her. But, God, he couldn't. He was the Grim Reaper. How did the Chief do it? Swiftly, cleanly; just say it, release the guillotine blade, pull the trigger.

"Delilah?"

She glared at him. Impatient to get back to the jam.

"Tess and Greg are dead."

Her eyes widened; they were more white than brown, and then all white. She dropped to the floor. Fainted away.

THE CHIEF

He had two major problems. Three. Four, actually. The first was his wife, whom he still loved deeply. She was in a black tank suit, howling, shivering, convulsing, alternately crying like a baby and screaming, and making other noises he couldn't begin to describe. If someone had asked him before today how Andrea would take the news of her cousin's sudden, tragic death, he would have said she would have handled it exactly this way, which meant sadness and upset and shock and horror of a quality no one could bear to imagine. However, a part of him had hoped that Andrea would be better than this, stronger. God, he felt evil and unfair for even wishing this. But Andrea had seen a lot over the years. She understood accidents and tragedy: they did not discriminate. They could happen to anyone. Andrea was the Chief's first responsibility. He kept his arms around her, he absorbed her shudders and screams. She was all he could handle.

And yet, on his hip, his phone was jumping. He was one of a handful of people who had any details at all. He had gone to the Coast Guard station to speak to Joe. Joe had the bodies. The Chief went to identify them. They were covered with orange tarps down in the basement of the Coast Guard station, where it was cool. After the Chief identified them, they would be picked up by the funeral home. The Chief descended the stairs to the basement and it was, honestly, like being in a horror film, like descending into a nightmare. The bodies lay side by side on boards. The Chief felt his heart going crazy. He had to get hold of himself; he did things like this all the time, by which he meant he dealt with the things that no one else wanted to deal with. He was a disaster specialist. Joe did him the favor of accompanying him—Joe had seen a drowned man before, many drowned men, he knew what to expect, but the Chief did not. Joe pulled the first tarp aside, and—bad luck—it was Tess. She was bloated; her skin was the color of putty, and her hair had a patch torn out in front. She looked childlike in death; she looked a little like the Chief's daughter. Okay, that was enough, cover her back up, he couldn't stand it, but then, too, he couldn't bear to think that this was the last he'd ever see of her.

He nodded.

Then on to Greg. Greg had a cut on his forehead, a gash that must have bled like a geyser, but because of the water it looked like a shriveled weal. His nose was out of place, too. The Chief had spent some time over the past nine months studying Greg's face, trying to figure out if the man was telling the truth about what happened with the girl at school. Was Greg a man of honor or a creep? The Chief was notoriously stingy with the benefit of the doubt, but he had given it to Greg—because of Andrea, yes, and Tess, but also because he loved Greg. Greg was like his feckless little brother, the talented one, the handsome one, the one who was chased by women old and young. Greg had wept openly when Tess walked down the aisle toward him on their wedding day, and then again when his twins were born. He had wept less openly that night at the Begonia when the Chief took him for drinks and said, *I'm not sure if I believe you, but I'm going to stick my neck out for you anyway.*

Now he was dead.

The Chief nodded. Joe covered Greg back up.

"Are you worried about that cut on his head?" the Chief asked. "Or about how Tess lost that hair?"

"I can't decide."

"What do we think happened?" He looked at Joe Finch, the commanding officer out on the water, a man he considered not a friend, exactly, but a colleague, steady and true. "What's your best guess?"

"I'd say they caught a gust the wrong way," Joe said. "He got hit in the head by the boom and went down. She was either thrown from the boat or she went after him. They got disoriented— people do, underwater—she hit her head on the bottom of the boat, or for some other reason couldn't make her way to the surface. His right foot was snarled in the ropes. My crew found a broken bottle of champagne floating with their personal effects. So they were drinking. Maybe they were drunk. If they were drunk and they fell and he was tangled and she was trying to reach him and got confused, or if she panicked . . . there are a million reasons it could have ended up this way. Neither of them was wearing a life preserver. And they were way out in the middle of nowhere, about a mile north of Muskegut. If the guy couldn't sail, he had no business being all the way out there, not on a day like today, not unless he was very well acquainted with the wind and what it could do."

The Chief nodded and made a motion with his hand to cut Joe off. He didn't want to hear Joe pin the blame on Greg. The guy was dead, lying under a tarp. And yet the Chief knew that

Joe was right. Greg was an overconfident sailor, always had been. The Chief had capsized with him on a Sunfish on Coskata Pond two summers earlier. Greg's understanding of the wind and the jib and when to tack was muddled, but even when the Chief got dumped into the pond, he didn't upbraid Greg the way he should have. At the time, he hadn't seen the point. Greg sailed by instinct instead of by following the rules, and that meant occasionally ending up wet. So what?

So now he was dead. He had tried going all the way to the Vineyard in 30-mile gusts, and he had been drinking. It didn't take a Rhodes scholar to figure out how they lost control of the boat. The boom swung around in a gust and caught Greg unaware, and off he went, and his leg was caught in the ropes and he couldn't get loose. Tess tried to save him, but she was afraid of the water, had been since she was a kid; she was no match for a grown man sinking in choppy waves. They both went down. Or Tess was thrown and Greg tried to save her. He tried to pull her up by the hair, which would explain the patch of bald scalp.

"We put the time of death at one-thirty, maybe two. Another sailor put in the call about an abandoned capsize at quarter to three and gave us the coordinates. We got there forty minutes later, at three twenty-five. They were both trapped under the boat."

"And that doesn't seem strange to you? There are a million ways that could have happened?"

Joe removed his glasses and rubbed his eyes, which were such a pale gray they were almost clear, the color of water. Joe was probably, like Ed, still shy of his fiftieth birthday, but something made him seem older—his beard, his uniform, his title. He knew these waters, he knew the wind, and he knew the craft. Tess and Greg had been sailing on a 12-meter sloop, a bigger boat than Greg was used to, by far.

"I just wonder what happened. Why they couldn't get to the surface."

"Let's say they were drinking. Their judgment was impaired, and their motor skills. Would one bottle of champagne and a few beers have incapacitated them? Well, it wouldn't help matters. This could have happened sober, too. One of them got knocked unconscious, or lost their balance. She was taking a leak off the back of the boat and fell in and he went after her, got caught in the ropes, couldn't fight his way to the surface. I could have the ME run toxicology. Do you want me to ask him to do that?"

Did the Chief want to do that? Would it help to know that Tess was drunk or Greg was high? God, no. It wouldn't help him and it wouldn't help the kids. He could ask Joe to run the toxicology in confidence. The only people who would see the results were himself and the ME, Danny Browne. But somehow, someway, rumors would fly. They always did. The Chief had seen it time and time again. You thought something was locked up in the vault when it turned out that everyone, including the girls who made pizza at the Muse, were talking about it. Getting the story right enough to maim, and wrong enough to kill. Tess and Greg had just had their lives examined under a microscope with the goddamn April Peck thing. Some child in Finn's second-grade class had told Finn that his father was a cradle robber. A second-grader! It made the Chief angry enough to want to throw somebody in the slammer—the second-grader or Greg, the Chief wasn't sure. Gossip was insidious. The Chief could not, in good conscience, create more gossip. And yet he was the police chief. He had to know what had happened.

"Run toxicology," he said.

"Will do," Joe said.

"On the down low," the Chief said.

"Absolutely."

"No, I mean it."

"I understand," Joe said. He was looking at the Chief steadily. "You have my word."

"That'll do," the Chief said.

The Chief followed Joe upstairs to sign the paperwork. Joe brought out two heavy-duty clear plastic bags with *USCG* stamped on them. One of them contained Greg's guitar case.

"This is what my guys found at the scene," Joe said. "We divided it into personal effects and what appears to be rubbish. But look through the rubbish to be sure we didn't accidentally throw away something important."

This was all standard operating procedure, but the Chief wasn't sure he could follow through. But if not him, then who? He couldn't ask Andrea to go through these bags, or Delilah or Jeffrey or Phoebe. The sight of Greg's guitar case made him queasy. He opened it up. The guitar was surprisingly dry, light, intact. The Chief held it the way he'd seen Greg do hundreds of times, and felt like a fool. Still, he was certain that if he strummed a chord, it would sound clear and untroubled. The guitar had survived the capsize, but two strong, capable adults were dead.

The Chief resisted the urge to play the guitar incorrectly. He set it down.

Joe Finch excused himself to make the phone call to the medical examiner. The Chief dug through the bag of rubbish first, thinking that would be easier. There was a bottle of Moët & Chandon, broken at the neck and side. Also the cork, the wrapper, the cage. There were two plastic cups, both cracked. Two empty bottles of Heineken, no caps. Two glass cereal bowls that the Chief recognized as those from his own kitchen, cracked. Two halves of a soggy paperback book, *Life's a Beach*, by Claire Cook. The book was saturated like a sponge, more pulp than pages. But it had been Tess's, and the Chief had to ask himself, Would Andrea want it? He decided not. He left it with the broken glass. On to the personal effects.

The Chief removed a woven picnic basket, another denizen of the Kapenash household (it had been a wedding present and had spent nearly all of its eighteen years languishing on a shelf in the basement), and its component parts, secured to the top of the basket by leather straps: the plastic plates, the inexpensive forks and knives, the cloth napkins, the corkscrew. There were various pieces of Tupperware which the Chief also vaguely recognized, one containing half a lobster salad sandwich, another containing a dozen or more of Andrea's macaroons. The macaroons had survived, but Greg and Tess were dead. The Chief took a minute after setting aside the macaroons. His eyes were dry, but his insides were dissolving. Tess's flip-flops were in the bag, and one of Greg's battered dock shoes. Greg had been famous for buying a new pair of shoes every ten years. There were sodden beach towels, two unopened bottles of Evian, a zippered leather suitcase that when opened revealed toothbrushes, deodorant, a change of clothes, a negligee.

Okay, enough. The Chief zipped it back up.

A pair of sunglasses, snapped in half. Red frames with white polka dots. Tess's. The Chief considered pitching them in the trash. But then he thought he might be able to glue them back together and give them to Chloe.

He did not want to think about Chloe.

Greg's BlackBerry was cold and dead. It was a piece of burned toast. Throw it away? The Chief decided to keep it. He would place it in a bag of rice (a trick taught to him by their worldwise dispatcher, Molly) and see if he could bring it back from the dead.

The cell phone could be brought back, but not Greg or Tess.

At the bottom of the bag of personal effects was a Ziploc freezer bag holding Tess's iPhone with its signature lemon yellow skin. She was a woman, a mother; it wasn't exactly surprising that she took better care of her electronics than Greg did of his. She would have needed her phone to check on the kids.

Carefully, the Chief removed the phone from the bag. It sprang to life under his touch. It flashed a bright picture of Chloe and Finn. The twins were sitting at the breakfast bar in their summer pajamas, eating pancakes. Finn was holding the curve of a banana where his smile should be, and seeing this, the Chief laughed. Then he felt himself coming apart again. This picture had been taken recently. It could have been taken that very morning.

Put the phone away! He could "investigate" later. But he was the police chief. He checked Tess's incoming calls. There was a call from Andrea at 8:04 that morning (to say, *I'm coming to drop off the picnic!* The Chief had still been home when Andrea made that call). There were incoming calls from Addison at 9:00, 9:03, 9:10, 9:16, and 9:24 A.M. Those calls might have been from Phoebe, but when the Chief checked, he saw it was Addison's cell phone number and not the number of the house. Why had Addison called five times? God only knew. The Chief checked Tess's outgoing calls. He was looking for what, clues? It would be elucidating if Tess had tried to call someone from the boat, if she felt . . . Jesus, if she felt like she was in danger with Greg. But the last outgoing calls had been placed the day before—Addison, Delilah, Andrea, Addison, Tess's friend Lisa Shumacher, Andrea, Delilah, a Vineyard number, Addison, Addison, Addison.

Lots of calls to and from Addison, the Chief thought.

It felt suddenly like what he was doing was not looking for clues but rather invading the woman's privacy. He felt monstrous. Tess was dead and here he was probing the tender, private insides of her life—fingering the lingerie she'd planned to wear the night of her anniversary, checking into whom she'd called and who had called her. Ordering that her blood be tested so they could determine how much champagne she'd drunk. The Chief had the impulse then to call off the toxicology, but by now Joe would have spoken to Danny or left a message, and calling it off might raise more eyebrows than ordering it in the first place.

The Chief palmed Tess's phone. What did he know? The calls to Addison may have been calls to Phoebe. There might be text messages, text messages would tell him more . . . but the Chief had to stop poking around like this. What had happened out on the water? He would never know for sure. No one would ever know. The wondering would drive him crazy.

The Chief left the Coast Guard station and headed straight for the south shore, to Andrea. But the fact was, he needed to return to the station to deal with this procedurally. To talk about "procedure" right now would be to commit a sin that Andrea would never forgive, so he sat holding her tight, wondering how to transport her and where to take her. Home? Jeffrey and Delilah's house? Greg and Tess's house?

His third problem: the children, Chloe and Finn. There was a will somewhere, but had Greg and Tess named guardians? The logical thing would have been for Greg and Tess to name Andrea and the Chief as guardians, but the Chief did not recall ever being asked or consulted about this. Andrea was the godmother of both kids, but that didn't mean anything beyond the scope of the church. Tess's father, Giancarlo, was dead; her mother, Vivian, had Alzheimer's and lived in a home in Duxbury. Tess had three older brothers, one living in Amsterdam with his Indonesian wife, one an undercover narcotics detective with the BPD, and the third the twice-divorced general manager of a Loews Cineplex in Pembroke. The only family Greg had that the Chief knew of was a sister in Vermont who was a weaver and who lived, romantically, with another woman.

He and Andrea would take the children.

The Chief's fourth problem was everyone else. His own kids for starters, and the rest of the group—Addison, Phoebe, Jeffrey, Delilah—and everyone beyond. The community, the people at the schools, the entire island. The island would be shaken, devastated; people would come out of the woodwork with food, donations for the kids, and offers of help and support. The Chief had seen it before—when the eight-year-old boy shot himself in the face, it was the sheer number of people who had demonstrated acts of human kindness that made the Chief decide that no matter what happened, he would stay on this island forever. It was an island of good people.

The Chief slowly, carefully, got Andrea to her feet, wrapped her in a beach towel, and collected her things: the trash from her lunch, her goggles, her injured book. He pointed her toward the car, he held her up, he showed her how to walk. *This way, up here, just a little bit farther, I've got you.* His wife, whom he still loved deeply, hobbled along like she was ninety years old.

His fifth problem was his own grief. But he would deal with that later. There would be plenty of time.

DELILAH

It was Delilah who had come up with the name. The Castaways.

Why did they need a name? It was something street gangs did, and sororities. But Phoebe insisted. (Did Delilah need to point out here that Phoebe had been an Alpha Kappa Delta at the University of Wisconsin?) Phoebe had been in charge of organizing their first trip together, to Las Vegas. She was having hats made, baseball caps in denim blue with electric green embroidery. *Las Vegas 2000* for the front, and over the vent in the back, Phoebe wanted a group name. In her life before meeting Addison, Phoebe had facilitated trips for Elderhostel USA. The Elderhostel groups had hats for each trip.

We need a name! Phoebe implored, clapping her hands.

They came up with a bunch of ideas, the most appealing of which was the Porn Stars, suggested by Greg—but then he let it slip that this had been the name of his first garage band. They dismissed it immediately on the grounds that they did *not* want to name themselves after any of Greg's failed musical endeavors.

They tried to incorporate Nantucket, the island, the beach, the first letters of all their names, GATEPADJ, JEDAGATP. Nothing worked.

Delilah came up with the Castaways as she was falling asleep, which was when she had all of her brilliant ideas. She had always meant to keep a notepad on her nightstand so she could write her thoughts down, or words that would cue her thoughts. Even in this instance, she woke up not remembering her idea for the perfect name. But then it surfaced: the Castaways.

The Castaways: Because Delilah had run away from her parents and found Nantucket, because Jeffrey had inherited a farm from an uncle he barely knew, because Greg had played in a (different) band with a guy whose parents owned a house in Sconset, because Andrea had been recruited to be the head lifeguard in the summer of 1988 and where Andrea went, Tess was sure to follow. Because Addison had scoped out the community with the most valuable real estate on the East Coast, and he had brought his new bride, Phoebe. Because the Chief had been transferred from Swampscott to shape up the police department. They had all washed up on the shores of Nantucket, and they had stayed and made it their home. They had found each other.

Everyone agreed it was the right name. It was embroidered on the hats, and Phoebe was happy.

Back then, they had all been happy.

Las Vegas! Vegas, baby! What happens in Vegas stays in Vegas!

January 2000: They had been talking about traveling together for months, but it took forever to decide where to go, and when. They chose Vegas because it was the place in the world that was the most unlike Nantucket Island. Nantucket was historic, pristinely preserved and maintained, it was quiet, it was gray and staid and safe, it was an island surrounded by chilly waters, it was a Quaker woman wearing a dress with fifty eye-hook buttons and a wide lace collar. Vegas was flashing lights and cigarette smoke, it was overchlorinated swimming pools, bulimic slot machines binging and spitting up change, it was point spreads and neon signs and cleavage, marble floors, fountains, bourbon on the rocks, it was an island of electricity surrounded by orange dust, it was a nineteen-year-old showgirl wearing red fringe, five-inch stilettos, and pasties.

Nantucket was an authentic place, a place largely unchanged since 1845, with its cobblestone streets, whaling captains' homes with widow's walks and cedar shingles, leaded transom windows, back staircases with rope banisters, brick fireplaces with cooking pots hanging from iron hooks. The storefronts, the churches, the banks, the Pacific Club at the bottom of Main Street, were all as they had been a hundred and fifty years ago.

Vegas was a studied mimic, it was three miles of trompe l'oeil. It mocked the rest of the world—Paris, New York, Venice. It tried to out-authenticate the authentic. What did Addison say as they strolled through the Aladdin? *This place looks more like Morocco than Morocco itself.*

All the clichés about Vegas were true, and they loved it!

They stayed at Caesars Palace, in the newly renovated tower. They had four rooms in a row on the nineteenth floor. The Kapenash room and the MacAvoy room connected—and Delilah and Phoebe joked that this was because Tess might wake up in the middle of the night and want her mommy. They had all been happy then, but there were still jokes and pokes shared sotto voce. This was the nature of the beast, the nature of women. The four women were two couples: Andrea and Tess, Phoebe and Delilah. Andrea and Tess were a couple because they were first cousins. Andrea had been a nine-year-old girl sitting on a front stoop in Dorchester the day Tess was brought home from the hospital in her baby bunting. Andrea owned Tess; she constantly lapsed into conversations that Delilah and Phoebe couldn't follow—about Sister Maria José, or Aunt Agropina, or Crazy Richard from Harborview Avenue and his plot of marijuana out back amid the basil and spring onions. Delilah and Phoebe had had no choice but to buddy up themselves, to prick their fingers, mingle their blood, exchange vows—best friends forever—although both of them, deep down, wanted to get close to Tess. Wanted to be her favorite. Well, you know, her favorite after Andrea.

They had all been happy then. The Chief and Andrea had kids in elementary school, left behind with Mrs. Parks, the retired dispatcher from the police department. No one else had kids, though Delilah and Jeffrey were talking about it—or, put more accurately, Jeffrey was talking about it and Delilah was avoiding talking about it. Tess and Greg were thinking about it, too; they may even have been trying. They disappeared to their room when they thought no one would notice. Addison had a daughter, who lived with his first wife. Phoebe had no desire to get pregnant. She was into her "business"—she still consulted for Elderhostel and other tour groups for the active aged—and she was into her body.

In Las Vegas, Phoebe jogged along the Strip each morning, all the way down to the Stratosphere and back; she worked out in the gym, she tanned by the pool, she had a bikini wax and a facial and a hot stone massage. She dragged the rest of the girls to Ferragamo and Elie Tahari and Prada and Armani and Gucci and Ralph Lauren. Phoebe was a size 2 and Addison made millions of dollars—why wouldn't she go shopping? Andrea tired of it first; she would stand in the concourse and call Mrs. Parks from her cell phone to check on the kids. Delilah and Tess hung in there a little longer. Tess could fit in things, but she had no money (teacher's salary, she moaned). Phoebe offered to buy her whatever she wanted, but they had a rule among the group about no gifts. It was a good rule, Delilah decided, especially since she sensed Phoebe trying to buy Tess's love. That wasn't exactly a fair assessment, because Phoebe offered to buy things for Delilah, too, but Delilah had full breasts and a curvy ass that Versace didn't design for. Eventually Delilah and Tess started going for gelato while Phoebe shopped and Andrea phoned, and when they reunited, they were happy. Tess and Delilah shared their gelato, Phoebe showed off what she had bought, Andrea gave them the lowdown on the kids.

They were happy in different configurations. Jeffrey wanted to see the Hoover Dam. So he and Delilah rented a burgundy Ford Mustang convertible and asked who else wanted to go. Phoebe was a no, and Addison decided to stay with Phoebe. Tess was a no, and Andrea decided to stay with Tess. Greg wanted to go and so did the Chief. The Chief drove because he was the Chief, and Jeffrey sat up front because he had rented the car. Delilah and Greg sat in the back, taking in the sun and the wind and the desert.

The dam was astounding, mind-blowing, 726 feet of concrete holding back a biblical amount of water. Delilah stood in genuine awe. She had gone along because her husband was keen on it and because she couldn't take any more shopping or smoke or signage, and as they descended down the middle of the dam with a tour guide, she congratulated herself on her fine decision. What if she had *missed* this?

As they waited for the elevator that would take them back up to the top of the Dam, Greg whispered in Delilah's ear, "I should have brought a joint."

Delilah giggled, less out of amusement than out of a sense of conspiracy, because she and Greg were the only two of the group who smoked dope, much to the dismay of their respective spouses.

Jeffrey looked at Delilah sharply—the tour guide was in the middle of a discourse on the WPA—and Delilah felt bonded to Greg even more. They were the bad teenagers disrupting class. Hadn't it always been that way when Delilah was growing up? She had led boys astray or she had let them lead her astray; she was always pushing the envelope, forever getting into trouble.

They stopped for a late lunch at a roadhouse on the way back to Vegas, and Delilah and Greg polished off three Coronas apiece and started telling stories about the sexual mishaps of their younger years. They laughed like fools, spurting beer all over the table, while the Chief looked on with mild indulgence (sex wasn't against the law, after all) and Jeffrey glowered.

"Why don't you guys tell stories?" Delilah asked.

They were embarrassed by the question, and Delilah knew why. It was Andrea, the woman they'd shared. The Chief would not tell any stories about other women for fear of disrespecting Andrea in front of Jeffrey. Jeffrey, Delilah knew, had only slept with two women, herself and Andrea, and that sewed that up pretty tight. It was not funny to tell stories about his own wife, nor about the wife of someone else at the table.

Jeffrey motioned for the check; Delilah excused herself for the bathroom.

Twenty minutes beyond the roadhouse, Delilah had to pee again.

"You just went," Jeffrey snapped.

Delilah had read somewhere that the human bladder could expand to the size of a grapefruit; hers was a basketball, a wobbly and distended water balloon. She had to go *now,* she was seconds away from letting the stream go, hot and grateful, all over the backseat of the rental car. She intoned as much.

The Chief pulled over and Delilah climbed out of the Mustang without using the door. She crouched behind the exhaust pipe and lifted her prairie skirt. Her flow ran in rivulets over the hard red dirt. Jeffrey held his forehead in his hand; he couldn't believe she was doing this, even though it was the kind of thing she was always doing. She climbed back into the car, grinning.

"Okay," she said. "Ready to go."

Delilah leaned her head back against the seat, catching the last angled rays of sun on her face. She was happy. The afternoon she went to see the Hoover Dam remained one of the singular afternoons of her life.

*   *   *

Greg and the Chief and Andrea got up early and walked to New York New York for Krispy Kreme doughnuts. Addison and Tess and Delilah went to the Bellagio to see the impressionist collection. Andrea and Addison and Delilah and Greg were addicted to the slot machines; they each walked around carrying a plastic cup of quarters and would stop to play when someone else in the group went to the bathroom. In the MGM Grand, Addison hit it big. The coins splashed down. He won seventeen hundred dollars. Everyone else groaned. Of all of them, Addison needed the money the least! He seemed abashed by the win; he pinkened all the way over his bald pate—or maybe he'd gotten too much sun by the pool with Phoebe.

I'll buy dinner! he said. *Wherever you want to go!*

They all agreed this was a wonderful idea, despite the rule of no gifts.

They went to Le Cirque, because they had all heard of it—even the Chief, who claimed to know nothing about the finer things in life. Addison had actually been to the original Le Cirque in New York with his first wife. (She had gone to boarding school with one of Sirio Maccioni's sons.) Phoebe complained that it was no fun to be the second wife and lead the second life with a person who had done it all—and done it well—the first time around. She complained privately to Delilah as they moved en masse down the strip through the throngs of people, sidestepping the short immigrant men who handed out cheap business cards about massage and dancing girls. Delilah was only half listening. She had had a fight with Jeffrey and could not stop fretting about it.

The fight had taken place as they were getting ready for dinner. Delilah ordered a bottle of Sancerre from room service. It arrived, elegant and cold, and Delilah, wrapped in her white waffled robe, waited as the bellman poured two glasses. She tipped him ten dollars.

Jeffrey was soaking, dutifully, in the two-person tub. The tub was merely atmosphere, it was foreplay. Delilah had it all planned out: wine together in the tub, wild sex either on the impressive acreage of their California king bed or on the plush bathroom rug, followed by a long shower for Delilah. She wanted to get the cigarette smoke and the twenty-four-hour miasma of the casino out of her hair and off her skin. But when she submerged in the tub and handed Jeffrey his wine, he said, "You really disappoint me. You know that?"

It was his choice of the word *disappoint* that struck Delilah first. It was such a parental word. "Why?" Delilah said.

"Carrying on like you did with Greg at the Hoover Dam."

"Carrying on?"

"You were like a couple of kids. The pot joke. The sex stories. And then you lifted your skirt in front of everyone. You pissed in front of everyone. I was embarrassed."

"Embarrassed?"

"Mortified. You're a grown woman. You're my wife."

"So?"

"You have no idea how to behave. No sense of decorum."

"Decorum?"

"It was disgusting. Three beers at lunch and a shot of tequila?"

She didn't realize he'd seen the shot of tequila, but yes, Greg had shanghaied her on the way back from the ladies' room and they'd each thrown back a shot of Patrón silver, quick and neat.

"I can't stand this," she said.

"What?"

"Being *monitored* like this. Being lectured on *decorum*. We're on vacation, Jeffrey. We're in *Las Vegas*."

"That's no excuse."

She stood up, unsteadily, and climbed out of the tub.

"Fuck you," she said, though she meant the opposite. There would be no wild sex. She stepped into the shower. When she emerged, Jeffrey was sitting on the edge of the bed, dressed in his navy suit, looking somber and morose, like a funeral director.

"I want an apology," he said.

"Apology?" Delilah said. "Ha! I'm the one who deserves an apology."

"And why is that?" He turned his head stiffly, like a ventriloquist's dummy.

"Because you're acting like my father," she said. She pulled a dress on over her head. Phoebe would have something new for tonight, a thought that was both demoralizing and infuriating. Phoebe had worn a new dress every night of the trip so far. "And don't forget, I ran away from my father."

"Meaning what?" Jeffrey said.

"Meaning what do you think?" Delilah said. She foraged through her suitcase for her other black slingback. There was a knock at the door.

It was Tess, fresh-faced and grinning like a Girl Scout.

"Ready?" she said.

Still, they were happy at dinner. Le Cirque was as glamorous a place as Delilah had ever eaten in, and she was relaxed knowing that Addison would take the bill. He ordered two bottles of Cristal. Delilah's spirits rose. Greg was to her left, Jeffrey to her right, and Andrea on Jeffrey's other side. Tess was next to Greg, Addison between Tess and Phoebe, the Chief between Phoebe and Andrea. The vacation had them breaking up into small groups, it had them rearranging and forging unusual allies, but when they sat down for a meal together, they always sat like this.

It was curious.

The champagne came and Phoebe, assuming the role of first lady (because Addison was paying for dinner or because she had organized the trip, Delilah wasn't sure), wanted to make a toast.

"To us," she said. "The Castaways."

"The Castaways!" everyone said. Glasses clinked, none crossing! (Phoebe swore it was bad luck.) Delilah sipped her Cristal.

She was normally counted on to get the conversation rolling, but tonight she wouldn't do it. She wasn't in the mood. No one understood how difficult it was to come up with new, interesting things to talk about with people who had exhausted every topic under the sun. No one gave her any credit for her conversational gymnastics, and she was pretty sure Jeffrey resented it. How many times had she heard it? *You talked a lot at dinner.* Tonight she would observe all the rules of proper decorum. She would not get bawdy. She would not be the first one to bring up sex, or drinking, or other lewd topics. She pressed her lips shut.

There was a lull at the table. They were waiting for her. *What is the greatest song the Rolling Stones ever recorded? I say "Loving Cup." Andrea, how about you?* No, she wouldn't. Was anyone looking at her? She didn't care. She didn't care if they ate their whole meal in awkward silence. She studied her menu.

Out of the blue, the Chief started talking. This was truly amazing, as the Chief normally said very little, in the way that serious men who had important, quasi-confidential jobs said very little. The Chief had apparently bumped into an officer with the LVPD at the roulette wheel. The Chief showed his badge. The other officer was on the vice squad, he said. The Chief and this officer chatted it up for quite a while.

"You would not believe the things he told me," the Chief said.

"Like what?" Delilah said, forgetting to keep her mouth shut.

The Chief drank from his beer bottle (the waiter had wanted to pour the beer in a glass, but the Chief held his palm up and said, *It comes in a glass,* in a way that was very Chief-like). He shook his head at Delilah. He wasn't going to tell them anything else. He was famous for bringing up teasers like that and letting them drop.

Okay, fine, forget it, Delilah wouldn't push it, though the life of a Las Vegas vice squad officer sounded fascinating if you loved the raw and the raunchy, which Delilah did—and it would be relevant besides. But she'd taken a vow of silence and she meant to stick to it.

Phoebe regaled the table with details of her hours by the pool—*Okay, does everyone in this town have fake boobs or what?*—and Delilah's mind wandered. It became clear, now that she had stepped out of her role as the conversational master of ceremonies, how firmly established that role was. They all had their roles, each one of them; they had their personalities, proclivities, interests, likes and dislikes. They were adults, they were known quantities. Was this good or bad? They could not surprise each other. They were not likely to change or act out of character. Like the Chief insisting on drinking his beer from a bottle, even here at Le Cirque, because that was how he drank his beer. Utterly predictable.

But the roles gave them comfort, the lack of surprise lent security, a sense of understanding, friendship, family, acceptance. Right?

The Chief was their spiritual leader. He was their man in case of emergency; he was the best problem solver (though Jeffrey was a damn close second). He was the police chief, he knew everything and he knew it first, but he gave nothing away. The man was a vault. If they ever broke him open, what would they find? A treasure trove of secrets and confidences bound up by his honor. The Chief was principled and discreet. He was part of a fraternity across the country, across the world. Law enforcement. The earth's finest.

Andrea was the den mother, Mother Earth, Mother Nature. Delilah had always thought it would be boring to be Andrea—she was matronly, sexless, she wore skirts to the knee and one-piece bathing suits, she wore comfortable shoes—but Andrea seemed content. She wasn't looking for anything, she wasn't searching for herself, trying on identities or attitudes the way Delilah sometimes did, the way Tess and Phoebe did, too. Andrea had a firm grip on who she was, and this left her plenty of time and energy to focus on others (the Chief, her kids, Tess). When Delilah was sixty or seventy, she wanted to be just like Andrea. She said this once to Jeffrey, and Jeffrey made a face indicating that he found this statement ridiculous or inappropriate. Jeffrey had been in love with Andrea years and years ago; they had dated, kissed, groped, copulated, fallen in love, moved in together. They had talked about marriage and kids. But back then, Jeffrey wasn't ready. Andrea was the first woman he'd made love to (Jeffrey's long-time girlfriend in high school and college, Felicity Hammer, was a devout Baptist, determined to remain chaste until her wedding day, and so for six years Jeffrey was dragged along on that virginal ride). But Jeffrey didn't leave Andrea because he had wild oats to sow; he left her because he had real oats to sow, real corn, real vegetables. He'd inherited a hundred and sixty-two acres of fertile farmland, a legitimate business opportunity, and he wanted to succeed. He could not put the farm first and put Andrea first. They broke up. It was, in his words, very sad.

This could have moved Delilah right along to thinking about Jeffrey, but she couldn't allow herself to deconstruct him. He was her husband, she knew him too well, and she was angry. She would skip him. *You really disappoint me.* God, it infuriated her, but it did not surprise her.

Addison was talking now, rescuing them from Phoebe's discourse on life as seen from the chaise longue. He was describing Las Vegas real estate trends (Addison loved trends) and how the old casinos—the Sands, the Golden Nugget, the Desert Inn—were being medicine-balled and replaced by theme-park giants—the Luxor, the Venetian, Treasure Island.

The waiter reappeared, and they ordered. Delilah ordered the salade frisée avec lardons and the steak. Jeffrey wanted the beets, but would not order them because they were out of season. And so he went with the grapefruit and avocado salad and the pasta with lump crabmeat. (Even their ordering could not surprise her.

Phoebe ordered a salad with roasted vegetables. Addison and the Chief got the steak, like Delilah.)

Addison was the businessman, the money man. His last name was Wheeler, and every single person on Nantucket called him "Wheeler Dealer." Addison was tall and thin and bald; he wore horn-rimmed glasses. He was part nerd, part aristocrat. His father had owned a carpet and flooring business in New Brunswick; his mother had been a nurse in the infirmary at Rutgers. Until high school, Addison's life had been very Exit 8. It had been McDonald's after football games; it had been Bruce Springsteen and summers spent "down the shore." But like cream, Addison rose to the top. If you believed him, he did so without trying. He was bright, polite, and charming. He had a silver tongue. He was a social genius, and because of this, he stood out. The junior high school principal suggested that Addison make a run at boarding school, where he could take advantage of some real opportunities.

He got into Lawrenceville based on his interview alone. From Lawrenceville he went to Princeton, where he was president of his eating club, Cottage. There was something funny about his graduation, and by funny Delilah meant peculiar—he hadn't had the correct credits at the end of his senior year to get his diploma. He had finished up the following summer at Rutgers. Had he graduated from Rutgers, then, technically? Or was it a Princeton diploma with a Rutgers asterisk? Delilah had also heard that Addison had been *thrown out* of Princeton for conducting an affair with the wife of the dean of arts and sciences, whom Addison had met at a faculty cocktail party he'd crashed. Now *that* sounded like Addison, but Delilah did not have confirmation of that story, and the one time she had been brave enough to ask Phoebe, Phoebe had said dismissively, *I can't keep track of all the stories. The man has had nine lives.*

That was the truth about Addison: he had had nine lives. The stories were too numerous and byzantine to keep track of. Which were real and which were lore? He claimed to have lived in Belfast, Naples, and Paris while working as a broker for Coldwell Banker. But he had only just turned forty: how had he possibly fit it all in? He spoke fluent French and Italian, he spoke *Gaelic,* he knew everything there was to know about food and wine, painting, sculpture, architecture, classical music, literature. His first wife was an anorexically thin rubber heiress named Mary Rose Garth, who had a brownstone on Gramercy Park and a penchant for younger men—her personal trainer, the handsome Puerto Rican doorman. Mary Rose had taken Addison for the ride of his life; she had shown him all of the best ways in the world to spend money. But she had been too much even for Addison; they divorced amicably, and Mary Rose now lived in Malibu with their daughter, Vanessa. If you were to believe Addison, Mary Rose and Vanessa shared boyfriends.

Delilah ate her steak. She had asked for it rare and it had come perfectly cooked, seared on the outside, dark pink on the inside. Addison had also ordered his steak rare, but the Chief had ordered his well done. (Predictable.) They had moved on to drinking a red wine from Argentina—shocking, since Addison was a Francophile. But it was the most incredible wine Delilah had ever tasted. It was like drinking velvet. It was like drinking the blood of your one true love. If she said this, everyone would laugh. Phoebe would say, *God, Delilah, you are so clever,* and mean it, and Jeffrey would shake his head, embarrassed.

Andrea was talking about her kids. Dullsville. But Delilah would not save her.

In her mind, she moved on to Phoebe. Phoebe was Delilah's best friend, though they were an odd match. Phoebe was blond, stick-thin, never caught in public without perfectly applied Chanel lipstick. She was a cruise director, a cheerleader; she was the pep squad. She was a trophy wife. She liked being all these things; the stereotype was her identity and she relished it. The shopping, the waxing, the Valentino heels, the Dior perfume, her slavish devotion to *Sex and the City*. She did not cook, she did not clean or do laundry, but she did take spinning and yoga classes, she did avoid red meat, as well as chicken and fish and all starches. It seemed like she ate the same way that she drank champagne: sparingly, on special occasions. Tonight she had ordered a beautiful leafy salad with a timbale of roasted vegetables, but at home it was all rice cakes, navel oranges, and mineral water.

What Delilah had learned, however, was that there was depth to Phoebe. The woman was a fantastic administrator. She sat on the boards of directors of two charities, she cochaired events that raised ludicrous amounts of money. She ran her consulting business with acuity; she was as shrewd as Addison—shrewder, perhaps, because whereas Addison was acknowledged as being shrewd, Phoebe was considered ditzy and vacuous.

Phoebe came from a close-knit family from Milwaukee. She had grown up with loving parents and a twin brother, Reed, whom she adored. They were the kind of twins who created their own language; they were, in Phoebe's words, "just like the twins in *Flowers in the Attic*, minus all the nasty stuff." Her parents, Joan and Phil, were still married, still living in a center-hall colonial in Whitefish Bay, still sustaining themselves on the milk and cheese of Phoebe and Reed's youth. Reed was a fantastically successful bond trader in New York. Phoebe talked to him at least twice a day. He invested her money. He had made her millions.

Something fell and hit Delilah's foot. It was . . . Greg's spoon, one of Greg's many spoons. (This dinner required the full Emily Post lineup of utensils.) He bent down to retrieve it, a very un-Emily-Post-like move. (How many times had Delilah's mother told her that when you dropped a utensil, you were to leave it be and ask the server to bring you another one?) Delilah felt Greg's fingers fondling her left heel. She was shocked, but she kept her expression steady. His fingers kept going; he dragged them up the back of Delilah's calf to the crease in her knee. This was out-rageous. It was unprecedented. There had been new allies forged on this trip, yes, and maybe Greg, like Jeffrey, was recalling their flirtatious afternoon at the Hoover Dam—but to fondle her foot under the table during dinner?

Greg surfaced like a kid trolling the bottom of a swimming pool for coins, holding his spoon aloft.

"Got it!"

It might seem like Addison and Phoebe were the couple who were the most mysterious, respectively unknowable and misunderstood, but Delilah was baffled by Greg and Tess. Because they, somehow, had won. They were everybody's favorites. They were Boy Bright and Suzie Sunshine; they had what everybody wanted.

With Greg, it was easy to understand. Greg was, after all, their rock star. He played guitar and piano; he sang. He had shaggy brown hair and intense green eyes and a day of growth on his face. He was six feet tall—shorter than Jeffrey by five inches and Addison by three—but his body was that of a professional surfer. He had six-pack abs and the shoulders of Adonis. He had a vine tattoo encircling his left bicep. He wore two silver hoops in his left ear and a silver ring on the second toe of his left foot, which only someone like Greg could pull off. If there was a woman in the world who was resistant to the charms of Greg MacAvoy, Delilah had yet to meet her. In a way, Delilah was immune. (His looks and charm were a virus she had encountered many times before.) She prided herself on being Greg's buddy, his partner in crime. She did not fantasize about Greg; she did not desire him.

(But this thing that had just transpired under the table—what was this? A joke, she decided. A harmless funny.) She looked at Tess. Had Tess noticed anything strange? She had not. She was listening with ridiculous, eager attention to Andrea talk about Eric's crush on the elementary school art teacher.

Tess was the ingenue, the baby sister. She was Amy in *Little Women;* she was Franny Glass. Adored, coddled, spoiled, adored some more.

It helped that she was small—five feet tall, ninety-seven pounds—and it helped that she had thick dark hair cut into a bob and tucked behind her ears, showing off her pearl earrings or her microscopic diamond studs. It helped that she had freckles and a Minnie Mouse voice. It helped that she was the nicest, kindest, most generous person on the face of the earth. She loved babies and animals. She cried at movies and AT&T long-distance commercials. She sponsored an orphan in Brazil, an eight-year-old girl named Esmeralda, and in addition to sending regular checks, Tess sent boxes packed with brown rice, muesli, coloring books, Crayola markers and colored pencils, jigsaw puzzles, modeling clay, a hairbrush, barrettes, packages of new underwear, a toothbrush, floss, toothpaste, stickers, a flashlight, and a special-ordered copy of *A Little Princess* in Portuguese.

Only Tess.

She was a good egg, for real. She never had a mean word for anyone; she loved Greg and Andrea and the Chief and the rest of them with unbridled intensity. It felt good to have Tess like you, to have Tess love you; it felt like sunshine, it felt like warm chocolate sauce over your ice cream.

Greg was no dummy. He could have had any woman he wanted and so he snapped up the prize: Tess DiRosa. He had been playing with his band at the Muse and Tess had been in the front row, wearing—how many times had Delilah heard the story?—jeans and a green bandanna on her hair. And Greg said to his bass player, *Hey, that little Gidget girl is hot.*

They were, now, the perfect couple.

Or were they? Delilah was suspicious. She didn't believe in perfect couples. She didn't believe in perfect families. Delilah told off-color jokes and stories, she threw decorum to the wind, and people liked this about her because on some level everyone related. Life was messy. It did fart and burp, it left a stink in the bathroom and bloodstains on the sheets. Polite society had an underbelly. People led complicated, secret lives, and this fascinated Delilah.

But what did she know?

Greg's hand on her foot. Her leg!

Dessert was served, and Delilah was tired of thinking. She wanted to talk. She cleared her throat, and everyone at the table looked at her. They were hungry for her.

"Greatest band of all time," Delilah said. "Who is it?" She pointed at Greg. "You're not allowed to say the Porn Stars."

"Or the European Bikinis," Addison said.

They were off and running.

By the time they left Le Cirque, they were all drunk. Happy drunk! Too drunk for Wayne Newton, too drunk for Barry Manilow, too drunk for O. Too drunk for the crooner in the cheesy lounge at Caesars who liked to end his cabaret show with "Someone Left the Cake Out in the Rain."

But not ready for bed. Not yet! It wasn't even midnight!

What to do? The Bellagio fountains—again? No. The white tigers at the Mirage? No. A drink at the Venetian? No. Slots? Maybe, just for a minute. Howie Mandel? No.

They decided to go to Circus Circus to ride the roller coaster. This was Tess's idea, and since she was Cindy Brady, and since she never got to decide anything, that was what they did. They were all dressed up, but no matter. They filed two by two (couples only this time) into the roller-coaster cars, with Delilah and Jeffrey up front. Delilah leaned her head against Jeffrey's shoulder; she squeezed the hell out of Jeffrey's farmer hand, which was as wide and sturdy as a spade. No one would believe this, it would in fact *surprise* them, but Delilah was afraid of roller coasters. Terrified. And not just in the way that normal people were afraid of roller coasters. She was in full freak-out mode. Her heart was a crazed animal that had been zapped with high-voltage electricity; she thought she might cry, or insist on staying on the ground where it was safe, but this was a group thing, Tess had picked it, and Delilah would not be the spoiler.

She clung to Jeffrey. The man was a walking, talking security blanket. He was not going to let anything happen to Delilah. That, in the end, was why she had married him. She didn't need excitement or trouble from a man; she created enough of that on her own.

"You're the best person in the world to ride a roller coaster with," she said to her husband.

It seemed he did not need this explained to him. He took it the way it was meant. As an apology.

"Thank you," he said.

The roller coaster lurched forward. Delilah shrieked. They hadn't even gone anywhere. *Here we go! Eeeeeeeeeeeeee!* The roller coaster jerked upward, it ticked ominously up the incline. Delilah had her back braced against the seat. Her heart wanted out. Oh my God. It would be thrilling, she thought, a thrill all the better because it was so damn scary. They crested, the car hesitating at the top. Delilah could not see the bottom of the chute but she could sense it. The air beneath her, the breath-stealing trajectory.

They plunged. Delilah's stomach fell away; it was somewhere over her head. She screamed. They all screamed.

(They hadn't known, then, what was coming. They didn't know about September 11, Phoebe's twin brother jumping from the hundred and first floor; they didn't know about lost pregnancies; they didn't know about the pharmaceutical cornucopia targeted at post-traumatic stress disorder; they didn't know about the ways their marriages would fall apart and then be saved; they didn't know about affairs or love realigning; they didn't know about a girl named April Peck or the shitstorm she would create; they didn't know they were going to leave and be left. They didn't know they were going to die.)

They screamed. Back then, they had all been happy.

ADDISON

For maybe ten years now, Addison Wheeler had considered himself a rich man. He had a beautiful home, four cars, membership in two private clubs, a case of 1967 port in his wine cellar, and eight figures invested with his broker in New York. He had a sixteen-year-old daughter in the best private school in southern California, and an ex-wife who was so wealthy on her own that all she asked Addison for were special favors. (He had a client who could get him tickets to anything, anywhere—the Super Bowl, the Academy Awards.) But from now on, money would mean nothing. Money couldn't help him. Money didn't matter.

Tess was dead.

They gathered at the Drake house, because they always gathered at the Drake house. Greg and Tess's house was too small, Andrea and the Chief's house was too police-chiefy (there was a scanner in their house that squawked all the live-long day, and somewhere in the house, everyone knew, the Chief kept guns). Addison and Phoebe had the biggest house, with views over Sesachacha Pond. From their widow's walk, you could see all three of Nantucket's lighthouses. Addison and Phoebe had tried to host gatherings in the past, but these gatherings were never quite right. Phoebe raided the fancy Italian cheese store for hundreds of dollars' worth of asiago and salumi, and Addison, hands down, had the best wine, not to mention the most sophisticated stereo and TV, but something was missing. Their house was too cold, too formal. They had no kids; that might have been the problem. And yet in their basement was a home theater with every DVD from *The Breakfast Club* to *Bee Movie*, as well as a pool table. They had beanbag chairs, a basketball hoop, and a swimming pool, half of which was only three feet deep. It was heaven for kids, so that wasn't the problem. The problem was something else.

Or maybe this was just Addison's insecurity talking (he was rich, yes, but not rich enough to quiet the voice in his head that constantly reminded him of his shortcomings). Maybe it wasn't that there was anything wrong with Addison and Phoebe's house; the Drake house was simply better. It was warmer. It was, in essence, a farmhouse, with a captivating mix of woods and woven rugs, bright fabrics, copper pots, a fire in the fireplace or the grill smoking on the deck. Delilah made everything from scratch rather than buying it prepared; she was an easy, natural hostess, pouring your drink before your coat was off. She made the most delicious cocktails, she had the funniest cocktail napkins, she cooked with cream and butter, herbs and just-picked produce. She had the best mixes on her iPod, and she was always, always ready to turn it up a notch. Addison loved it at the Drake house, and Phoebe would have put their own house on the market and moved in with the Drakes at the drop of a hat. There was just something about it. It was happy, balanced.

But not, of course, today.

Addison and Phoebe arrived at ten minutes to seven, though it felt much earlier. It was the longest day of the year. The Chief and Andrea had arrived, and instinctively Addison looked for Tess's Kia. For the past six months, when he had pulled into this driveway, he had looked for Tess's car. He had her license plate memorized: K22 M3E. He had waited, dozens of times over the past winter, for that car to pull into the driveway of the cottage in Quaise, an exclusive listing of his, where they used to meet.

Tess's car wasn't there. It was in the lot across from the town pier.

Next to him, Phoebe was as still and quiet as a statue in a garden. She had self-medicated, which was dangerous after an event like this, but Addison hadn't had the wherewithal to check what she had put in her mouth. He tried to monitor what Dr. Field prescribed her, what she took, what she stashed away, what she gave to Delilah (Phoebe was a very generous woman, even with her pharmaceuticals)—but this had dropped off in recent months, partly because of Tess, and partly because the responsibility of being on constant watch with his wife was wearying. He had tried lecturing, he had tried an intervention (a mini-intervention, him and Dr. Field, explaining to Phoebe that she was becoming dependent on these drugs and she had to wean herself off them—the antidepressants, the pain meds, the sleep aides). Nothing worked. Phoebe popped pills, and rather than killing her, they seemed to be keeping her alive. So whereas Addison felt like he wanted to take a steak knife and eviscerate his insides, cut his heart out so it would stop hurting—Tess was dead!—Phoebe was as calm as a houseplant. She wasn't a person so much as a topiary.

Addison turned off the car. He wasn't sure that he could go into that house and pull off the acting job that was required.

"He killed her," Addison said.

Phoebe turned to him. "What?" she said.

There had been a text message, sent to his phone at quarter to ten that morning. Addison had been in his office, reviewing the purchase-and-sale agreement for the big deal. He saw that the text was from Tess and he willed it to say *I love you*—he found he needed constant reassurance of this from her—but when he opened it, it said, *I'm afraid.*

He had stared at the message, wondering how to respond. Tess was right to be afraid. Addison himself was terrified. Greg was pulling out all the stops to win her back. She had to be careful, she had to resist him! The text came just as they would have been sailing out of the harbor, so Addison thought that Tess meant she was afraid of the water. She had nearly drowned in Dorchester Bay as a child. She swam with her kids at the beach, but only on the north shore, where the water was placid, and even then she went right in and came right out. When her kids were swimming in Addison's pool, she stood at the side, vigilant, even though Chloe and Finn had suffered through years of swimming lessons, born from this very same fear. Sailing, fishing, boating, snorkeling, scuba diving, even the ferry back and forth to the mainland, made Tess uncomfortable. She remembered what it had been like, at age nine, to slip under the water's surface and not be able to fight her way back up.

Addison shuddered.

Phoebe said, "I think we should offer to take the kids."

"Let's go in," Addison said.

The Drake house was not the Drake house. There was no food or drink, no music, no Delilah. In the living room, Jeffrey sat with the Chief, face-to-face, saying nothing.

Addison said, "We're here."

The two men nodded.

Phoebe said, "Where's Delilah?"

"In our bedroom," Jeffrey said. "Waiting for you."

Phoebe said, "Where are the kids?"

"Downstairs."

"Do they know?" Addison asked.

"Not yet," the Chief said.

"We'll take them," Phoebe said. "We have lots of room."

"Phoebe—" Addison said. He should have headed off this notion while they were still outside. No one was going to be comfortable with Addison and Phoebe taking even temporary custody of the kids.

"One step at a time," the Chief said.

"Where's Andrea?" Addison said.

"Asleep upstairs," the Chief said.

"Asleep?"

"The doctor gave her something. She can't handle it. Tess was . . . everything to her."

She was everything to me, Addison thought. And no one will ever know it.

I'm afraid, the text had said.

Phoebe tiptoed down the hall to Delilah. Downstairs, Addison could hear the kids.

"What happened, exactly?" Addison said.

"It's not clear," the Chief said. "The boat capsized, they drowned. They got caught underneath the boat. Greg's foot was tangled in the ropes. They had been drinking."

Addison pictured Tess and Greg on the deck of the boat, drinking champagne, eating strawberries, kissing. Talking—about what? There was so much anger between the two of them, so much suspicion and confusion about what had happened the previous fall with April Peck. Greg had never come clean; he stuck to his preposterous story. Addison had asked him once when they were both very drunk: "Tell me what happened, man. The truth."

And Greg had hesitated, as if thinking about it. Could he trust Addison? He and Addison were very close friends. But in the end, the answer must have been no. He said, "Man, I already told everybody the truth."

It ate away at Tess. Her trust in Greg had been destroyed. She didn't believe in anything anymore: not marriage, not friendship. She had fallen in love with Addison. Or she claimed to have fallen in love. Addison worried that Tess was using him unconsciously (God, of course unconsciously, the woman didn't have a mean bone in her body) to get back at Greg. She still cared what Greg thought; she worried what Greg did, where he went, whom he saw.

"The Coast Guard retrieved their things. Greg's guitar, the picnic basket, their shoes . . ."

"He killed her," Addison whispered. He said this to himself. He was in such agony he couldn't help it, and he didn't care if they knew what he thought. They did not hear him.

The Chief said, "Greg thought he was a better sailor than he was. He had no business trying to get them to the Vineyard. I should have stopped them."

"I should have stopped them," Addison said. He had been dying to tell her not to go; he had wanted to give her an ultimatum. *If you love me, you won't go.* But at the time he hadn't seen that this would accomplish anything besides upsetting Tess and, possibly, learning some things he didn't want to know. Such as that she still loved Greg, despite her anger and distrust. Such as that if Addison forced her to choose—him or me—she would choose him.

But if he'd insisted, she might still be alive.

"I'm going downstairs now to tell the kids," the Chief said.

"Or I could do it," Jeffrey offered.

"I had pictured this as Andrea's territory," the Chief said. "But she isn't capable."

"And neither is Delilah," Jeffrey said.

"I'm their uncle," the Chief said. He took an audible breath, and Addison noticed how old he looked—a bad sign, since he and Addison were the same age. Forty-nine. "I've done a lot of crappy duties with this job, but . . ."

"This is the worst," Jeffrey said.

"The worst," Addison echoed. He was so, so upset, but there was no way for him to express it. Should he be the one going down to tell Chloe and Finn their parents were dead? Absolutely not. And yet he and Tess had been so intimate. For the past six months, it had been just the two of them in a make-believe world, a carefully preserved fantasy, touching, kissing, experiencing unprecedented tenderness. They were simpatico. He held her while she slept, he listened to her, he bought her cookies and marzipan and truffles for her sweet tooth. He tickled her, they laughed, he combed her hair, she rubbed his back, and when they parted, she cried. *I don't want to go back to him.*

After Easter, they had begun to talk about running away. Living together. Addison was the one who broached the subject first. He had loads of money, he could make anything happen, he could pay lawyers, he could leave Phoebe the house and they could buy a new house together. They could buy the cottage. Then they would never have to leave, never have to say goodbye.

Tess played along, but not wholeheartedly. Addison sensed she was repeating his words back to him because she knew it made him happy. *Never have to leave. Never have to say goodbye.*

He loved her more than he had ever loved anyone else, including fiery Mary Rose Garth, including Phoebe, including his own daughter. Tess unlocked something in him. Everything he'd done, everything he'd seen, everything he owned, had meant nothing until she became his. She gave him a reason.

But would Tess want him to be the one to tell her kids that she was dead?

He was sure the answer was no.

The Chief went downstairs.

Addison and Jeffrey sat together in awkward silence. They were waiting. Listening for . . . what? Addison's own daughter, Vanessa, was high-strung and prone to melodrama. If informed that he or Mary Rose was dead, Vanessa would shriek to break glass. She would climb into her Miata and drive like Richard Petty through Beverly Hills, wailing to her friends on her cell phone. But how would two sweet, levelheaded seven-year-olds react? Addison and Jeffrey waited. The happy noise downstairs quieted. Then Addison heard footsteps on the stairs. He turned. It was Jeffrey's boys, Drew and Barney. They were crying the way boys cried once they'd outgrown the baby stuff. Red eyes, tears, but no noise.

Jeffrey said, "Come here," and opened his arms.

"The Chief told us," Drew said. "Then he asked us to come upstairs."

"He needs time with Chloe and Finn," Jeffrey said. He hugged his boys fiercely and made a grunting noise. Addison both recognized it—*I love you guys, I will always love you, we are so lucky this isn't us*—and was made uncomfortable by it. The emotion was so raw, he felt voyeuristic. Addison stood up.

In the mudroom, he found the bag the Chief had collected from the Coast Guard. The personal effects. Addison lifted Greg's guitar out of the bag.

I'm afraid.

Greg had killed her.

But to say so would only damage the kids.

Addison rooted through the bag. He needed something to do. Andrea was asleep, Delilah and Phoebe were cloistered away in a lair of female bonding. The Chief had the twins and Jeffrey was consumed with his own boys. From the bag Addison removed pieces of Tupperware, some still containing food. He inspected the contents of one: a half-eaten lobster sandwich. Had this been Tess's sandwich? Had her lips touched the bread? Addison lifted out the picnic basket; the fibers were waterlogged and disintegrating. He pulled out Tess's flip-flops. Size five and a half J.Crew flip-flops in red and navy grosgrain ribbon. He turned them. Her tiny, doll-like feet had been in these shoes this morning. Her feet were so small, she had a hard time finding shoes that fit. He would keep these flip-flops. But no, he couldn't. Where would he put them? What would he do with them? He yanked out Greg's deck shoe, which most closely resembled an overcooked steak; two striped beach towels; a small suitcase. Did Addison dare open it? He did not. Then he came across Tess's iPhone wrapped in its sunny yellow prophylactic. Addison didn't think. This was her cell phone, it was important, it was evidence; there was the text, *I'm afraid,* and who knew what else she'd kept or erased? Addison crammed the phone into his pants pocket. He pitched the Ziploc bag into the trash. Would the Chief notice that the phone was missing? He might. If he'd had the chance to study the contents of the bag of personal effects, he would notice. Would he have had that chance? The Chief's afternoon had been frantic. He had gotten the whole story from the Coast Guard, more of the story than he was telling, certainly. Knowing Ed as Addison did, Addison realized that yes, Ed would have found time to go through this bag. He may even have documented the contents. He would notice that the phone was missing.

Well, that was too bad. If he wanted it, he could fight Addison for it.

Addison needed air. The house was too warm; the wind had died down and the heat of the day was sticky and uncomfortable. Addison was going to vomit or faint. Tess was dead. She had been trapped under the boat, unable to swim out from under it. She had been afraid. God, just the thought of her fear and her panic, her struggle against the water, her need for air, her lungs about to explode, her cries for her kids. *Chloe! Finn!* She would have been thinking only of them in the end.

Addison wanted to take the pilfered phone and get in his car and drive. Drive away, heedless and fast.

He erupted with a broken shout, and tears blurred his vision. He stepped out onto the deck. All their cars were there in the driveway, except for the one that mattered. *Never have to leave. Never have to say goodbye.*

He pulled the felt heart out of his pocket, and sure enough, it ripped.

No! His heart!

He held the two pieces together. Could it be glued? It looked like an apple with a bite missing. He put the two pieces of the torn heart in his pocket. It was the only thing Tess had ever given him.

This, she'd said, *is my heart.*

PHOEBE

Phoebe envied Delilah for many reasons, and today another reason was added to that list: Delilah was able to express her grief
fully and plainly, like a child. She was in her bed, curled in the
fetal position, crying like a baby, sobbing, hiccupping, catching
her breath, wiping her nose and face, and then collapsing all over
again. She was hysterical, nothing would stop her, and that had
to feel good.

Phoebe lay on the other side of Delilah's bed. She stretched
out and covered Delilah's body with her own. She made a shushing sound as she might for a baby. These gestures didn't seem to
be making any difference to Delilah, but Phoebe stayed there.
She felt, as ever, that she was watching the rest of the world from
behind frosted glass; there was a barrier between her and everyone else. That barrier had come down for the first time in eight
years today, when she had gone to find Addison. She had *lost it.*
The news of Greg and Tess dead—delivered by Sophie from her
Pilates class, whose husband served in the Coast Guard—had
shattered the frosted window, and Phoebe had found herself
face-to-face with horror.

Phoebe had been through it all before.

Reed!

Her twin brother had been . . . how to explain? The dearest
person in her life. He had always been there. Since Phoebe was
conceived, since the womb, since her first day on earth, the two
of them had been a pair, pink and blue, a matched set, meant to
be together. The twin relationship sometimes backfired; Phoebe
had heard all kinds of weird, twisted stories. When Phoebe was in
her twenties, she finally heard her parents speak of the concerns
they had had when Phoebe and Reed were young. *You were too
close—you spoke only to each other. We wanted to take you to see
a therapist.* Phoebe and Reed had developed their own language,

which their mother feared was meant to keep the rest of the world at a distance. But when Phoebe thought back to her childhood, there was only peace, comfort, and constant, safe companionship. She and Reed liked each other, they were considerate of each other—even as teenagers. They realized that hurting each other would be akin to hurting themselves. Reed was handsome and popular and smart; he played soccer, basketball, lacrosse. Phoebe was beautiful and popular and smart; she was editor of the yearbook and she was a cheerleader.

Reed helped Phoebe with her trig; she helped him with his paper for American lit. He was math and science, she was English and history. Reed could draw; Phoebe could sing. They both sucked at French. Phoebe called him Reedy, Reeder, Freebird, Sweet Reedy Bird. He in turn called her Twist, short for Twister, short for "twin sister."

Did people tease them? It was possible, behind their backs. They were too good, too cute and perfect, too close. One night after basketball practice, Reed came home with a swollen eye. Something had happened, a fight with Todd Carrell, a boy Phoebe had broken up with before Christmas. In the locker room, Todd had said something crass about Reed and Phoebe, and Reed had gone wild. Todd Carrell had been sent to the hospital with a broken arm. Rather than being upset, Phoebe was dismissive.

The rest of the world doesn't understand, she said.

Later that year Phoebe and Reed were in danger of being voted homecoming king and queen. They both won, but after the Todd Carrell incident, Phoebe understood that the student body wouldn't be able to handle it. Since Phoebe was on the homecoming committee, she fixed the vote so that Shelby Duncan, who was Reed's girlfriend and had come in second place, was named the winner.

Phoebe and Reed went to college at the University of Wisconsin. They led separate lives in a natural way. Reed played varsity soccer, majored in business admin, and pledged TKE. Phoebe majored in communications and pledged Alpha Kappa Delta. They spoke on the phone daily and met for lunch at the Dairy every Wednesday, just the two of them. After college, they both moved to New York City. Phoebe lived in Chelsea and slugged it out as a catalogue model for nearly a year before she got a job with Elderhostel. Reed lived on the Upper East Side. He worked for Goldman Sachs first, then went to Columbia Business School, then got a job with Cantor Fitzgerald. They still talked on the phone every day (and with the convenience of cell phones, it was usually two and three times a day), and they had lunch every Wednesday at Pastis. Their grandfather died; they drove back to Wisconsin for the funeral together. Reed went through a bad breakup with a woman ten years older than he who happened to be number three on the masthead at *Vogue;* Phoebe met him at McSorley's, and they got wickedly drunk and hung out on the swings at the Bleecker Street playground until four in the morning.

Phoebe could go on and on explaining and still not quite capture what she was trying to get across. She did not fight with Reed. When they disagreed, they did so nicely. They knew each other too well to fight; they understood each other completely. The bottom line was: Phoebe had never in her life felt lonely. Because she always had Reed. Her best friend. Her double. He was she, she was he, they were pink and blue, two halves of a whole.

Reed met a girl and got married. Moved to Connecticut. Phoebe loved her sister-in-law, Ellen Paige, and helped her organize Junior League luncheons in New Canaan. Phoebe then met Addison and moved to Nantucket. The Wednesday lunches became a thing of the past, but Phoebe and Reed still talked on the phone two or three times a day. They spent a week together in Wisconsin at Christmas. Reed and Ellen Paige came to Nantucket for a week in June; Phoebe and Addison went to Connecticut for a week in October.

Ellen Paige got pregnant and had a baby boy. His name was

Domino, but Phoebe called him Sweet Reedy Junior. She spoiled him rotten, sending him a monogrammed bathrobe, a full Brio train set, a four-foot stuffed giraffe from FAO Schwarz. *I'm an auntie! The auntie.* Reed's baby was her baby.

In my will, Phoebe said, *everything goes to him.*

What could Phoebe say about September 11 that hadn't already been said in sixty languages? It was a beautiful day. Addison got up early to go shark fishing with Bobby D. Phoebe was headed to the gym, but she gagged and spit in the kitchen sink over the smell of her usual espresso. She was grossed out, but she was happy, too.

She was pregnant! She, Phoebe Wheeler, was going to have a baby!

Phoebe hadn't even realized she wanted a baby. In fact, when asked, she was adamant that she *didn't* want a baby. She didn't want to ruin her body, she didn't want to cramp the lifestyle that she and Addison had cultivated, she didn't want to deal with poop or vomit or her own filled-to-bursting milkmaid breasts, which would undoubtedly leak all over her Elie Tahari camisole tops. But since Domino had come into the world, Phoebe had softened toward the idea. She would have a baby girl, and her daughter and Domino would be Reed and Phoebe, the next generation. On September 11, she was eleven weeks and four days along. She and Addison had gone for an amniocentesis and found out that the baby was perfectly healthy, and yes, it was a girl.

There was no reason Phoebe couldn't exercise, the doctor said. In fact, she should exercise. *Just don't overdo it, and be sure to eat!* (Phoebe blanched; she was not a big eater. She feared calories as if they were poisonous spiders, and now, with the nausea, even her usual diet of espresso, celery sticks, and fat-free yogurt dip wouldn't stay down.)

At the gym, Phoebe got on the treadmill. Only three days until her first trimester was over and she could tell people she was pregnant. She had told her parents, of course, and Reed and

Ellen Paige, and Delilah and Jeffrey and Tess and Greg and Andrea and the Chief. But, for example, Jeremy, the adorable boy who checked IDs at the front desk of the gym, didn't know. He must have looked at the slight swell of Phoebe's belly and thought she was eating too much banana pudding, complete with Nilla Wafers and whipped cream. (This was Phoebe's favorite dessert, but she didn't let herself get within a hundred yards of it.) Phoebe wanted to stick by the first-trimester rule, because she felt that the only thing worse than miscarrying would be people pitying her for miscarrying. Phoebe had always been lucky and blessed; her life had been happy. Pity was foreign and horrible to her; she feared it more than calories or poisonous spiders.

As Phoebe ran, she watched the *Today* show. It was eight-thirty. There was a half-hour limit on the machines at the gym, but if there wasn't a line (which there wouldn't be, now that all of the summer people had gone home), she could push it to sixty minutes. At five minutes to nine, Phoebe was hitting a wall. She was feeling worn down, shaky, short of breath. The doctor had told her not to overdo it. She should stop. She had a Pilates class at four, anyway. But she put on her headphones and kept going.

She was listening to Taylor Dayne sing "Tell It to My Heart," and her feet were moving now. She had her second wind; she was feeling better than she had all summer. And this was what all the pregnancy books said: the day will come when the nausea and fatigue will end and the pregnant woman will feel good. Phoebe was thinking about this, wondering if it was okay to believe that her turning point had arrived today, Tuesday, September something, when she noticed something happening on TV. The *Today* show was cut short; they had Tom Brokaw on, looking very serious. Then there was footage—a plane flying into the side of a tall building. People crowded in among the treadmills, trying to see the TV. Jeremy from the desk was among them.

Phoebe was hesitant to slow down or stop; her pace was perfect. She was having that experience when her body and the machine were working optimally together.

She kept going. Again they showed the plane flying into the building. More people crowded in. They didn't want to use the treadmill, they just wanted to watch the news. Phoebe removed her right earbud and said to Jeremy, "What's going on?"

"A plane hit the World Trade Center," he said.

Phoebe gagged. Okay, wait. Wait! She punched the correct sequence of buttons on the treadmill to make it slow down, then stop. Her insides were a brewing storm; she was going to lose her bowels right there on the treadmill in front of everyone. Another indignity of the pregnant body. She could not get her breath. She had that shaky, hot, diarrhea feeling. She was afraid to move for fear of erupting. There was a word on her tongue, one word, but she had to deal with her personal emergency first. Get out of the gym! She had to get her bag, her *phone,* she had to get to her car. Before leaving the gym, she checked the TV screen again. The World Trade Center? In New York City? Of course that's what the building was. She had been watching the screen just like everybody else, she had seen the plane fly into the building—through the building—just like everybody else, but she had been so inward-looking, so consumed with the cardiovascular and reproductive systems of her own body, that she had not thought to wonder where the building was. If pressed, she would have said Jerusalem or Lebanon, or some other part of the world where planes flew into buildings, either because political strife was a part of the everyday or because they just weren't as careful as Americans. But New York City? The World Trade Center?

She was holding the word in her mouth like a piece of hard candy. She spit it out.

Reed!

She ran down the stairs to her car, dialing. Number one on her speed dial, before Addison even, was Reed at work. Cantor Fitzgerald, hundred and first floor, the World Trade Center, Tower One.

She got his voicemail.

"Jesus, Reed, call me!" she screamed.

Two women Phoebe knew vaguely were getting out of their cars in the parking lot. One of them, Jamie, said, "Hey, Phoebe! Are you okay?"

Phoebe waved, got into her car. Call Addison! The receptionist at Addison's office, Florabel, answered the phone. Phoebe detested Florabel and suspected the feeling was mutual.

Phoebe said, "Addison, please?"

Florabel didn't recognize Phoebe's voice, because Phoebe's voice was held hostage by panic. Florabel said, "Mr. Wheeler is out of the office today. Would you like his voicemail?"

Shit! Addison was fishing! Phoebe hung up. She tried Addison's cell phone and got his voicemail. He was so far offshore, he would never have reception.

She called Reed back. It was five after nine.

"Hey, Twist," he said. His voice was calm, but in the background Phoebe could hear shouting, which seemed more frenzied than the usual Cantor shouting. "You would not believe what is happening here. Have you seen the news?"

"Sort of," she said. "Are you okay?"

"Well, I just threw up in my trash can," he said. "Because I tell you what, people are *dead* over in that other building. You should see the smoke. It stinks, even in here."

"What are they . . . are they saying anything?"

"We're supposed to sit tight. Some of the guys—Ernie, Jake, you know—they want to go to the ground to watch, but there's debris falling. It's safer, I think, to stay put."

"You think?"

"That's what . . ."

"What?" Phoebe said. She couldn't hear.

"I'll call you back when the dust settles, okay? I love you. I'm going to be fine, I promise."

"Okay," Phoebe said.

"I have to call Ellen Paige. She's at play group with Domino, but when she hears about this, she's going to freak."

"Okay. I love you," Phoebe said.

"Hey," he said. "How are you feeling?"

"Me?" Phoebe said. "I feel fine."

There was a noise. Honestly, it sounded like a lion roaring, or a wave crashing over her head. The line went dead. Phoebe nearly sideswiped the mailman, who was filling boxes on Old South Road.

She watched footage of the plane hitting the second tower on Addison's sixty-inch plasma TV, in the closed-up, air-conditioned, professionally decorated comfort of her own home. Outside, the day shimmered. Nantucket was as tranquil and lovely as it had ever been. Phoebe turned her stare outside, in a daze. According to Tom Brokaw, America was under attack. Phoebe waited for the planes to come screaming over the ocean. Nothing. A monarch butterfly settled momentarily on the picnic table, then flew away.

On the TV a plane hit the second tower, which was Tower One. Again and again. Phoebe was riveted. Show it again! She was counting floors and dialing Reed from her landline.

"Pick up!" she screamed into the phone. No one was around, no one could hear her. Their neighbors on both sides had left after Labor Day.

Her call went to Reed's voicemail. "Call me!" she screamed.

It looked like the plane had hit the second tower, Tower One, about two thirds of the way up. Definitely lower than the hundred and first floor. Were there a hundred and five floors or a hundred and ten? She couldn't remember.

Her phone rang. Delilah. Phoebe let it go. She could not talk to Delilah.

She counted floors down from the top. They flashed back to Tom Brokaw.

"Show the building!" she screamed. No one on TV could hear her.

Another channel, CNN, showed the towers smoking, blazing. This channel showed people hanging out their windows. Hanging out their windows so far up? What if they fell? They were waiting for the helicopters to come. Where were the helicopters? Was the National Guard going to send in helicopters for the people who were trapped above the flames? Phoebe had seen it countless times in the movies. This was the United States. The government, the military, the people in fucking charge would use their expensive, cutting-edge technology to rescue the people hanging from their windows.

"Send the helicopters!" she screamed. Where were the fucking helicopters?

At some point it hit her. This was real. Reed was in that building, he was clinging to that office window—the very same window that for years had afforded him what he called the billion-dollar view—because the temperature inside, they said, was three thousand degrees. Was that correct? Was there even such a thing as three thousand degrees?

Phoebe was on her knees. She was freezing, shivering, convulsing. The TV showed people jumping. Jumping from the hundred and first floor? Was there a team of firemen on the ground holding one of those inflatable parachutes that would catch these people, that would make their landing marshmallow-soft?

No. The TV said the jumpers most likely would suffer a heart attack on the way down. They were dead on arrival. They splattered like a watermelon falling off the back of the farm truck. The jumpers had so much velocity, the TV said, that they were killing bystanders at the bottom.

At that moment, or a moment later, Reed jumped.

Phoebe felt it. She, too, was falling.

In high school, in the French class that Phoebe and Reed detested, both of them barely hanging on to a B minus, their teacher showed a film called *The Corsican Brothers*. About twins who felt each other's pain. One breaks his arm, the other screams. Reed and Phoebe developed a Corsican Brother shtick for a while—Reed would bump his shin, Phoebe would howl.

You're a regular vaudeville act, their father said.

Was there a spiritual connection between them? Did they feel each other's pain? Sometimes people asked this. (Just as people always asked if they were fraternal or identical. Hello! World's dumbest question!)

No, they said.

And yet there was something.

A few years earlier, Reed had gone skiing in Telluride with Cantor clients and something went wrong on one of the runs. There was an avalanche of sorts, leaving Reed buried to his waist, unable to move or even reach his cell phone, for ninety minutes. Phoebe, who was on Paradise Island in the Bahamas with Addison, felt her feet go numb. She could not feel her feet, not even when she grabbed her toes or walked over the scorching tiles around the swimming pool.

Something's wrong with Reed, she said. She called him, and his cell phone rang and rang. She made Addison go to the concierge desk to track down the number of the mountain in Telluride.

Later, when Reed was nursing his frostbite, wrapped in blankets in front of the lodge fire with a hot toddy, they laughed over the phone and said, "Corsican Brothers."

So, yes, there was something.

But never anything as powerful as the feeling that overcame Phoebe at that moment on September 11. She had leaped out into the billion-dollar view. She was floating. And then there was a rush, friction like she was being sucked through a tunnel. The air was devouring her. She tried to fight back but couldn't move her arms. Her arms were pinned to her side, and then suddenly her arms were over her head, she was upside down, she was going off the high dive at the Whitefish Bay pool club, she was going to hit any second, break the surface with a resounding splash, and have a strawberry back from the impact. But there was no impact. She was still falling, keening, the air ripped her hair out, her teeth out, she was blind, she was deaf. There was so much air, she couldn't breathe. The wind ripped her up. It rubbed against her like flint and she ignited. She burst into flame, like a star.

Reed was gone. And so was she.

She did not cry. She curled up on the sofa and shivered. The phone rang. At first she checked the display in case it was Reed, in case he had decided in a rush of fraternity-brother camaraderie to go downstairs with Ernie and Jake to watch from the ground, but it was everyone else calling. Delilah again. Ellen Paige. The Chief. Andrea. Tess. Phoebe's mother. Ellen Paige. And finally Addison. She did not answer. These people left messages on her machine. She sensed concern (the Chief), she sensed hysteria (Ellen Paige, her mother), but she could not hear anything clearly. She was deaf from the wind in her ears.

She couldn't watch the TV anymore, but she couldn't stop watching. The plane hit the building; it pushed right through it like a poison dart through the wall of a straw hut. She thought of people jumping. It was jump or melt, and Reed, whose life had been just as blessed as Phoebe's until this very morning, would have weighed two impossible options and decided to jump. Would his red cape work? He chose to believe it would—for Domino's sake, Ellen Paige's sake, their mother's sake, Phoebe's sake.

Freebird. Sweet Reedy Bird.

I'll call you back when the dust settles here.

When the dust settles.

On TV, the buildings collapsed like a house of cards.

By the time Addison got home, sunburned and smelling strongly of fish, Phoebe had vomited all over their seventeen-thousand-dollar silk Oriental rug, hand-knotted in Tehran, and she had wet herself. Her gym shorts were soaked. She didn't care. Nothing mattered anymore, not even when Addison gasped and said, "Jesus, Phoebe!" And she realized that she had not wet herself. She was sitting in a pool of her own blood.

It was now eight years later, and everyone had healed and moved on. Phoebe's parents had started a scholarship at Reed and Phoebe's high school in Reed's name. It was a large scholarship with elaborate requirements, and they spent many of their postretirement hours administering it.

Keeps me busy, Phoebe's father said.

Domino was in fourth grade, living with Ellen Paige and her new husband, Randy, whose wife had been a restaurant manager at Windows on the World. They met at a support group.

It was only Phoebe who was stuck in an acrylic box. She could see out, but she was alone. Untouchable.

It was the drugs. Phoebe was on antidepressants, pain medication, and sleep aides. She had the drugs that Dr. Field liberally prescribed, and she had black-market drugs that she got from Brandon Callahan, Reed's roommate at Wisconsin, who was a drug rep with—well, Phoebe was hesitant to name the company that Brandon worked for. It was a big company; the drugs were good.

There were those people—Addison, Phoebe's mother, and to some extent Delilah—who felt that the drugs were harming Phoebe, killing her even. Look what they had stolen from her already—her consulting business had gone under; her body, once fit and toned, was now a bunch of twigs with skin hanging off them like cobwebs. And her personality had vanished. She smiled once a month, she never cried, she never laughed. She had, however, become an excellent listener. Listening was something she could do; many times the drugs made her feel lofty, like she was floating on air above everyone else, a Buddha on a pedestal, a deity calling in from the clouds. She gave sage advice now, everyone (meaning Delilah) said so, because she had no ego. She spoke only the truth because she no longer cared.

Addison and Dr. Field had tried to get her off the drugs. They wanted her to cut back with the eventual goal of quitting altogether. She could see their point. They would wean her off a little at a time, the way one treated frostbite. You warm the feet gradually by rubbing, and the blood returns, the tissue pinkens and comes back to life. This was how it would work with Phoebe. She would go off the drugs and things would come back into focus. She would get an appetite back, she would return to the gym, she would take on a small consulting project or agree to chair a brunch for donors to the Atheneum, she would agree to take tennis lessons with Delilah, she would shop for a dress or a belt, she would be able to watch TV, make love to her husband, bite into a peach, take a swim on a hot day, read a magazine—and enjoy it.

Life is out there waiting for you, Addison said, with Dr. Field nodding beside him. Addison sounded like a TV evangelist, a motivational speaker with a best-selling book. Phoebe understood that Addison was right. Life *was* waiting for her, she could see it through the clear walls of her box. But she didn't want to give up the drugs. The drugs were Phoebe's life support, they were the bubble wrap that kept her from breaking. Reed was dead, he was never coming back; she would *never see him again.* Even now, eight years later, that fact took her breath away. It was the vertigo. She was falling!

Life was out there waiting for Phoebe, but it was not waiting for Reed, and therefore Phoebe would not, could not, take advantage of it. This seemed childish to the rest of the world, but that was because the rest of the world did not understand what it was like to have a twin like Reed.

Phoebe remained locked in her museum case.

Labeled "Twin sister of September 11 victim."

* * *

Phoebe lay against Delilah, absorbing her sadness. Delilah was rocking and rolling with it; she was hot and heaving. Her grief was pornographic. She was showing Phoebe the raw, pink, gaping, oozing parts of herself.

Tess and Greg were dead. Phoebe had taken four Ativans between the time Sophie had told her the news and the time she reached the Galley to tell Addison. The drugs were clothing her now, covering her like a protective suit. The fascinating thing had been her exhibition in the restaurant parking lot. She had emoted like a regular person—screaming, yelling, crying.

She had been convincing, even to herself.

THE CHIEF

The call from Danny Browne, the medical examiner, came while the Chief was standing behind Finn at the mirror, doing his necktie.

The funeral was in an hour.

Andrea was with Chloe, upstairs. The hair dryer was droning, Andrea wouldn't have heard the phone, and so the Chief answered the call—leaving Finn's tie dangling—despite the fact that Andrea would have said, "Now is *not* the time, Ed."

He had to know.

"You're not going to believe this," Danny Browne said.

Which was not what the Chief wanted to hear. He had been hoping for a glass of cold water, clean and transparent. He didn't want murkiness, he didn't want a goddamn detective story, he didn't want something he wasn't going to believe.

And yet he'd had a feeling. Two people trapped under a boat, unable to grapple for the edges or swim until they were free of it?

"His blood alcohol was at .09. Hers was at .06—but she was on other junk."

"Other junk?"

"Opiates. Your normal cause for finding opiates of this strength in the blood is heroin use."

Finn stood morosely at the mirror, staring into his own freckled face, which looked exactly like his mother's, and then, noticing the Chief's gaze, he fingered the limp tie around his neck as if wondering what to do with it.

Now is not *the time, Ed.* Andrea was always right.

"Send a copy to me at the station. In a sealed envelope, please, marked 'Confidential.' Do you understand me?"

"Yes," Danny Browne said.

"I mean it," the Chief said. The Chief did not like to pull rank, but in this instance he had no choice.

"No one else will see it," Danny said.

The church was filled to overflowing. The Chief had ordered Federal Street closed on the block the church occupied, between Main Street and India Street. People spilled out of the church onto Federal Street, and then around both sides of the church like an apron. The Chief would have said he knew everyone who lived on this island, but he was wrong, apparently. Outside the church were groups of high school students. These were the girls from the singing group and their friends, and Greg's guitar students—they were easy to pick out, with the long hair and the look of discontent. The Chief knew many of them, recognized others, but that was because he had two kids in high school himself. Kacy and Eric's close friends had taken seats inside, but these other kids—the Chief could not, in his present state, put a name to a single one—either did not feel worthy of a seat inside or liked the freedom of remaining outdoors. There was another group, young mothers and fathers with small children. These would be Tess's kindergarten students and their families, past and present. There was a whole generation of parents bringing up kids on this island who were strangers to the Chief. Did they know who he was? He supposed they did.

All in all, the Chief estimated, there must have been a thousand people.

It was hotter than Hades. Bright and sunny, without a trace of the wind that had capsized Greg and Tess's boat. The island was teeming with tourists. At the edge of Main Street there was a clear delineation between those vacationing and those grieving. The summer people wore their Lilly Pulitzer prints and carried lightship baskets as they shopped for hydrangea bouquets. The locals were somber and subdued, wearing a depressing amount of black. Nearly all of them were weeping behind their sunglasses.

The Chief was wearing civilian clothes, a black suit bought for civilian funerals. He was working, too, trying to supervise crowd control (this would have been easier in his uniform) and teaching his summer cops, who had been on the job exactly nine days, which street was India and which was Federal. The hearse was parked in front of the church. The Chief was to be a pallbearer in addition to everything else. It might have been easier to delegate someone to take his place, but Andrea insisted that he carry Tess into the church and then again to her grave. He would do it.

Once the service started, things were easier. The Chief and Andrea were up front with Kacy and Eric, and Delilah and Jeffrey and their boys, and Phoebe and Addison. Chloe and Finn had asked to be allowed to sit in the very first row, all by themselves.

You're sure? the Chief asked.

Nods. Then, from Chloe, the self-appointed spokesperson, "We're sure."

Those two kids were wiser and more composed than many of the people sitting behind them. They were holding hands (again, it seemed, at Chloe's insistence). Finn was wearing khakis, white shirt, navy blazer, and navy tie, the exact outfit he had taken his first communion in two months earlier. Chloe was wearing a navy sailor dress that she *deplored* (her word, used this morning, with Andrea). It was her parents' funeral; she was supposed to wear black. But her closet revealed nothing black except a velvet Christmas dress two sizes too small, and so Andrea had steered her toward the navy sailor dress. There were, predictably, tears, and a lot of misplaced anger directed at Andrea, but Andrea had emerged from her cocoon of despair to deal with the kids, especially Chloe, with kindness and patience. Chloe put on the navy sailor dress, and as consolation Andrea allowed her to carry a black sequined cocktail purse. The result, in Andrea's words, was part Shirley Temple, part Coco Chanel. In the purse, Chloe had put Tess's broken red sunglasses with the white polka dots, Tess's gold cross from her confirmation at St. Eleanor's in Dorchester, a package of Kleenex (at Andrea's suggestion), a Chapstick, a copy of the picture of herself and Finn that she had slipped into Tess's casket, and a copy of the letter she had written for Tess, ditto. Nothing of Greg's. She'd put nothing in Greg's casket, and neither had Finn. Andrea must have noticed this, but did not comment on it, and the Chief followed suit. Both kids had been very attached to their mother. Greg had been a good father, though he had complained to the Chief and everyone else that Tess loved the kids so completely that there was no room for Greg to parent them, except around the edges. He played lullabies for them on his guitar, he read them *Harry Potter* (though Tess disapproved, she thought it was beyond them and scary to boot), he helped them do flips off his shoulders at the beach, he took them to the Scarlet Begonia, where he bought them a lunch of cheddar potato skins and Coke. Tess complained to Andrea and everyone else that Greg was less like the twins' father and more like some prodigal uncle just returned from following the Grateful Dead, who showed up to break the rules and disrupt routine.

Tess and Greg had had their battles, just like everyone else. And now here they were, in caskets, side by side, as the organ played the processional hymn and the ushers checked each pew for empty space. Could they squeeze in one more person? The church was like a Cineplex during the 8 P.M. showing of a block-buster movie.

A ripple went through the church. The Chief did not like ripples; a ripple meant an assassin in the crowd. He craned his neck. April Peck and her mother were headed down the left aisle. Andrea dug her fingernails into the soft underside of the Chief's thumb. Delilah groaned. Even Phoebe pursed her lips and shook her head.

April Peck was wearing a denim halter dress, as though she were ready for a day at the Hyannis mall. Her mother, Donna, wore a black floral caftan that flowed to her ankles and a black scarf wound around her head. The Chief did a double-take: Donna had lost all her hair, it looked like. Cancer? This was a momentary distraction. The Chief could not believe the girl had had the guts to show up. What exactly was she trying to prove? The Chief had half a mind to escort the little minx right back out of the church. She could stand in the street, where Greg's other students had gathered. April Peck thought she was special, she thought she deserved a seat inside. Had the mother not been wearing that headscarf, the Chief would have made a move.

The priest reached the altar. *In the name of the Father . . .* Everyone genuflected, but not the Chief. He had been raised a Unitarian and did not love all the high-church rigmarole—the hands, the prayers, the responses that everyone else seemed to know.

"A light has gone out," Father Dominic said. "Two lights. It is a beautiful day of sunshine, but we spend it in darkness."

The Chief tried to concentrate on the service, but then, too, he wanted to monitor the twins. All he could see of Finn was an inch of pale neck caught between the straight line of his summer hair-cut and the starched collar of his shirt. Chloe turned frequently to whisper to him, though Finn did not react. What was Chloe saying? She had developed a fearsome personality already; she was quick and clever, polite with adults, bossy with her brother. The Chief smiled. The twins were an example of the miracle of life. They were healthy, intelligent, complex human beings. But for so long they had been nothing but an idea, a yearning, a project, a wish helped along by the daily lighting of candles and a prayer chain. Tess had lost three pregnancies, one of them in a terrible accident, well into the second trimester. The twins, when they arrived, were a gift, and Tess never let herself forget it.

The priest finished. Delilah stood to give the readings. Andrea did the prayers with a stiff upper lip, and then Jeffrey rose to do the eulogy. The church was silent. Jeffrey had the bearing of Abraham Lincoln—tall, lean, stately—and he was an orator, too. That was a Cornell education for you. Jeffrey talked about meeting Tess for the first time when she was fifteen years old, a sophomore at Boston Latin, and so naive about the world that at dinner that first night, while helping Andrea set the table, she put ice cubes in Jeffrey's beer.

The church laughed. It was so Tess. Even at thirty-five, there had been things she was so naive about.

April Peck was in the church. The Chief, who liked to know where his sniper was, had her pegged in row nine.

Danny Browne had found opiates in the blood. Tess shooting heroin? This was impossible; there was a mistake with the tox report.

The night before, the Chief and Andrea had gone through the Coast Guard bag. Andrea took the broken sunglasses for Chloe and Tess's flip-flops for Kacy, but they were way too small. Together they asked Eric if he wanted Greg's guitar—there had been a period of time when Eric was keen for Greg to teach him to play—but Eric said he wanted to think about it. When Andrea saw the macaroons still watertight in their Tupperware, she burst into sobs. The delicate emotional business of going through the personal effects ended then and there. The Chief pitched everything else, except for the guitar and the overnight bag. There was a whole house full of stuff to be gone through, and the will to administer. Addison had been named executor back in 2000,

when Greg and Tess bought their house. The will had been written before Chloe and Finn were born and had never been updated. Never been updated! No guardians named! This was an
egregious oversight on Greg's part; it was one of a million loose
ends that would surface, the Chief was sure, once the man's life
was examined. Andrea was adamant about taking the kids. Tess's
brother Anthony agreed, saying, *You were not only her family, you
were her best friend.*

And heaven help the poor soul now who tried to take those
kids away from Andrea.

As the Chief was dealing with the remains of the personal effects, he noticed that the Ziploc bag with Tess's iPhone was missing. He rummaged through what he had already pitched into the
trash, thinking the bag might have gotten mixed in accidentally.
He didn't see it. He checked through the overnight bag—Greg's
boxers, the black lace lingerie thingie of Tess's, toothbrushes, hairbrush, polo shirt, khaki shorts, Noxema, Advil. No phone. What
had happened to the Ziploc? The Chief checked the mudroom.
His family stowed every last pair of shoes they owned in there,
so in total maybe fifty pairs of shoes were jumbled in baskets that
Andrea bought from Holdeverything to contain the mess. The
Chief sat down and dutifully emptied the boxes of shoes—nothing—and then got on his hands and knees and checked under
the cast-iron radiator. Nothing. He checked the trash again.

Okay, the iPhone was gone. Someone had taken it. Andrea?
She had been avoiding the bag of personal effects as if it contained the Ebola virus. So no. Kacy or Eric? It wasn't impossible,
but both Kacy and Eric had been quiet and introspective since
the deaths, and considerate of their mother. They wouldn't have
removed anything from the Coast Guard bag without asking.
Chloe or Finn? Chloe, maybe—she was seven going on seventeen—but was she sneaky or curious enough to lift her mother's
phone? There had been people in and out of the house for the
past five days. It could have been anyone.

The cell phone. Jeffrey was still up there talking, now about Chloe and Finn and how it was the responsibility of everyone in the church to raise them into adults and remind them each and every day how much their parents had loved them.

Amen. There wasn't a dry eye in the house. Including the Chief's own. He pulled out a handkerchief. He had the summer cops outside to worry about, and opiates in Tess's bloodstream, and two more children to raise when his own two were nearly out of the house, and a wife who would hit the anger stage of grief prematurely if April Peck and her mother dared to show up at the reception. She would attack like a Siberian tiger who hadn't been fed in two weeks. And the cell phone (five calls from Addison in half an hour) was missing.

But the funeral was almost over; those caskets were going into the ground. It was unspeakably sad and awful and unfair, and the Chief was going to shed a few tears. He deserved it.

PHOEBE

She couldn't make herself cry during the funeral, no matter how hard she tried. She was rummaging for anything, even horror—after all, the dead bodies of her friends, Tess and Greg MacAvoy, were moldering in those caskets. But no, nothing. If she had feelings, they were shriveled and cold, hiding in a dark corner somewhere.

The recessional hymn played. Phoebe caught a glimpse of Chloe and Finn from the side. Finn was crying, and Chloe had her arms around him as if he were her child. She was whispering something. Phoebe watched her lips. She was singing the hymn. *And I will raise you up. On the last day.*

Phoebe was rapt. Something inside her peeled back, revealing . . .

In another second the priest would head down the aisle and the caskets would follow.

Phoebe got out of her seat. She scurried over to Chloe and Finn. She said something, inaudible to her own ears over the organ and the halfhearted singing, but Chloe and Finn seemed to hear her. They seemed to understand. They were nodding.

They understood her! Really understood. Phoebe could see it in their eyes.

You still have each other, she'd said. *You still have each other.*

JEFFREY

He had given the eulogy because that was what had been decided on by the group. He said "the group," but what he really meant was Andrea. Andrea had the final word on all things Tess-and-Greg-related. Andrea wanted Jeffrey to do the eulogy; he did the eulogy.

Now, as they were filing out of the church, Andrea approached him again.

"I need your help."

Something other than delivering the eulogy? Something other than serving as a pallbearer for Greg's casket?

"Anything," he said.

"I need you to make sure that April Peck does not come to the reception."

Uhhhhhhhh. Jeffrey had already received an earful of April Peck–inspired invective from Delilah when the girl and her mother had entered the church. *Little slut, what makes her think, I mean, Jesus, she has to know she doesn't belong here, she is the last person, all the lies she told, the heartbreak she caused, and I'm not only talking about Tess, I'm talking about Greg, too . . .*

Jeffrey had shushed her.

To which she'd hissed, *You are not my father!*

Now Jeffrey made a pained face.

"I can't have her there," Andrea said. Despite her grief, or maybe because of it, Jeffrey thought Andrea looked especially beautiful. She looked twenty-five years old, not forty-four. Her face was thin. She was very tanned.

What exactly was he supposed to say to April Peck? On the night that Andrea had asked him to do the eulogy, she had told him, *You always know just what to say.*

And everyone, except for Delilah, had agreed.

"I'd have Ed do it," Andrea said now. "But he's . . . oh, hell, he's busy being the police chief."

"Okay," Jeffrey said.

Andrea said, "Thank you, Peach." Which was what she used to call him, twenty years ago.

"No problem," he said.

He found April Peck and her mother, Donna, talking with Mrs. Parks, the former police dispatcher, who had to be eighty years old by now. Mrs. Parks, it seemed, had mistaken April and Donna for MacAvoy relatives—April a niece of Greg's, perhaps, or Donna a cousin. Jeffrey loitered awkwardly at the edge of their conversation, waiting for April and her mother to separate so he could do the dirty business of letting them know they would not be welcome at the Westmoor Club. Jeffrey wasn't sure if April Peck knew who he was. Would she know that Jeffrey and Greg had been friends? Obviously—he had just given the eulogy! He didn't realize the kind of celebrity this would temporarily lend him until April's mother stepped out of the chitchat with Mrs. Parks, touched Jeffrey's arm, and said, "You did a wonderful job."

Jeffrey was flustered. How to respond? "Thank you," he said. He had Donna's full attention now—Mrs. Parks had moved on to someone else—with April standing at her mother's right elbow. "Listen, I don't know quite how to say this . . ."

"I came out of respect for Mr. MacAvoy," April snapped. She was just a floating head over her mother's shoulder. Blond hair upswept, mascara appealingly smudged, transparent pink lip gloss glistening. April Peck was a knockout. That was the problem.

"Yes," Jeffrey said. "Thank you." He let this expression of appreciation rest for a moment before he continued. "But because of the difficult situation—last year, I mean—the family has asked that you forgo attending the reception. They feel your presence would be inappropriate."

Donna seemed truly astonished by this statement. She took a stutter-step backward, narrowly missing colliding with Mrs. Parks behind her, and her black headscarf slipped, revealing her bald scalp.

"I'm sorry," Jeffrey said. "It's just that it's . . . difficult for the family."

"It's difficult for me!" April said. "He's dead and I want to pay my respects! You think I don't *know* my presence is 'inappropriate'? You think I didn't feel a thousand eyes on me? Of course I did!" April's voice was loud. Her mother's expression was one of horror, but whether that was because of April's outburst or because of her own exposed scalp, Jeffrey could not tell. He was grateful that the church was emptying out. He didn't want a scene, and he was sure Andrea didn't want a scene either—but what had she expected when she had sent him on this mission?

"Okay, listen . . ." he said.

"And for the record, you can't actually keep me out of the reception."

"Well, it's private."

"Well, I don't want to go anyway. I never had any *intention* of going. My mother is sick." Donna, meanwhile, had made her way unsteadily to the back of the church and was standing in front of the rows of candles as if debating whether or not to light one.

"I'm sorry to hear that—"

"She has cancer!" April said. And since her mother was out of earshot, she added, "The chemo may not work."

Jeffrey nodded solemnly. The unfortunate truth about April Peck was that she had lost all credibility.

"And one more thing," April said. She took a step toward Jeffrey. She was officially too close. God, if Delilah saw them, she would have a conniption. Jeffrey didn't want to know one more thing. He had done his duty; April Peck would not come to the reception. Now all he had to do was get out of the church. But April Peck was not willing to let him go. There was something she was determined to tell him. She was so close to him, he could smell her breath: bubble gum. Her sooty eyes were narrowed. She was going to have the last word. "I was with him the night before he died."

DELILAH

Delilah hated Andrea Kapenash.

Hated her!

She may have hated Andrea for years but had only now, with the event of Tess and Greg's death, admitted it to herself. How could she hate someone she was such good friends with? It was all of a sudden obvious: Delilah hated Andrea because they were such good friends. Because for years she had spent hours and days and weeks in Andrea's infuriating presence. Andrea always had the answer. Tess had been Andrea's handmaiden, eager to please her, eager for everyone to please her. And so, for the years that they'd been friends, Andrea had controlled everyone's lives. Andrea was always right, she was the oldest, she had raised her children first, she would tell you how it was done. Andrea was married to the police chief. That gave her power, two feet firmly planted on the Moral High Ground.

But now Tess was dead and certain things were going to change. For starters, Delilah was going to express her true feelings about Andrea.

Or maybe not. The fact of the matter was, Delilah was great at articulating anger in her mind, but in real life she found confrontation difficult and unpleasant. Especially with women. Delilah had never argued with Phoebe or Tess, and she had never overtly argued with Andrea (disagreed strongly, maybe, but Andrea had steamrolled her every time). Delilah had no problem fighting with Jeffrey. All they did was fight! She'd had no problem fighting with Greg, either. They had had a fight the night before he died. A fight that she couldn't bear to think about.

Delilah was hosting the reception-after-the-reception, which meant the six of them and the four younger kids. She had a bowl of chicken salad, a platter of cold cuts, slices of watermelon, a big bowl of potato chips, and a blender full of stiff daiquiris made from the strawberries she had picked at the farm with the kids. The food was the same as always, the drink was the same, the setting the same—her back deck with the two chaises and the six Adirondack chairs, the croquet wickets set up in the lawn, the mermaid fountain gurgling, the cosmos and snapdragons blooming, butterflies and bumblebees hovering—but of course nothing was the same. Delilah found herself unable to put on music. Music would remind them all of Greg. Would they ever be able to listen to music again? Addison had turned down her offer of a strawberry daiquiri and joined the Chief in drinking Jack Daniels over ice. Addison was already quite drunk. They were all quite drunk, like characters from a Hemingway novel. Andrea was in a chardonnay stupor. Phoebe was nursing a daiquiri, which she had topped off with more rum. Delilah was practically reeling from the daiquiris—in addition, she had had three glasses of pinot gris and (stupidly) a dirty martini at the Westmoor Club. Jeffrey was drinking beer and was probably monitoring how many he'd had over what time period. But upon closer inspection, Addison was the worst of them all. He was muttering nonsense into his drink, his glasses were slipping, his hair—the fringe around the edge of his scalp that he claimed as hair—was mussed. All of his usual Princetonian deportment had flown away like a flock of birds frightened at the sight of him.

"No one's eating," Delilah complained. She picked a chip out of the bowl, but couldn't bring herself to eat it.

"I don't know why you went to so much trouble," Andrea said. "We all ate at the reception."

Or you could say thank you, Delilah thought. But instead she decided to step on Andrea's shoulder and go over her head. "Chief, would you like a sandwich?"

"Sure," the Chief said.

The kids were down in the basement, watching *Cars* for the umpteenth time, despite the fact that it was a beautiful evening and wouldn't get dark until nine. Delilah had even given them free run of the PlayStation, but they said they didn't want to play.

"We just want to be quiet, Mom," said Barney, Delilah's six-year-old, in a way that killed her.

The usual rules didn't apply. The world was upside down. Her kids didn't want to play PlayStation, Addison wasn't piling Delilah's chicken salad onto a baguette, there was no music.

Delilah sidled up to Andrea and lowered her voice in a way that indicated intimacy between two women friends. "There's something I want to talk to you about . . ."

Andrea was having none of the cuddly stuff. Her eyes, when she turned to Delilah, were bright blue and cutting. Her face was a shiny, impenetrable force field. "What is it?"

"I'd like to take the kids for the summer."

"The kids?"

"Chloe and Finn."

"Out of the question."

Now, see? Who said things like that?

"Hear me out," Delilah said.

Andrea raised her eyebrows and pursed her lips in a way that made it look like she was whistling. Delilah tried to think back to a time when she had really liked Andrea. Well, when Drew was born, Andrea had come to the house and cleaned and done laundry and roasted a chicken. She had monitored Delilah's milk flow; she had reached right in and fixed the way Drew was sucking. She had pinched Delilah's nipple with gentle authority, as if she were a nurse.

Better? she'd said.

Miraculously, it was better. The nursing didn't hurt anymore. Drew took in long drafts of milk; Delilah felt her breasts thrumming along like a machine. Better!

Andrea had checked in on Delilah for weeks. She offered to baby-sit so that Delilah and Jeffrey could go out to dinner. She had, Delilah realized, filled the space where Delilah's mother should have been.

Then there was the kiss, South Beach 2005. They had all been at a dance club in the wee hours, Delilah was drunk on champagne and Andrea on vodka; they had both been eating cashews that they later found out were laced with ecstasy. Andrea and Delilah had been dancing on a stage with poles; it was fun and sexy, and although Delilah had very little memory of the details, she did remember that she had kissed Andrea in front of three hundred writhing bodies, and the kiss had been passionate.

But thinking about that now was only puzzling.

Andrea could be fun; she could be kind and reasonable. Phoebe believed that when you had faith in a person, he or she responded by rising up to meet that faith. Okay, fine: Delilah would test out that theory. She would have faith that Andrea was a reasonable woman who would see that Chloe and Finn should spend the summer here. If Andrea wanted them in September, so be it.

"Just for the summer," Delilah said. "I have the boys at home all day anyway. Finn is in the same camps, the kids are on the same schedule. They're best friends. I have all the toys, all the books, all the games, inside and out. We have the empty guest room, or they can do air mattresses and sleeping bags on the floor of the boys' room. Like summer camp. It will be fun."

"They need to be with family," Andrea said.

"But you and Ed don't need two seven-year-olds underfoot all summer. You were just starting to enjoy yourself."

"It's safe to say that enjoying myself is a thing of the past," Andrea said. Her nose reddened and started to run. "It's over."

"Let me take them for the summer," Delilah said. "You'll see them all the time. Whenever you're here and any other time you want. Then, at the end of August, we can transition them to your house."

"One transition and then another?" Andrea said. "It will be too difficult for them. Think of the kids."

"I am thinking of the kids."

"You're thinking of yourself. You want to be the one who swings in on a vine and saves the day by taking in the orphans."

Delilah's faith was gone; she was back to anger. "I don't think of it like that at all. I was thinking of the kids, what would be the most fun for them . . ."

"Fun?" Andrea said.

"Yes, fun. There's nothing wrong with fun. They're *seven,* Andrea."

"They need to be with family."

It was time for her big gun. Her sure thing. But first she looked around. Jeffrey and the Chief were out on the deck. Delilah had forgotten about the Chief's sandwich. She panicked for a second, the panic of a waitress who'd neglected to put in an order. Well, she would get to it in a second. Then she checked on Phoebe and Addison. Phoebe was asleep, stretched out on the sofa—Delilah watched for a second to make sure she was breathing—and

Addison was slumped in the club chair, still muttering into his chest like a homeless person on the street.

Delilah said, "Why don't we ask the kids? See if they'd rather stay with us or with you?" *Ba-boom.* She could almost hear the gun's report, smell the bitter smoke.

But Andrea did not surrender. She said, "Why don't we ask ourselves what Tess would have wanted? Would she have wanted the kids to spend even *one night* here?"

Delilah laughed. "Ha!" And busied herself with making the Chief's sandwich. She was stunned silly by Andrea's counterattack. Delilah had left herself open for this. Tess did *not* like the kids to spend the night at Delilah's house. She had always been funny-strange about letting Delilah take the kids at all. Delilah knew that Tess believed the kids ate too much junk at this house (if you called freshly popped popcorn topped with freshly grated Parmesan cheese junk), they played too much PlayStation (though there was a house rule of one hour at a time, two hours if it was inclement weather), they didn't get enough sleep (at home Chloe and Finn were in bed at six-thirty, a fact Delilah found unfathomable). Tess basically let it be known, without actually saying it, that she did not approve of Delilah's parenting or the way Delilah ran her household. It was too free-form for Tess; there was too much left to chance. Tess had been extremely vigilant in the parenting department. Delilah had once watched her clean the inside of the twins' ears with a Q-tip soaked in rubbing alcohol. Tess did not allow the twins to eat food from the school cafeteria. She did not allow PG movies.

But Delilah's supervision had been okay with Tess—it had been a *complete lifesaver*—whenever Tess was in a jam. When she and Greg had in-service days at school and no one to baby-sit, who did Tess call? Did she call Andrea? No! She called Delilah. Who had Tess called when she and Greg had wanted to go on an anniversary sail, with a possible overnight on the Vineyard? She had called Delilah. Delilah rued her decision to allow Andrea and the Chief to take Chloe and Finn out of here that first night. She should have held on; possession was nine tenths of ownership.

Delilah said, "Let me take them for the summer. Please, Andrea? I'm not interested in a custody battle. I just think—"

Andrea said, "What about your work?"

Delilah smoothed mayonnaise over the Chief's bread in careful stages, as if she were painting a wall. "What *about* my work?"

"You plan to work four nights a week, work *late,* and then come home and take care of four kids all day?"

Delilah laid down slices of Black Forest ham, Genoa salami, Lorraine Swiss, hothouse tomato and baby mâche from the farm, roasted red peppers, a few thinly sliced marinated artichokes. Perfection between two slices of country loaf. Okay, so now Andrea was going to attack Delilah's job. Why not? Delilah's job was as embattled as the Gaza Strip. Jeffrey resented it, he thought it was beneath her, he thought it was shabby. Delilah was little more than a glorified hostess in his eyes, her job was nothing more than a flimsy ploy devised to escape the kids and get free drinks at the end of the night. Delilah had stated her case again and again: She had been the dining room manager at the Scarlet Begonia for six years. She held the number-four position, behind Thom and Faith, the owners, and Donaldo, the general manager. She headed the waitstaff, she squared the bills, she tipped out Graham, the bartender, and the Salvadoran busboys. She made the deposit at the bank in the morning. She helped Donaldo sift through ninety or so applications when the college kids arrived in May, and she helped him fire anyone who didn't work out. The Scarlet Begonia was a vibrant year-round business, it made buckets of money, and Delilah was a crucial part of the team.

"I'm thinking of quitting," Delilah said. Her head was spinning. She was drunk. One of the signs of Delilah drunk was that she disclosed pieces of classified information prematurely. She hadn't discussed quitting the Begonia with Jeffrey, nor with

Phoebe—nor, properly, with herself. The thought was just float-ing around in her mind with sad inevitability. At the funeral re-ception, Thom and Faith had approached her together and told her to take as much time as she needed before she came back to work. They had been drunk at the reception. They were more or less always drunk or hung over, which was what gave the Begonia the whiff of disrepute among people like Jeffrey and An-drea. But Thom and Faith were good citizens, community peo-ple. They loved Delilah and they had loved Greg, who had played the guitar there for over ten years. Thom and Faith had, in their hippie, hazy, funky, freewheeling way, always treated Delilah and Greg as part of their family.

They had also had the misfortune of being present for the fiasco that was Sunday night, Greg's last night alive. But Delilah wasn't willing to discuss it with them; she wasn't going to think about it. She looked at Thom and Faith—Thom with his gray ponytail and John Lennon glasses, and Faith with her signature rouge (some days it was applied more evenly than others). Delilah had tried many times over the years to imagine Thom and Faith making love, and had failed. Likewise, she could not imagine herself ever working a shift at the Begonia again. Thom and Faith feared this, maybe, and hence were offering her lots of leeway—anything to keep the door open. If Delilah could just be honest with herself, she would say that for her, the Scarlet Begonia had always been about Greg, and Greg was dead.

Andrea did not respond to Delilah's revelation. No surprise there. She just closed the book on the conversation by saying, "The kids will live with us. We're their family."

Delilah cut through the Chief's sandwich with her serrated bread knife and arranged it on a plate with a handful of chips. Jeffrey stepped in off the back deck and said, "What are you girls talking about?"

"Nothing," they said together, and Delilah was grateful. She had concocted the whole notion of taking Chloe and Finn without consulting Jeffrey. She was a horrible wife. And she was drunker than she thought.

ADDISON

Addison's memory, in regard to Tess, went back only as far as the first time he had kissed her. December 27, in Stowe, Vermont.

He wasn't sure if he could go back and think about it. Well, wait, maybe, give him a minute. It was sort of like asking him if he could go down and touch his toes now that his femur was broken. But then it occurred to him that all he had left of Tess were these memories, and since no one knew about their relationship, there was no one in the world to talk to about it other than himself. It had crossed his mind to make a truly mind-blowing announcement at Jeffrey and Delilah's house following the reception. Why not just confess? Make a scene? But Addison loathed scenes. Even now, when he thought about Phoebe shrieking in the parking lot of the Galley, he closed his eyes and breathed in deeply. Never mind the way she'd shattered like a teacup on September 11. Addison decided not to come out with the truth for many reasons—and really, his distaste for scenes was at the bottom of the list. First of all, he didn't want to hurt Phoebe. Second, he loved his friends, and he wanted to keep them. And somewhere in there was another niggling reason: he feared that if he told everyone that he and Tess had fallen in love, no one would believe him.

Why? Because Tess was married to Greg, who had muscles chiseled out of mahogany, a voice that fell somewhere between Frank Sinatra and John Mayer, eyes that made even Florabel, the receptionist in Addison's office, who was a lesbian, tremble with nerves and excitement so that she almost spilled her coffee every time Greg walked in. Why why *why* would Tess turn around and have an affair with Addison, who was bald and bespectacled, and who could not even get his own wife to kiss him with tongue?

No one would believe it. They would laugh.

In your dreams!

But it had happened. It was real.

They had all gone to Stowe on the day after Christmas, for what was their sixth (and final) group vacation. Adults only, five days of ski and après-ski. Addison had gotten hold of the 4BR condo for free in the usual way, which was to say that a man who had bought a five-million-dollar piece of land on Pocomo Point from Addison in the fall had offered the condo to Addison as a thank-you for doing the deal.

Addison said, *Oh, really, Jack, it was nothing.*

Jack said, *Take the condo. Week after Christmas, it's yours. Wife and I are going to St. Barts.*

The group vacations were always fun. They were always the *best* (though in Addison's mind the best of the best had been Vegas, and every trip since had been an earnest attempt to live up to Vegas). This trip to Stowe was especially handicapped because of what had transpired between Tess and Greg. The whole mess with April Peck had been murderous. Addison had heard only Greg's side of the story: Tess would not forgive him. She would act like she'd forgiven him and then either something would happen (she'd bump into someone at the grocery store who would want to vent their feelings on the topic) or nothing would happen—out of the blue, she would just flip out. She would make Greg tell her the whole story *again,* she would get angry *again,* she would declare that she could never trust him *again.* She wanted him to quit his job, she wanted to move away, she wanted to move out.

Still, they had agreed to the trip to Stowe; they asked Cassidy Montero, on Christmas break from her freshman year at Dartmouth, to baby-sit. Greg was gung-ho about the skiing in a way that made Addison nervous. Addison, despite his many other talents and accomplishments, did not ski. He liked the atmosphere of skiing—the fire-warmed lodge, the view of a snowy mountainside, the clean air, the drinks—but not the sport itself. Addison suspected that Greg's opinion of his own prowess was inflated—this was generally the case—but at any rate, Greg's enthusiasm fueled a sense of great expectation for the trip.

So there they were, the eight of them, in colorful Gore-Tex parkas and snow pants, with probably a hundred zippered pockets among them. The Chief and Andrea had their own skis and boots, as did Greg, as did Jeffrey and Delilah. Phoebe had brought her ice skates and her cross-country skis and boots, all carefully preserved relics from her high school years in Wisconsin.

The condo was located two hundred yards from the parking lot of the mountain. It had two stone fireplaces, four sumptuous bedrooms, each with its own marble bath, a gourmet kitchen that Jack the Client had, as a surprise, stocked with Swiss Miss and marshmallows, fondue cheese, exotic salamis, olives, white wine, champagne, and a handle of spiced rum. A deck with an eight-person hot tub overlooked the face of the mountain; from the deck, Addison could pick out tiny figures whooshing down the trails. The furnishings were "luxe lodge"—suede sofas and deep armchairs, a coffee table fashioned from a tree trunk. There were two flat-screen TVs and a sound system with speakers throughout the house.

It was impossible to walk into that condo and feel like anyone except the luckiest person alive. If the fluffy duvet sheathed in English flannel on your bed wasn't enough, if the deep shearling throw rugs under your feet weren't enough (it was as if there were fur coats strewn across the floor), then step out onto the deck, where the hot tub was steaming like a cauldron, take a hot buttered rum from the tray Delilah was passing around, help yourself to a cracker topped with goat cheese and hot pepper jelly and look at the mountain while snow fell gently onto the shoulders of your Spyder ski jacket.

"Are you happy?" Addison had asked Tess. He had asked her randomly, because she happened to be standing next to him.

"Deliriously," she had said.

Had it started there? Not quite. But Addison had been affected by that answer. Something had bloomed under his layers of goosedown, Gore-Tex, cashmere, and 100 percent cotton. He had, via the unexpected perks of his profession, been able to make Tess, who had been sad and anxiety-ridden for months, *deliriously happy*. What had bloomed in Addison's chest was not love, but self-congratulation. It was a start.

In the morning, everyone drank coffee, munched toast, grabbed bananas or stored them in one of their many zippered pockets for later. Off to the mountain! The ski car—the Chief's Yukon—was leaving.

Phoebe would take the other car, her and Addison's Range Rover, up to the Trapp Family Lodge, where she would cross-country ski, get lunch, and have a massage. Phoebe had a little duffel packed with all her stuff, she had her boots hanging over her shoulder by the laces, and her hair was done in two braids, just like the Swiss Miss.

"Okay!" she said. "See you later!"

She looked fine, normal, happy—a woman out to relive the winter sports experiences of her youth and then indulge in the pleasures she had discovered as an adult. Addison would have been fooled had it not been for the tinny quality that her voice took on when she was medicated, as opposed to the pure, melodic silver of her actual voice, though Addison heard that sterling quality so rarely anymore that he wondered if he would even recognize it.

When he checked in the trash of their bathroom, he saw that she'd taken two Percocets (prescribed to her "for pain") as well as her Ativan—and he knew she had secret stashes of oxycontin, valium, and Ambien with her at all times. But he wasn't going to waste time hunting them down. He hoped she didn't fall through a hole in the ice or get lost in the woods.

That left Addison in the condo . . . with Tess. He hadn't realized it, but Tess did not end up going along with the others. She didn't ski, though Greg had spent much of their four-hour, wine-soaked fondue dinner the night before trying to convince her to take a private lesson. Tess had been reluctant, but Greg seemed to have persuaded her in the end. And yet when Addison closed the door behind Phoebe (he stayed at the sidelight until Phoebe pulled away, wondering if it was wise even to let her drive in the snow, much less ski) and returned to the kitchen to his coffee and the *Wall Street Journal,* there was Tess at the table, wearing a heather gray Nordic sweater and black leggings and socks, assiduously punching numbers into her cell phone again and again.

"There's no reception here," she said.

"Who are you trying to call?"

"The kids. The baby-sitter." Tess smiled, then flushed, embarrassed. "I know they're fine, but . . ."

"You're a good mother," Addison said. "And good mothers worry."

She set the phone down on the kitchen table and looked at him. Really looked at him with her wide blue eyes. It took him by surprise.

"Thank you," she said. "Thank you for saying that." She cast her eyes down at the table. "Greg thinks it's ridiculous how much I worry. But they're my children. I like to know they're okay. I like to know what they're doing, what they're eating, if they slept well, what they dreamed about."

"They're lucky to have you," Addison said.

"I don't want them to think I've just abandoned them, the day after Christmas. And the tree is still up with the lights on it, and I told Cassidy not to build a fire, but it gets so cold in our house, so then at the last minute I told her that if it was freezing then it was okay for her to build a fire, and I was up half the night worried that she *would* build a fire and the house would burn down . . ."

"You don't have to explain it to me," Addison said. "I get it."

Tess sighed. "I guess I'll have to call them from town. What are you up to today?"

"I'm going to the fitness center right now," Addison said. "Then I thought I might walk into town for some lunch."

Tess was staring at him. She was pretty, like a doll. Of course, Phoebe was pretty like a doll, too. Phoebe was an exquisite china doll, delicate, fragile. Tess was pretty like a Bobbsey Twin, like Mary Ann from *Gilligan's Island.* She was cute, perky, freckled, kindergarten-teacher pretty.

"What?" he said.

"I like it that you made a plan for yourself," she said. "You're not worried about the others, you're not worried about Phoebe—"

I'm always worried about Phoebe, he thought. But he would never say this to Tess.

"You just asked yourself what you wanted to do today, and you're going to do it."

"Yes," he said. "I'm very selfish."

"My New Year's resolution is to be more selfish," Tess said. "To do things that I want to do—not that the kids want me to do, or Greg wants me to do. What I realized—this year, you know—is that I put far too much time and effort into looking out for Greg. And meanwhile, Greg is looking out for Greg. He's doing a terrible job, of course."

Here Tess gave a weak laugh, and Addison thought, *Are we going to talk about it?*

Tess paused. She looked for a moment like she was sizing him up. Was he worthy of a conversation about the big, forbidden topic?

He was not.

She said, "So one of the things I decided is that I'm going to spend more time and energy taking care of myself." She fiddled with her iPhone; with its yellow cover, it was as bright as a child's toy. "I don't even know where to start." She glanced up. "So for today, can I tag around with you?"

Had it started then? Getting closer.

Addison filled with warmth. And anticipation. Would it seem odd to the others if he and Tess spent the day together? The hallmark of these group trips had always been unexpected alliances. Addison remembered the four-hour canoe trip he and the Chief had taken during their vacation at the Point, on Saranac Lake. They had gotten lost somehow, had debarked and carried the canoe over their heads like Indians until they came across a dirt road, where they hitched a ride back to the Point with two dope-smoking hippies who seemed markedly less jolly when they discovered Ed was a police chief. That story was now legend. It remained the touchstone of Addison and Ed's friendship.

So today would be his day with Tess.

"I'd love it," he said.

They went to the fitness center, which was down the hill, at the base of the condo complex. Addison signed them in under Jack's name. The place was deserted except for a very fit-looking older gentleman on the elliptical and a muscle-bound kid of about twenty-five who was wearing a complicated knee brace and pumping iron. Both the older man and the kid eyed Tess in the mirror as she stripped down to her workout clothes—a pair of incredibly flattering yoga pants and a jog bra that left the pale, toned plane of her abdomen bare. Addison wore gym shorts and the tattered gray Princeton T-shirt that he'd ordered ten years earlier from the back of the alumni magazine. It was a revolting spectacle, according to Phoebe, but it was the T-shirt he liked to work out in.

He got on the treadmill. Forty minutes, level 7 with hills, just as he did six days a week at the gym. Why did he feel like a stranger to this machine? Why did he feel self-conscious and uncoordinated? Tess was on the mat in front of the mirror, stretching. Or doing yoga—Addison couldn't tell. She was incredibly flexible. The young guy was watching her, too; Addison was surreptitiously watching him watching her. Okay, it was impossible to exercise this way. Addison put on his headphones and tried to keep up with the pace he'd set.

He gave it more than usual. He gave it too much. He was running at a 9 with hills, he was sweating like a wild boar, the Princeton T-shirt was dark and sopping. Addison's face was red, and he was forced to remove his glasses because they kept slipping down his nose. He set them on the tray next to the *Newsweek* he was too pumped up even to open, but without his glasses, he couldn't see Tess. Or rather, he could see her—first on the exercise bike, then doing sit-ups on the inclined bench, then lifting weights and chatting with the young stud in between sets. But Addison's eyes were very bad (everyone told him to get Lasik surgery, but he could not abide the thought of a laser or anything else touching his eye), and hence he could not see Tess's facial expression, he could not see the muscles in her stomach tense and release with the sit-ups, and he could not hear clearly what she was saying to the young stud. Blind people, apparently, had a keen sense of hearing to compensate for not being able to see, but without his eyeglasses, Addison felt completely adrift. He might as well have been up on the mountain, buried in a snowbank. He heard Tess laugh, heard her say "Nantucket," heard her say, "Oh, that's too bad. Such bad luck." Maybe this guy was telling her the reason for the knee brace. (Ski accident, Addison guessed. Torn ACL.) It was as if Tess and the guy were speaking a foreign language, and not one of the three Addison was fluent in.

Had Tess noticed him? Did she see how fast he was flying up one electronic hill after another?

He realized simultaneously that he was trying to impress Tess and that he was jealous of the kid with biceps the size of grapefruits and a sympathy-evoking knee injury. Jealous! But no, not possible. He asked himself: if some blond, hulking Adonis on the cross-country trail decided to accompany Phoebe and then later join her for lunch, would Addison be jealous? The answer was no. Men hit on Phoebe regularly because she was so beautiful, and Addison's prevailing emotion for these men was pity.

She doesn't see you. And even if she does see you, she won't let you in. She lives in a chamber where there is only enough oxygen for one.

Addison got off the treadmill shakily. He was going to have a heart attack. He staggered around on the AstroTurf carpet, disoriented for a second about which way was up. He collapsed onto the floor and put his head between his knees. His vision was blurred. Then he realized he needed his glasses! But he didn't have the energy to stand up and retrieve them.

He felt a hand on his shoulder. He looked up to see the older gentleman.

"Are you okay?" the gentleman asked.

There was an audible gasp in the gym. Tess set her weights down on the bench.

"Addison!" she said. "What's wrong?"

Well, he had trumped the kid in the knee brace. But Addison wasn't after Tess's sympathy; he had wanted to be impressive. He had wanted Tess to see that although he wasn't careening down the side of a mountain at thirty miles per hour with two Popsicle sticks strapped to his feet, he was still an athlete.

"I'm fine," he said, smiling. He could not see her expression, though she was standing right over him. "Never better. That was a great workout!"

Tess said, "You sure?"

"Sure I'm sure. I'm just cooling down."

"Okay," she said. "Great! I have three sets left. Bill is helping me with my form. He was on the ski patrol here, but he hurt his knee jumping from the lift. He was trying to rescue a little boy."

Sounded like a load of shit to Addison, but he said, "Wow!

Okay, I'm going to do some stretching and we'll leave when you're ready."

No doubt about it: Addison was jealous.

Tess giggled. "It was so cute. Bill thought you were my *husband*."

They walked out of the fitness center into a light snow. With the fir trees and the condo units looking like Alpine chalets, and the snow coming down so softly that the flakes seemed suspended in the air, it was so lovely and peaceful that when Addison spoke, he whispered so as not to disturb the silence.

"Do you want to go back to the condo to shower, or should we just go for our walk?"

"Let's walk," Tess said.

There was a path that led out of the condo complex and headed down, parallel to the mountain road. The path was in the woods, and there were small footbridges that delivered them over tiny streams.

"It will lead us into town eventually," Addison said. "And you can call your kids and we can get some lunch."

Tess linked her arm through his. "You are such a prince."

"I aim to please."

They walked along ten steps, and then twenty, with Tess's arm twined through his.

This, for Addison anyway, was when it began. Because this was when he started to feel like he was fourteen years old. Tess's arm through his was a distraction, but he realized he would be crushed if she separated from him. But then he worried: did she *want* to separate from him?

This was also when Tess asked, "How is Phoebe doing?" in a grave way, as though Phoebe had cancer. And instead of giving his usual sunshine-and-butterfly answer of *She's fine, great, really great,* Addison expelled what felt like all the air from his lungs and said, "I just don't know." It was the honesty of his answer that opened the floodgates between them. They were going to talk, really talk, really open up, really share things about their respective marriages that they would never think of sharing with the rest of the group. He told Tess everything as they walked. It was easy, the words flowed out of him; he told her everything he would have told a therapist, but both he and Phoebe had given up hope in therapists. Addison and Tess crossed bridges and left matching sets of footprints in the snow. Addison found he couldn't talk fast enough.

Addison told the truth. He said things like *Phoebe is not the woman I married. She's changed. But that doesn't do it justice. She emigrated. She's a refugee of her grief. It has colonized her, reorganized her. She's different down to her cells, her molecules. And it's eight years later. So it's not grief anymore, it's the drugs. The so-called medication, the substances applied to her pain. They are her captor now, and she suffers from Stockholm syndrome. She loves the drugs. They are more important to her than Reed ever was.*

Tess knew how to listen (perhaps this was a result of having a classroom full of five-year-olds vie for her attention one hundred and eighty days a year). She did not automatically take Phoebe's side, as Addison had expected ("Let me play devil's advocate here . . ."). She was hearing Addison's side; she was—still!—holding on to Addison's arm.

Addison said, *Our sex life is a shambles. Once, twice a year, and only when she's been drinking.*

Tess said, *That must be difficult. To have this gorgeous woman right there in your bed and not be able to touch her.*

I'm used to it, Addison said. *That is the screwed-up thing. I am used to a crippled marriage.*

They reached town—a charming covered bridge, a steepled church. Because it was a heavy-lidded, gray day, all of the twinkling Christmas lights were on. Snow-dusted wreaths hung from lampposts. They strolled past shops with cheese and chutney, maple syrup, nutcrackers, wind chimes, pottery, wine and spirits, specialty kitchen equipment, woolen hats, gloves, scarves, sweaters.

"Anywhere you want to go in?" Addison asked.

"Maybe later," she said.

"Want to call your kids?" he asked.

"Yes!" she said. She decided to call from the middle of the covered bridge, leaning on the railing, overlooking the river. "It is so liberating to be here with you. Every time I call the kids around Greg, I feel guilty, like I'm sneaking a cigarette. Ridiculous, right? Because if anyone should feel guilty, it's Greg."

Addison let that comment hang for a second. Were they going to talk about it?

But at that second the baby-sitter answered, and Tess said, "Cassidy? Hi, it's Tess! How is everything?"

She was visibly lighter when she got off the phone. "It's snowing at home! Cassidy is taking them to sled at Dead Horse Valley, and then home to have hot chocolate and change into dry clothes. Then she's taking them for dinner and a movie at the Starlight. They'll be in bed at eight-thirty, which is very late, but what the heck, it's vacation!" She grinned at Addison. She was wearing a red cashmere hat, and the curled ends of her dark hair poked out beneath it. She was lovely. Addison was overcome with the desire to kiss her. Kiss Tess MacAvoy! He was sure he would be struck by lightning or the railing he was leaning on (indeed, depending on for support—after the treadmill and three miles of walking, his legs were shot) would give way, dumping him into the icy river.

"What do you want to do now?" he asked.

"Lunch!" she said.

It was, they agreed afterward, the lunch of a lifetime. They went to a small French café called Nous Deux (We Two) that had a blackboard menu and banquettes that used to be church pews and were now upholstered in bright Provençal fabrics. The woman who seated them was the owner, Sandrine, a Quebecoise,

Addison discovered, as he and Sandrine chatted for a moment in French. Sandrine was visibly delighted by Addison's French. He asked for a table in the corner. He and Tess each slid onto a pew and Sandrine left them with the menus and the wine list.

Tess said, "You speak French so beautifully."

"Six strict years with Madame Vergenot and two and a half years in Paris working for Coldwell. Would you like wine?"

"Wine?" she said, as if he were suggesting an all-night rave at an underground club on the Boulevard Saint-Germain. He remembered suddenly that this was *Tess,* who during the course of a normal week drank milk at lunch, out of one of the small cartons they gave the kids. But then she said, "Sure. Why not?" with a wicked little grin on her face.

So, really, *really really,* it had started then, with Tess's renegade decision to throw caution to the wind and drink wine at lunch with Addison. Addison ordered the most expensive bottle on the menu, a Mersault he positively adored but that one could rarely find on a wine list. Ordering this wine and then praising Sandrine for the fine selections on her list incurred even more favor with this woman than speaking French had. She loved Addison and Tess! She brought them the wine, she poured it lavishly. Then she whisked away their menus and said to Addison, "Allow me."

A succession of marvels came out of the kitchen—duck confit on a gaufrette, endive stuffed with aged chèvre and a balsamic fig, a platter of petits croque-monsieurs, an asparagus salad topped with a quivering poached egg. Tiny ramekins of the most decadent onion soup gratinée Addison had ever tasted. Sandrine, Quebecoise goddess, treated Addison and Tess not like husband and wife but like lovers. She set plates down, she gave a sly smile or a wink, she disappeared.

Tess, defying all precedent, was an accomplished student of such debauchery. She not only drank the wine, she savored it the way it was meant to be savored—mouthful by mouthful, over the tongue, eyes fluttering. (Addison could not help drawing a comparison. Phoebe drank wine the way she took pills: she threw it back with purpose rather than joy, then waited for the numbness to take effect.) Tess ate her food in tiny, delicate tastes. She had a child's hands; he had always been aware of this, but what he hadn't realized was how deft her hands were. Addison fumbled with his food (he was nervous, despite the loosening effect of the Mersault), but Tess cut little bites and popped them into her mouth quickly and neatly.

During all this time—the wine being savored (Addison bravely ordered a second bottle), the courses devoured, Sandrine appearing, then disappearing—Tess was talking. She talked about the problems she'd had getting pregnant—the two miscarriages, the baby lost at twenty-one weeks. Then she talked about the twins. She loved the twins too much, maybe, and this was what had caused her problems with Greg.

Again Addison held his breath. Were they going to talk about it? Sandrine popped the cork on the second bottle of Mersault and Tess reached for her glass and drank. And then she started to talk about It, that Sunday Night, April Peck, What April Said, What Greg Said, Holes in April's Story, Holes in Greg's Story. How Tess Knew Greg Was Lying. How She Begged Him to Tell the Truth, How He Stupidly Stuck by the Asinine Lies He Concocted.

Addison nodded; he tried to mirror Tess's own listening techniques. He did not defend Greg's side of the story. Instead, it felt like he had been looking through the wrong end of a kaleidoscope. Only now, when hearing the story from Tess, did it all make sense.

"We've been married eleven and a half years," Tess said. "Andrea tells me not to let one measly night ruin so many years of hard work and devotion. But what Andrea doesn't understand is that the 'one measly night' was representative of so many underlying problems in our marriage. The fact that I can't get the truth. Greg won't come clean! What Andrea doesn't understand

is that the hard work and devotion have been one-sided. Me giving to him." She carefully constructed a masterpiece bite out of
farmhouse bread, Roquefort, apricot preserves, and a candied
pecan. Sandrine had just dropped off a cheese plate worthy of
Auguste Renoir. Tess eyed the morsel thoughtfully, then looked at
Addison. She had tears in her eyes.

Oh no! he thought. She was going to cry!

"I want to leave him," she said.

"And go where?" Addison said.

Tears dripped down her face. "I don't know," she said.
"Paris?"

It had started there. They did not need the petites tartes Tatin
with Calvados ice cream that Sandrine sent out, nor did they
need the chocolate truffles or the slender flutes of rose champagne. ("Billecart-Salmon," Sandrine said. "Un cadeau." A gift.)
But they enjoyed them anyway.

Addison paid the bill with five one-hundred-dollar bills, which
made Tess gasp even louder than she had at the gym when she
thought he was in cardiac arrest. He whisked her out of there,
stopping only to kiss Sandrine on both cheeks and say, "Le
déjeuner de ma vie."

He and Tess were holding hands as they left the restaurant. Nous Deux. *We Two.* That morning at eight o'clock, Tess
MacAvoy had been Phoebe's friend and, more saliently for
Addison, Greg's wife. She had been a secondary or tertiary theme
in the symphony of Addison's life; she had been a figure in the
background.

Now, however, she was his.

They stood under the awning at the back door of the café, facing a small parking area where there was only one car, an ancient
silver Peugeot—most likely Sandrine's. Addison bent down and
kissed Tess—and yes, it did occur to him that he'd consumed an
entire bottle of wine, followed by a glass of champagne. He was
drunk and so was she. The kiss could fail. It could be like kissing

his little sister. But their lips connected and there was a spark, an electric charge, a surge of attraction. The kiss was the right thing. He kissed her again. And again. And again, and then they were kissing in the back parking lot of Nous Deux. Tess's arms locked around him. He pulled her in. She was his now. Did she know this?

So that there was no mistaking what all this meant, he said, "I may have just fallen in love with you. Okay?"

And she said, "Okay."

Addison was crying now. Of course he was crying. The silly, sad tears of a little boy, though he had no recollection of feeling like this as a child. This feeling was adult. There were so many things he could never bring himself to do again: he would never go to Stowe, he would never order that bottle of Mersault, he would never eat a croque-monsieur. He would never kiss anyone for the first time.

He had Tess's iPhone, pilfered from the Coast Guard's bag of her personal effects. He felt guilty for stealing it. But then, guess what? The Chief called to inform him that he was the executor of the MacAvoy wills.

"What?" Addison said. And because his memories of Tess started this past December, it took a while to come back to him.

He *had* agreed to serve as executor. Back in 2000, when Greg and Tess bought their house on Blueberry Lane. Addison was their Realtor, he was at the closing with their attorney, Barry Karsten, a big, affable fellow of Danish descent. When the papers were all signed, Barry suggested that Greg and Tess make wills. He could write them up.

"Right now?" Greg said.

"All you need to figure out is who you'd like to be the executor and what happens to the house if you both die at the same time."

Tess said, "We're trying to get pregnant."

Barry Karsten said, "Okay! We'll account for that."

Addison had barely been listening, but he had been at the right place at the right time (or, as he'd thought of it then, the wrong place at the wrong time). Greg asked him to serve as executor. Since Greg and Tess had both taken the day off from teaching to attend the closing, Barry ended up printing out a boilerplate will for each of them. They all signed.

"And you mean to say that Greg and Tess never signed another will?" Addison said.

The Chief muttered something, throwing in the words "goddamn careless," but under the terms of the existing wills, the twins got everything anyway. No guardians had been named for the children, and this was the thing that the Chief didn't understand. It was an egregious oversight. But the last thing Tess and Greg had planned on was . . . dying.

So, put honestly, Addison knew he was the executor of Greg's and Tess's wills, but, like being the permanent treasurer for the Class of 1977 at Lawrenceville, he'd forgotten, because he never expected the job to have any responsibilities.

Tess's iPhone was suddenly under his jurisdiction. All of the MacAvoy property was under his control. He would go through the house, see what was there; he would have free rein over the most intimate nooks and crannies of Tess's and Greg's life—the bank statements, the drawers of the bedside tables, the diaries.

It terrified him.

ANDREA

Twice she had the same dream. Then three times. It was such a stupid way to manifest her grief. So clichéd and predictable that Andrea was too embarrassed to tell anyone about it. There was no one to tell anyway, since Tess was dead.

The dream was real, though. This was to say, she was really having it. Once. Then again. Then a third time, with a variation.

It went as follows: Andrea was her normal self, sitting in her chair on the beach, reading her book. There was shouting from offshore. Someone was drowning. Andrea ran to the shoreline. It was a man caught in the riptide. Andrea motioned with her arms; she shouted: *Swim with it—it will carry you down the beach, but you'll be okay.* She was a lifeguard, with a lifeguard's instincts and knowledge. She did not want to go in to save this man; he was too big. In a rip like this, he would take her down. She cupped her hands around her mouth and shouted. She had faith that the man would get it; he would save himself! But he was going under. She lost sight of his face. She started swimming. She reached him, got him under the chin. She could do this. In lifesaving class, Andrea had practiced on dummies that weighed twice as much as she did.

It was when they were almost to the shore, when Andrea knew they were both going to be safe, that she allowed herself to look at the man's face. He had blue eyes, the most piercing eyes she had ever seen. He was, this man, disturbingly handsome. When they reached shore, Andrea waited for him to thank her, but instead the man turned and walked down the beach, away from her. Andrea watched his buttocks in a black Speedo and the triangle of his upper body. His hair was salt-and-pepper curls; he wore a silver hoop earring. He walked toward a woman lying on a towel, a woman who most definitely had not been present when he was shouting for help in the water. The woman raised her head at his approach. It was Phoebe. Andrea thought, *Of course, Phoebe.* She was heartbroken.

Then, seconds later, Andrea and the man—Pyotr, his name was, he spoke only Russian, though she had no idea how she knew this—were making love against the side of her Jeep. They were, put more accurately, *fucking.* Because it was wild, tear-at-your-clothes, breathless, stranger sex, sex such as Andrea had never experienced in her life. Pyotr opened the passenger side of Andrea's Jeep. Andrea sat in the seat while he tasted her.

The Jeep was the same Jeep she had owned during her first summer on Nantucket. She was confused. She asked Pyotr where it had come from. In Russian, which she somehow understood, he said, *It's okay, it's your Jeep, you can do what you want in it.*

Andrea woke up in a panic, her heart shrieking, her hormones raging. She looked at Ed, asleep like a grizzly bear next to her. She filled with guilt. She was riled up, as sexually aroused as she had ever been in her life. Should she wake Ed? And do what? Tell him that she'd had an erotic dream about a man that she'd saved from drowning? A Russian man named Pyotr who was having a relationship with Phoebe? She thought, *He was drowning. Of course he was drowning.* But that wasn't what made her sad. What made her sad was that Jeep, the black Jeep she'd bought off the lot at Don Allen Ford in the middle of her first summer, when she was so flush with cash she didn't know what to do with it. She had driven the Jeep from the dealership straight to the ferry dock, where she picked up Tess, who was fifteen years old, leaving home alone for the first time.

Tess had been wowed by the island, the gray-shingled, cobblestoned quaintness of it, and she had screamed for joy about the black Jeep with the top down. A beach buggy that they could ride in with their dark DiRosa hair flying out behind them.

The dream came again four nights later, at the end of a particularly brutal day, and Andrea recognized it. She knew what was going to happen. She knew the man would shout for help, she knew she would save him, she knew he would leave her for Phoebe, she knew he would come back to her and they would mate like wild animals. In the Jeep, with Andrea's legs hooked up over the roll bar. This time there was more shame, more worry. She was worried about indecent exposure; she was worried about the police showing up! *The police.*

Pyotr said, "It's your car. You can do what you want in it."

Once she'd had the dream a second time, it was like a TV show she'd become addicted to, or a novel she was reading. The details plagued and baffled her. She thought about the dream for four or five minutes of every hour. Pyotr—who was he? Andrea had never known anyone like him. But that wasn't possible, was it? Her mind's eye couldn't just create a person out of thin air. Pyotr must have been a person she'd seen somewhere, at some point during her life. He was sitting at a café during her semester in Florence; he was in her subway car one of the thousands of times she'd ridden the T; she had seen him with his wife at a restaurant. At Straight Wharf, perhaps, where she and Ed went every year on her birthday. The identity of Pyotr nagged at her, as did her mounting sexual energy. She and Ed made love when the spirit moved them—once every two weeks, say, normally in the morning when they woke up together and sunlight was pouring through their bedroom windows, or rain was tapping, and Ed found himself with an erection and, being the practical man that he was, decided it shouldn't go to waste. The sex was nice. It was familiar and pleasant. Ed knew what Andrea liked; he got the job done.

They had not had sex since Tess died. Ed had assumed sex was the furthest thing from Andrea's mind. (She would have thought this way, too, if she were Ed.) Plus they now had two little kids in the house, and whereas Finn slept soundly, Chloe was sometimes up three and four times in the night, searching the house for her parents.

Maybe the lack of sex was to blame for these dreams, then?

Maybe Andrea was, at the age of forty-four, about to hit meno-pause, and so her body was throwing itself a surprise party?

Or it was grief. Which, like every other human emotion, revealed itself in ways that made sense and ways that didn't.

They were, all of them, drowning. Ed was drowning in work. Andrea was drowning in meanness.

Delilah had asked for Greg's guitar. Barney wanted to learn to play it, she said.

Although Addison was the executor (a fact that made Andrea feel like she was choking on her son's gym sock), the bag of per-sonal effects from the Coast Guard was at the Chief and Andrea's house. What remained were the leather overnight bag and the guitar. The guitar was something of a golden egg.

"Barney really wants it," Delilah said. "He's dying to learn."

Andrea had seen Barney, Delilah's younger son, sit at Greg's feet every single time Greg played. He was the most devoted worshipper at Greg's temple. He was probably the only six-year-old who knew all the lyrics to "Bell Bottom Blues." Andrea was not surprised that Barney wanted the guitar. They had all joked about how Barney would be the next Greg. Greg, but famous. Ha!

"Eric has asked for the guitar," Andrea said. "We gave it to Eric."

This was not true. Andrea had asked Eric if he wanted the gui-tar, and Eric said he'd have to think about it. When Andrea asked him again, Eric said he didn't want the guitar. He wasn't musical, could not carry a tune, would be mortified to play in front of any-one. He didn't want it. *Give it to someone else,* he said.

Andrea, frankly, had been glad. She thought Greg's temple was a cult. It sucked you in, but it wasn't real.

So here was Andrea drowning in meanness: Barney wanted the guitar, he was the correct spiritual heir, Eric did not want the guitar, Andrea was glad Eric did not want the guitar. And still she would not give the guitar to Delilah.

Despicable! Andrea kept a firm line over the phone, but inside she was cringing at her behavior. Tess had died and Andrea was turning into a witch.

Delilah was upset. She pleaded again on Barney's behalf, but halfheartedly. She hung up without saying goodbye. Andrea supposed she would go to Addison. Get a court order, maybe, for the guitar. Fine! Let her!

Andrea had a moment of weakness. Or was it strength? (Everything was so inside out, she could not tell the difference.) She would call Delilah back and offer Barney the guitar.

But no, she wouldn't.

Andrea's copy of *The English Patient* with its cover and the first eighteen pages ripped out lay on the counter. She could still finish it, Ed pointed out, since the part she had yet to read was unharmed.

She threw the book in the trash, then started wailing. Didn't he see? Didn't he see the way everything was ruined?

Andrea tried to put her energies elsewhere. She tried to focus on the twins. But the twins were like little goblins; they both looked so much like Tess that they scared Andrea. Andrea was losing hold of her sanity; she was frightened by two seven-year-olds. Looking at them was like looking at Tess, and Tess was dead. She was never coming back. Andrea would never see her again. She was *dead.* The reality gripped Andrea around the neck like two bony hands. She avoided looking at the twins. She was barely able to pour their Cheerios, pack their lunch boxes, and get them to camp. Once they were gone (running from the car, exhilarated by their freedom), Andrea drove aimlessly around the island. She was searching for something. What would help? She pulled into an unfamiliar driveway and burst into tears. She screamed with her fist jammed in her mouth.

She went to the grocery store to buy steaks. This was a normal, everyday act. This was what people did when they were alive:

they went to the market to shop for food, which they turned into meals. The grocery store was chilly and indifferent. The produce section featured neat pyramids of plums, peaches, nectarines, grapes, wedges of watermelon. Knobs of gingerroot, bags of coleslaw mix. How could any of this matter? Tess was *dead,* she was in a *coffin,* in the *ground* not a half-mile away. But she was gone. That smiling face, that perky voice. Dead. Andrea hurried through the store to the butcher shop. If Andrea had died and Tess was alive, would Tess be able to make a trip to the store? Yes, of course. But Andrea was not Tess. She felt like she was going to asphyxiate. Air, she needed air; she needed to be outside. But being outside felt wrong, too. How could Andrea enjoy sunshine and the breeze when Tess was in the ground? She couldn't be inside and she couldn't be outside. She was a mess.

She grabbed six rib-eye steaks. They were far more expensive than the steaks she usually bought, but who cared anymore about money? Andrea cut down the cereal aisle to the cashier—and bad luck. In front of her in line was Heather Dickson, wife of one of Ed's sergeants, whom Andrea had not seen since this happened. When Heather saw Andrea, her face instantly registered that cross between sympathy and pity that Andrea so detested.

Andrea held up a hand, not in greeting but in traffic-cop sign language. *STOP. Please don't speak. I cannot handle the kindest words.*

Although Heather's husband was a policeman who did occasionally direct traffic outside the Boys & Girls Club, Heather did not pick up on the meaning of Andrea's sign language. She said, "Oh, God, Andrea, how are you? I've been thinking of you."

How am I? Andrea thought. *I am a stark raving lunatic. Look at me: I can't even draw the breath to answer you. I am going to try a nod and a whispered lie.* "I'm okay, thanks."

Heather stared intently. She hadn't heard. But she got the message, maybe, that Andrea was losing her marbles and should be dropped like a hot potato. "Please let me know if you need anything," she said as she piled her bags into her cart and rolled out of the store.

Andrea stared at the steaks wrapped in plastic. Need anything?

That night Ed was late. Kacy had been entertaining the twins outside with Frisbee, but she had been promoted to the evening shift at the Juice Bar and had to get to work. Eric was playing in the adult softball league for the bike shop team. Andrea marveled at the difference between two children with their own lives and two children who needed everything done for them. Finn, Andrea had learned, couldn't even tie his shoes.

You're seven years old! Andrea had said. *And you can't tie your shoes?*

Mom always did it, he said.

This was true. Tess was guilty as charged. She babied the kids. She did everything for them, even to their own detriment. Finn could not tie his shoes. He could not pick out his own pajamas or pour a glass of milk.

Andrea lit the grill. She had too much food; she had not realized that both Eric and Kacy would miss dinner. Although, really, she thought, when was the last time either of them had been home for dinner? They were putting themselves outside the house on purpose. They didn't want to be at home with their deranged mother.

The flames jumped as Andrea laid the steaks down.

Was there a hell? She wondered. Really, was there? She had been a Catholic for forty-four years, educated by the nuns and the Jesuits, and this was the first time she'd thought to ask.

Chloe came out on the deck, holding a piece of robin's-egg-blue construction paper folded in half. Andrea took the paper but did not look at Chloe.

"What have we here?" Andrea asked.

"A formal request," Chloe said.

This should have been enough to make Andrea smile, but it was beyond her. She opened the paper. It had been decorated around the edges with curlicues, flowers, and birds. At the top, Chloe had written: *A Formal Request.*

Can we please go to Auntie Dee's house tomorrow after camp and perhaps spend the night?

Andrea was speechless. She resisted the urge to throw the formal request onto the grill flames. It was innocent, she reminded herself. Chloe and Finn wanted to see their friends. But still, the "formal request" was for "Auntie Dee's house." Auntie Dee would cut their grilled cheese into fun shapes; she would permit them to run through the sprinkler until the fireflies came out. The twins did not want Andrea. They wanted Delilah. She couldn't blame them, but it infuriated her.

She handed the formal request back to Chloe, not able to look her in the eye. "We'll see," she said.

Chloe stood before her for one resigned moment. "That means no."

"That means we'll see."

Chloe fled.

Andrea collapsed onto a deck chair and sank her face in her hands. *Need anything?*

"I need Tess back," she whispered. Denial was such a stupid phase of grief, especially for a forty-four-year-old woman who had lost both her parents and well knew that death happened to each and every one of us. And yet at any second the finality of Tess's death could level Andrea. She wanted to rip her hair out, tear her clothes, get on her knees and beg the sky, *Bring her back!*

The grill was smoking. Andrea pulled the steaks off just as the Chief walked onto the deck.

"Hey," he said. "Those smell good." His voice was light and chipper. How could he be chipper? It was twenty minutes to eight. He had stayed at work for twelve hours. He didn't want to be at home with her either.

Andrea stared at the platter of steaks. They did smell good, and they had cost her seventy dollars. The grocery store was booby-trapped with land mines. She couldn't stand to see anybody she knew. She didn't want pity or sympathy or understanding. But neither could she tolerate cheerful, normal life moving on. She was falling apart. Couldn't anyone see that she was *falling apart?*

She flipped the steaks off the deck, and they landed in her unwatered perennial bed.

"Jesus!" the Chief said. He grabbed her arm. "Andrea! What the *hell?*"

Need anything? She crumpled.

That night, after the Chief had pulled the steaks out of the garden dirt and washed them off, sliced them thinly, and cajoled both the twins and Andrea to eat, Andrea wandered into her bedroom, lay down on her bed fully clothed, and fell immediately to sleep.

She had the dream a third time. The man shouting for help, shouting in a language she didn't understand, but no matter, she understood the urgency. She swam out, she grabbed hold of him, she said, *Just float. I'll get us in. I'm a lifeguard!* She noticed his deep blue eyes. And then later, when he was walking away, she noticed his salt-and-pepper curls, his earring. When Phoebe lifted her face from the towel, Andrea felt her heart break. Of course he belonged to someone else. He belonged to Phoebe. But she felt something else, too: hope, anticipation.

And there they were, in the Jeep, clawing at one another, sucking, biting. He was behind her, but she didn't like it. *I want to see you!* she said. *I want to see your face!* She could feel his fingers on her nipples, his mouth on her neck. But she wanted to see his face! She turned.

It was Jeffrey.

DELILAH

Delilah was the best storyteller, and so she would tell the story of Greg and April Peck, the whole sphere of it—Greg's side, April's side, Tess's side. That was the only way to understand. To hear only Greg's side or only April's side was like taking one slice out of an apple and claiming the rest of it wasn't rotten.

Delilah considered herself a neutral third party, a Switzerland, a safe place for either Tess or Greg to go. But really, it was so much more complicated than that. (The most frustrating thing about being an adult was, indeed, how complicated everything was. Throw a party, write a letter to the editor, buy your children a PlayStation—there would be consequences and repercussions you never expected.) The Greg-and-April-Peck story was complicated by the fact that Delilah was in love with Greg.

Okay, there, she'd said it.

She was in love with Greg MacAvoy, who was now dead. And would it be flattering herself to say that he had been in love with her, too? Halfway in love? Delilah had been his confidante, his almost-lover. They were always *this close* to crossing the line into *that territory.*

It had started in Vegas, at Le Cirque, with his hand on her foot and then trilling up the back of her leg. This had tipped her off: Greg was interested. His interest made her interested. His interest had, tangentially, been responsible for her taking the dining room manager position at the Begonia. She wanted to be close to Greg outside of the scope of their group friendship. How? The Scarlet Begonia. Delilah worked four nights a week, most of them nights when Greg played and sang. It was officially impossible to watch Greg up onstage with his dark hair flopping in his eyes and his vine tattoo encircling his biceps and his feet in deck shoes no matter what the weather and listen to him sing "You Can't Always Get What You Want" and feel anything except powerless against his charms. Every woman in that bar, on any given night, would sleep with him. Delilah placed herself in a distinct category from these women; she was his friend.

But just admit it, Delilah!

No, it was more than that. To sleep with Greg MacAvoy would be a disaster. She had slept with his type before—nascent rock stars, athletes just off the winning field. They looked at Delilah like she was a juicy cheeseburger, they devoured her . . . and then they wiped their mouths with a napkin and walked away.

She wanted Greg to love her, to value her—someday—more than he valued Tess.

They hung out nearly every night after closing. Greg drank copiously and played a private concert for Delilah, Thom and Faith, Graham the bartender, and whoever else happened to be lingering. He and Delilah talked, he told her everything—or if not everything, then most things, things he did not tell Tess. It happened organically. They started talking about their kids. Barney had been only eight months old when Delilah went to work, the twins were a year and a half, Drew was two. Talking about the kids, after a few drinks, morphed into talking about their spouses. How long had it been before both of them realized there was no forbidden territory? Delilah complained: *Jeffrey acts like my father! I did not want to marry my father!* Greg complained: *Tess treats me like one of the children! She thinks I am completely incompetent!* They were simpatico in their restlessness. And where did this lead them? It led to nights when, at three in the morning, Delilah would drive Greg home. Greg would sometimes sit in the passenger seat oblivious to the world before stumbling to his front door, his guitar in its case banging into him like an inebriated sidekick. But he would sometimes direct Delilah to Cisco Beach, where they would watch the waves. Greg would tell her how much he wanted to touch her, kiss her, make love to her, and Delilah would stave him off. *We can't, it will end up in such a mess, our incredible friendship trashed, the guilt will kill you, you don't think so now, but trust me.*

A few nights he shushed her, his finger, callused from too many E minor chords, lightly touching her lips. And then he cupped his hand around her neck and pressed his face to her ear. He breathed into her until she thought, *Okay. Just this one time, okay.* But they had never so much as kissed. Not even one kiss. She held steady. Her body was the Hoover Dam, resisting the force of all that water. It *could* hurt. It would hurt Tess and Jeffrey and the four little children at home; it would hurt Greg and Delilah's friendship. Once Greg had her, he would weary of her. It wouldn't be as great as he hoped. Whereas to keep him at bay, to keep him always wanting this thing that was just beyond his reach, was to hold him captive.

He sent her love notes on cocktail napkins and cardboard coasters: *You look beautiful tonight. Will you run away with me?* He made her CDs and left them in her car; he sent her text messages from school: *U staying late 2nite?* He dedicated songs from the stage: *This one's for you, Ash* (because her maiden name was Ashby). He told her dirty jokes, he noticed when she got a pedicure. He said, *You are my best friend.* When they were all together, the eight of them, the group, he sent her a signal—two fingers, crossed. *You and me, babe.*

Then came April Peck.

Greg had a day job. He was the high school music teacher. It should not have been allowed—to put someone so goddamn good-looking, with so much magnetism and talent, in that position. But there it was. Greg taught music appreciation to all ninth-graders, he taught guitar to juniors and seniors (this was mostly boys), and he directed the exclusive all-girls a capella group, the High Priorities. It was the girls who were the problem. These were girls with voices like angels, with perfect pitch. When a girl made it into the High Priorities—it was fiercely competitive; try-outs were the first week of May every year, and the whole student body held its breath to find out who made it—she stayed until she graduated. The High Priorities, the twelve of them, were Greg's darlings. They were all in love with Greg; that was no secret. They were his groupies, his harem. They baked him cookies, they left elaborate illustrated notes like "We ♥ U, Mr. Mac!" on his chalkboard while he was at lunch, they endured painful scales and voice exercises *("Red leather, yellow leather!")*. They memorized lyrics in twenty-four hours. Greg lifted his hands and they sang; he brought his hands down and they stopped.

All the girls were beautiful. Even if they were heavy (and yes, it did seem like the best singers were heavy) or had acne or wore braces or their toes turned in. They were all beautiful when they were onstage in their white jeans and pink cashmere twinsets. They were sassy and sexy, they were luminous, aglow. So much feminine beauty and energy and talent, those bodies blossoming, those hearts unfolding, the desire and the jealousy and the yearning for praise, for distinction and admiration—God, it was a time bomb. Delilah had warned Greg about this: all those girls with their raging hormones, their new breasts, their asses squeezed into skin-tight jeans, all falling over themselves to make Greg MacAvoy happy, to be chosen for solos, to sing like a nightingale. It would get him in trouble one day. He had to be careful.

But Greg *was* careful. Delilah had for years watched him be careful. He taught his girls to sing together, to practice blending their voices. *Harmony!* he shouted. *Listen to one another!* He agonized over who to give solos to; he never played favorites. *You're all my favorites*, he told them again and again. *You're all my highest priority.*

But teenage girls were fragile. They were both brave and stupid. They were innocent and cunning. A few girls, over the years, had fallen so in love with Greg they nearly drowned in it. Greg was always kind, always firm, always funny and avuncular. *You feel this way now, but you'll get over it. You'll grow up and shine your light and I will seem very small and faraway to you, I prom-ise.*

Sometimes the girls showed up at the Begonia "for dinner" in low-cut tops and lower-cut jeans, and when Delilah told them, at ten when the kitchen closed, that they had to leave because they were underage, they—well, they whined. *I want to see Mr. Mac play. Just one song. Please?* Delilah had small children at home, she knew how to deal with whiners. *Off you go. Come back when you're twenty-one.*

They really love you, Delilah said to Greg.

Yes, he said. *But do you?*

Delilah swatted him, sashayed away. People talked about Greg and those girls, but the crushes were innocent and funny; it was an after-school special.

Until April Peck.

Why April Peck and not some other girl? Like anything, most of it was timing. Delilah had sensed things coming to a head be-tween Greg and Tess. He complained about Tess all the time, and his complaints were angry and mean-spirited. He and Tess were in a rut—sexually and emotionally. The summer had brought the Debacle of the Roof. (Greg dwelled on the roof more than Delilah thought necessary. It was a home improvement project! Could it really fell a marriage?) Tess and Greg had had some serious leak-ing in the spring rains, and they'd discovered they needed a new roof. They were quoted a price of thirty-seven thousand dollars to replace the roof, which they couldn't afford. Greg decided to replace the roof himself. He hired two Lithuanian day laborers; he bought twenty-two bundles of shingles at Marine Home Cen-ter. He rented the tools and the ladders, and with a DIY website as his professional reference, he got to work. They spent a week getting the old shingles off and a thousand dollars dropping them at the dump, then another two weeks reshingling in the brutal July sun, only to discover that the roof still leaked and had to be torn off and redone by professionals. Tess did not handle this well. There was a lot of innuendo about the roof caving in on the marriage, literally and figuratively. By the time school started in September, Tess and Greg were depleted, stressed out, and sick of each other.

There had been a lot of drives to Cisco Beach to talk that September, a lot of Greg pushing and Delilah resisting. He grew belligerent.

You don't care about me.

Because I won't sleep with you, I don't care about you? Even you, Greg MacAvoy, are too emotionally mature to believe that.

I need . . . he said.

What? she said.

Something, he said.

April Peck was a senior. She had lived on Nantucket for two years. She lived with her mother in a huge beach house owned by her mother's parents. There was a father and a brother in New York City. A bad divorce, apparently.

The night in question was October 23, a Sunday night. According to Greg, things at home had been okay: they were having a fire, Tess had roasted a chicken, football was on. Tess wanted to read the rest of the Sunday paper and watch *60 Minutes,* and she had to make the kids' lunches and get her lesson plans straight for the week. Chloe had a fever of 100.7—not anything to worry about, but still. They, the MacAvoys, had not gone over to Delilah and Jeffrey's house for cocktails and a six-foot sub for the usual Sunday afternoon drunken free-for-all because of Chloe's fever. If she had something, Tess didn't want her to pass it on to the other kids. Tess also didn't want Chloe to get run down. They were staying home, Tess had told Delilah over the phone, to have a "family night." Delilah had been disappointed and a little hurt—weren't they all family?

Greg had not wanted to stay home. He loved their friends and the tradition of the free-for-all Sundays. He loved Delilah and Jeffrey's house, he adored Delilah's cooking (her repertoire was straight off a sports bar menu—stuffed potato skins, Reuben sandwiches), he loved taking his guitar and getting everyone singing. Sundays, he said, were the days that made him glad to be alive—the drinking, the music, their friends, the kids running around. He could not believe they were turning down a Sunday just because Chloe felt a little warm.

"A hundred point seven is more than just 'a little warm,'" Tess said.

Greg huffed and considered slamming around the house to demonstrate how pissed off he was, but then he got the great idea that he would put the kids to bed and head over to Jeffrey and Delilah's alone. He switched immediately into model parent mode. He got the kids in the bath, he gave Chloe a dose of Motrin, he supervised the tooth-brushing and hunkered down with them through three chapters of *Charlie and the Chocolate Factory*. Downstairs, Tess finished the newspaper, made herself a cup of chamomile tea, and watched *60 Minutes*.

Greg came down from reading to the kids, but he did not speak to Tess. If he told her he was going to Jeffrey and Delilah's, they would fight. He didn't want to fight. He wanted to be free. He felt like he was shackled to the house. He opened the fridge and got a beer.

Tess said, "Are the kids asleep?"

Greg said, "What do you think?"

He was angry. And resentful. He felt like a sullen teenager that Tess had grounded.

"Go over there if you want," she said.

He did not appreciate the way she'd read his mind. She was so sure she was always one step ahead of him. He said, "I'm going into work."

"Work?" she said.

"I want to play," he said. "If I play here, I'll wake up the kids."

Sheer brilliance. Tess did not like it when Greg played the guitar or the piano at night because the kids *did* wake up, every time.

They loved to listen to him, and would not go back to sleep until he was finished.

"Fine," said Tess, and Greg left.

Greg's official version of what happened that night went as follows: He arrived at the school; he played the piano in his room. He figured he had been playing for an hour or so when April Peck walked in. She was wet, he said. Her blond hair was matted and dripping; the soles of her shoes squeaked against the tile floor. When Greg looked out the window, he saw that it had started to rain. Then he realized April was upset; she was crying. She was wearing a jean jacket and a denim miniskirt. The jean jacket was soaked. April took it off and laid it across his piano. Underneath her jacket she wore a white T-shirt, which was also wet. He looked down at his hands, arched over the keys. (In the unedited version, he told Delilah he knew right then that he was in trouble.) He stopped playing.

He said, "What are you doing here, April? It's nine o'clock."

April said, still crying, "Play me something."

Greg said, "You don't belong in the school after-hours without a reason. Do you have a way home, or would you like me to call your mother?"

April said, "I don't have a way home. Derek dropped me."

"Why did he drop you *here?*"

"I saw the light on in your room. I thought you would be here."

Greg said, "I'm going to call your mother and have her come get you."

April broke into hysterical sobs. In Greg's words, she threw herself into Greg's arms. (*Meaning what?* Delilah asked. Meaning he was sitting on the piano bench and she lobbed herself into his lap. *So she was sitting on your lap? Sort of, yes. It was awkward. I was trying to get her up, get her off me.*) Her white T-shirt was wet and she "did not seem to be wearing a bra." He said he "patted" April's back and then tried to ease her up. *Up onto your feet!*

he said. *Let's go.* He said she put her arms around his neck and pressed her breasts against his shoulder. He said he jumped up with such force that he dumped April onto the ground and she bumped her shin on the leg of the piano. She howled in pain, even though it was just a bump and couldn't have hurt that much.

She said, "I just want to talk to you."

Greg said again, "You don't belong here."

She said, "I want you to take me somewhere."

Greg said, "I'm calling your mother." He dug out the phone book, but the number wasn't listed under Peck. The house belonged to April's grandparents. Greg asked April for the number; she would not tell him. Greg picked April's jean jacket up off the piano and found her cell phone in the pocket. He scrolled through it for her home number. April grabbed for her cell phone, he held it up over his head, and in trying to get the phone back from Greg, she scratched his face. He gave her the cell phone and said, "Fine. You deal with it, then." The scratch on his face was bleeding. He ushered April out of the room, turned off the light, locked the door, and headed down the corridor, leaving April behind. April followed him, crying, pleading. *Take me home. Please don't call my mother. She thinks I'm here with you, practicing.*

"What?" Greg said. He was very, very angry now. He was afraid, too, and incredulous. What must April's mother think about a so-called practice at nine o'clock on a Sunday night? Greg said, "I can't take you home, I've been drinking." As soon as he said it, he realized it was a huge mistake, and it was at that point that he wondered if April had been drinking or if she was on something. He hurried out to his car in the rain. Parked next to him was the car he knew to be April's, a white Jeep Cherokee. He said he peered into the front seat to check that it was indeed April's car, and he saw a bra lying across the driver's seat. He got into his car and drove home, leaving April in the rain in front of the school, crying.

He should have gone home, he said. He should have crawled

into bed next to Tess and told her exactly what had happened. But he did not do that, because he did not want to go home to Tess, and he knew that if he told her what had happened, she would blow a gasket. She would find something wrong with the way he'd handled things (indeed, he felt he'd handled things badly, but the situation had been impossible). Tess would berate him, they would fight. Which was why he'd left home in the first place.

So he went to Jeffrey and Delilah's. Everyone was still there: Addison and Phoebe, the Chief and Andrea. Delilah was buzzed; she'd shrieked enthusiastically when he walked in. She fixed him a plate of food, which he was too agitated to consider eating, but he sucked down a cocktail pronto.

Jeffrey said, "Where've you been?"

Addison said, "It's Phoebe's Packers, so we decided to stay."

Andrea said, "Where's Tess?"

"Home with the kids," Greg said. "Chloe has a little fever."

Jeffrey said, "Are you okay? You look terrible."

They all turned to look at him. This, he told Delilah, was the moment when he should have told them what happened. Full disclosure.

"What happened to your face?" Andrea said. She inspected the place where April had scratched him. "You're bleeding."

He didn't know what to say. At that moment the real story seemed grotesque and not remotely feasible. "The goddamn cherry tree in my yard," he said. "I didn't see the branch."

Andrea gave him a funny look. She didn't believe him. She thought something else had happened. She thought . . . what? That *Tess* had scratched him? Now was the time to set things straight, but Greg didn't want to lend his encounter with April Peck any more energy than it already had. Was there a crime in that?

So he lied. And lying begat more lying.

"It's fine," he said. He cleared his throat. "I think I might be coming down with a little something myself."

The following afternoon April Peck filed a complaint with the superintendent's office.

April's story went like this: She had left a book that she really needed in her locker, and she had swung by school to pick it up. Luckily, the men's basketball team was playing and the door to the school was open. Since April's boyfriend, Derek, who had graduated the year before, played in the men's league, she stopped by the gym to look for him, but he wasn't there. She saw a light on in the music room, peeked through the window, saw Mr. Mac, and decided to say hi.

She said it had been raining and Mr. Mac encouraged her to take off her wet jacket. She said Greg patted the spot next to him on the piano bench. "I'll play you something," he said.

She said she declined. She told him she had just come by to say hi. She had to pick up her book and get home to study.

He said, "Won't you just stay and listen to one song? No one at home wants to listen to me play."

She said she didn't want to, but she agreed. She said she felt self-conscious without her jacket on because her T-shirt was so wet it was see-through and she wasn't wearing a bra. She said that the song Mr. Mac played, "Tiny Dancer," made her uncomfortable. She said he was more than singing it. He was singing it *to her* in a way that seemed to mean something. April said when she went to stand up, Mr. Mac stopped playing, grabbed her arm, and kissed her. She said he tasted like beer. She said he touched one of her breasts through the wet T-shirt. She said she could tell he had an erection. He said, "I know why you came here." She turned to leave—to run!—and stumbled over the piano bench. She said he reached out for her, saying, *Please don't leave. I need . . . I need . . . I need . . .* He had her by the arm again. She said she was afraid, so she scratched him, hard, on the face. She dashed out of the room, out of the school, to her car. She said as she pulled away, Mr. Mac was standing in the rain, calling her name.

Delilah heard the two stories, in tandem, on Monday night. Delilah was horrified. She was—how else could she say it?—crushed.

Jeffrey said, "We have to support Greg in this. He needs us. This is going to blow up into one of those huge, ugly stories that ruins his reputation."

Jeffrey was, as ever, correct. The stories traveled around the island like an infectious disease. *Everyone* was talking about it. Delilah knew this because for the remainder of the week, wherever she went—the post office, dry cleaners, Stop & Shop, the Begonia—people clammed up when she approached.

We have to support Greg, Jeffrey said. *He needs us.*

Delilah was furious. Whereas Tess was heartbroken, devastated, incredulous, and confused, Delilah was just angry. She believed April Peck.

Greg said, *No one at home wants to hear me play.*

True.

Greg tasted like beer.

True.

Greg played her "Tiny Dancer." This was Greg's favorite song. It was his theme song. It was the best song in his repertoire, his sexiest, most soulful song. It was the song he sang when he wanted something from his audience. It was his seduction song.

Greg said, *Please don't leave. I need . . . I need . . . I need . . .*

What?

Delilah knew what the next word was. He had said it to her only a few weeks before.

Something.

Greg was suspended from his teaching position for two weeks. "Suspended" was the word that went around town, with all its negative connotations. Greg was a restless teenage boy who had gone looking for trouble and found it. The school administration called the suspension a "temporary leave of absence."

Dr. Flanders, the superintendent (who, Delilah knew through Thom and Faith, had more than a few skeletons dangling in his own closet), said, "Mr. MacAvoy is taking a leave of absence while we sort the matter out."

April Peck took a "leave of absence" also. Her mother, Donna Peck, who had encouraged April to confront the administration, whisked her away to Hawaii. The Four Seasons, Maui.

Delilah felt betrayed. Greg needed "something," but why did that "something" have to be April Peck, a seventeen-year-old siren with a voice that was a cross between Renée Fleming's and Alicia Keys's? April Peck was too obvious. She showed up at nine o'clock on a Sunday night, a contestant from a wet T-shirt contest and crying to boot, and Greg didn't have the willpower or the common sense to kick her out?

Well, he said he did, but Delilah didn't believe him.

I need . . . I need . . . I need . . .

What Delilah thought was, *He was supposed to need me.*

What certain people knew (Delilah, Jeffrey, Addison, and Phoebe) was that the Chief had had a private chat with Dr. Flanders on Greg's behalf. The two men had met in a secret chamber at the police station. The Chief either slipped Flanders the equivalent of a maître d's fifty-dollar bill or he exerted his considerable authority. The Chief talked to Flanders as a favor to Andrea, who wanted it for Tess, who wanted it for her kids.

This has to get swept under the rug. He can't lose his job. What will we do for money? He has to be fully exonerated.

And in fact the school administration decided to believe Greg. Not in absolute terms, perhaps, but enough to salvage his job and dismiss April Peck from the High Priorities. Both Donna Peck and Derek Foster, April's boyfriend, protested this ruling, but they had no clout. Greg had tenure, he had worked in the school for twelve years without incident, he was the father of two young children, he was well respected and well liked in the community, his wife was a teacher in the district, he was a fine musician and an all-around asset to the music department, and the High Priorities were a source of local pride: they had won competitions at the state and national levels; they had traveled to Italy and Luxembourg.

And there was the chief of police factor.

And what the administration knew that no one else did was that the high school phys ed teacher, Bob Casey, had long been complaining to the superintendent's office that April Peck was lascivious, her behavior in school inappropriate and dangerous to teachers who were only trying to help her.

And and *and!* When the superintendent and his "inquiry team" asked April Peck which book she had gone to retrieve from her locker on the night in question, Sunday, October 23, April Peck floundered.

"Which *book?*"

"That's the question, Miss Peck. Which book were you coming to school to get?"

"You mean the title?"

The inquiry team frantically scribbled notes.

She said, "Why do you want to know that?"

"It's just a question," Flanders said. "We're asking you the title of the book you came to get."

Finally she said, *"A Separate Peace."*

Which was required reading for freshmen. Not seniors.

With news of this prime-time flub, the plaintiff caught in a lie, Greg crowed his innocence with a previously unseen confidence and vigor. *The girl's a liar! She's been lying all along!*

What Delilah chose to believe was that Greg was both lying and telling the truth, as was April. The truth fell somewhere in between. The truth was an amalgam of his details and hers. But the truth had been burned in the incinerator, dumped in the ocean a hundred miles off the coast. They would never know the truth.

For weeks and then months, Delilah was cool and distant with Greg. She had been denying him for years, yes, but for all of those years she had been in love with him. Surely he realized this? Surely he understood that turning to April Peck would wound her? The cocktail napkins and cardboard coasters that came to her now said, *Do you still hate me?*

Onstage, he said, *This song is for you, Ash.* And it was Natalie Merchant's "Kind and Generous." Or it was "Landslide," Delilah's all-time sentimental favorite.

In February, once the matter was dead and buried in the public eye and almost so among the eight of them, Delilah said, "You had everyone else fooled, but not me."

And he said, "That's too bad. You're the only person who matters."

Which sounded like total bullshit, but she was won over anyway.

If the story had ended there, it would still have been awful, but ultimately it would have been forgivable. It would have been catalogued under *We all fuck up. So what?*

But then.

Fast-forward almost as far as you could go (there was an end point now, because Greg was dead), to the night before Greg died. Another Sunday night. It was now June 19, and the Begonia was filled with tourists whom Delilah didn't know. It was a blah night; Delilah was feeling a little flat, a little premenstrual, a little down. Greg and Tess's anniversary was the following day, they were going on a sail to the Vineyard, they were taking a champagne picnic, Greg was taking his guitar, he had written Tess a song, they were going to stay overnight in a Relais & Châteaux property. Fabulous.

Would Delilah watch the twins while they were gone?

Delilah had a Cinderella complex going; her ego was hurt, and her heart, and her hopes. Nine months earlier Greg's marriage to Tess had been looking like a terminal case, but now here it was, rising like a phoenix out of the ashes. She pretended to be happy for them, but she wasn't.

At five minutes to ten, April Peck walked into the Begonia. Delilah nearly stumbled in her very high and wicked Jimmy Choos. She was surprised the alarms weren't going off. The little-lying-bitch alarms.

Delilah rushed her. April was wearing a shell-pink slip dress embroidered all over with tiny flowers and a pair of expensive-looking silver stilettos. She looked stunning and mature and confident—nothing like the other girls who had tried to pass themselves off in here. If Delilah hadn't known better, she would have said the girl was of age, or close enough to let slide. But she did know better.

"The kitchen just closed, April," Delilah said. "And you're underage. So I can't let you in."

April stared. "How do you know my name?"

Delilah stared back. What was the savvy answer? The truth? They lived on an island where everyone sort of knew everyone else. Delilah and Jeffrey went to all of the High Priorities concerts to support Greg, so Delilah supposed the first time she had seen April Peck was in the high school auditorium two springs earlier. Even among all the lovely songbirds, April Peck had stood out. She was the most beautiful of the beautiful, and she had a solo in "Fire." Her voice had been rich and smoky and simmering and strong. Before all this shit with Greg, April Peck had been the kind of teenager adults noticed because she had star quality. And after all this shit with Greg, Delilah was mortified to admit, she had stalked April Peck a time or two.

Once she had seen April standing in front of the magazine rack at the Hub (paging through *Elle*—predictable), and Delilah had lingered on the other side of the store, fingering the polished shells they sold from barrels. She studied April Peck, she deconstructed her: the hair, the jeans, the ass, the breasts, the lips (moving ever so slightly as she read, which made Delilah feel sorry for her). April's cell phone rang—it sounded like the bells of Westminster Abbey—and April answered in her silk-sheets voice. "Allo?"

She left the store, and Delilah followed her. April Peck was fascinating. Why? She was the object of Greg's desire. Greg had been so bitter and banged up on that Sunday night in October that he might have made a pass at anyone. But it had been April Peck for good reason. She was flawless. Delilah allowed herself a few seconds of sheer envy, then decided she would find a flaw. She followed April Peck up Main Street. April climbed into a white Jeep Cherokee while she was still on the phone. She backed up without looking in her rearview mirror and nearly rammed into a guy in a Ford F-350. The guy opened his window to shout, but then he saw April and whistled instead.

There you had it.

How do I know your name? Delilah thought. *When you pulled a stunt like you did with Greg, you instantly became famous.* Surely April realized that. Still, the question threw Delilah. It made her feel defensive and weirdly at a disadvantage. She knew April Peck, but April Peck did not know her. April Peck was a celebrity and Delilah was a nobody. But this was a ploy by April Peck, a stall tactic.

"I can't let you in," Delilah said. "You're underage."

"No, I'm not," April said.

"You—"

April opened her straw clutch purse and produced an ID. A Massachusetts license that furnished her name, April Peck, her address, 999 Polpis Road, and her birth date, June 1, 1988. Which made her twenty-one years and eighteen days old. Delilah peered at the license closely. It was a fake, of course. It looked real, but it was fake.

"You're handing me a fake ID?"

"It's not fake. It's real. I'm twenty-one."

Delilah laughed. "You just graduated from high school. I know who you are, April, and I know how old you are."

"It's a long story," April said wearily. "I don't need to eat. I ate. I just want to sit and listen to Greg play."

Greg. That was a nice touch, calling him Greg. Delilah was wearing a Diane von Furstenberg dress that put her boobs on magnificent display. (When she'd walked into the Begonia earlier that evening, Greg had said, "Would you wear that dress every night for the rest of your life? Please?") But the dress also stretched tight against the premenstrual bloating at her abdomen. Compared to April Peck in her sleek size zero, Delilah felt like a lumpy cow. She crossed her arms.

"I'm not letting you in."

April Peck exhaled in one long stream, to let the world know she was growing impatient. "Call the police. Have them run the license." She stared defiantly at Delilah. "Be my guest. I'm serious."

Delilah had been fantasizing about a showdown, but now that it was happening, she was uncomfortable. She had been ambushed; she didn't have her footing. It was a tug of war, and Delilah was about to end up facedown in the mud.

There was a hand on her back. Greg.

"Let her in," he said.

Delilah turned to him, stunned.

"She's not of age," Delilah said.

"Delilah," Greg said. "Let her in."

April sidestepped her way around Delilah and walked into the bar. She took a seat, alone, at the table closest to the stage. Delilah felt like she was watching a horror film. Greg followed April and talked with her for a minute. April said something, and he laughed. He laughed! Then he climbed up onstage, and with the predictable toss of his hair, he sat down in the chair and started singing.

Delilah never drank during service. It was a good rule, adhered to even when Addison and Phoebe were in, or the Chief, even when a table full of college boys offered to buy her what they called a glass of "chardonnay wine." But now Delilah hipchecked Graham aside and poured herself a goblet of cabernet and a shot of Wild Turkey and carried both of them to the ladies' room. She locked herself in the handicapped stall and threw back the whiskey first—awful—then chased it with a deep swallow of wine.

This was hideous, right? Greg had trampled Delilah's authority; he had humiliated her. And for whom? For April Peck bin Laden, the lying bitch seductress with her fake ID. The very same woman—girl!—who had trashed his marriage and his reputation. She had nearly cost him his job, and his life here, and yet there was Greg defending her, ushering her in, then laughing at whatever insipid thing she'd said. He was up onstage playing for her now.

Delilah strained to listen from the confines of the bathroom stall. "Tiny Dancer." Impossible. But yes, he was singing it. He had not sung that song since the mess with April Peck had occurred back in the fall. But he was playing it now. Delilah sucked down more wine, but the wine only fueled the fire of her rage. It was absconding with the last shreds of patience and understanding that she had left. Should she call the Chief? Have him send someone down to charge April with identity fraud? Should she call Tess? And say, *Greg is onstage right now singing that song to April Peck.*

The door to the ladies' room swung open and Delilah could hear Greg singing more clearly. The second verse.

The head waitress, Amelia, who was a real hard-ass, barked, "Delilah? Are you in here?"

Delilah drank more wine. "Yeah."

"Are you planning on coming back out?"

Delilah left her wine on top of the toilet paper dispenser. She did not want a scene where April became the adult and Delilah the adolescent.

"Yes," she said.

April Peck left at midnight, when Greg took his break. She had consumed three glasses of pinot grigio; one of them, Graham told Delilah, had been comped by Greg. April left a huge tip—forty bucks—which made her Queen for a Day in Graham's mercenary eyes. April had slipped out while Delilah was in the ladies' room polishing off yet another shot of Wild Turkey chased by yet another goblet of cabernet, and Delilah did not see her go and did not have the opportunity for another parry. Which was good or bad? Good, she decided. She was drunk by closing time; she couldn't do the counting that cashing out required, and so she had Graham do it and slipped him twenty bucks for the trouble.

Thom and Faith were at one end of the boomerang bar with their sixteenth or seventeenth vodkas, and Greg was at the other end brooding over a Sam Adams draft. Delilah had seen Greg's brooding act a million times before; he used it like a petulant twelve-year-old girl. *If I make moody, faraway eyes, someone will ask me what's wrong.* Delilah had meant to storm out of the Begonia after closing without a word to anyone. But she was just drunk enough to want another drink. Greg was dopily sitting there and Delilah could not control her urge to vent.

She took the stool next to him, asked Graham for a glass of cabernet, and whispered viciously, "I just don't get it."

"I know," Greg murmured.

"Have you been . . . talking to her?"

"Sort of," he said.

"Sort of!" Delilah said. She sounded like the indignant wife, the shrew. She was supposed to be the cool girl, the one who could take any news and shrug it off.

"She came in to talk right before she graduated," he said. "And we decided to mend the fence."

"Mend the fence," Delilah repeated.

"Put everything behind us. She asked for forgiveness."

Delilah narrowed her eyes. "She's a liar."

Greg sipped his beer. The mooniness was disappearing. "Well, she's not twenty-one."

"No shit," Delilah said. "And you made me let her into the bar. I could be fired for that. The Begonia could be shut down."

"Oh, please," Greg said.

"I just don't *get* you," Delilah said.

"Sure you do, Ash."

"No," Delilah said. "I don't. Were you telling me the truth about that night with April? The whole fucking truth?"

"Yes," he said.

"I don't believe you."

"Nobody believes me."

"I would like you so much better if you just admitted you were lying. I wouldn't even care if you said you fucked her that night. Just as long as you told me the truth."

"Tess feels the same way," Greg said. "But I have nothing to add or detract from my story. It stands. And at this point, it is dried up. It is *burned*, Delilah. There is no reason to talk about it any further."

"Except that April came in tonight."

"Like I said, we mended the fence."

Delilah's head was spinning. Graham, behind the bar, was a hologram. Thom and Faith were studiously pretending to watch a rerun of *Law & Order* which was playing on the TV over the bar, but really, Delilah knew, they were listening to every word. She didn't care. She put her head down on the bar.

"You have no idea how much I love you," she said.

Greg rubbed her back, but his touch lacked intention. "Sure I do, Ash," he said. He finished his beer and set the glass down with some purpose.

"Will you play for me?" Delilah asked.

"Not tonight," he said. "Tonight I have to get home."

Right, she thought. Big anniversary tomorrow. He had made it by the skin of his teeth through year number twelve.

He stood to leave and Delilah stood as well, thinking, *Change your mind! Stay here! Play for me!* Would he change his mind? Sometime before he reached his car, would he call out to her?

He did not. He climbed into his beat-up 4Runner, which was parked down the block from Delilah's Rubicon, and he drove out of town.

She did not mean to follow him. They lived only half a mile away from each other, and even though he was way up ahead, she noticed that he did not turn left onto Somerset Lane the way he would have to to go home. He kept going straight. He was headed for Cisco Beach.

Was this it, then? Her cue? Did he know she was behind him? Was she supposed to follow him? She checked her cell phone for a text message: nothing. She followed him anyway, around a bend that gave her vertigo. She put on her turn signal and pulled over to the side of the road. She was very drunk; she should not be driving. If the police got hold of her, she would fail the breathalyzer. She was so drunk she would break the thing. Greg sped away, oblivious. In so many ways he was just a boy. What was she doing? She had a man at home—Jeffrey. Jeffrey was too old and Greg was too young. This was ridiculous. She couldn't chase Greg like this. She had to get home to bed, she had the twins tomorrow, and she liked to be on top of her game when she had the twins. If she gave the kids free run of the PlayStation while she took a nap, Tess would hear about it. Delilah was so drunk, she could not trust herself to be fortresslike with Greg. She would give in to him tonight, of all nights, and it would end up a mess. It would ruin everything.

Turn around!

Such good advice, but Delilah ignored it. Greg's taillights were two red pinpricks in the distance, and then he rounded the curve by Sandole's fish store and disappeared from view. Delilah followed at a law-abiding pace.

She was a cat, Jeffrey always said, because she could see in the dark. It was one of her many unsung talents, and tonight it was a talent she was grateful for. She was four or five hundred yards away when she spotted two cars parked at the end of Cisco Beach. Two cars: one was Greg's 4Runner, and the other was a white Jeep Cherokee.

Delilah swung into the next driveway. A voice was screaming in her head—no words, just screaming. She looked again. She was very, very drunk, an unreliable witness. Yes, it was a white Jeep Cherokee. April's car. Greg had come to Cisco Beach, to *their* spot—his and Delilah's—to meet April Peck, and . . . what? Mend some more of that fence?

Screaming.

Delilah backed the car out of the driveway, turned around, and headed for home.

She vowed she would never speak to him again. She didn't care what kind of rift it caused within the group. Greg MacAvoy was a rat bastard and Delilah would not speak to him.

The next morning Tess showed up at a little after nine to drop off the twins. Delilah felt like absolute crap; she had vomited up the contents of her stomach in a lurid cabernet hue. She had cried, and spilled her guts to Jeffrey. She was leaden, her head ached, her stomach was puckered like a lemon, her balance was off, she was exhausted. She had not slept for a minute. She could not stop thinking of the two cars, side by side, and then the imagined scene between Greg and April Peck that followed.

Delilah had showered and dressed and made the kids Belgian waffles with caramelized bananas and whipped cream for breakfast. She had to put up a front for Tess. Delilah would take the kids to the beach, then to the farm for strawberry-picking, then home to make jam and eat cheeseburgers, and perhaps end the day with ice cream sandwiches, sparklers on the back deck, and a game of Monopoly.

Tess, when she arrived with the kids, seemed a little off. She looked adorable in a red bikini top and white denim shorts, cutesy flip-flops, starlet sunglasses, but her smile was tentative. Something was on her mind. What was it? She was in full apoplectic mode as far as leaving the children was concerned. She kissed them half a dozen times each, she said *I love you* fourteen times, and she came back from the car for one more hug apiece. *I love you so much, please, please be good, make healthy choices, I'll be back tonight or tomorrow morning at the latest, depends on how your father does with the sailing. It's pretty windy.*

Delilah knew Tess was ambivalent about sailing, and every other sport that involved the open water. She said, "Are you nervous, Tess, about the sail?"

"Terrified," Tess said plainly. She met Delilah's eyes with what felt like an indecent amount of honesty.

Delilah hung in the balance for a suspended moment. Shouldn't honesty be met with honesty?

She couldn't bear to think about it now. Could not bear it! Delilah's decision could not be taken back, any more than Greg's indiscretions could be taken back, any more than Tess and Greg could be brought back from the dead. It was all over and done.

And yet the whole mess festered in Delilah. Physically she was healthy, but her emotional state was frayed. Two weeks after Greg and Tess died, she had nearly caused four catastrophic car crashes. She drove, but she did not pay attention. She did not sleep. Phoebe gave her enough Ambiens to euthanize an army battalion and still she did not sleep. She was tired all day with the kids; she dropped the boys off at camp and then had to set the kitchen timer to remind herself to pick them up. She did not have the energy for fishing or hiking around Quaise Swamp or taking a kayak off the Jetties. She gave the kids too much money for the snack bar, or she dropped them at the movies, and then she sat listlessly in her car for two hours with the air-conditioning on, watching people go into and come out of the Begonia. She had not given Thom and Faith an answer about her job, but she would have to tell them soon that she was not coming back.

She stopped cooking. Every night it was pizza or prepared food from the farm. And she had stopped drinking. This last change may have sounded like it was for the best—better, certainly, than Delilah drinking herself into a coma every night. But Delilah's relationship with alcohol had always been positive, and now alcohol was one more thing she couldn't bring herself to enjoy.

She tried to be kind to Jeffrey, and he in turn was extraordinarily solicitous with her. He brought her flowers and just-picked vegetables and jars of preserves that the girls in the farm kitchen had put up. He took the kids and let her sleep. He did not say, "Pizza, again?" He looked at her grieving and considered it normal. He was wary of the sleeping pills and happy about her abstinence. He knew there was something else, but he did not ask her what it was.

That she had loved Greg and Greg had loved her, but they had not acted on this love.

That Greg had had a relationship of some sort with the little blond bin Laden.

That Delilah had not been brave enough to speak the truth.

ANDREA

The first week of July was too hot to sleep. Normally the Chief and Andrea installed an air conditioner in their bedroom window, but this year they did not. The twins were up many times in the night, and Andrea wanted to be able to hear them. Andrea took sleeping pills, but they didn't work. She lay in bed, sweaty and drugged and so psychologically addled that she could not sleep.

During the day she was a zombie.

She had moved on from denial, or so she thought. She knew, intellectually, that Tess was dead and not coming back. She resisted the urge to call Tess's house to see if she would pick up; she did not drive by the house to see if Tess was out in the front garden, deadheading the daylilies. Ed was at work all the time. It was his job to insure the island's public safety 24/7. Additionally, he was thinking about Tess and Greg. He was trying to figure out what happened. Didn't she want to know what happened?

No, she didn't. She just wanted it to unhappen.

Andrea was in some other stage of grief, one not previously documented by the authors of grief books. She was in a stage that should be known as Long Periods of Exhausted Stupor Punctuated by Psychotic Episodes.

One day, however, she got herself to the beach to swim. This was Ed's idea. Ed was a big proponent of getting-back-to-normal. Even if Andrea didn't feel normal, she could do normal things, and this might help.

Go to the beach, he said. Swim.

She put on her tank suit. She packed a towel and her goggles. She settled in her usual spot on the beach. It was the first week of July, and the beach was crowded with people getting on with their normal, happy lives on vacation. How could they do it? Andrea walked to the water's edge. She filled with a terrible dread, a sickening revelation, which was by no means new, but which struck her in a new way.

She had not become a nun.

She had stood at the foot of Tess's prostrate nine-year-old body and she had prayed to God. She had in fact made a pact: *Spare Tess and I will devote my life to you.*

But how easy it had been to let her end of the bargain go once it turned out that Tess was okay. What happened to people who did that? They ended up in hell.

She, Andrea, was in hell.

She could not swim. She could not even make it back to the bluff to her car. She was going to have to call Ed and have him come get her. He had come nearly two weeks earlier to tell her the news. (She could not think about it.) She retrieved her cell phone from her bag to call the station, but there was no reception. She couldn't call Tess at home, because no one would answer.

Andrea pitched her cell phone into the ocean.

A guy on a towel a few yards away from her said, "Whoa!"

Ed was at work trying to figure out "what happened," but Andrea already knew what happened. She had made a promise and then not upheld it. God had waited years and years, but he had come back for Tess.

Andrea looked blankly at the guy on the towel.

She needed help.

This was rock bottom. It had been two weeks since Tess and Greg had died. Molly, the dispatcher, dropped off a book about grieving, which Andrea had been unable to read, but she was pretty sure that if she read it, it would tell her that grief had a trajectory and that two weeks after a death a mourner hit bottom. Dumped a platter of rib-eyes into the garden. Threw her cell phone into the ocean.

But then the next day Andrea woke up feeling worse. How could she feel worse when she had already hit rock bottom? She was despondent and restless. She could not pour the children's cereal or pack their lunches. She asked Kacy to do it, and Kacy did it without complaint while Andrea sat on the edge of her bed, paralyzed. The bed was unmade, she should make it; Ed would tolerate many things, but not an unmade bed. She could not make it. Kacy was such a good kid. She must have her own grief, she must miss Tess and Greg, too, but Andrea couldn't ask. She started to cry.

Kacy came into the bedroom and said, "I'll bike with the kids to camp."

Andrea nodded. Kacy did not leave. She said, "But they want to go to the beach this afternoon, Mom. And you promised you'd take them."

"Did I?" Andrea had no recollection.

"You did."

She took a deep breath. Air. Sometimes air helped. Like right this second. Andrea believed she could take the kids to the beach—the north shore, where it was placid—and watch them like a hawk while they swam. And then later, tonight maybe, she would ask Kacy how she was feeling about things. Ed was a big believer in reaching out. *Step outside of yourself for a minute,* he said. *Call Delilah, or Phoebe.*

But Delilah and Phoebe didn't matter anymore. The only person who mattered was gone.

When the kids came home from camp, Andrea was ready. She was wearing her bathing suit and a pareo. She had packed juice boxes and Fritos. She had done nothing all morning except sit on the edge of the bed, breathing in, then out, trying to prepare herself for an afternoon at the beach with the kids.

There really was no explanation for what happened. The kids got into their suits, put on their flip-flops, and waited by the mud-room door. Eric was home, making himself a ham sandwich before heading to work. Andrea stuffed beach toys into a mesh bag for the kids. She felt a sudden burst of anxiety, as if someone were blowing up a balloon in her chest cavity.

She said, "We'll go to the beach, but you kids are not allowed to set foot in the water."

"What?" Chloe said.

"We want to swim," Finn said.

"No," Andrea said. How to explain her cold, clear panic? If they swam, they would drown. Andrea had been a lifeguard for years. She knew what she was talking about. They would drown and she would not be able to save them. It was beyond her to save anyone.

She cast around the mudroom for something to throw. She saw Greg's guitar. She was not thinking. She was not, at that moment, a human being. She was a robot with a short circuit. She took the guitar out of its case, carried it into the kitchen, and smashed it against the countertop.

It cracked, the strings popped; the cacophonous noise was satisfying to Andrea, the destruction met a need somewhere in her dark insides. Smash it, smash it! She was so angry.

The twins were crying. Andrea did not realize this until Eric brought it to her attention. Eric, her fifteen-year-old son, had her in some kind of death grip that he must have learned either from his father or from watching wrestling on TV.

"Drop the guitar, Mom. The twins are crying."

She dropped the guitar. It fell to the floor with a racket. The twins clung to each other.

This was rock bottom, Andrea thought. The lowest point on any grief's trajectory.

Right?

THE CHIEF

Every free minute he had, he studied the toxicology report. Willing it to make sense. Willing it to say something different. Tess had had opiates in her bloodstream. The kind of opiate that was most commonly found in heroin. Heroin! But there had been no needle marks, Danny Browne said.

So, what? the Chief asked. *She snorted it?*

Doesn't look like it, Danny said.

It didn't matter. The Chief repeated this phrase. Greg and Tess were dead and nothing would bring them back. But the Chief hated to think that Tess had been high on something. Had Greg drugged her? Had he taken her out on a sail because he wanted to hurt her? She had been missing that hank of hair. But maybe he had been trying to save her. It didn't matter, but it did matter. A sequence of events had unfolded out on the water and nobody knew what they were. They had both been drinking; Tess had been high. There was so much anger between them. But it was their anniversary and Andrea had made that picnic. Five calls from Addison in half an hour. See? The Chief ordered himself to stop thinking about it, but he couldn't. And there was nobody to talk it over with.

Jeffrey, maybe. The Chief would think about it.

His phone buzzed. Molly, the dispatcher, said, "Chief, your son is on line three."

He tucked the tox report into his desk drawer and locked it.

It was not a phone call he had hoped for. Eric said, "Mom has officially lost it."

And the Chief, steeling himself, said, "What do you mean?"

"She smashed Greg's guitar to bits in front of the twins, and now she's locked herself in her room. The twins are crying."

"Where's Kacy?"

"She's at work. I was getting ready to leave for work, too, but then Mom flipped out so I called the shop and told them I would be a little late."

"Did something trigger your mother?"

Eric said, "Would you please come home?"

He had a ton of work to do. He had his entire summer force to place on their assignments for the Fourth of July. He had parking tape to secure, barriers to erect, and there was a party on Hulbert Avenue that former president Clinton would be attending, so he would be dealing with the Secret Service. The Chief had not even planned on taking a lunch, but now . . . Well, this didn't sound like something he could ignore.

"I have to go out," he told Molly. "Back shortly."

Things at home were just as Eric had reported. The kids were in their bathing suits with towels around their necks, sitting in front of the television eating blindly from a bag of Fritos. Their breathing was ragged and hiccuppy. The guitar lay in the middle of the kitchen floor, smashed, its strings broken and haywire.

The Chief marched back to the bedroom. It was locked. He knocked once, to be considerate.

"Andrea? Open up."

Nothing. His heartrate picked up. Andrea would never, ever do anything to hurt herself. She didn't have it in her. But apparently she had it in her to do a Mötley Crüe destruction number on the guitar, which he would also have said was beyond the pale. He reached up to the lintel and pulled down the pin that would open the door.

He stepped inside. Andrea was on the bed facedown, her head under a landslide of pillows. She was wearing her black tank suit and a black, orange, and hot pink pareo that she had bought during their group trip to Sayulita, Mexico.

"Andrea?"

She didn't move. She was, however, breathing. The Chief sat down next to her. His hands were ice-cold; he was afraid to touch her with such cold hands. He was afraid to touch her at all. She was formidable in her grief, terrifying. Anything he or the kids said or did could set her off—she would shout or berate them or start to cry so hard it resembled an epileptic seizure. It unnerved the kids—his own kids and Chloe and Finn—and it made the Chief feel both angry and helpless. Andrea was grieving more deeply than the rest of them because Tess had been her cousin and her best friend and everything else in between. There was guilt mixed in there, too, about the swimming accident twenty-six years earlier, about bringing Tess to Nantucket at all. *I couldn't save her, Ed! I couldn't keep her safe!* He heard her talking to him while he was falling asleep, but clearly he didn't have the words to comfort her, because her sadness only grew worse and manifested itself in more disturbing ways.

Smashing Greg's guitar against the kitchen countertop?

The Chief had tried, gently, to remind her that she was responsible for two more lives now—young, impressionable lives. She had demanded custody of the kids, she had requisitioned them, and now she had to *raise* them. She had to deal with her grief reasonably; she had to lead by example. If pressed to share his truest thoughts, the Chief would say that Andrea was not fit to bring up the twins, not right now. She should have let Delilah take them for the summer when Delilah offered. She would then have had the time and space to exorcise the demon of her grief.

"Andrea?" he said.

She didn't respond. He lifted the pillows until she was exposed. Her eyes were open.

"I need help," she said.

PHOEBE

She had done the unthinkable.

An invitation had come for a Fourth of July party on Hulbert Avenue, a big, splashy party thrown by summer resident Caroline Nieve Masters, and Phoebe had accepted.

Caroline and Phoebe had served together on the board of directors of the Atheneum a decade earlier; they had been friends. In the intervening years, since September 11, when Phoebe resigned from the Atheneum board and the two other boards she sat on, she and Caroline had lost touch. There had been one awkward encounter when Caroline saw Addison and Phoebe out to dinner at 21 Federal, and she had approached the table cheerfully and asked Phoebe if she would consider sitting on the Circus Flora committee. Phoebe and Addison were out celebrating Phoebe's thirty-fifth birthday, which was also Reed's thirty-fifth birthday, but Reed would not be turning thirty-five because he was dust, and to compensate for this fact Phoebe had taken three valiums and, to numb herself further, one of the contraband pills that she had gotten from Brandon, which Brandon referred to only as the Number Nine. Throw in a glass and a half of the outrageously expensive Mersault that Addison had ordered to blur his own edges and you had Phoebe in such a haze that she was barely able to keep her head off the table. She looked at Caroline, but did not see her. She spoke, but did not say anything intelligible.

Caroline seemed confused. Addison said, "Phoebe is trying to keep her plate clear these days."

Caroline said of course, she understood, and beat a hasty retreat. Phoebe had not heard from her since, and had seen her only in passing. Just like the rest of the women from her previous life.

So the invitation came as a surprise. And even more unlikely was the burst of anticipation Phoebe felt. She wanted to go to this party. She asked Addison if they could go to Caroline Masters's party on the Fourth and he looked at her dully, then shrugged. Addison was the emotionally hobbled one now. Since Greg and Tess had died, he had done little more than drink whiskey, stare out the window, and cry in his sleep.

Phoebe couldn't help him. He was on his own. Phoebe had not been able to grieve for Greg and Tess since her outburst in the Galley parking lot. She had used up her sadness and horror and now she was empty. If anything, she felt better than she had in years. It was backward. She felt almost normal. She looked at her bottles of scrips and thought, *I really don't need these.* But she took them anyway, just in case.

The best thing about Caroline Masters's party was that it would be a reprieve from the torrent of misery about Tess and Greg. Caroline Masters hadn't known Tess and Greg, and her fancy New York friends and Nantucket summer neighbors hadn't known Tess and Greg, nor did they know that Phoebe had lost friends named Tess and Greg. Phoebe would be free.

She bought a red cocktail dress at Eye of the Needle and made a hair appointment. And at six o'clock on the Fourth, when Addison slumped in the club chair with his Jack Daniels and turned on Wimbledon, Phoebe declared that if he wasn't going to shower and change, she would go by herself.

Fine, he said. *Go.*

He was saying it as a challenge, a dare. He thought she would chicken out. Phoebe had not been out at night without Addison since Reed died. But tonight, yes, she would go, with or without him. It was so weird, the way she felt. She felt reborn, as though she had been preserved in ice all these years and was just now thawing out. She felt liberated! She could not help Addison with his grief, but she could be kind. After all, he had stuck by her for years and years.

"You're sure you don't want to come?" she said. "It will be fun, Add. Swede and Jennifer will probably be there. And their friend Hank. We used to have fun with them, remember? Maybe Hank will invite us on his boat again."

"No boats," Addison said. He was like an autistic person, with his short sentences repeated over and again. The phrase he muttered most often under his breath, which Phoebe knew she wasn't supposed to hear, was, *He killed her.*

Meaning Greg killed Tess. But Phoebe had a different idea about that.

"Okay, no boats," she said. No sailing, no sailboats, no boats of any kind. "Sorry." Dealing with Addison now was like dealing with a child. He was so drunk all the time that she had to undress him most nights, direct him to the shower, and put him to bed. The more she thought about it, the more firmly she believed that it would be a terrible idea to drag Addison to this party. He would drink too much and embarrass them both.

Phoebe kissed the top of his bald head. "I'm going. I'll be home . . . well, when I get home."

He nodded, then muttered something she didn't hear, and she didn't ask him to repeat it.

She was free! She was (slightly) high on her happy pills and she had drunk a slender flute of champagne in the bathroom as she dressed, and these combined to provide a warm, optimistic buzz. She was suffused with the holiday spirit. What was that song she and Reed had blared in high school? *Hey, baby, it's the Fourth of July!* Their father, Phil, had bought them a bona-fide mail Jeep and presented it to them on their sixteenth birthday. It had a cassette deck and crummy speakers, which they pushed to the limit. Phoebe had her license, but she always let Reed drive. Who knows where they had ever been headed, but Phoebe could say for certain that those rides with Reed driving and the window open to the dairyland smell of the Wisconsin dusk and the music blaring had been the happiest rides of her life.

She felt almost that happy now.

When Phoebe found out about Addison and Tess, she thought it was just a sex thing. She was no dummy. She understood men's needs, and since for years she had been unable to climax, she assumed that Addison would discreetly go elsewhere. Phoebe had gotten the tip-off from Addison's receptionist, Florabel, about the cottage in Quaise. Addison "showed the cottage to clients" several times a week, Florabel said, but strangely, no one ever wanted to rent it. When Phoebe went to look for Addison there ("He's there all the time," Florabel said), she saw Tess's car parked in the dirt driveway. Phoebe could not believe it, so she had tiptoed right up to the window and had seen them together. Through a little detective work, she figured out that Addison and Tess were in love. Phoebe had been too hampered by the confines of her own mind to summon the anger she knew she was supposed to feel about this. Instead she watched (silently, secretly) as their love unfolded. She watched it like a TV program. Addison was more in love than Tess was; Phoebe could tell the affair was going to end badly. As indeed it had.

Traffic was being redirected at Hulbert Avenue. It was a mess, and Phoebe feared her good mood would be thwarted by something as mundane as a long and winding detour. But there, standing on the corner in his spiffy black-and-white uniform, was the Chief. Phoebe rolled down her window.

"Ed!" she cried. "Eddie!"

He smiled and came striding over. Phoebe adored the Chief. He had gone to Ground Zero to help in the search effort. He had seen it firsthand, he had spent a week inhaling the toxic fumes, he had dealt with one one-trillionth of the debris. He felt one one-trillionth of Phoebe's pain, but that was more than anyone else.

"Where are you going?" he said. "Where's Addison?"

"He's at home," she said. "I'm going to the party on Hulbert."

"President Clinton is going to that party," the Chief said. "Which explains why this mess is even bigger than the usual mess. I'll have one of my guys wave you through."

"Thanks, Eddie," she said.

"Anything for you, babe," he said. He winked and made a clicking noise. She loved him. She feared that one day he would be gravely disappointed in her, but she wasn't going to let that ruin her good mood right now.

She drove past with a wave.

At the party, there was champagne served from a tray and yummy things to eat: crab cakes, corn fritters, oysters, tenderloin on French bread, phyllo filled with spinach and feta, stuffed mushrooms. Phoebe was eating more at this party than she'd eaten since her sophomore year in high school. A band played Sinatra, Bobby Darin, Boz Scaggs. Phoebe saw people she knew but had not seen in centuries.

You're back! Where have you been?

Oh, I've been around, she said. She would have to come up with a better answer. She would tell people she had taken eight years in silence at a Buddhist monastery. She had been in the South of France, or Santa Fe; she had been on Martha's Vineyard! When Caroline Masters saw Phoebe, she took her by the arm and escorted her around. Reintroduced her.

This gorgeous creature is Phoebe Wheeler, the best cochair I ever had.

Phoebe met President Clinton! He asked her where she was from and she said, "I live on the island year-round. My husband owns a real estate agency here. But I was born and raised in Whitefish Bay, outside Milwaukee."

Milwaukee! President Clinton loved Wisconsin, loved Whitefish Bay, loved this certain kind of cheddar they made at the university, loved the Green Bay Packers. Brett Favre had been to the White House twice during his administration.

After the president moved on, Phoebe was swamped. People seemed to be standing in line to talk to her. Swede and Jennifer monopolized her. They had missed her so much! Remember all those Sunday sails on Hank's boat? Jennifer asked Phoebe if she would cochair a cocktail party for Island Conservation, to be held out on the savannah in August. *I know you've dialed back, but . . .*

Phoebe panicked. She felt like she was falling. *Reed!* Her feet were numb with frostbite. She was stuck in the snow and could not move her arms or legs; she could not reach her cell phone. Phoebe's excellent mental health this evening had been an illusion; it was some kind of spell that was now wearing off.

Phoebe opened her mouth to speak, but no sound came out. She felt like a fish.

The Chief had been at Ground Zero. He got it. He had seen it and smelled it. Addison had never understood, but he had stuck with her. He had stood by her until Tess. Okay, see, Phoebe needed to get hold of herself. She should not be thinking of Reed and she should not be thinking of Tess. She was at a lovely, upbeat social function on a beautiful evening and she was being asked a simple question. Cochair a cocktail party on the savannah for Island Conservation? In her previous life, this would have been a layup.

But what about now? Was she a normal person? Could she do it?

"I'd love to help," Phoebe said. "Call me."

Jennifer was happy. Her husband, Swede, was happy. Their friend Hank who had a billion dollars and that beautiful sailboat was happy. Hank was there with his new French girlfriend, Legris, who complimented Phoebe on her dress.

Jack, who had given Addison the keys to his house in Stowe last Christmas, approached Phoebe and asked her to dance. Again Phoebe felt like she was being pushed right to the edge of what she was capable of. She was going to fall . . .

Dance?

"They're playing 'Mack the Knife,'" Jack said.

She loved "Mack the Knife." She would dance. She would watch the fireworks. She did not have to think about Reed or about Tess and Greg, or even about Addison. She was a person having fun.

She was getting better.

DELILAH

Every night when Delilah tucked Barney into bed, he asked about Greg's guitar.

"Can I have it, Mom? Please?"

"I'm working on it," Delilah said, though this was not exactly true. Delilah hadn't spoken to Andrea in over a week. She avoided her at drop-off and pick-up from camp, though more than half the time Kacy biked in with the kids.

"I want it really bad," Barney said.

"I know, honey," Delilah said, kissing his forehead. Barney was six and a half, with the sensibilities of an evolved forty-year-old man. He did not ask for things gratuitously. He only became emotionally invested in things that were meaningful. Delilah had offered Barney a brand-new guitar, but that wasn't what he was after. He wanted Greg's guitar, the well-worn, honey-toned instrument they all loved and recognized. It was the only guitar he had ever heard played.

An idea formed in Delilah's mind. She would steal Greg's guitar out of the Kapenash house and give it to Barney. Steal Greg's guitar out of the police chief's house! This was, she realized, the only way she was going to get her hands on it.

When?

Anytime! It would be easy! Ed and Andrea left their house unlocked, and in the summertime wide open! Delilah would slip in in the middle of the night, take the guitar, and slip out. The last time Delilah had been to the house, the guitar had been collecting dust in the mudroom. It would be so easy and yet so subversive! One naughty step that Delilah could take to make Barney, and herself, feel better.

And so, on the fifth of July, Delilah set her alarm for 2 A.M. She slid out of bed, tiptoed out of her house, got in the car, and drove to the Kapenash house. She parked down the street and strolled through the balmy night. The sky was clear and there were a million stars, and the stars made Delilah think of heaven. Was there a heaven, and were Greg and Tess in it?

Delilah crunched up the Chief's shell driveway. She had thought she might feel afraid. What if the Chief mistook her for a burglar and appeared with his gun? But she was as calm as a nun. If the Chief or Andrea woke up, Delilah would declare herself, and as odd as it would seem, she would tell them she was there for Greg's guitar.

As predicted, the door to the mudroom was wide open. Delilah pulled back the screen door and stepped inside. The house hummed with sleeping people. Delilah had picked the fifth of July because the Fourth was the Chief's most arduous day of the year—thirty thousand people descended on Jetties Beach, the traffic alone was a migraine—and he would be exhausted.

For the first time since moving to Nantucket, Delilah had skipped the Fourth of July celebration; she was too downtrodden to deal with the frivolity or the crowds. And so she'd taken the boys to Addison and Phoebe's house. Phoebe was out at some big, splashy party, but Addison was home. He escorted Delilah and the boys to the widow's walk, where he drunkenly belted out "The Star-Spangled Banner" once the fireworks started. Delilah found the occasion depressing, and the boys seemed antsy and unimpressed. Andrea was supposed to come with the twins, but she didn't show up, and when Delilah called, Kacy answered and said that Andrea was "under the weather."

Right, Delilah thought as she shifted feet, praying for the fireworks to end so she could get home to bed. They were all under the weather.

There in the corner of the Kapenashes' mudroom was the guitar case. Delilah reached for it, giddy. The whole operation would take less than thirty seconds. But when Delilah grabbed the case, it swung open and banged against the trunk that held the Kapenash family's winter boots. Delilah looked: the guitar case was empty. It was a casket without a body.

No! Arrgh! It would have been too easy. Delilah propped the guitar case back in the corner and waited a few seconds to see if the banging noise had woken anyone. The house was silent. Where was the guitar? Delilah tiptoed into the living room, through the kitchen, down the hall. She opened the door to the coat closet. Was the guitar in here? No. Just the Christmas decorations and the hideous fur that Andrea had inherited from her mother. (Okay, they all knew each other too well.) Delilah stood for a second outside the Chief and Andrea's bedroom. She could hear the Chief snoring. She realized that if the guitar were anywhere it was probably in Eric's room, but even Delilah had no intention of entering the bedroom of a fifteen-year-old boy. Ha! If Andrea caught Delilah in there, she would have her arrested.

As Delilah turned to leave, she heard a feathery noise. The Kapenashes had a cat named Arthur who was breaking all kinds of feline longevity records. Was it Arthur?

Delilah peeked up the stairs and caught her breath.

Jesus!

Chloe was floating down the stairs in a white nightie. A ghost, an angel. Her eyes were open, her face placid, even as she saw Delilah.

"Oh, honey," Delilah whispered.

Chloe held out her arms and Delilah reached for her. Chloe was petite, like Tess; she was a featherweight compared to Delilah's boys.

Chloe said, "Where's my mom?"

Delilah's heart was a berry, crushed underfoot. She hugged Chloe. This poor child. No mother, no father, no Fourth of July fireworks. Delilah carried her back upstairs to the guest room, where Finn lay, growling like a Tonka truck in his sleep. Delilah laid Chloe down in bed and smoothed her dark hair and stroked her cheek, the perfect pink little girl cheek, dotted with light freckles. She kissed Chloe's temple. Delilah had never wanted a little girl; she had been too afraid that the girl would turn out to be like her. But Delilah wanted this little girl, and her brother, too.

She cast her eyes around the room for the guitar—the twins' room was another place it would likely be—but she didn't see it.

She stood up and gazed at the twins. Tonight she had come for the guitar. But the next time she would come for them.

ADDISON

He needed a book. *Executoring for Dummies.*

The Chief had been into Tess and Greg's house twice to get the kids' belongings, the first time for shorts, shirts, bathing suits, pajamas, underwear, toothbrushes, and the second time for toys: the Nintendo DS, the DVD collection, the bikes, the boogie boards, the stuffed animals. Both times the Chief went, he called Addison to clear it.

I'm only going upstairs, the Chief said. *To the kids' rooms. For the kids' things. Okay?*

Okay, said Addison.

Implicit in the Chief's asking was the fact that Addison had yet to do anything about the rest of the house. He was the executor, it was his job, he'd better get on it.

Executoring for Dummies did not exist. He checked.

So, then, maybe he would write it.

He listed his duties in a notebook.

- Give away or dispose of (sell?) furnishings (china, silver, etc., to Chloe)
- Give away or dispose of personal effects
- Clean house (call Nicole at Swept Away)
- Sell cars (call Don Allen Ford)
- Put house on market/sell house
- Pay debts (credit card, mortgage, etc.)
- Set up college/trust funds

Figuring out exactly what had happened out on the water was *not* on this list. Naming Greg MacAvoy as Tess's murderer was *not* on this list.

Addison had a hard time getting past Tess's iPhone. He looked through the calls: all those calls from him, in addition to calls from Andrea, Delilah, Phoebe, Lisa Shumacher. And the text messages troubled him. The night before the sail, a Sunday night, a night when Addison knew Tess had been with the kids because Greg was singing at the Begonia, Phoebe had sent Tess a text message that said, *I'll be over in five minutes.*

Addison did not remember Phoebe going over to Tess's house or leaving home at all for any other reason. But Addison was having a hard time remembering that Sunday night in any detail. What had happened? Where had he been? Then he recalled the deal, the big deal, $9.2 million on Polpis Harbor, and he realized that he and Phoebe had eaten takeout Greek salads and then Addison had gone back into town to his office to write up the purchase-and-sale agreement. Furthermore, he remembered seeing both Greg's car and Delilah's car outside the Begonia, and he considered stopping in for a presigning, anticipatory celebratory drink, but he'd decided against it because he didn't want to jinx himself. So Phoebe must have gone to Tess's house while Addison was at the office.

He couldn't keep himself from asking Phoebe about it. But he had to be casual. He did not want to raise any red flags. (Though really, he thought, it was impossible to raise any red flags with Phoebe. It was impossible to make her curious or suspicious. She simply did not care.)

He said, "Did you see Tess the night before she died?"

Phoebe was lying by the pool with a wet washcloth over her eyes. She kept half a dozen washcloths in a bucket of ice water by the side of her chaise.

She said, "I did."

"Did you go to her house?"

"I did."

He did not think she was being coy. She simply could not, in her drug-muddled state, bring herself to wonder why he was asking.

"What for?"

She sighed. "I needed to drop something off."

"Oh, really?" Addison said. "What?"

"An anniversary present." She removed the washcloth and squinted at him. "Do you think we should get a dog?"

"A dog?"

Washcloth discarded. There was a pile of warm, soggy washcloths by the side of the pool, which unsettled Addison in the way that used tissues or soiled sanitary napkins would. Phoebe wrung out a new icy cold washcloth and secured it over her eyes, just so.

"I wouldn't be able to take care of it," she said. "Maybe I'll buy a dog for Domino. Do you think Ellen Paige would throw a fit?"

Addison was dying to revisit the anniversary present. Anniversary present? That didn't sound right. Between the eight of them there was a rule about no gifts; they all strictly adhered to it.

"What was the present?" Addison asked.

Phoebe said, "She probably would. A dog is so much work. Maybe next year."

Also in Tess's text messages was the message she had sent him at 8:45 A.M. *I'm afraid.*

Addison only checked Tess's outbox as a lark. Because what moldered in one's outbox? Texts that were unfinished or unable to be sent. But Addison checked anyway, to be thorough—and there was a text that Tess had tried to send Addison three times. Eleven-oh-five, eleven forty-three, twelve-ten. During the sail. Before they capsized.

The text said, *I'm afraid you won't get it.*

She was afraid he wouldn't get what? She was afraid he wouldn't get something, as in an object she had left behind for him? Or she was afraid he wouldn't understand. Get what? Why she was going on this sail in the first place? (He in fact didn't get it, though he pretended he did.) Or why she couldn't tell Greg that she was in love with Addison? Or something else entirely? Wondering about this would drive him mad. He put the phone in his pocket with the two pieces of his felt heart.

The job of executor was overwhelming. Addison had to dismantle two lives, four lives, really, a family's life, a home. He had the keys to the house; he could go over there anytime. But he made excuses. He wasn't ready.

The Chief stopped into Addison's office. This wasn't exactly a big deal, because Wheeler Realty and the police station were only a block and a half away from each other.

The Chief said, "How's it coming with the house?"

Addison fell back in his swivel chair. "It isn't coming. I've been so busy."

The Chief said, "That may be. But you have to think of the kids. They need closure."

The Saturday after the Fourth of July, Phoebe announced she was going on a day sail with Swede and Jennifer on Hank's boat. She had seen them at Caroline Masters's party and they had invited her, as predicted. She accepted, she wanted to go, she knew Addison felt differently, she knew Addison didn't want to sail again as long as he lived. So she was going alone.

He looked at her. She was in a swimsuit and a matching coverup, she had a bag packed, she was eating a bagel with cream cheese. A bagel with cream cheese? Was that actually a wheel of carbohydrate slathered with fat going into her body, or was it an illusion? Who was this woman? Was it Phoebe Jurgen, the twenty-six-year-old hotshot whom Addison had seen for the first time sunning herself in Bryant Park? It *was*—he could see her, his wife, the woman he had been waiting so long for. But honestly, he could barely bring himself to care. This would be one of those tragic/ironic love stories where they missed each other coming and going.

"Okay," he said. "Have fun."

He went over to the MacAvoy house with his list. Where to begin?

I'm afraid you won't get it.

Are you going to tell him? Are you going to tell him you love me?

You have to think of the kids. They need closure.

He had brought a bottle of Jack Daniels.

He would write the book. *How to Be the Executor of a Will, Even When One of the Deceased Was Your Lover.*

It was ten-fifteen in the morning. He poured himself a drink and got to work.

He was a real estate agent. Houses and the things in them were his area of expertise. Greg and Tess's house was small, but it was cute, in a garage-sale-find sort of way. He did not mean to sound condescending. He would gladly have lived in this house with Tess; he would have lived with Tess in a shack with papier-mâché walls and a corrugated tin roof.

He finished his first drink by ten-thirty, then vowed to slow down.

The fireplace was the house's best feature; it was made of stacked fieldstone. The furniture in the living room, Addison knew, was a combination of purchases from Pottery Barn (Addison loathed Pottery Barn and the resulting homogenization of American interiors) and pieces Tess had salvaged from the take-it-or-leave-it pile at the dump: a tall cabinet that held her candles and her table linens, a pine bar that she had painstakingly stripped and refinished. Tess had a touch of Charlie-Brown-Christmas-tree syndrome. If she saw something pathetic or abandoned, she brought it home.

Stray animals, friends of Chloe's and Finn's from dysfunctional families, pieces of crap furniture from the dump—and Addison.

He would save nothing from the living room, he decided, except for the pine bar.

He felt much the same way about the rest of the house. There were no treasures, nothing that Addison could present to the experts on *Antiques Roadshow,* only to discover that it was worth tens of thousands of dollars. Tess had been a big fan of inexpensive embellishments—candles, throw pillows, paper lanterns, glass vases, seashell collections, houseplants (all of these were dead from lack of water, except the cactus), handmade curtains, her children's artwork, and photographs. Tess and Greg had poured much of their disposable income into sitting for Cary Hazlegrove every year and then having the prints enlarged and lavishly framed. There were black-and-whites of the twins, together and separately, and of the whole family spanning the course of seven years. Tess and Greg hugging, the whole family in a pig pile, smiling, gorgeous, happy.

Addison finished his second drink. Eleven-ten.

There were photographs of the group, too. The entire surface of another take-it-or-leave-it table was dedicated to displaying framed pictures of the eight of them on vacation—in Las Vegas, in London, on Saranac Lake, in Sayulita, Mexico, in South Beach, in Stowe. Addison stacked these pictures and carried them to the slipcovered sofa. He meant to savor these photographs as if each one were a novel.

And indeed, each one was.

In his edition of *Executoring for Dummies,* Addison would warn about getting too caught up in your own role in the life of the deceased.

He took special interest in the photograph of them (well, all of them except Phoebe) in London. London had, hands down, been the worst of the six vacations. Andrea had picked it. She had never been to London, but it topped her list of places to see before she died. They went in March of 2002. Phoebe was still so raw from September 11 that taking her to a major metropolis with traffic and skyscrapers and mandatory sights that attracted crowds and long lines was a terrible idea. Andrea had booked them into an adequate hotel near Selfridges, and when Phoebe checked into their room and saw the chintz polyester spread and smelled room freshener over cigarettes, she cried. Of course, she had been crying for six months, but this crying had seemed to be caused by something Addison could fix. And so he picked up the phone and booked a room at the Connaught. When he told the rest of the group that he and Phoebe were moving to the Connaught, they were thunderstruck. The hotel Andrea had booked was expensive already, considering the price was in sterling. None of them could afford the Connaught. Tess tried to talk Addison out of moving, because this was a group vacation and the whole point was to be together. He remembered Tess pleading, *Don't go! We have to stay together!* But Addison's first priority was Phoebe. They made a deal: they would all move to the Connaught, and Addison, who had plenty of money, who had nothing *but* money, would pay the difference. The Connaught was the ultimate in luxury, it was the best of London all by itself, and yet once they were all settled in, Phoebe cried harder. The vacation to London was hallmarked by this realization: Addison could not make Phoebe happy. He could not do anything, say anything, spend anything. He tried, but he could not break through. Phoebe spent the week alternately soaking in the clawfoot tub, sleeping facedown in bed, and staring dumbly at the comedies on the BBC, whose humor was inscrutable to Americans. She was on her pills; she was at all times stoned.

Addison joined the rest of the group as they trudged dutifully to St. Paul's, Westminster Abbey, the Tate, and Buckingham Palace for the godforsaken changing of the guard in sideways sleet. They went to the British Museum, where Greg spent the whole time ogling the handwritten lyrics of John Lennon and Paul

McCartney. They went to Madame Tussaud's and Churchill's War Rooms, they rode a double-decker bus in thirty-mile-an-hour wind. They ate shepherd's pie and Welsh rarebit lunches in pubs. They got half-price tickets to a mediocre production of *The Bald Soprano.* They went to Harrods, where Tess bought an electric tea kettle like the one in her hotel room and a tin of Indian curry powder that set her back nine pounds sterling. They went to a dance club in Covent Garden where the band played really good covers of U2 and the Police and AC/DC and they danced with punkish teenagers from the East End, and Greg glowered from a solitary spot at the bar because the lead singer wouldn't let him sit in. When they stumbled out onto the street, they found that the tube had long since stopped running, so Addison called the Connaught and had it send a couple of cars. Right before he unlocked the door to his hotel room, feeling sweaty and tired and good for the first time since they had boarded the plane, he became convinced that he was going to open the door and find Phoebe dead. ODed like a rock star. He nearly turned around and retreated to the lobby. He nearly cried. It had been six whole months; he couldn't *do* this anymore. Was she ever going to snap out of it? Get better?

He opened the door and found Phoebe asleep facedown on the bed, right where he'd left her that evening at seven. And whereas he was relieved, he also wasn't.

Addison finished another drink. Nearly noon. And that, he thought, was London.

The other picture that grabbed him, of course, was the photograph taken in Stowe. Taken on the last day, out in front of Jack-the-client's condo.

In this picture, he and Tess were newly and tenderly a couple. They had only shared the kisses in the parking lot at Nous Deux and then a lot of long, meaningful looks, a few hand squeezes, and innuendo.

How was your day, you two? Greg had asked upon his return from the slopes. He was so high from his own experience of skiing and the demonstration of his prowess that he wasn't really listening for an answer. He didn't care how their day had been.

It was heaven, Tess said.

And Addison's heart floated.

They belonged to each other in that picture. Addison was standing behind Tess, his hand resting lightly on her shoulder. If a stranger looked at that photograph, he would think Addison and Tess were husband and wife.

It is important not to get too caught up in your role in the lives of the deceased.

But come on! That was all Addison cared about! The house and its furnishings were boring (he would list the house at $750,000; he would get rid of everything except the pine bar and the photographs). He wanted to find himself in this house, proof of his relationship with Tess, of her love for him. Where was the proof, the evidence only he would recognize? He was drunk enough now to admit that the Tess-and-Greg-ness of this house was gut-wrenching: the photographs of them smiling, Greg's piano, a framed copy of their wedding invitation. Addison couldn't take any more. He wanted to find Addison and Tess. Where was Addison? Where was *he?*

He went into their bedroom. Which was dangerous, he knew. It was a bad neighborhood where his feelings would likely get mugged. He armed himself with a stiff drink.

He ransacked the place. First her dresser. In her top drawer, he recognized her underwear, the bras, the belts, the bathing suits. But there was other lingerie in there that he'd never seen before. Lingerie she wore for Greg. There were pajamas and nighties that he'd never seen because he and Tess had never spent the night together.

In the other drawers were shirts, shorts and skirts, pants and jeans. No Addison. Her side of the closet? Dresses, sweaters, shoes. No Addison.

Her bedside table. A book called *Exploring Nature on Nantucket,* with pages folded down and passages highlighted. A copy of *Olivia Forms a Band.* A novel called *The Good Wife.* Addison scanned the back. The title to this one was too rich to ignore. But Addison was too drunk to make sense of the jacket copy. And, too, he was distracted by the fact that he was sitting on Tess and Greg's bed. He had never sat on this bed. He had not ever realized that Tess and Greg slept in a regular double bed. They must have slept on top of each other, or at the very least in each other's arms. A demoralizing thought. He abandoned the bedside table for the desks. There was Greg's desk, with the laptop computer, which contained, Addison knew, a music library of over fifty thousand songs. And then there was Tess's desk and Tess's computer. He turned her computer on.

He was shaking. The desk drawers were right there at his fingertips; he could open them. He would have to open them and decide what to do with the contents—he was the executor! He opened the drawer at the bottom. Hanging folders held . . . ABCs, counting, colors, shapes: kindergarten lesson plans. He shut this drawer. The other side contained more hanging folders—the twins' birth certificates, the paperwork for the house, their medical insurance, car insurance, her diploma from Boston College, her Massachusetts teaching certificate . . . but no certificate of Being in Love with Addison. No Appeal to the Commonwealth for a Divorce from Greg MacAvoy.

He moved up a drawer. It was stuffed with kids' drawings, snapshots, birthday cards, Mother's Day cards, end-of-the-year-you're-a-great-teacher cards. In the opposite drawer, Addison found a stack of journals. Pay dirt! With Parkinson hands, Addison lifted the journal that was on top. Open it? He did not *have* to open it as executor. In fact, he was pretty sure that as the sage author of *Executoring for Dummies* he should advise readers *not* to open it. It was an invasion of privacy. He should give the journals to the next of kin, unread.

Addison opened the journal. *Where was he?*

The handwriting was odd. It was different. It was, he realized after wiping his glasses on his shirt (as if it were his smudged lenses and not half a bottle of Jack Daniels that was keeping him from understanding just what was going on here), a *child's* handwriting. And then Addison saw the date: May 1981. Tess wrote about her first communion. The wafer, she wrote, tasted like cardboard, when all along she had thought it would taste like peppermint.

He riffled through the other journals. All from her life Before. Tess's youth and adolescence had been well documented. She despised her mother, worshipped her father, her grandmother was sick, the priest came to the house to administer last rites, her grandmother died. She loved her mother again; she did not want her mother to die! She was in love with a boy named Tanner who played kick ball at recess. In 1987 she wrote: *When I grow up I want to be a teacher. Kindergarten or first grade. I want two kids, a boy and a girl.*

Check, check. Did she want a husband who would lie to her? Did she want a bald, bespectacled lover with his own business and a heart full of love and generosity, who would worship at her feet? She did not specify.

In 1990 she wrote: *This summer I want to go visit Andrea on Nantucket.*

Check.

Okay, he'd had enough. The top drawers of the desk revealed compact disks, a calculator, stationery, paper clips, string, a highlighter, index cards, some of which had grocery lists scribbled on them. He, Addison, was nowhere.

But it was impossible, right, to have been involved in a love affair as intense and consuming as theirs was and not discover a trace of it *somewhere?*

The computer booted. The screensaver was a picture of Greg and the kids on a bench on Main Street, the three of them blowing pink Bazooka bubbles.

Pop. There went his heart.

I'm afraid you won't get it.

Addison shut the computer off. He was forty-nine years old and had been classically educated—literature, painting, architecture, sculpture, music, history. The computer, however, was beyond him. At the office he had to ask Florabel for help with anything more involved than e-mail or a standard listing sheet. More to the point, he wanted Greg and the twins to stop ogling him. He was in crisis here! He had been madly, crazily, stupidly in love with a woman. That woman was now dead. He had been named executor of her will; he was in charge of all her earthly possessions. Among them he had expected to find proof, however well coded, that she had been madly, crazily, stupidly in love with him, too. Admit it! He had expected to find Tess's heart in an envelope that was addressed to him.

Also on Tess's desk was her engagement calendar. Okay! Maybe here . . . ? Addison shoved aside the computer keyboard, nearly toppling his drink, and scooted the engagement calendar forward. It was open to the week of June 20, and there on the Monday square was a big heart and inside the heart it said: *12th anniversary!* Also in this square it said *Charlotte Inn* and listed the phone number.

Which part of this was the poisoned tip of the arrow? The adorable hand-drawn heart? The exclamation point? Or the name of the charming inn where Tess was planning on making love to her husband?

Addison flipped back through the calendar to January 7, the day Addison had called Tess and told her to meet him at the cottage in Quaise. She had been anxious on the phone. She had said to him, *Jesus, Add, I am so nervous.*

And he had said, *Just meet me. Nothing has to happen.*

She showed up late. She had lost her way, she said. She missed the dirt road and had to double back, then she missed it again. When finally she found it, when she pulled the Kia into the driveway of the cottage, Addison understood what she meant by nervous. Whoa! He had been married twice, and he had bedded many other women in his lifetime, but when Tess stepped out of the car, Addison didn't know what to do. He wanted to blink them back to the parking lot behind Nous Deux. He wanted to conjure the magic they had felt there. Could he do it?

He didn't know what to say, so he reverted to real estate agent mode, which put both Tess and himself at ease.

Let me show you the house!

The cottage somehow did the trick. Addison had brought in small bouquets of hothouse flowers, put scented soap in the bathroom, put Vivaldi on the stereo. The cottage had pale pink walls and exposed beams and large windows looking out into the bare woods with a blue ribbon of the ocean beyond. The brass bed had forty pillows stacked up at either end. It was a love nest. Tess gasped, then cooed.

Is this yours?

Oh, you know, he said, and he laughed. It was a joke, especially after Stowe, how Addison could make a house appear anywhere in the world. *It's on loan.*

There was silence between them. Awkward. God, what to say? What to do? *The Four Seasons* trilled along in the background. And then, just when Addison was afraid that he had made a monumental mistake (what had happened the week before in Stowe was a fluke, an illusion created by the circumstances), Tess ran toward him and jumped into his arms. She wrapped her legs around him.

Was it okay to call that the happiest moment of his life?

They had made love on top of the bed and it was . . . well, think about it! Addison had made love to his wife only a handful of times in the previous eight years, and even then the lovemaking fell somewhere between fair and marginal. To have a whole, happy, warm, responsive, physically delectable woman, a woman he liked, for the first magical and romantic time was . . . yeah.

Later, when they lay there, gazing out the window at the stark beauty of the daylight fading between the bare, slender trees, Tess admitted that she had not gotten lost at all. His directions had been perfect. She was late because she'd sat in her car at the end of the road, collecting her nerves, and checking in with Greg, who had the kids at the dentist.

It was a day he would never forget, January 7. On Tess's calendar what it said was: *Chloe + Finn, dentist, 3:30 P.M.*

Dentist! Addison thought. There should be a hand-drawn heart that said *Addison! The Day I Fell in Love!*

Addison flipped forward. February. Valentine's Day, another brutal holiday. Addison had bought Tess a book of love stories. He had driven to the elementary school and surreptitiously left the book on the driver's seat of Tess's Kia. Addison asked Tess if she would read the stories. She said she would, but to his knowledge, she hadn't read a single one.

The square for February 14 said: *LoLa 41. 7 P.M.*

Which was where she and Greg had gone to dinner.

On March 3, Addison had told Tess he loved her for the first time. They were in the cottage, listening to Billie Holiday. It was pouring rain outside. Addison lit a fire and made two mugs of coffee with Baileys. It was as perfect a scene as he could imagine. When he lay dying, this would be the moment he reflected on.

He set his mug down. He ran a fingertip along Tess's jawline. He said, "I love you, Tess."

That day should have a hand-drawn heart!

Tess had said, "I love you, too." Her eyes were clear and dry.

But the square for March 3 was empty.

Addison's birthday, April 23, said: *Addison b-day (49).* Greg had been at a singing competition in Lenox with the High Priorities and Tess had, as a surprise, called in sick to school so she could spend the day with Addison at the cottage.

Was it necessary to mention that this was the best present he had ever been given?

She had bagels and cream cheese waiting, and a steaming carafe of coffee, and his newspapers: the *New York Times,* the *Wall Street Journal,* and *USA Today* for the sports. She had ordered, online, the entire catalogue of the Rolling Stones and said they were going to listen to each of the albums all the way through, in order. They made love. They played chess in bed, then took a tiny nap. They had lunch: somehow she had gotten hold of two bottles of the impossible-to-procure Mersault, which they drank with croque-monsieurs that she whipped up at the stove. And real dill pickles, his favorite! They watched *Casino Royale* and she cried in his arms. They ate two brownie sundaes, one of which had a candle, and Tess sang "Happy Birthday" to him, and at the end she added on the kindergarten chant, *Are you one? Are you two? Are you three?* All the way to forty-nine.

Then she gave him his present: it was a heart cut out of red felt.

She said, "This is my heart."

Now, he touched the pieces of the heart in his pocket. He had never been without it. He wished he had given her something like this instead of a hardback tome of fusty love stories she would never read. He should have given her a token of his love that she could hold on to, touch so much it fell apart. Why had he not done that?

May 10 was the day he first broached the topic of leaving their respective spouses. *I can't do this anymore,* he'd said. *I need to be with you. I can make anything happen. Just give me the okay.*

She had bit her bottom lip. She was conflicted!

I know what you mean. I know. But . . .

But: the twins, their friends, their lives. She couldn't pull the pin.

But: she agreed. She loved him. She would think about it.

On Tess's calendar, it said: *Meeting w/principal, 4 P.M.*

Addison flipped back to the twentieth of June and the insidious heart. A slip of paper fell to the floor. He picked it up. It was a poem, ripped, not cut, from a magazine. From *The New Yorker.* He recognized the type.

The poem was by Michael Ryan, the title was "Sixtieth Birthday Dinner." What interested Addison, of course, were the lines that Tess had underlined. Here it was—finally!—a message.

> *My life with you has been beyond beyond*
> *And there's nothing beyond it I'm seeking*
>
>   . . .
>
> *I wouldn't mind being dead*
> *If I could still be with you.*

Addison read the lines, then read them again. His heart floated. It was all he'd been looking for, a snippet like this. A love note.

He folded the poem and slid it into his front pocket. He looked at the heart, enthusiastically marking their twelfth anniversary. He pulled the poem back out. Had she clipped this for Greg? As an anniversary present? To write in his card? Or was it meant to be for Addison? *Oh, please,* he thought. It was a love poem, a beautiful sentiment, it was *them. Their* life together, short as it was, had been "beyond beyond." There was nothing beyond it Addison was seeking.

I wouldn't mind being dead/If I could still be with you.

He couldn't process that, for the obvious reasons.

For Greg? For Addison? There was nothing else for him here—nothing else! And so, fuck it, Addison was going to claim the poem. Tess had read it and thought of him, she had impulsively torn it out of the magazine to give to him or recite to him over the phone. He was fooling himself, maybe, but he was keeping the poem.

He rinsed his glass and tucked the bottle of Jack under his arm. As he was walking out of the house, he realized he hadn't found the present Phoebe had given to Tess.

What was it?

JEFFREY

On the fifteenth of July, the corn was ready. It had been the perfect growing season; everything was ahead and bountiful. The strawberries were finished now, but the crop had been legendary; the squash and zucchini and cukes were runaways, multiplying faster than rabbits.

And on July 15, corn. The earliest ready date in twenty-five years. Jeffrey almost didn't believe it, but he peeled the husks back on ten ears of butter and sugar, all of them pearly and mature, bursting, ready to go. He tasted them raw. Sweet. He sent pickers out and went upstairs to his office to notify his accounts—thirty-two accounts on Nantucket alone, and another dozen on the Cape. There were local farms on the Cape, but many places preferred his corn, grown thirty miles out to sea in that sandy soil. There was something about it.

Jeffrey's office was above the retail space of the farm market. It was, properly, the attic. It had open studs on a wicked slanted ceiling and it was hotter than hell, despite the efforts of strategically positioned fans. The sun beat down on the roof and Jeffrey was directly underneath. This kept it toasty warm in winter, but it was a frying pan today, July 15, the official first day of corn.

"Whew!" he said aloud when he reached the top of the stairs. To no one, because Jeffrey's office was his and his alone. He worked without an assistant, and everyone else—the farm market manager, the marketing person, the head chef, the buyer—all had offices on the first floor, which was air-conditioned. Jeffrey had segregated himself on purpose because he was a serious person who savored silence and his privacy.

It was beastly hot. There was sweat in his eyes. He pulled a bandanna out of his back jeans pocket (yes, a real red bandanna—Delilah teased him, but he didn't care) and wiped his face.

There was someone sitting in his chair. Andrea.

He was speechless. But not surprised. Somehow he'd expected her. The other day he'd spied a beat-up black Jeep Wrangler in the parking lot and his heart had sung out a short, sweet tune because he thought it was Andrea's—but then he realized that Andrea no longer drove a Jeep. She hadn't driven one in over fifteen years. He was losing his mind.

"Hey," he said.

"Hey, Peach," she said. She was wearing a white T-shirt and jean shorts. Her dark hair was in a ponytail. There were flip-flops on the floor, but her bare feet were tucked under her bare, tanned legs. Andrea's legs were her best feature; they were very strong, taut, powerful. They weren't sexy to look at, maybe, but they were sexy for sex—she used to tense and kick and fight him off. He remembered this instantly and it embarrassed him, and then he thought about how her showing up here in this dim, sultry room was like the beginning of one of the porn movies Delilah tried to get him to watch to spice up their sex life. He felt a surge of energy. Entirely inappropriate. He forgot all about the corn.

She was sitting in his chair, so there was nothing for him to do but stand. But he couldn't stand. It was too hot and he was too rattled by this unexpected visit. He pulled a milk crate out of the shadowy eaves, flipped it over, and sat down at her feet.

They had been a couple for twenty-six months. From May of 1990 until July of 1992. They had met on the steamship on a chilly, miserable, slate-gray day. They had each bought a discolored, overcooked hot dog at the snack bar and were standing together at the ketchup dispenser as the boat lurched like a drunk through the chop. Jeffrey was feeling a little green; he was a man of the land, not the water. He thought maybe his stomach needed food, hence the hot dog, but the ketchup managed to make the hot dog seem less appetizing instead of more. He smiled weakly at Andrea. She was beautiful, raven-haired, robust, surefooted even as the boat rocked. She was confident, a queen. She regally inhaled her hot dog before Jeffrey could even wrap his properly in a napkin.

"Is it your first time on this boat?" she asked. She seemed genuinely concerned for him. He must have looked as bad as he felt.

He nodded. He handed Andrea his hot dog, staggered to the men's room, and vomited in the toilet.

When he emerged, she was sitting on a bench holding his hot dog gently, like it was a child in her custody.

"You want?" she said.

He shook his head and discreetly (he thought) sucked on a Life Saver.

She said, "Okay if I eat it?"

He nodded.

She said, "Do you talk?"

He whispered, "I do *not* feel well."

She beamed at him. "You *do* talk!"

He was an ag student, newly graduated from Cornell. She was three years out of BC, a championship swimmer, and this summer she was to be Nantucket's head lifeguard. It was her third summer on the island. Jeffrey had a deed to a farm left to him by his grandmother's unmarried half-brother—a great-uncle he hadn't seen in years.

"I thought that kind of thing only happened in the movies," Andrea said.

"Me, too," Jeffrey said. The deed to the farm from Uncle Ted had come as a whopping surprise. Jeffrey's parents had been astounded. Ted Korkoran had been the only son of Jeffrey's great-grandfather's second wife; Ted was a bit of a black sheep, declaring himself homosexual and as such escaping duty in World War II. He moved from Fredonia to Nantucket in 1950. He and his partner, Caleb Mills, bought a farm and worked it together. They had cows that supplied 70 percent of the island's milk, they had chickens for eggs, pigs for bacon and ham. They slaughtered turkeys at Thanksgiving, and made their own goat cheese long before the public had cultivated a taste for it. Jeffrey had heard these stories from his grandmother, and Jeffrey would see Uncle Ted and his friend Caleb every summer at the Korkoran family reunions, Ted and Caleb as sober and grouchy and properly masculine as all the rest of the Korkoran men. But then Caleb got mysteriously sick and died—this was in the mid-eighties, and it was all kept very quiet—and Uncle Ted stopped attending the reunions. And then, five years later, Uncle Ted died and left his farm to Jeffrey. No one could figure out why. All Jeffrey remembered were Caleb's recipe for baked beans with brown sugar and Uncle Ted's dead eye in horseshoes. Ted had left Jeffrey the farm because he received a Christmas card from Jeffrey's mother every year. He knew Jeffrey was an ag student at Cornell, a farmer-to-be in need of a farm.

And here was a farm.

Andrea listened as she polished off the second hot dog, and then a soft pretzel dripping with yellow mustard. She had been an English major at BC; she loved sprawling family sagas. She came from a large and storied Roman Catholic background herself, complete with closeted priests and nuns living in the basement and undercover cops and Mafia ties.

"And when you get a free century," she said, "I'll tell you all about it."

Meeting Andrea had been all bundled up with Jeffrey's meeting Nantucket. He set eyes on the quaint gray-shingled town first, then took in the scope of the farm that was now his. A hundred and sixty-two acres of fields—his! A greenhouse and barn, tractors, combines, plows—his! A dilapidated little house that had not been cleaned out and hence still contained the day-to-day detritus of a lonely bachelor. Andrea was there with him when he first set foot in Uncle Ted's house. She saw the dishes in the rack by the kitchen sink, the pie-crust table that supported a rotary phone and the King James Bible, the two single beds side by side in the house's only bedroom. On the bedside table was a photograph of Ted and Caleb in front of the barn, holding chickens in their arms like babies. Andrea was there because she decided before the steamship even docked that Jeffrey needed her help. What he was doing—seeing the farm for the first time, taking inventory, and uncovering the life of the man who had left it to him—was not something he should do without a friend.

She was right. She helped him find someone to clean out the house, she showed him where the Town Building was so he could register the deed in his name, she drove him around in her black Jeep with the top down, even though Nantucket in May was cold and windy and rainy. (Did anything grow here? Jeffrey had to wonder. Maybe the farm was a joke.) She took him for chowder and steamed lobsters and scallops wrapped in bacon. She let him crash on the floor of her room in the rental house that she shared with two other lifeguards. And then, after a full week of this platonic, almost sisterly help, she invited him into her bed and took his virginity.

Because, yes, Jeffrey had been a virgin at twenty-two. Owing to his girlfriend Felicity Hammer's love of Jesus and her refusal to make love to him until the day they were married.

Andrea was different from Felicity in every way. Andrea was strong and athletic and dark-haired and capable and Italian and Catholic and confident of her many talents and charms. Felicity was blond and petite and meek and easily frightened; she was shy and God-fearing, she was a small-town Baptist whose father had sent her to community college. She was a baker and a knitter. She wanted six children. Felicity had thought that once Jeffrey got settled with the farm, he would send for her and they would get married.

But meeting Andrea at the ketchup dispenser changed that. Andrea was a storm, a force of nature. He could not resist her any more than he could stop the rain. They fell in love. In October they moved in to the tiny farmhouse, now clean, cozy, and all fixed up. They made love, they made pasta, they made curtains for the windows. Jeffrey made a plan for the farm. He got rid of all the livestock except for the chickens. Chickens and eggs he could handle; everything else was too expensive and beyond the perimeters of his expertise. He wanted to grow things: corn, vegetables, flowers. He had no money. He went to the bank for a loan way beyond what he would be able to pay back in this lifetime, but they gave him the money eagerly, with the land as collateral. Andrea got a job teaching private swim lessons at the community pool.

They were happy. They talked about getting married. They talked about kids. They ate a lot of eggs. They had nicknames for each other. He called her Andy. She called him Peach, which had something to do with sex—how he tasted, or the fact that he'd been a virgin until she took a bite out of him.

Life was weird, right? It was weird because Jeffrey and Andrea had been happy, they had been a couple on their way to matrimony and wedded bliss, until somehow it unraveled. As though a sweater had a snag and he pulled at it, or she did, and one by one the stitches came undone until it was a pile of yarn at their feet. Jeffrey was obsessed with the farm, consumed by it; he could not give Andrea his full attention, he could not give her any attention. She complained, he heard her complaining, but he could do nothing about it. He was single-minded, he always had been, and his mind was on the farm, the fields, the crops, the business of it.

At the beginning of their third summer together, Andrea, once again Nantucket's head lifeguard, went to a party for town employees, where she met the new police chief. Young guy, she said. Single. From Swampscott.

And two weeks later she moved out.

In all honesty, Jeffrey was too busy to do anything to stop her. By the time he got off his goddamn tractor in the figurative sense, Andrea and the new police chief, Ed Kapenash, were engaged.

Life was weird, because instead of Jeffrey's relationship with Andrea ending, it started a new incarnation. At first Jeffrey was tentatively friends with the newlywed Kapenashes; then Jeffrey met Delilah and they became couple-friends with Ed and Andrea. Andrea's cousin Tess started dating Greg, and they moved to the island permanently, then Phoebe and Addison joined the scene and the eight of them, over time, developed an insanely tight bond. What did Delilah call them? The Castaways. And it did, at times, seem like just the eight of them alone on a deserted island.

Life was weird because although Jeffrey had seen Andrea every week for nearly twenty years, seeing her now sitting in his chair was sort of like seeing her for the first time. On a rolling boat, by the ketchup dispenser. *You do talk!* It was as if he'd looked up, finally, after getting the farm running, profitable, and fully staffed, and noticed that she was gone. And he went looking for her. And he found her here, in his chair. Because there was something about her that transported him back. The nickname, Peach. Or the way it was just the two of them here, alone, unlikely to be interrupted. (Had that happened even once since they split?) Or it was the way she was looking at him.

"What are you doing here?" he asked her.

She said, "I'm having a hard time."

He said, "She worshipped you, Andrea. You were her friend and her sister and her mother wrapped up into one. You did right by her."

Her tears were silent. "How can you say that? She's dead."

"It was an accident."

"Was it?"

"Wasn't it?" Jeffrey said. He shifted on the milk crate. He had a nugget of classified information that no one else knew, that had been lobbed at him like a hand grenade by April Peck. *I was with him the night before he died.* But what did that mean? Did it mean anything? Was it even true? (In his heart, Jeffrey felt it was true. He realized now that Greg had been hiding something.) One thing was for sure: Jeffrey was not going to share this radioactive nugget with Andrea.

"I don't know," Andrea said. "All I can tell you is that I'm in agony. I am hurting worse than I could ever imagine I could hurt. Like I lost one of the kids. Like a stranger came into my house and held Kacy's head under the bathwater until she died. And I wasn't around. I let it happen."

"Greg was the stranger?" Jeffrey said. "He was Tess's husband. Twelve years they were married."

"He made her miserable."

"Did he?" Jeffrey said. Jeffrey's understanding of Greg and Tess's marriage—before April Peck—was that Tess had loved Greg with the same ardor and enthusiasm that she loved everyone else in her life. "So you wish you'd . . . what? Spoken up at their wedding, when the priest offered the chance?"

"He hurt her," Andrea said. "Last fall, that whole thing? He cut her heart out. And she was never the same. The week they separated? God, Jeffrey. We talked for hours. She was trying to make sense of it. *Do you think he lied to me? Do you think he lied to Flanders? Do you think something happened between him and that girl?* And the answer is, Yes, of course. *Something* happened, we don't know what, we'll never know exactly what. And there's Greg, sending flowers and hounding her cell phone and calling the house begging and pleading . . ."

"Yeah," Jeffrey said. "That was a weird week."

While Tess was at the Kapenash house with the twins, Greg had taken refuge at Jeffrey and Delilah's. It was, of all awful things, the week of Thanksgiving, the holiest family holiday, but despite that, or maybe because of that, Tess decided to take the kids and leave. She had meant to go to her brother's house in Pembroke, to visit her mother at the nursing home in Duxbury, but in the end she had simply sought refuge with Andrea. She slept with Andrea in Andrea's bed and the kids slept in the guest room. And Greg, although he had his house to himself, slept on Jeffrey and Delilah's leather couch each night. He never stayed over intentionally—otherwise he would have used the guest room. He came over for dinner and drinks, and he and Delilah stayed up so late talking and he was so drunk that he ended up crashing on the couch. And in the morning he would be awakened by Drew and Barney and SpongeBob SquarePants. He would eat Delilah's delicious breakfasts, talk about going home to grab a shower, but then there would be college football and lunch and Barney begging him to play the guitar . . . and he just stayed on and on. A few of those nights, Greg and Delilah worked at the Begonia and came home absurdly late. Jeffrey was busy at the farm market—the kitchen had orders for three hundred fresh turkeys and six times that many side dishes—and if he didn't catch every nuanced detail of what was going on, could anyone blame him? Delilah was the head paramedic of this particular train wreck; she was in charge of tending to Greg. Jeffrey noted Greg's attempts to reach Tess, but she was not taking his calls. He heard about a bouquet of flowers sent, and returned to the florist by Tess. Jeffrey wasn't sure how he felt about the whole thing; what he wanted was to stay out of it. This was, no doubt, what the Chief was doing, and this was what Addison and Phoebe were doing. The prizefight was between Tess (and her trainer, Andrea) and Greg (and his trainer, Delilah) in the opposite corner. Jeffrey did not love it that his house had inadvertently become Greg's camp; he felt like he was harboring a fugitive.

There had been one night in particular that bothered Jeffrey. It was four-thirty in the morning and Jeffrey was rising for the day when he noticed that Delilah was not in bed. He tiptoed out to the kitchen for coffee and he heard Greg's voice. Greg was murmuring to someone. Although Jeffrey was the last person to eavesdrop, he couldn't help it—and goddamn it, this was his house. Jeffrey thought, *If he is talking to Delilah like that, I am going to throw him out.* Because, really, Jeffrey had had enough of the Greg and Delilah confidante thing. Greg was not good for Delilah, or for Jeffrey and Delilah's marriage.

But when Jeffrey reached the kitchen, he saw that Greg was on his cell phone. Greg noticed Jeffrey and said quickly, "I'll call you later." And hung up. And then, despite the fact that Greg had seen Jeffrey and Jeffrey had seen Greg, Greg closed his eyes and pretended to be asleep.

Delilah, as it turned out, was upstairs sleeping with Barney, who tended to wake up in the middle of the night and want his mother.

Jeffrey did not say anything to Greg about the phone call, but he knew it wasn't Tess on the other end.

Then there was Thanksgiving itself. Tess had ceded a little ground and allowed Greg to see the kids in the morning. Greg had hoped for a family reconciliation for the holiday, and learning that he was only gaining custody for four hours like the divorced man he was sure to become depressed him. He had nothing planned. Delilah suggested that he take the kids to breakfast at the Downyflake, or for a walk on the beach, but Greg seemed eager to avoid quality time when the twins might have a chance to ask him questions he was ill-equipped to answer, such as *Why is Mom so mad at you?* or *Why are we living at Auntie's house?*

Instead Greg took the twins over to the Drake house, and this, in combination with the overheard phone call, led Jeffrey to understand that Greg was lost, hapless, and in possession of the maturity of a twelve-year-old boy. Jeffrey therefore took over. He rescued the kids from the PlayStation by driving everyone to the farm, where they went for a hayride. Jeffrey drove the tractor, and Delilah and Greg sat in the back with the kids. The kids liked the bumps, and Jeffrey obliged them. The day was sunny but cold. Jeffrey took the long way, all the way around the edge of the property. Time and circumstances were suspended. Everyone had fun, and at the end of the ride they drank apple cider and ate moist pumpkin muffins, and then suddenly it was one o'clock. Delilah had to get home to check on the turkey, and Greg had to get the kids back to the Kapenash house.

Normally the eight of them, plus the six kids, had Thanksgiving dinner together, and Delilah and Andrea alternated years hosting. This year it felt like they had all divorced. The Chief and Andrea had Tess and the kids. Jeffrey and Delilah had Greg. Phoebe and Addison, not wanting to take sides, went to the Ship's Inn by themselves. It felt awful. Jeffrey, Delilah, Greg, and Drew and Barney held hands around the table and said grace, but when they looked up, they could see how wrong everything was. Jeffrey thought about Ed and Andrea's table, with Eric and Kacy and Tess and the twins, and he wondered if things felt wrong there, too. He hoped they did.

Jeffrey never found out how or why, but by Sunday night Greg and Tess were back at home with the kids. Four weeks later, the eight of them were on vacation in Stowe and everything was back to normal. Tess had forgiven Greg, forgotten April Peck, and moved on.

Now Andrea was taking the credit for this—or the blame.

"I convinced Tess to take him back. For the kids' sake. Ed and I both thought that was the best thing."

"It was the best thing," Jeffrey said.

"How can you say that?" Andrea said. She was shaking and crying. Her face was wet with tears. Jeffrey wanted to reach out to her, to hold her. He had lost her so long ago, when he wasn't watching, and although it was his fault completely, it had never seemed fair. Now she was back. She needed something and he would try like hell to give it to her. "How can you say that when she's dead?"

"Remember when Tess came to visit us?" Jeffrey said. "And she borrowed my bike?"

Andrea wiped at her tears. "And she insisted on riding it barefoot? And she fell and—"

"Broke her arm," Jeffrey said.

"But we didn't believe her," Andrea said. "We didn't believe her when she said how much it hurt. We made her go to the movies."

"And we saw *The Player.*"

"And it was the best movie of all time."

"And we couldn't figure out why Tess was crying at the end . . ."

"And it was because of her arm."

"We took her to the hospital," Jeffrey said. "You stayed by her side while they X-rayed her and set it."

"You stayed in the waiting room," Andrea said. "And fell asleep across four chairs."

"I felt so guilty," Jeffrey said. "It was my bike."

"I felt so guilty," Andrea said. "She told me her arm was broken and I gave her some Advil and told her to toughen up."

"We made her sit through that movie."

Andrea was quiet. She stared at her legs. Her strong, beautiful legs that had nearly gotten her to the Olympics, that had locked around him when they were making love. This was the pornography of grief—going back and remembering a moment in a dead person's life, step by step. So few people were willing to comb back through it like this, because it was too intimate or too painful or it wouldn't help anything, it wouldn't bring the person back. But this, perhaps, was what Andrea needed. Let Tess live in the minute detail of their memories. Jeffrey could see Tess's teenaged face, as plain as day. He could see her bare toes on the spiky pedals of his Cannondale.

"Thank you, Peach," Andrea said, as she stood up to go. "Thank you."

Jeffrey was at a loss, because of both her arrival and her departure. "You're welcome."

Andrea continued to appear in Jeffrey's office. Jeffrey never knew when she would show; she didn't call or forewarn. He would climb the stairs to the attic, and there she would be, sitting in his chair. She always came in the morning, after she dropped off the twins at camp. Jeffrey started to anticipate her visits and look forward to them; on days she didn't come, he felt let down. He worried, stupidly, that he would never see her again.

He had stumbled across what she wanted. She wanted someone else to remember Tess, to miss Tess, to tell stories about Tess. She wanted a partner in her grief. Not a sympathetic listener—any poor motherfucker could listen. She needed someone to share the burden, to do the talking and remembering for her. No one wanted to do this.

There were certain ways in which Jeffrey didn't want to do this either. Or couldn't do it. How much attention had he really given Tess, after all? But he would try, for Andrea.

He was methodical in all things, and so in this endeavor he moved chronologically. The broken arm story led to the story of Tess's first beer. Tess's first true, cold beer had been consumed at a bonfire on Ladies Beach under the careful, almost parental watch of Jeffrey and Andrea. A Coors Light in a frosty silver can. Tess's arm was in a sling, her drinking arm, her everything arm. Jeffrey had to open the can for her and put it in her left hand.

"Had she asked for a beer?" Jeffrey said. "Or did we force it on her?"

"She asked for it," Andrea said.

Jeffrey did not remember it that way. He remembered that they had packed a cooler for a beach barbecue, and when they opened the cooler, they found they had nothing to drink *except* beer. They weren't used to hanging out with teenagers. He remembered saying to Tess, *Looks like it's beer or ocean water.*

Andrea covered her eyes. "Oh, God," she said. "You're right."

"And she drank the whole thing down right away and let out that burp they could hear in Portugal."

"Yes!" Andrea said. She was most delighted by the details she had forgotten. "And we gave her another one and another one and another one."

"She drank five," Jeffrey said. "And then she—"

"Puked in the dunes," Andrea said.

"And we took her home and she passed out on the bathroom floor. And when she woke up in the morning, there were tile marks on her face."

"Yes!" Andrea shouted. She put her hands up in the air. He had scored again.

"And you made her sign that slip of paper," Jeffrey said.

"Promising she wouldn't tell my aunt and uncle," Andrea said. She was laughing, then crying. Sweetly weeping. "Thank you, Peach," she said. "Goddamn it, thank you."

"You're welcome," he said.

How about the night Tess met Greg? Could Andrea handle that one? She looked dubious, but Jeffrey pointed out that he wasn't going to be able to tell stories for very long if he couldn't mention Greg.

"Okay," she said. Then she cocked her head. "Wait a minute. You weren't even there that night."

"I still know the story. I've heard it a hundred times. Do you want me to tell it or not?"

"Tell it."

Girls' night out, summer 1995. Andrea, Tess, Delilah, Lisa Shumacher, who waitressed with Tess at the RopeWalk that summer, and Karin Poleman, who had taken over the head lifeguard position from Andrea when Andrea got pregnant with Kacy. The girls went to dinner at the Boarding House, they went for drinks at 21 Federal, drinks at the Club Car, drinks at the RopeWalk, where Lisa and Tess, on their night off, were treated like royalty and plied with tequila shots. Then, finally, they went to the Muse to hear this band everyone was talking about called the Velociraptors.

The Velociraptors were five guys who had done a PG year together at the Berkshire School and who had then done separate tours of duty at egregiously preppy colleges like Colgate and Bates and Middlebury, and who had reunited on Nantucket. Greg MacAvoy (Hamilton College) was the lead singer. He was twenty-three years old, he jogged and surfed and lifted weights, he wore a white rope bracelet and a shark's tooth on a leather choker, he sang while holding a Corona, he sang with his hair in his eyes. He sang "Loving Cup" by the Stones and "Sheena Is a Punk Rocker" by the Ramones, he sang "The Core" by Eric Clapton with a hot redhead who tended bar and only came up onstage for that one song. It was well documented that Greg MacAvoy, currently of the Velociraptors (formerly of the garage bands the Porn Stars and Eklipse), could have any woman he wanted. The band house behind the Muse, where the Velociraptors had pretty much taken up residence (though the drummer Beckett Steed's parents owned a house in Sconset where they technically lived), had a throng of girls teeming around it every night after-hours, like bacteria around a fresh cut. What happened in the band house? Well, pretty much what you'd expect.

On the night in question, Tess was drunk.

"We were all drunk," Andrea chimed in.

Tess was wearing jeans, flip-flops, a white T-shirt, a green bandanna in her hair, and dangly silver earrings. She and the rest of the girls were dancing right up front; their beers were sitting on the edge of the stage, next to the amplifiers. With all the girls on the dance floor and the promise of yet more girls banging down the door of the band house, what was it about Tess that caught Greg's attention? The green bandanna? The sparkling earrings? The freckles on her nose or her big blue eyes or her tiny feet with nails painted a color called Cherry Pie?

She knew *all* the words to "Low Spark of High Heeled Boys." He noticed that. He smiled at her, winked at her. At the break, he said to his bass player, "Hey, that little Gidget girl is hot." He dispatched a roadie to speak to her.

"Greg wants to know if you'll join him in the band house later."

Roadie asked Tess this in front of all the girls. Roadie offered Tess a cold Corona, a present from Greg. The girls stared, speechless.

Tess said, "The band house? No way."

Delilah said, "Are you crazy? Every woman on Nantucket wants that guy."

But Andrea approved of Tess's answer. Andrea had a baby and a two-year-old at home; she was mother superior. She was drinking and having fun like the rest of them—more than the rest of them—but she did not want to see her beloved younger cousin, Tess, disappear into the opium den/syphilis shack that was the band house.

Tess said no, and Greg was fired up. The hunt was on!

"What did he do to get her?" Andrea scanned Jeffrey's desk for a piece of paper. She wanted to make a list.

"He tried to find out her last name," Jeffrey said.

"Failed," Andrea said.

"He tried to get her phone number."

"Failed."

"But then someone told him where she waitressed . . ."

"He showed up at the RopeWalk with flowers."

"Didn't work."

"The next time he showed up with that CD he made her. With 'Romeo and Juliet' by Dire Straits on it."

"Didn't work."

"He ordered the lobster dinner to impress her."

"It was just like Greg to be so misguided," Andrea said. "Ordering the lobster was not impressive."

He asked her out each and every time. Where did she want to go? The Chanticleer? The Wauwinet? Beckett Steed's parents had a Boston Whaler. Did she want to go out on the Whaler?

"She told him she was afraid of the water," Andrea said quietly.

Did she want to go on a picnic? Would she meet him for breakfast? Coffee?

He showed up at her yoga class; he did all the positions, hoping she was watching him in her peripheral vision. He waited for her by the water cooler, but she breezed past him.

"He borrowed a dog," Andrea said. "That golden retriever."

Jeffrey shook his head. "Jesus. I forgot about the dog."

"She almost fell for it," Andrea said. "But when she found out it wasn't his, it set him back."

"So what was it, in the end?" Jeffrey said. The Greg-in-pursuit-of-Tess story was in fact a well-documented and much-laughed-about legend, and the first-night-at-the-Muse story could easily be told by people (like himself) who hadn't even been there. But what had flipped her? What had changed her mind? Jeffrey couldn't remember, or didn't know.

"I gave her permission," Andrea said. "I told her the guy clearly deserved a chance, he was going to so much trouble. I told her it was okay to relent. To say yes. And that was all she needed. She did."

"Oh," Jeffrey said.

"Thank you, Peach."

Jeffrey nodded. "You're welcome."

He did not tell anyone about Andrea's visits or about the recounting of Tess's life in obscene detail. Meaning he did not tell Delilah. This was unprecedented, because one of Jeffrey's hallmark qualities was that he was an open book. His accounts were honest, his slate clean. He hid nothing; he had no secrets. He prided himself on operating this way; he felt it gave him the upper hand. Delilah had secrets; she had hundreds of hours unaccounted for that fell under the category of "time to myself" and was therefore unimpeachable. She was always hiding something, covering up, making excuses. It was exhausting to live that way; Jeffrey could see the toll it took on her, harboring an entire emotional life she refused to share with him.

He decided to keep Andrea's visits a secret, not for his sake but for Andrea's sake. It went unspoken, but Jeffrey was pretty sure the Chief knew nothing about the hours she whiled away in the farm attic. Delilah, if she knew, would get mad, she would feel threatened (though she claimed again and again that it was *impossible* to feel jealous of someone like Andrea); she would ridicule Jeffrey first, then Andrea; she would degrade their attempts at self-help, at memory as therapy. She would misunderstand it and misrepresent it to others and ruin it.

It was working. Jeffrey could tell just by looking at Andrea that she felt better.

And so did he.

PHOEBE

Her days grew happier and happier. She woke up and brewed an espresso. She had renewed her membership at the gym; she ran on the treadmill and lifted weights three times a week and attended Pilates twice a week. On Saturdays and Sundays she tried to get Addison to walk with her to the beach, but he usually said no, he didn't feel like it, he was too tired, too hungover, too lazy. So Phoebe went alone.

She was secretly taking herself off her drugs. Back in 2001, after Reed died, she had been diagnosed with post-traumatic stress disorder and then, in short order, depression. She took all the drugs prescribed to her and then some, twice as often as she was supposed to, and in this way the pain had subsided. But along with the pain went everything else. Along with the pain went her personhood. Goodbye, Phoebe.

In coming off the drugs, the whole thing was working in reverse. She could think, she could feel. She had appetites. This, she thought, was a basket of raspberries. Yum! This was an egg salad sandwich with arugula on wheat bread. She wanted to eat it, in alternating bites, with crisp, salty gourmet potato chips, the juicy berries, and sips of iced tea with mint. Eating lunch, for the first time in years, gave her joy. Her pathological fear of calories was gone, too. She had desires. On a sunny day she liked to sit for an hour or two by the pool. She liked the warm sun; she liked the cool water. While on the drugs, she had barely been able to tell the difference between the two.

She called Delilah. She wanted to hang out with the kids.

You're kidding, Delilah said.

Phoebe wanted to go to the beach, ride a boogie board to the shore on a monster wave, and eat a faceful of sand. She wanted to pick a Popsicle out of the cooler and let it drip down her hands. The colors of the water and the sand and the eelgrass in the dunes and even of the Popsicle startled her. Such deep, vibrant color! She could see it, she could appreciate it. It was as if she had been blind and only now was her sight restored. The pink of the raspberries, the deep brown of her espresso, the turquoise of the swimming pool. Amazing!

The sound of the boys, Drew and Barney, laughing. The sound of the waves crashing against the shore. The hum of airplanes making a landing. The James Taylor song on the boom box three towels down. She used to love that song; she still did.

"I can't believe how wonderful I feel," Phoebe said.

"That makes one of you," Delilah said.

It was wrong, all wrong. It was backward. Addison was a shell, a husk. He was miserable and toadish. He was an abuser of alcohol. His lover had died and he was undergoing the predictable decline. Delilah, too, was suffering from nuclear fallout. Her hair was wild and haglike; she admitted she could muster the energy to get in the shower only once a week. Once a week! She was getting dreadlocks. She had put on weight. Delilah had a very sexy, curvy figure, but she stuffed her face mindlessly with the Doritos and Chips Ahoy that she took to the beach for the kids, which went right to her ass. She complained about her ass and her dimpled thighs, she had a harder time getting out of her beach chair, she waddled to the water line, but she kept on snarfing down the snacks. Phoebe invited her to go for walks to the beach, or to Pilates class when the kids were in camp, but Delilah turned her down. *I don't have it in me, Phoebe.* And she had quit her job. She couldn't work at the Begonia anymore, now that Greg was gone. Thom and Faith had replaced Greg with an Irish trio; Delilah had gone in to work one shift to see if she could do it, but when the girl started crooning in her Gaelic accent, Delilah ran out of the bar in tears. She went through her closet and took all her hostessing dresses to the hospital thrift shop.

"But why?" Phoebe said. "They were so pretty."

"Because," Delilah said, "I'm never going to wear them again."

She was declaring her life over, and her sense of fun—which had always been her guiding principle—defeated. All she wanted to talk about was how much she hated Andrea and whether Greg had been screwing April Peck, neither of which interested Phoebe in the slightest. This was how people acted when two of their best friends died tragically—they suffered, they retreated, they regressed. Phoebe was the oddball. She did not want to dwell on Greg and April Peck or Addison and Tess falling in love in the Quaise cottage, or about her visit to Greg and Tess's house the night before their sail, or about the drowning.

She wanted to move on!

But it looked like she was going alone.

Phoebe wanted something to do. She had agreed to cochair the cocktail party for Island Conservation on August 15. With ten phone calls, the whole event was organized—tent, tables and chairs, caterer, donated beer and wine from Cisco Brewery, swing band, invites. Wheeler Realty was going to be a major underwriter, though Phoebe had cleared this only with Florabel, the receptionist. Addison did not have the attention span to take in the details.

That accomplished, she was ready for the next thing. What was the next thing? She had nearly eight years of energy stored up. Should she resurrect her business? Arrange group cruises through the Mediterranean for the over-sixty-fives? Perhaps join them on the cruise, jump off the ship at the Amalfi coast, and take a young Italian lover?

Phoebe ran across the twins by accident. They were in Nantucket Bookworks, standing quietly shoulder to shoulder in front of the chapter books. Phoebe had been adrift in paperback fiction. She thought maybe what her soul was craving was an education. There were so many books she hadn't read. *Madame Bovary, Deliverance, A Room with a View, The Ice Storm, The Corrections, A Handmaid's Tale, A Thousand Acres, Bastard Out of Carolina, The Emperor's Children, Bel Canto*—God, the list was endless. She picked a pile to start with: *I Cannot Get You Close Enough, Prep, The Brambles, Beautiful Children,* all from the staff-favorites shelf. Someday in the near future, Phoebe would have her own shelf of favorites. It was a goal. She was all about goals. She wanted to add *Catcher in the Rye* to the pile, because that had been Reed's favorite book. Phoebe had read it—it had been required their sophomore year of high school—but she could not remember one single thing about it except for the boy in Holden's class who would shout "Digression!" whenever the teacher got off the topic. (But Phoebe thought she might even have been remembering that wrong.)

She could not find *Catcher in the Rye* on the shelf with the other Salinger novels. The woman behind the counter told her it was in the young adult section because it was on so many summer reading lists—and that was how Phoebe discovered the twins. Side by side, dark head buzz cut (Finn) next to dark head bob (Chloe), both in stripy T-shirts and shorts. Phoebe nearly cried out at how darling they were, how quiet and serious. Finn was looking at something called *Captain Underpants* and Chloe was flipping through *A to Z Mysteries*. There was something about their silence and composure that made them seem like little adults, a husband and wife, selecting books for a week of evening reading. Because they were twins, Phoebe had an incredibly tender spot in her heart for them. She felt connected to them in a way that she did not feel connected to Drew and Barney. Chloe and Finn were like Phoebe and Reed: a pair, a couple, connected at the hip. At the funeral, Phoebe had said to them, *You still have each other.* And they had nodded in their composed, adult way. They didn't need her to tell them what they already knew.

Phoebe did not speak to the twins in the bookstore, or make herself known. They were too perfect. Phoebe wanted to gobble them up; she wanted to vaporize herself and inhabit their flawless bodies.

They were so sad. They were babies abandoned in a basket. Tears welled in Phoebe's eyes. Could anyone help? Could Phoebe help? Was this it—the thing she was seeking? Was it the twins?

She paid for her stack of books and scanned the store. Where was Andrea? Or . . . the Chief?

Later, Phoebe called Delilah on the phone and said, "I saw the twins at Bookworks by themselves. As in all alone. Does this seem right to you?"

Delilah said, "It seems negligent. Andrea is unfit. Finn told

Barney that Andrea smashed Greg's guitar against the kitchen counter, right in front of the kids."

"You're kidding," Phoebe said.

"They should be living with us," Delilah said. "I should have fought for them."

Fought for them, Phoebe thought.

Phoebe saw the twins again a few days later, out in Sconset. They were eating ice-cream cones on a bench in the pocket park adjacent to the Sconset Market. Phoebe was in her car; she had just enjoyed the world's most elegant lunch of lobster and mango salad, crème caramel, and a crisp Sancerre with her cochair, Jennifer. Phoebe was a little high from the wine; she wasn't certain at first that the two children on the bench were the twins. Out of the corner of her eye . . . yes, she thought so. She looped around, enjoying Sconset. It was adorable, this little town, with its rose-covered cottages and the cafés and the tennis club, and the magnificent summer homes on the bluff, which ended with the candy-striped lighthouse and the rolling green acreage of Sankaty Head golf course. Phoebe only came to Sconset on special occasions, and there hadn't been many special occasions in the past eight years.

The second time she passed the park, she saw the twins clearly. Again sitting in silence, alone with their ice cream, staring straight ahead, licking. Phoebe slowed down. She looked for Andrea's car—or the Chief's?—because what would the twins be doing all the way out here on their own? Phoebe parked in front of the market. It felt like her heart had a zipper that was being pulled up—and down. Up—and down. She did not see Andrea's car. Nor the Chief's. So maybe the kids had come on their bikes. All the way to Sconset? *Was* Andrea negligent?

The twins did not see Phoebe. They did not appear to see anything except their ice cream. Phoebe was overcome with the desire to make them smile. To make them happy. Could she do it? If she approached them, would they acknowledge her? Of course they would—she had known them their entire lives, she had spent countless Sundays in their presence. But how did they think of her? They called her *Phoebe,* not *Auntie Phoebe,* even though Delilah was *Auntie Dee* and Andrea was simply *Auntie.* So Phoebe was not *Auntie Phoebe,* that was okay, she wasn't their aunt like Andrea was, nor was she the mother of their dearest friends like Delilah was. She was just some strange childless woman who hung out with their parents and who spent most of her time checked into the Dope Motel.

She was different now. Would they be able to tell?

Should she offer to take them to her house and let them swim in the pool? Up—and down. The twins! The thought thrilled her.

A girl walked out of the Sconset Market swigging from a bottle of Diet Pepsi, and the kids stood up and threw away their soiled napkins and the nubs of their cones. The girl was . . . Andrea. No. It was Kacy. Phoebe's heart whistled. She let out a soft Sancerre burp. She was relieved that there was a responsible person out here with the twins. But she was deflated, too. The twins were darling and wholesome. They were Hansel and Gretel, and she, Phoebe, was some kind of witch.

Kacy and the twins extracted their bikes from the rack. The twins mounted their bikes and the bikes wobbled, like fawns standing on new legs. Then they balanced themselves, they pedaled and gained speed. They were steady and confident, and Phoebe smiled as she watched them go.

She wanted something, but it was not the twins.

It was like a bad dream. It was the middle of the night, pitch-black. Now that Phoebe was off the Ambien, she needed the shades drawn and the air-conditioning on full blast in order to sleep. But the storm woke her up. Lightning flashed around the edges of the shades and the thunder sounded like someone on the second floor was picking up large pieces of furniture and then letting them drop. That wasn't the scary part, however. The scary part was

Addison sitting up, eyes wide open, watching her. He was not wearing his glasses, and for a second, she didn't recognize him.

"Jesus, Add!" she said. She liked even this, however: the ability to be startled, to be frightened.

He said, "The present."

She said, "What?" Though she knew, right away.

"What was the anniversary present?" he said. "That you gave Tess?"

She looked at her husband. He was staring at her, but could he see her? She had an urge to . . . what? Jump out of bed and run into the storm? Run down to the basement and hide in her cedar closet?

"It's none of your business," Phoebe said. "Is it?" This last little bit was a dare on her part. *If Tess is your business, tell me why. Tell me she was your lover. Tell me you were in love with her.* But Phoebe didn't want to hear him confess. She knew what she knew, but he didn't know what she knew, and that meant it wasn't real. Phoebe realized in that instant that with or without the drugs, she had always chosen to live in a fantasy world, and she wanted to keep it that way.

She touched Addison's shoulder. He wore a long-sleeved T-shirt and his flannel pajama pants; the AC was set at something like fifty degrees. It was so cold he claimed he could see his breath. He did not respond to her touch, even though it had become some kind of crazy rule (established, she knew, by crazy Phoebe) that they did not touch in bed. Her medication had not only sapped her sex drive, it had made her irrationally afraid of sex. Or she was afraid of sex because in recent years Addison had only pursued her when very drunk, when he was rough and he hurt her. They had had a lovely, tender sex life years and years ago, back when they were both different people. Now, along with everything else, Phoebe found herself interested in sex again. Her body resumed its humming rhythm; she had actually gotten a period, and even the blood and the cramping had seemed, if not wonderful, then at least natural and right. A return to life. She was a woman again.

It had occurred to her that what she wanted was a sex life, a sensual life. Hours with Addison where they touched and teased, kissed and stroked, gave each other massages and took candlelit baths. She wanted to climax under his finger, or with him pumping inside her. Would it be difficult to get something like this under way? Addison had tried everything both holistic and black-market to get Phoebe interested in sex again—porn videos, vibrators, scented oils, Barry White CDs, Anaïs Nin—and nothing had worked. Would it be the same now, only in reverse?

She stroked his arm with what she meant to be a suggestive up-and-down motion. Again her heart did its zippering and unzippering. Up—and down. She was pulsing between the legs.

"Do you want to make love?" she asked.

He looked at her. Again the empty, blind-man gaze. "I want you to tell me about the present."

Thunder. A crack like a very big bone breaking, and then the rumble.

"I won't."

He fell onto his side as if shot. Phoebe would not accept this. She crossed the invisible boundary into Addison territory (he had the western half of the bed, she the eastern) and slid her hand beneath the drawstring waistband of his pajama pants. She touched him, hoping. But he was shriveled, flaccid. She retracted her hand and thought of apologizing.

And then Addison started to sob.

Still, she thought, she wanted something. If that something was Addison, she could wait it out; she could be as patient as he had been. She could fix their relationship—sew the head back onto the doll, rescue the fallen soufflé.

*   *   *

She found the poem—or it found her—on the hottest day of the summer. Addison came home from the office at four and said he wanted to stay in the pool until nightfall.

"Okay," Phoebe said. "Just as long as you keep your head above water." This was said lightly, though Phoebe worried that Addison would pour himself four or five bourbons, lie on his inflatable raft, fall asleep, and inadvertently slip to the bottom of the pool without her noticing. Another drowning.

He couldn't get into his swim trunks fast enough. Addison, who was always fastidious, very sloppily emptied his pockets all over the granite countertops too close to where Phoebe was attempting both to brew iced tea and to shred a rotisserie chicken for chicken salad. Phoebe had never been much of a cook, but she had watched Delilah make chicken salad a hundred times (watched her through someone else's prescription eyeglasses, it seemed now). It was easy. Shredded chicken, celery, chives, mayonnaise, salt, pepper, and the secret ingredient, straight out of Mary Poppins—a spoonful of sugar. Tonight, Phoebe thought triumphantly, they would eat a dinner she'd prepared herself.

When Addison opened the door to go out to the pool (full Jack-over-ice in hand), the hot wind lifted the poem off the pile of debris evacuated from his pockets—the money, the change, the business cards, the single piece of root-beer-flavored hard candy, a couple of pieces of pilled red felt—and it wafted into the melee of ingredients that was to become the chicken salad.

Phoebe lifted the poem with her nails; her fingers were coated with chicken grease.

A poem! Ripped from somewhere.

She read the poem, keen to understand it. Literature was her friend now; she had finished *Catcher in the Rye* and was halfway through the Ellen Gilchrist. The poem was straightforward; she got it, but not really. A birthday party in a restaurant, the men's room, someone pissing Asti Spumante. Macho! Then Phoebe came to the underlined verses. *My life with you has been beyond*

beyond/And there's nothing beyond it I'm seeking/I wouldn't mind being dead/If I could still be with you.

Phoebe set the poem back down on the pile of Addison's things and weighted it with his keys.

She had seen the poem before. She had seen it at Tess's house. Tess had handed it to her. She'd said, *Look at this.* Phoebe had pretended to read it, but of course the words had been little more than ants on sugar.

It's beautiful, she had told Tess.

Tess had sniffled a little bit. Everything made that woman cry.

Phoebe scooped mayonnaise into the bowl with abandon. Addison could not be saved. She would have to find something else to want.

THE CHIEF

He summoned them to the Begonia because he didn't know where else to go. And because he hadn't yet decided whether he should tell them about the tox report or keep it a secret. If they went to the Begonia, it could be passed off as simply the three of them meeting for beers. Since the evening after Greg and Tess's funeral, they had done nothing as a group. Nothing—it was odd, and the unexpected thing was, the Chief missed it. He missed gathering, he missed drinking cold beer out on the Drakes' deck, he missed being invited to swim in Addison's pool, he missed Delilah's cooking (she had a knack for always knowing what he was craving), he missed sitting on the beach in a semicircle, talking about boats and listening to the Sox game on the last transistor radio in America, which he had bought on eBay. Delilah called the house once to invite them and the twins over for a barbecue, but Andrea had said no. When the Chief asked why, Andrea said, *I don't care if I ever go over there again.*

So along with Greg and Tess, something else had died.

The Chief got to the Begonia first, and Faith greeted him at the door. He kissed her rouged cheek. She said, "How you doin'?" in a way that seemed to be asking more than the obvious, and he said, "Oh, Jesus, Faith. As well as can be expected, I guess."

Faith said, "We sure do miss him."

He could do a little detective work here; the Begonia had been Greg's "third place," after home and the school. If Greg had been talking to someone who sold drugs, Faith might know about it. But it was imperative to keep things under wraps, and Faith, while a decent woman, was Nantucket's answer to a daily newspaper. If it was happening, she would tell you about it.

He asked to be seated at the back table, the one that was shielded by half-walls. Everyone called it the Mafia Table. Normally the Chief liked to sit at the bar where he could see the TV and lend an air of neighborhood security to the establishment, but tonight he needed the Mafia Table.

He said to Faith, "I'm meeting Add and Jeffrey."

She nodded, set down menus, and said, "Please know that Thom and I are thinking of you. And we're thinking of Andrea."

The Chief said, "Appreciate that."

Faith lingered a second and the Chief panicked. He did not want to get involved in a conversation. He picked up his menu even though he always ordered the bleu burger, and Faith reluctantly wandered away.

He took a deep breath. Beer, onion rings, exhaust from the stove. The Sox were on TV and the jukebox was playing Tom Petty. He was in the Scarlet Begonia. He was okay, despite the fact that the tox report was eating at him like a tapeworm, despite the fact that Andrea was certifiably nuts and needed a padded room on a quiet farm in central Pennsylvania. Andrea thought about nothing other than Tess: Tess drowning in Nantucket

Sound, Tess almost drowning in Boston Harbor as a child, Tess miscarrying once, losing the second baby in a fall, miscarrying again, Tess suffering through the weeks of Greg's inquisition, Tess withdrawing from Andrea right after Christmas. This last thing seemed to be the corn kernel stuck in Andrea's back molar: for the six months prior to Tess's death, Tess had been distant and strange. Andrea had felt her pulling away. It would have been imperceptible to anyone other than Andrea, but Andrea had sensed that something was wrong. Tess didn't confide in Andrea, she went two and three days without checking in, and, worst of all, she had stopped going to mass with Andrea on Saturday evenings, which was the one hour of the week that they reserved not only for the Lord but for each other.

Andrea was so consumed with her interior life that she didn't always notice what was going on around her. The twins had their own set of complicated needs—food, clothing, a chauffeur service, enriching ways to pass the time indoors and outdoors, athletic and educational, for all of their waking hours. Andrea could barely meet the minimum requirements: drop off, pick up, breakfast, lunch, dinner, bath, bedtime. If there were to be outings, if there was to be fun, it had to be provided by Eric, Kacy, or the Chief. Eric and Kacy had jobs and friends. The Chief had a police force to run and an island to keep safe. They did what they could, but it was clear the twins were unhappy. Not only devastated by the tragic loss of both their parents, but bored and uninspired by their new life in the Kapenash house. On Sundays, when the Chief was in charge, he asked the twins what they wanted to do and they invariably said they wanted to play with Drew and Barney; they wanted to go to Auntie Dee's house. And though that would have been killing two birds with one stone—he would be making the kids happy *and* resurrecting some of his lost social life (his mouth watered at the thought of grilled corn, cherry tomatoes stuffed with guacamole, the wickedly spicy tuna tartare that Delilah made in the summer)—he could not in good conscience take the kids over there. Andrea would unhinge. This happened more and more frequently—the guitar smashing had been the worst, followed by dumping a platter of perfectly grilled rib-eye steaks into her perennial bed, followed by throwing her cell phone into the ocean. The kids were terrified of Andrea. One morning Finn ate his Cheerios without milk because he was afraid to ask for some.

Chloe had a bad case of the night terrors. She woke up calling for her mom, and Andrea lay there with her eyes open but made no move to deal with it, so the Chief would walk Chloe back to bed, find her doll, and try to make a convincing whispered argument that everything was going to be okay. The poor kid was craving her mother, a woman with peppy energy and feminine warmth, and what she got was her gruff uncle who had a big, scary job and carried a gun.

In a brave moment, the Chief had told Andrea that the best way to honor Tess now was to concentrate on caring for the children.

Andrea had basically spit on him for that. She said, "I *am* caring for them, Ed."

But she wasn't. She was too caught up in her grief. It was backward, upside down, inside out.

Here at the Begonia, the Chief stroked the scarred tabletop. Addison was next to arrive, and he must have stopped at the bar, because he was carrying a drink. The Chief stood, they shook hands, Addison sat down opposite, and the Chief felt nervous suddenly, like he was on a blind date. He and Addison had been friends for eons. It was true that he and Addison did not have a whole heck of a lot in common; Addison was slippery like a fish. Impossible to grasp. He had had a fancy education, he'd lived and worked in other countries, he had a daughter who lived in California like a character in one of those Teen Disney shows that Chloe wanted to watch but Andrea prohibited. Addison was a businessman; he was Nantucket's real estate magnate. He did deals where he made so much money it felt illegal. He made connections, he culled favors, he lived in a six-thousand-square-foot house with his fragile wife.

The Chief had always respected the way Addison fretted over Phoebe. Especially now that the Chief had his own wife to worry about.

The Chief and Addison had once been lost in the woods together. They had rented a canoe during their group trip to Saranac Lake, paddled around the wrong bend (the Chief had chosen incorrectly; he'd insisted, despite Addison's protests), and ended up in East Who-the-fuck-knows. They had no map (two big strong men, no need for a map), half a bottle of Evian, and no food except for breath mints. They each had a cell phone, but no goddamn reception. They were out on the lake for hours, and when they were supposed to meet the hotel pickup truck at the end point, they were lost. They decided to pull onto land and carry the canoe and look for a road. Hitch a ride back to the refuge of their elegant resort, the Point, where everyone else was getting ready for dinner and most likely starting to worry.

They pulled off into thick, almost impenetrable woods. They considered getting back into the canoe, but that felt like regressing. They battled through the brush while holding the canoe over their heads. The Chief had worked with guys who had been to Vietnam; he'd heard stories just like everyone else about the dense jungle, the bugs, the snakes, the booby traps. What the Chief and Addison were dealing with now was, of course, not warfare, but the conditions weren't much more favorable. The mosquitoes were thick and whining; there were thorns everywhere, and mud. Addison was, ridiculously, wearing Ferragamo loafers. The canoe hindered them tremendously; at one point they were tempted just to ditch it, but it belonged to the resort, it was a beautiful wooden canoe and had probably cost thousands of dollars. It was growing dark, they couldn't see, the mosquitoes were like motherfucking tigers, the Chief was dying of thirst. He was so thirsty he would gladly have drunk lake water, despite whatever kind of gut-rotting dysentery it would give him, but by now, he estimated, they were at least a quarter-mile inland.

They were both tired; they decided to rest. They had been paddling all day in the sun; the resort had packed them an excellent picnic lunch, which they had devoured six hours earlier. They sat on top of the overturned canoe and swatted at mosquitoes and caught their breath and surveyed their surroundings. Woods and more woods. The Chief was trying not to panic. He was a policeman; he had heard countless stories just like this—man out enjoying nature for the day—that ended in tragedy.

They had to keep going. They *had* to ditch the canoe; it was too cumbersome. Addison said that he would pay for it. The Chief said they could argue about that later, once they found some goddamn civilization that included a hot shower, clean sheets, and a cold beer. Once it was just the two of them, minus the albatross of the canoe, they moved much faster. They ran in places. They had decided to move in only one direction, toward the sunset, west, which was, theoretically, the direction in which the resort was located. But west went on forever.

To keep from getting discouraged, Addison told the Chief stories of the wild days when he was married to the stick-thin, chain-smoking socialite Mary Rose Garth, who loved seeking out scandal the way other women loved chocolate, and then he told the real story of why he got kicked out of Princeton the week before he graduated. (The Chief swore never to divulge the details.) These were fantastic stories, they passed the time, and the Chief tried to come up with his own stories, but he had never been married to a woman who liked to bring another woman home to bed or throw last year's couture on the library fire, and so what he realized in the woods was that although he was a police chief, his life had been pretty dull.

They noticed the woods starting to thin out. Then they hit a road. "A road! A motherfucking road!" They'd hit the jackpot: all roads led to somewhere.

But maybe not this one. It was a dirt road, and half an hour later, not a single vehicle had driven past. Addison tried his phone and got a cell signal. While he was dialing the hotel—all he would be able to tell everyone was that they were alive—the Chief saw headlights, and along came an honest-to-God VW bus with two hippies inside smoking a doobie as if they had arrived straight out of 1967. Addison and the Chief gratefully climbed into the green haze of the backseat.

There were two men sitting up front, if kids in their twenties with wispy beards and remnants of acne could be called men. They were listening to John Hiatt on the radio, and the Chief said happily upon settling in his seat, "Love the music!"

"Where we dropping you?" the driver asked. He was wearing a purple T-shirt and a pair of John Lennon sunglasses with purple tinted lenses.

"The Point," Addison said with obnoxious authority, as though they were in Manhattan and this was their cab.

"Whoa-ho!" the passenger up front said. He was the one actually holding the joint, and after hearing the name of their hotel, he inhaled again and while holding his smoke said, "Sweet place."

The Point was sweet—it was the finest place the Chief and Andrea had ever stayed at, with its rustic luxury, every detail attended to, including the temperature at which the red wine was served and the type of pillow each guest preferred. The Point was a resort for the rich. The Chief understood that Cheech and Chong here would now mistake him and Addison for wealthy men, and while this bothered him and he yearned to set the record straight, he really just wanted to get back.

"Can you take us there?" he asked.

"No prob," the driver said. He looked at his companion and said, "Want to offer our friends a taste?"

The passenger, who looked like he was trying to grow in

muttonchop sideburns, passed the joint back over the seat. Addison took it without hesitation.

"I haven't smoked in twenty years," he said. "But I have just been lost in the wilderness and experienced what I can most accurately describe as fear for my life, and a little spliff feels like exactly what I need right now."

"Amen," the passenger said.

Addison inhaled deeply with his eyes closed, held the smoke, and then let the stream go. "Smooth as silk," he said. The Chief looked upon Addison not with shock or disgust, but rather with envy. He wanted to smoke, to have a looseness enter his stiff and sore muscles—but he just couldn't.

"No, thanks," said the Chief.

"Come on!" the passenger said.

"Can't, really. Random drug testing at work." The random drug testing among Nantucket's police officers had been the Chief's idea.

"Bummer!" the driver said. "What's your line of work?"

"He's a police chief," Addison said.

There was a pause. One beat, then two. The song changed to Paul McCartney and Wings singing "Band on the Run." The Chief wanted to deck Addison. What if these potheads got unnecessarily paranoid and decided to dump them? They would be only half a mile closer to home.

But instead the passenger, Master Scrawny Sideburns, burst out laughing. It was a giggly and girlish sound. And this set the driver laughing. Then, in a drug-induced delayed reaction, Addison laughed. He laughed so hard he held his stomach.

"Police chief," he said. "Heeheeheeheeheehee."

The driver could barely keep the van on the road. His tiny glasses slipped down his nose. He hunched over the steering wheel. Hahahahahahaha.

It took several minutes for them to collect their wits, but

when they did, Master Scrawny Sideburns said, "Well, there, Mr. PO-lice Chief, would you like a beer?"

The Chief said, "Yes. Please."

And that was now the Chief's own best story.

Addison looked worse sitting across the table at the Begonia than he had after being lost in the woods for three hours and enduring what had ended up being a forty-five-minute drive back to the secure luxury of the Point. Then he had been mussed and torn and mud-caked and mosquito-bitten and sunburned and stoned out of his mind, and now, although his shirt was pressed and his hair tidy, he looked bloated and pale and tragically sad. He looked, the Chief thought, like a bald male version of Andrea. There had been a guy in the force in Swampscott who had lost his partner in a botched arrest, and as a sign of his grief he had tattooed half his face. The grief of the people close to the Chief was just as clear and indelible as Sergeant Cutone's tattoo. And as with the sergeant, the Chief could barely stand to look at Addison. He had to avert his eyes.

In this part of the restaurant there were only two tables seated, and the Chief did not recognize the people. Tourists. The TV set was too far away to see the score of the Sox game. A waitress approached with a Budweiser for the Chief and another drink for Addison, even though he already had a healthy drink in front of him. She set the drinks down and said, "Would you like to place an order?"

Addison shook his head. "Nothing for me."

The Chief was starving. Andrea had fed the twins microwaved hot dogs on some stale-looking buns, along with a couple of slices of pale watermelon, and although the Chief liked kid food—chicken nuggets, mac and cheese—nothing about the twins' meal had appealed to him or to them. To be polite, he should wait for Jeffrey before he ordered, but etiquette was not the Chief's strong suit and everyone knew it.

"Bleu burger well done, please. Fries. Coleslaw with extra

horseradish. And start me with something . . . the jalapeño poppers."

"Will do," the waitress said.

"Jesus, Ed," Addison said.

"I know," the Chief said. "It's a one-way ticket on the Heart-
burn Express."

Addison swilled the rest of his drink as if it were water and
jostled the ice.

"Jesus yourself," the Chief said.

"Yeah," Addison said. "Phoebe thinks I have a problem."

"Do you?"

"Have a problem?" He laughed joylessly. "I have a few."

"I'm going to be honest with you," the Chief said. "You don't
look that great."

"Am I supposed to look great? It hasn't even been a month.
Can you believe it? It's only been twenty-six days, but it's like our
whole reality has changed."

"You're taking it hard?"

"Is there another way to take it?" Addison's eyes welled with
tears. The Chief had seen it all during his seventeen years on the
force, but one of his least favorite things was watching a grown
man cry. He thought about all the phone calls between Tess
and Addison on the day before Tess died. Five phone calls from
Addison to Tess on the final morning. He had been trying to
reach her. But why? Along with the tox report and what to do
about Andrea, this was one of the things the Chief turned over
incessantly in his mind. There had to be an explanation. Should
he ask?

Among the four men, Greg and Addison had been the closest
friends. They were the outgoing, party-all-the-time type who attended bachelor parties and took golf weekends, who went fishing
and sailing and played bocce on the beach, clinking beer bottles
after a good lie and offering high fives. When Addison got Celtics
tickets or front row to see Jimmy Buffett, he always took Greg.

Greg was his little buddy, his much younger fraternity brother; Addison told a joke and Greg was the first to laugh. That, perhaps, was the reason Addison looked like a jigsaw puzzle with a couple of pieces missing. He'd lost his sidekick, his Sundance Kid.

The Chief said, "Andrea's a mess. What about Phoebe?"

"Phoebe?" Addison said. He sucked down the first third of his second drink and said, "The strange thing is that Phoebe is just fine. She's actually better than she's been in a long time. I'm sure everyone thought Phoebe would collapse, this would be the last straw, but she's great. She's exercising, eating, smiling."

"Mmmm," the Chief said. He had seen Phoebe on the Fourth and had noticed how luminous she looked. "And how goes it with the estate?"

"The estate?" Addison looked perplexed. "Oh, fine. We're going to list the house at seven-fifty."

The Chief nodded. There were forty or fifty follow-up questions to ask about the house and the furnishings and the personal effects, the business of the deaths, the selling off and cleaning up of two full lives, but the Chief wanted to ask about the phone calls. Who knew when he would get another chance? He was a policeman; he had to know. He would be direct, no funny business, no innuendo.

"I noticed there were a bunch of calls from you to Tess on the morning she died. Five, to be exact."

Addison stared. The eye contact was reassuring, because what did a liar do? He dropped his eyes to his drink.

"Was something going on?" the Chief asked.

"Going on?"

"Happening? Was she thinking of selling the house or renting a place for her college roommate or . . ." He was giving Addison a chance to lie here, and put his mind at ease, at least temporarily. "Why so many phone calls?"

Addison shrugged; his stare did not relent. "We were friends."

"Well, obviously," the Chief said. "We were all friends. But why were you trying to reach her? Five phone calls in half an hour. What for?"

"What for?"

"Yeah."

Addison hunched his shoulders. "What are you asking me, Ed?"

"I'm asking what you wanted to talk to her about. If you saw half a dozen calls from me to Tess, you would want to know what was going on, wouldn't you? You would want to know what we were talking about."

"I would figure it was your business. I wouldn't interrogate you."

"That's not what I'm doing."

"It sure as hell sounds like it."

"Okay, well, while I'm at it, I have another question."

Addison held eye contact. "What would that be?"

"In the bag of the items the Coast Guard recovered was Tess's phone."

"You have the phone. You just said you checked it."

"It went missing the day she died. That night. And you were at the Drake house. Did you take Tess's cell phone? Do you have it?"

Addison's nostrils flared, ever so slightly. "No."

"I need you to tell me the truth. The phone could have clues still on it. I didn't look at her text messages, for example."

"Why not?"

"I didn't have time. I was dealing with Andrea." The Chief paused. "Do you have the phone, Addison? Just tell me."

"No."

"Okay," the Chief said. He was sure now that Addison did have the phone, but what could he do? Get a search warrant? Turn the phone into evidence? Let the whole island know that Tess's and Greg's deaths were, maybe, more than an accident?

"If you find the phone . . ." the Chief said. "If for some reason Phoebe has it, or it turns up . . ."

"You'll be the first to know," Addison said.

The waitress approached timidly with the jalapeño poppers. She looked nervous. It was the Mafia Table replete with men speaking in angry whispers. The Chief waved her in. Food, yes, hurry, put the plate down, the Chief was starving. He ate when he was nervous or stressed out, and he was both things in extremis right now. He popped a popper right away, then regretted it. The popper was filled with molten lava that branded his tongue with a sizzling hiss. He gasped and nearly spit the glowing coal into his napkin, but both the waitress and Addison were watching him. If Addison could bluff, so could he. Thumbs up! Delicious!

"Another beer," he whispered. "Please."

"And a drink for me," Addison said.

Just like that, the moment was past, the topic was kaput, and to revisit the question of the cell phone or the reason for Addison's phone calls would seem aggressive. The Chief would not be able to uncover anything. Addison, despite his diminished appearance, was cunning—that Ivy League education meant something, as did the charm, the business acumen, the money, the languages, the connections. Addison was as slippery as a fish, but he would not get caught like a fish. There were two types of men, cops and robbers, and Addison . . . well, the Chief hated to say it, but he was a robber. The kind who stole a man's money and his property. Greg had been a robber, too, the kind who stole a woman's heart. The Chief was a cop through and through, but that didn't mean he would prevail. Going head to head with Addison, he almost certainly would not.

"Want a popper?" the Chief asked, secretly wishing Addison would end up with a sore, dry spot on his tongue like the Chief now had.

"God, no," Addison said.

And they both chuckled.

Jeffrey said, "Sorry I'm late."

He had not left Delilah at home at night since Greg and Tess had died, he said, because he was worried about her. Crackerjack Delilah, the bat out of hell, Joan Jett meets Julia Child, a woman formidable in a dozen different ways—and she was a mess now.

"I can only stay for one beer," Jeffrey said.

Jeffrey was a cop also, the Chief thought. He was a cop's cop, incorruptible.

"I'm sorry to hear about Delilah," the Chief said. "I miss her cooking."

"I miss her cooking, too," Jeffrey said.

"Have a burger," the Chief said, nodding at his own plate, half demolished.

"I can't stay that long," Jeffrey said. The man was a Supreme Court justice.

"Right," the Chief said. He had to put aside his feeding trough—the extra horseradish in the coleslaw had his mouth buzzing in a way that made him want to shovel in more and more food—and deal with the unpleasant business of the evening. Or he could just forget about it. He had a *choice* here—he could open up the Pandora's box that was the tox report—or he could let it go.

He cleared his throat. "I asked you both here for a reason."

Pause. Jeffrey and Addison leaned forward over the Mafia Table. The waitress again looked afraid to approach, but she had the extra mayonnaise for the Chief's burger and she wanted to get Jeffrey's drink order. Stella draft. Okay. She fled.

The Chief said, "The ME ran a toxicology report on the bodies. They had both been drinking. And Tess was high on something." The Chief paused. "The opiate most commonly found in heroin."

"Heroin?" Jeffrey said.

"Did either of you know about Greg or Tess mixed up with heroin? Or any other kind of street drug?"

"No," Addison said. "Well, Greg smoked weed. We all knew that. And he did cocaine back in his Velociraptor days."

The Chief looked at Addison and remembered his Ferragamo loafers iced with mud; a three-hundred-dollar pair of shoes had gone into the hotel trash without a second thought. The bill for the abandoned canoe had come in at a whopping forty-two hundred dollars, and Addison had paid it. (The Chief had always felt crummy about that, but Addison had the money and he'd convinced the Chief that it had been his idea to orphan the canoe. That was the robber in him; he'd saved the Chief two thousand dollars but stolen his dignity.) The Chief also remembered Addison toking up with Deep Purple and Scrawny Sideburns and how envious he'd felt. The lost-in-the-woods story with Addison was the Chief's best story, but right this second the Chief didn't find it amusing at all. Five phone calls to Tess on the day she died. Addison was hiding something.

"I just thought you both should know," the Chief said. "The accident can't be taken at face value. Something else was going on."

"Well . . ." Jeffrey said.

Pause. The waitress dropped off his Stella.

"Anything else I can get you?" she asked.

"No," they all said at once.

She scooted away.

"Well, what?" the Chief said. Something was coming. The Chief had heard hundreds of people bear witness, leak secrets, confess. The human need to spill the beans, to *tell,* could not be underestimated. Even Jeffrey, the judge, had this urge. He was about to share privileged information. But what the Chief had learned over the years was that his thirst to find out led him to be burdened with information he would have been better off not knowing.

"When I spoke to April Peck at the funeral," Jeffrey said, "she told me she'd been with Greg the night before he died."

Suddenly the Chief felt full. He pushed his plate away. He exhaled, burped beer and horseradish, felt nauseous. April Peck.

Yes, he thought.

Beautiful women were dangerous. But beautiful girls were even more dangerous, because they weren't seasoned; they didn't know that beauty was a weapon and so they flung it around carelessly. April Peck had been after Greg; she had been hunting him on the night of October 23. Of this, the Chief was convinced. He believed that April had gone into Greg's classroom on purpose, wearing a wet T-shirt without a bra; he believed that she had only been pretending to be upset; she needed an excuse for physical contact. The Chief believed that she had forced herself on Greg. The part the Chief had a harder time with was Greg's response to that. Had he resisted from the get-go? Or had he succumbed to what would have been as irresistible as a bowl full of juicy berries with whipped cream on top? Had he accidentally grazed a nipple? Had his skin heated up when April put her mouth on his neck? Had he responded, for even just a second? *Of course he had.*

In his seventeen years as police chief, Ed Kapenash had pressed the boundaries of his authority only once. That was on October 27, when he met clandestinely with school superintendent Dr. Richard Flanders at the station. The Chief and Flanders had gone over the details of both Greg's account of what happened and April's account. They came up with the following conclusion: April probably did initiate; Greg probably did, in some way, respond. (What man wouldn't respond to April Peck? Both men agreed it would take someone very strong—the pope, for example.) The important thing was that Greg had not capitulated, he had not crossed the line; he had not slept with the girl. Flanders said he would continue with the inquiry—he had to, for protocol's sake—but he assured the Chief that unless any new information was revealed, Greg would keep his job. Flanders shook the Chief's hand, looked him in the eye; they were men, they understood each other and they believed they understood Greg. The Chief was able to go home to Andrea and say he'd taken care of the problem.

But Greg had the temperament of a spoiled child. His whole life he had gotten whatever he wanted. He had gotten a taste of April Peck; it was not surprising to learn that he'd wanted more.

Greg was a robber.

There were two incidents that the Chief had chosen to overlook. The first was this: On the night of February 2, a domestic disturbance call had come into the station. It was a mother-daughter situation; the mother had stolen the daughter's car keys in order to keep her at home. The daughter was threatening to stab the mother; she had pulled a kitchen knife. The mother called the police. A squad car was sent to 999 Polpis Road, where they found Donna and April Peck in a messy catfight—hair-pulling, face-scratching, a strap ripped on an expensive camisole top (April's). There was a knife on the counter—a five-inch serrated sandwich knife—but no one had been cut or stabbed. There was screaming and name-calling, even after Walker and Dickson, the officers, separated the two women. Walker was a ten-year veteran, a deer hunter and early-morning fisherman; he lived alone and had neither the time nor the patience for hysterical women, even though April was, in his words, "one of the hottest chicks I have ever laid eyes on." Dickson, on the other hand, was the Chief's secret weapon. Dickson was too smart to be a policeman; the Chief had him marked for a detective in the near future. Dickson had an incredible memory. So he recalled for the Chief, later, word for word, what the women had said.

She put me under house arrest! I'm eighteen years old!

She's going to see HIM!

Him who, ma'am?

The teacher!

I am not!

Don't lie to me, April. I've checked your phone.

You don't know what you're talking about. The cancer has gone to your brain.

How dare you, young lady!

Dickson had it all written down in his report. They had concluded that as April was eighteen, she was free to leave the premises. The car in question was registered in April's name. It was hers, she could use it.

Do you have a safe place to go? Dickson asked her.

Yes, she said.

And the mother had said, *She's going to meet the teacher.*

Dickson had tried to hold the Chief's gaze after reporting this last bit, but the Chief would have none of it. Hearsay. Who knew which teacher she was talking about, or if it even was a teacher? It could have been Casey, the phys ed teacher, who had his own issues with April Peck. The Chief didn't want to speculate and he didn't want Dickson speculating.

But deep down, he knew. Of course he knew. And he thought, *Jesus, Greg!* And he thought about calling Greg up or surprising him at the Begonia and saying, *What the fuck are you doing?* But the Chief backed away from that particular ledge because it *was* hearsay and the anguish of the first accusation had just healed and who was the Chief to pull the scab off?

On the night of April 18, it was Dickson again, out cruising the tough Nantucket streets alone. It was the first night of spring break; many islanders were away on vacation. It was two-thirty in the morning, and Dickson came across two vehicles parked at the end of Hummock Pond Road, facing Cisco Beach. He pulled up, because there was no good reason for two cars to be parked at the beach in the middle of the night. Dickson was hoping for a drug deal, something he could really bust (it had been a dull winter). He touched his gun, though he'd been told in training that he had no prayer of ever using it. As Dickson was remembering this, there was movement. A figure moving from one car to the other. The car on the left, a silver 4Runner, plates Q22 DR9, backed up, turned around, and tore out of there in what Dickson would call a classic getaway. He climbed out of his car and poked his flashlight into the dark window of the other car.

And there she was. April Peck.

She looked at him. He indicated that she should roll down the window. She did, but only a crack.

He said, "What are you doing out here in the middle of the night, Miss Peck?"

And she said, "Looking at the ocean. Is that a crime?"

The plates had been Greg's. Dickson took this information to the Chief in the morning. The Chief said, "Well, the girl is right, there was no crime in her sitting there. Were you thinking of issuing a parking violation?"

Dickson said, "I just thought you should know."

Dickson walked out, and the Chief was left breathless. He picked up the phone, then dropped it. Greg and Tess had taken the kids to the Children's Museum in Boston. They had wanted to do Disney for spring break, but because of the roof replacement, there wasn't enough money. They would go next year, they said.

The Chief vowed that when Greg got back, he would talk to him. He would say, *If you don't stop this, I will tell Tess. I will tell Flanders. You will lose your wife, your kids, and your job.* He would say, *Stop this now. It isn't worth it.*

But the Chief had not spoken up, and it was a source of private shame. By the time Greg and Tess had gotten back from Boston, the incident seemed diminished, the urgency had passed. The Chief chose to believe that Dickson was bored and trying to drum up scandal.

"April Peck," the Chief said. The name itself conjured a vision of all that a good man was meant to avoid but could not.

Jeffrey nodded.

Addison said, "It's clear what happened." His neck was growing red from the collar up. He looked like he was going to boil. But his mopiness had disappeared, which made the Chief glad. "If there was heroin in Tess's blood, then Greg drugged her. He drugged her and dumped her off the boat."

"No," the Chief said.

"No," Jeffrey said.

"No?" Addison said. He jumped up and bumped the table. "How can you possibly believe otherwise? Isn't it obvious? Greg was trying to get rid of her so he could be with April!"

"Hey, now," the Chief said. "Respect."

Addison sat back down and put his head in his hands.

Five phone calls to Tess on the fateful morning. Had something been going on between Tess and Addison? Impossible. But Addison was a robber. Then there was Greg and April Peck. The Chief had lifted a rock and found bugs. Why was he surprised?

Addison said, "He killed her."

"He died, too."

"It went awry."

Was this possible? The Chief was losing his grip. April Peck, the tox report, Andrea crumbling at home. And he had eaten too much.

Jeffrey stood up. "I have to get back home." The man was Jesus Christ.

Addison said, "You think I'm right, don't you, Jeffrey? I mean, you're the one who just said he was still seeing April."

Jeffrey grimaced. "I can't say what happened on that boat, Add, and neither can you. The important thing here is the kids. Those kids *have* to believe it was an accident."

"But we don't have to believe that, do we?" Addison asked.

The Chief said, "I've got the bill."

Addison said, "No one's with me?"

"I'm sorry I brought it up," the Chief said. And he was.

"Me, too," Jeffrey said. "Truth be told, I just don't have the focus for a murder mystery here."

Addison stared at them both balefully. He said, "I'm leaving, too."

They all shook hands. Did the Chief need to remind them not to talk about this?

"So, for the kids' sake . . ."

Addison held up his palms.

Jeffrey said, "Not a word. Obviously."

Addison and Jeffrey weaved their way between the tables and out of the restaurant. Faith trailed them and kissed them both before they left. The waitress reappeared and cleared their glasses and the Chief's plate. She said, "Can I interest you in dessert?"

The Chief said, "Yes." And he ordered the mud pie.

ANDREA

The only time she felt like a human being was when she was up in the farm office with Jeffrey. It felt secret, illicit, affair-like, even though they never got close enough to each other to touch. But there was warmth, a connection, energy. They were on a mission: to remember everything they could about Tess DiRosa MacAvoy.

They had made it all the way to modern times. Tess and Greg were married, they were teaching, taking modest vacations, fixing up their house. They were getting ready for the next step.

"It's time," Andrea said, "to talk about the pregnancies."

Jeffrey paused. He looked squeamish. He didn't want to go there. He was a typical man; he couldn't do trimesters or blood, separated placenta or gushing miscarriage. It was feminine territory, like tampons and waxing. He wanted to skip it. He wanted, perhaps, to say, *It was a tough road, but eventually Chloe and Finn were born.*

Well, too bad! He had taken Andrea places during these conversations that she hadn't wanted to go. There were hours, for example, when they had to talk about Greg. So, yes, they were going to do the pregnancies; they couldn't talk about Tess without talking about her pregnancies.

Tess got pregnant for the first time in January of 2000; she and Greg conceived, most likely, in the high-gloss luxury of Room 1910 in Caesars Palace, Las Vegas. They had only just started trying to get pregnant, and voilà—pink stick. Tess jumped for joy; she had been put on earth to be a mother, she felt. She embraced her pregnancy. She talked about her sore breasts, her incessant nausea, her cravings (grilled cheese sandwiches, tomato soup), her complete and total exhaustion (she fell asleep with her head on her desk while her class was at music). In week eight, she announced to everyone, including the school custodian, that she was pregnant. There was no reason not to shout it from the mountaintops—pregnant! due September 30!—because Tess's life had been easy and blessed. She was secure and smug. She had been put on earth to be a mother.

The call came at four in the morning. Andrea picked it up thinking that it was a call for Ed, a police emergency, something bad happening to some poor nameless, faceless soul.

But it was Greg. It was dark and still and silent at four in the morning at the Kapenash house, but on Blueberry Lane, where Greg and Tess lived, all the lights were on and Greg was shouting.

"She's bleeding, Andrea! She's really fucking bleeding! There is blood *everywhere.*"

Andrea's heart fell through a hole and disappeared. Tess was losing the baby. She crossed herself and said to Greg, "I'll be right there."

"I've called 911. An ambulance is coming!"

"Okay, I'll meet you at the hospital." She hung up. Ed rolled over and said, "What's happening?"

"She's miscarrying," Andrea said.

"Shit," he said.

Ed and Andrea had two healthy kids asleep upstairs, ages seven and five and a half. They had been parents long enough to know how nature worked: one out of every five pregnancies terminated spontaneously in the first trimester. This didn't mean the woman wasn't healthy or couldn't go on to have six future children, all of them perfect and beautiful and headed to Ivy League colleges. It just meant that this one particular pregnancy wasn't meant to be.

Andrea tried this reasoning as she sat by Tess's bedside in the hospital. The ultrasound showed that the miscarriage had been complete and clean; there was no need for a D&C.

"That's good news," Andrea said.

Tess, who was lying in bed looking pale and despondent, said, "Good news? How can you *say* that?" She asked the question but did not wait for Andrea's reply. She burst into tears that became full-blown hysteria, sobbing and moaning about the lost life, the destroyed dream. Tess's vision of herself as a mother had popped like a soap bubble. Tess's tears were the most heartbreaking display of sorrow Andrea had ever seen, and she cried in sympathy, and apologized again and again because her words had been insensitive. Insensitive, but true. The pregnancy wasn't meant to be; there was no reason, these things just happened. It wasn't Tess's fault. It wasn't anybody's fault.

Tess got pregnant again two months later. She told only Andrea and the Chief. She was going to keep it a secret until she had her ultrasound at seventeen weeks. She did not talk about her nausea or her exhaustion or her leaden breasts; she wore smock tops over her swelling midsection. She looked positively morose and at times frightened, as though there were a man with a gun in her house, holding her hostage.

She and Greg heard the baby's heartbeat at each of their pre-natal appointments, but Tess would not crack a smile. She would not relax. She said to Andrea, "I am not going to let myself love this baby until he or she is born."

Andrea said, "Honey, everything is going to be fine."

And in fact, at the seventeen-week ultrasound, everything did look fine. Wonderful, even. The baby was a week ahead in its development. It was a little boy.

Everyone breathed a sigh of relief. Tess was able to tell every-body: it's a little boy, due the week before Christmas.

By then it was summer. School was out. Tess was feeling magnificent and happy, healthy and hungry. She power walked in the mornings, then ate scrambled eggs and a bran muffin with homemade peach jam. She would pack herself a lunch of tuna with pickles and a juicy plum and she would ride her bike to the beach, where she let her swollen belly absorb a moderate amount of sunshine before she carved a wide, shallow hole in the sand and turned over.

She was twenty-one weeks and four days along when she fell off her bike. Nothing happened—there was no oncoming car filled with hooting teenagers, no clap of lightning to startle her—she simply lost her balance, wobbled, and fell, just as she had years earlier when she broke her arm. She fell with a thud onto her side, crushing her swollen belly. She would later say that she knew in-stantly her baby was dead. There was blood everywhere and pain that made her knuckles turn white as she clenched her hands into fists and screamed without making a sound. Oncoming bikers called 911, the ambulance came, Tess was put on a jet and flown to Boston, and yes, the news was bad—the baby was dead—but it could have been worse. Tess could have died, too, from the hemorrhage.

When Tess gained consciousness, this time in a bigger, whiter, more sophisticated hospital, the Chief and Andrea were there—and Delilah and Jeffrey and Phoebe and Addison. They stood in a semicircle around the foot of the bed. And Father Dominic, the priest from St. Mary's, was there. Greg was there, too, looking baffled and helpless. He didn't know what to do. In the minutes before Tess came to, Greg had sung "Puff the Magic Dragon" softly, almost to himself. The song was a lullaby of sorts, meant to comfort, but it was a song of loss, too. By the last verse they were all singing along, even the Chief, even Father Dominic.

Tess opened her eyes. She had perhaps caught the tail end of their singing, and didn't understand it as a tribute. She ordered everyone out of the room except for Father Dominic.

"What about me?" Greg said, sounding like a jilted boyfriend.

"Go!" she screamed.

There was no consoling Tess this time. She was carrying sorrow *and* guilt. She had lost her balance and fallen off her bike. She had killed her son. She should never have been riding a bike, it was a lapse in judgment; she had been thinking of herself, the pleasures of a summer day, and not the baby. Her baby was dead, it was her fault, she would not hear otherwise.

There was a small graveside funeral, at which Tess and Greg buried a coffin the size of a shoebox. It was all too sad and too nebulous for anyone to handle; it was the loss of a life none of them had known, and yet this somehow made it worse. Or rather, what was worse was watching a part of their beloved Tess die, the part that was peppy and chipper, the part that was loving and kind and nurturing. She was sad now, unable to think or talk about anything but her loss; she was as crumpled and useless as wet tissue.

She saw a therapist. She went to a pregnancy loss group, where, she told Andrea, her story was by far the most gruesome. She quit attending the pregnancy loss group first, then she quit her therapist.

"Dr. Amlin keeps trying to tell me it was an *accident,*" Tess said. "If I hear the word *accident* one more time, I'm going to cut my ears off."

Andrea squandered her life savings taking Tess to Canyon Ranch in the Berkshires. Tess halfheartedly submitted to massage and facials while Andrea swam hundreds of laps in the pool. They ate poached salmon and lightly dressed greens in the dining room. When Andrea tried to start a conversation, Tess would shake her head. "I don't want to talk." As she and Andrea lay between 600-thread-count sheets in their beds, she said, "I'm not cut out for the whole maternal thing."

Andrea said, "Like hell you're not."

Andrea was spending damn near a thousand dollars a day and getting nowhere.

On the final morning, she dragged Tess out for a sunrise hike to the top of what they would later refer to as the "godforsaken mountain." All the swimming and weights and yoga and fresh fruit had worked on Andrea: she felt clean, light, and empowered. She basically dragged Tess up the damp, mossy trail, booby-trapped with tree roots and hidden rocks. They did not speak; the hike was too strenuous to spare the breath. It was still dark; they were making their way using a flashlight provided by the hotel. By the time they were a steep hundred yards from the peak (Andrea could spy the yellow banner flying from the pole that marked the top), Tess was bawling. She couldn't get to the top, and if she did, she was going to be so depleted of resources that she would only have the energy to throw herself off the mountain into the abyss.

Andrea kept going. Tess followed like a dog Andrea was dragging on a leash. They reached the peak and they watched the color of the sky warm and lighten. It was a moment from a commercial or a tear-jerker chick flick. It was the moment when everything was supposed to change. They would stand side by side with their arms flung around each other, their faces bathed in the buttery light of a new day, and it would be an epiphany. Tess would be cured. The realization would hit: it was time to move on.

Instead Tess found that her legs were unable to support her, and she collapsed on a rock. She was howling like a trapped animal. Andrea thought, *I have seriously fucked up. I made her hike up here, but she has no prayer of making it down. I am going to have to carry her.* And though Andrea would have said that she would be willing to carry Tess anywhere, she could not realistically get Tess down the mountain.

Andrea had to call the front desk at Canyon Ranch and have them send a rescue team. Andrea had had a speech written in her head, words she had planned to deliver at the summit. Something like this: *The baby is dead. It was not your fault—you have to deal with it like the reasonable, strong woman you are. You have to put the pieces back together and move forward.* The delivery was supposed to be no-nonsense and tough—but Andrea couldn't say the words to Tess in her current whimpering state. So they sat next to each other on the rock, waiting for nearly ninety minutes until two strapping men showed up with a stretcher, on which they carried Tess down the mountain.

The only thing Tess and Andrea talked about while they waited for the rescue team was what they would order for breakfast once they made it back to the dining room. Andrea was addicted to the Canyon Ranch granola (almonds, dried cherries, amber nuggets of dried apricots) with house-made yogurt.

Tess said she wanted four poached eggs with salt and pepper.

Which in itself felt like a victory.

In November, Tess got pregnant again and miscarried the day after she found out.

She said to Andrea, "I can't do this anymore. I'm going back to using my diaphragm."

Andrea said, "Okay."

Jeffrey jumped in here. He had been sitting quietly on his milk crate, but when Andrea reached this point, he sprang to life. Because wasn't it the painful truth that in the harrowing aftermath of Tess's second lost pregnancy, Delilah had gotten pregnant with Drew? The farmer and his wife were pregnant! It was happy news, except for the fact that they were intimate friends with a couple who had lost two, then three consecutive pregnancies. Delilah could not bring herself to tell Tess she was pregnant; and because she didn't want Tess to find out from a third party, she didn't tell anyone else, not even Phoebe. Jeffrey was angry about this. It was unfair that he and his wife could not celebrate their pregnancy because of Tess and Greg's difficulties. Jeffrey said, "Greg and Tess are going to understand. They're going to be *happy* for us."

Delilah said, "If you believe that, then you do not understand *anything* about human nature. She is going to hate me. I am going to lose one of my best friends."

Jeffrey and Delilah told Phoebe and Addison first, at a private dinner at 56 Union. Or rather, Phoebe guessed, because Delilah had ordered a club soda instead of her beloved espresso martini. Phoebe and Addison were happy for Jeffrey and Delilah. Phoebe had just watched her brother, Reed, and his wife go through the whole childbirth thing; she now had a nephew, and was enjoying being an auntie. And now Delilah! Phoebe couldn't wait; she hoped Delilah had a girl; she wanted to buy tutus and glow-in-the-dark nail polish. Jeffrey and Delilah drove home from that dinner feeling good about the pregnancy. Of course Greg and Tess would offer their blessing! Delilah picked up the phone as soon as she got home; it was ten-thirty on a Saturday night, but Delilah didn't care. The dread of telling Tess about the pregnancy was eating away at her; the anxiety had to be bad for the baby. Delilah was getting it over with *now!*

Greg picked up the phone.

Delilah said, "Greg, I'm pregnant."

There was silence.

Delilah said, "Would you put Tess on the phone, please?"

Greg said, "No, no, no. I'll tell her myself."

Delilah said, "*I'll* tell her. Put her on."

There was silence. A shuffling sound. Then Tess came on the phone, sounding very young and half asleep.

"Hello?"

"Tess? It's Delilah."

"Hi."

"Hi." Delilah swallowed. "Listen, I'm pregnant."

Silence.

Then Tess said, "I bet it wasn't easy for you to tell me that."

And Delilah burst into in tears.

Drew was born by cesarean section after eighteen hours of labor. He weighed ten pounds. Delilah was exhausted and in extreme pain; they put her on a morphine drip. She was the only person in the maternity ward, so Jeffrey left her and baby Drew in the capable hands of the labor and delivery nurses and went to the Begonia to meet Tess and Greg, the Chief and Andrea, and Addison and Phoebe. They had all been at the Begonia since the news of Drew's birth had reached them four hours earlier. They were in a festive mood, raising their glasses to toast Jeffrey as he walked in. Greg got up to play a set and started with "Danny's Song," dedicated to Andrew Jeffrey Drake, Nantucket's newest native son. Jeffrey was attentive to Tess; he was concerned about her, but she looked great, she looked happy. She kissed Jeffrey full on the lips; he tasted the sweet tang of the champagne she was drinking.

That night, Tess got so drunk that she (famously) forgot to put in her diaphragm. Nine months later, the twins were born.

Andrea sighed. She was teary. She was always teary during her time in the farm attic with Jeffrey, because it was like reliving secret, stolen time with Tess, but this story made her teary for a different reason. This was the Greatest Story Ever Told—the story of a woman who deserved something good who hung in there and persevered and got something miraculous. Not one healthy baby, but two, a boy and a girl, a perfect matched set. Andrea could remember holding Finn in his bunting at the hospital, and Tess was glowing like the Virgin Mary (never mind that the conception had been less than immaculate, including as it had six glasses of Moët & Chandon). Tess asked Andrea at that moment if she would be Finn's godmother and Andrea said, "Oh my God, I would be so honored." As if she hadn't been expecting it.

Tess said, "I'd like to thank you for not lecturing me when we were stuck on top of that godforsaken mountain at Canyon Ranch. I don't think I could have handled it."

Andrea said, "I had my speech all prepared."

Tess said, "I did okay without the speech. I finally, finally did okay."

Andrea said, "You did better than okay, honey. These children are beautiful."

Tess said, "So I just have one other question."

"Shoot."

"Will you be Chloe's godmother?"

"Oh my God," Andrea said as she sank onto the side of the bed next to Tess, because this she had not been expecting, this was an embarrassment of riches, two darling babies to guide spiritually, the way she had been guided by her mother's sister Katharine, the way Tess had been guided by her Aunt Agropina. They were, Andrea felt at that moment, all going to be okay. "I would be so honored."

JEFFREY

He was going to give them one shining moment together before things fell apart.

And really, it should be his wife telling this, she was better at it than he was, she remembered every last detail about each one of their group trips, down to what they ordered for dinner, who sat next to whom on the airplane, and what the bar bill was at the end of the night. But Delilah wasn't available and this story needed to be told, even purely as an antidote to the sad and difficult material that came before and to what was yet to come.

South Beach! Miami!

There had been so many great things about this trip, but perhaps the greatest thing was that it was spontaneous, pulled together in five days.

It had been the most brutal winter of all time. Brutal! The temperatures were in double-digit minus figures for a week straight. The harbor was frozen and the Coast Guard had to send an ice cutter through so the steamship could make it back with fuel and food. Even so, the Stop & Shop was poorly stocked and the butcher was closed. The Begonia was open, technically, though only half the menu was available, and one night they ran out of draft beer completely and there was nearly a riot. It was that awful second week of February when the realization hit: *there was no more football.* Nothing to do on Sundays but eat too much, drink too much, read the paper, and play Scrabble, which was what the eight of them did. Barney and Drew were four and two and the twins were three, and all of them had perpetual head colds and runny noses, which were impossible to beat. You kept them home, you gave them Campbell's chicken soup with stars and let them watch unlimited episodes of *Caillou* and *Miss Spider,* they got better, then you put them back into the petri dish that was preschool and they got sick again. The situation was wearing on everyone. Around their harvest table, Jeffrey saw his wife and their six dearest friends looking pudgy, pale, listless, and crabby. They each had a section of the *Times* (dealt out like poker hands; it was very much the luck of the draw, except that Phoebe always got Sunday Styles), and on that particular awful football-less slate-gray ten-below-zero day, Jeffrey had the Travel section. He was halfway through his third Kahlua coffee (to which he had, uncharacteristically, added a shot of whiskey) and the cover photo—a bunch of half-naked people drinking mango mojitos in South Beach—seemed to mock him.

That is where we should be, he thought.

Then he thought, *That is where we should be.*

He excused himself from the table. The Scrabble game was growing predictable anyway, with Addison trying to get away with the word *qat* once again. He claimed it was Russian for "hat," and since he was the linguistic expert among them, no one bothered to contest it. Though today Delilah was in a combative mood and said, "No foreign words."

"What?" Addison said. "You can't make that rule *now.*"

Delilah said, "I should have made it seven years ago."

Jeffrey slipped over to the computer in the corner of the kitchen, taking his Kahlúa/whiskey coffee and the Travel section with him. He proceeded cautiously; he read the fine print, he clicked on every link. South Beach: this was, he realized, simply a reinvented, reimagined version of the Miami Beach his parents and grandparents had visited a generation before. Except now it was Cuban food and nightclubs with monosyllabic names like The Drink and BED. Now it was cocktails made with freshly squeezed fruit and vegetable juices and art deco hotels with rooms draped in white Egyptian cotton. One might not think that South Beach was a farmer's kind of place, but it was eighty-seven degrees in South Beach and sunny. Jeffrey was going to make this happen.

Ninety minutes later (with breaks to refill his "coffee" and change the DVD for the kids, with seven answers over to the table of "I'm working on something here, give me a minute"), he had reserved eight tickets on American Airlines, Boston to Miami, for $237 per person. And he had, on hold, the penthouse suite at the Sagamore Hotel, which was locked in like a Lego between the art deco gems of the National and the Loews. The penthouse slept eight and cost $1050 per night. It was less per person than

the Radisson in Hyannis in the height of summer. The last piece
of the puzzle was baby-sitting. The Kapenashes always used
Mrs. Parks, the retired dispatcher, and for the other kids, Jeffrey
e-mailed the Bulgarian twins, Lana and Vesselina, who had worked
at the farm market the summer before and who had (unwisely)
decided to stay on Nantucket for the winter. To see what it was
like! (Did it rival a former Communist bloc country in the gray
and dismal department? How about twenty-four hours with no
bread at the supermarket?) Jeffrey and the Bulgarian twins joked
about how bad the winter was, how boring, how cold. Would
they want to make an extra five hundred bucks baby-sitting?

Their response came back: *We want to go to South Beach, too!
Only kidding! Yes to baby-sit!*

Jeffrey stood up from the computer with all the details written
down on a sheet from Delilah's to-do pad. He turned down the
music and cleared his throat. The five Kahlúa/whiskey coffees
made him feel light and giddy and unlike his usual self. He, the
parsimonious farmer, had single-handedly booked a trip to South
Beach, Miami! If he wanted to go, he knew they would want
to go.

He was right. They jumped for joy! They let go a group cheer.
They toasted one another and they toasted him. Imagine! Jeffrey!
Leaving Friday! They vowed to buy Lana and Vesselina and Mrs.
Parks truly fabulous thank-you gifts. Addison said he had a friend
who owned a sushi restaurant right there on Lincoln Road. Greg
had played in a band with a guy who was now the DJ at the underground club at the Delano. Whoo-hoo! It was the best vacation they'd ever taken, and they hadn't even left yet.

Phoebe went to the tanning booth twice the week before their
flight and burned the skin off her nose, but no matter. Tess didn't
have a single bikini that fit; the scale at the gym said she had gained
seven pounds since the summer. But who cared? It snowed again
on Wednesday and again school was canceled and again Jeffrey
and Delilah were trapped in the house with two rambunctious

little boys who wanted nothing more to do with Delilah's home-made Play-Doh and other indoor distractions. Delilah said, "I'm going to miss them so much! But not really." She made six dozen chocolate chip cookies and three dozen peanut butter cookies with chocolate kisses. "Mommy and Daddy are going to be gone for seven days!"

They arrived at the airport in full-length down coats. Phoebe wore her fur hat with the ear flaps, which the Chief jokingly called her Russian qat. Their flight to Boston was canceled because of weather in Boston, even though on Nantucket it was bright and sunny, with a wind-chill factor of minus twenty-two.

Addison worked his magic with the woman behind the Cape Air desk, and they were on the next flight to Providence and had been rerouted from Providence to Miami. Piece of cake. One stop at Au Bon Pain, an issue of the *Economist* front to back, and a twenty-minute nap later, Jeffrey's plan had come to fruition. They stepped off the plane in Miami, Florida. They shed their coats, gloves, scarves, and the Russian qat and followed the man holding the sign that said "The Castaways" to the limo.

Is it possible to tell a story that is happy from start to finish? Doesn't the word *story* mean that there is conflict, then resolution? Maybe the trip to South Beach didn't properly qualify as a story, because all Jeffrey remembered was good upon good, best upon better. They asked the limo driver to stop at the liquor store on the way to the hotel. They bought champagne, Patrón, Mount Gay, white wine, a case of Corona, tonic, seltzer, Coke, limes, lemons, bottled water, pretzels, peanuts, sesame sticks, potato chips, nacho chips, bottled salsa, bubble gum, and a scratch card. The scratch card was a winner, the Chief announced: five hundred dollars. Everyone thought he was kidding; each of them bought scratch cards from time to time, and no one had ever won more than two bucks.

"I'm serious," he said.

Delilah checked and let out a hoot. Five hundred dollars! They couldn't believe it! It was, at that moment, better than world peace. The Chief cashed the card, collected the money, and paid the bill. He had enough money left over to pay the limo driver and tip the bellman at the hotel who was responsible for their sixteen bags.

The Sagamore was cool and white and filled with avant-garde objets d'art. The concierge was a lean Frenchwoman named Geneviève who had platinum blond hair in a geometric cut. Upon their arrival, she handed out lasciviously pink raspberry caiprihanas, along with ripe pieces of mango dipped in sea salt. Geneviève led them through a secret passageway to a space-age elevator that jetted them up to the penthouse suite.

The penthouse suite was all white, as promised, with mirrors and sleek, cutting-edge electronics. There were four identical white bedrooms lined up to overlook the ocean. Each bedroom was dominated by a king bed iced with butter cream and dotted with fondant pillows. The bathrooms were white tile and white marble threaded with gold. There was a living area with white leather sofas and high-design glass tables; there was a "kitchen," which consisted of a fridge to store the liquor and a counter on which to cut the lime wedges and spill the snacks. Addison did both things in short order.

The place was heaven—not just heavenly, but heaven, as in the place Jeffrey wanted to go to when he died. Always when he checked into a hotel, his first instinct was to make love to his wife, and he had that instinct right now. He led Delilah wordlessly into their white bathroom, peeled off her winter clothes, and began to kiss her.

"Do you love it here?" he asked.

But she was too happy to answer.

Later he lounged on the green-and-white-striped canvas furniture on the impressive penthouse balcony, drinking a Corona, inhaling the view across the white beach and the ocean as if it were a drug.

He did not remember every hour of the vacation as clearly as those first hours, but he did remember certain things. Sprawling with Delilah on the white-cushioned papasan by the shimmering turquoise pool, debating the pros and cons of going to war with Iraq with Addison, who lay next to a sleeping Phoebe in the neighboring chaise. All the women—and the men—around the pool were beautiful. They were thin and tanned and wore designer sunglasses and sleek bathing suits and white, flowing coverups. They spoke French or Portuguese, they kissed on both cheeks, they ordered the huge salade Niçoise for lunch and ate only the olives. They ordered cold, sweating bottles of white wine and drank them the way Jeffrey and the others drank water (which came in cylindrical glass bottles that cost twelve dollars apiece). It was hot in South Beach, eighty-seven, eighty-nine, ninety-four. Delilah was Mediterranean, she turned brown as a nut in one afternoon, but Jeffrey was a farmer. He respected the sun, he knew what it could do. He dunked frequently in the pool, he drank four bottles of the expensive Dutch water, he moved under the umbrella to play dice with Greg and the Chief.

They always tried to fit in wherever they went, to respect the sense of place. In Vegas they had gambled and driven to see the Hoover Dam. In London it was Buckingham Palace and the crown jewels. At the Point, in Saranac Lake, they canoed and hiked and cooked over a fire. In South Beach, it was clear from the beginning, they did not blend. They were as obvious as a pack of grizzly bears—the unhealthy pallor, the flab, the Red Sox hats to shield their eyes from the sun. Andrea, in her black tank suit, did actual *laps* in the swimming pool, and their fabulous European fellow guests watched her with undisguised interest, as though she were some kind of curious wildlife.

A woman doing the butterfly stroke in the pool!

The ladies went shopping on Lincoln Road. They were in and out of BCBG, Ralph Lauren, Lilly Pulitzer, AG, Lucky Jeans, and a bunch of boutiques that sold sequined dresses and over-the-knee white snakeskin boots. All the women bought new sunglasses at Aspen Optical, even Andrea, who couldn't have told you whether Tom Ford was a fashion designer or a car salesman; even Tess, who couldn't afford them. The new sunglasses were big and round, with gold bling decorating the sides. The women put on their new sunglasses and mugged for the Chief's camera.

"We're getting there," Delilah said.

They had to change their internal clocks. They drank triple espressos in the morning, skipped breakfast, took a nap by the pool, drank iced tea and expensive Dutch water, picked at a light lunch (did they even serve carbohydrates in South Beach?), walked on the beach, shopped frivolously, savored a café con leche at the Cuban place on the corner, called the kids to check in, then . . .

Then the day began. They opened Coronas and slipped in wedges of lime, the girls popped champagne and filled up slender flutes, they toasted one another, they took deep, grateful drinks. They showered and lounged on the impressive balcony while wearing the hotel's waffled robes. They snacked on sesame sticks and sliced mango with sea salt. It was seven-thirty, the sun was setting, they made love discreetly behind closed doors while "getting dressed." Greg played Buffett and James Taylor's "Mexico" and then, once the sun set, he swung into Sinatra and Bobby Darin and they all gathered in their silk and sequins, heels and perfume, ready to leave for dinner. Their reservation was at nine o'clock.

Nine o'clock! At home they would have eaten pot roast at five-thirty, been finished and cleaned up by six, had the kids in bed with stories by six-thirty, and been back down with the dishwasher churning at seven, while outside snow piled up or the wind screamed like a woman in agony. Some nights they watched reruns of *The Sopranos,* some nights they rented movies, some nights they crawled into bed at seven-thirty with the latest David McCullough tome and fell asleep after ten pages. Some nights they cleaved to each other and made love despite being weighed down by the layers of flannel, chenille, and goose down. Every night, save for the ones when they gathered at the Begonia, they were fast asleep by nine o'clock.

But not in South Beach! In South Beach they arrived at the threshold of the restaurant at nine o'clock and were escorted to their table, where they sat, without deviation, in this order: Phoebe, Addison, Tess, Greg, Delilah, Jeffrey, Andrea, the Chief. They were a strand of DNA, repeated, then repeated again. They ate things like sushi and soft-shell crabs in a Meyer lemon reduction, and they shared desserts with passion-fruit foam and honeycombed pineapple. They drank wine at dinner and ended with shots of Sambuca or sips of tequila. And then, feeling happy-happyhappy and *ready to go,* they cabbed it to a nightclub. At the first nightclub, BED, the doorman had their names on a list, provided by Geneviève, and they were whisked past the waiting mob (made up mostly of teenagers, Jeffrey noticed; truly, to fit in in South Beach, they needed to be twenty years younger). They were shown to an alcove with two cocktail tables pushed together and four ultrasuede cubes where they could sit, should they want to sit.

They looked out over the dance floor, at more gorgeous Europeans lounging on round beds in the midst of a sea of gyrating young bodies.

Jeffrey ordered a bottle of champagne and a bottle of Grey Goose and tonic and lemons. A beer for the Chief (twenty dollars) and four bottles of Icelandic water. They came with a dish of salted cashews, presumably complimentary, delivered by their preternaturally beautiful (though scowling) cocktail waitress. She poured everyone a drink with disdain. (She knew their type—married thirty- and forty-somethings, probably with a stable of kids back home, wherever they lived, Peoria or East Bumblefuck, Idaho.) Jeffrey took a sip of his ice-cold vodka tonic with a twist and declared it an elixir of youth. He was ready to dance.

They let loose in a wild, free, sexual way. Jeffrey had never moved his body like this in public. There had been some crazy parties at Cornell, of course, but this was elemental, tribal, it was a trip to the moon. Jeffrey was released. Was he thirty-eight? The father of two small boys? The owner of a hundred and sixty-two acres of permafrosted land? It didn't matter. He took off his jacket, slid off his tie, unbuttoned his shirt. He was sweating, he was breathless, he was dancing, he was living!

And he was not alone. There, like satellite planets coming in and out of his orbit, were Greg, Phoebe, Delilah, the Chief, Tess—and a guy Jeffrey didn't recognize, an interloper who was getting awfully close to Phoebe. Jeffrey was aware of this much, and he was about to ask the guy to step back. Phoebe could not be counted upon to protect her own airspace; she seemed not even to notice this guy.

Then Jeffrey realized the interloper was Addison without his glasses. He had taken his glasses off, he was sweating too profusely, they would slip off, the dancing was so wild, they would fall off. The reason the interloper kept bumping into people was because it was Addison, the sight-impaired. He could not see a damn thing without his glasses, and Jeffrey wondered what it felt like to be dancing in a blur of bodies, to be reliant on sound, smell, touch. Jeffrey wanted to be Addison.

Just then a cry went up and Jeffrey was nudged in the ribs. He turned. It was the Chief, pointing. Across the dance floor there was an elevated stage with two poles. There were two women dancing, three women, four women.

"Look at the girls!" the Chief shouted.

The girls, the women—Delilah, Phoebe, Tess, and Andrea—were all up onstage, spinning around poles, lifting their legs, throwing their heads back. Phoebe was the most beautiful of the four women, and the best dressed, in a short go-go number of red-and-orange fringe. But she was the weakest dancer—spaced out, she was a cross between a Deadhead and bad Twyla Tharp.

Tess was adorable and Gidgety in her white pants and navy striped nautical top; she had been born to do the twist. These two used their good judgment and hopped down from the stage into the arms of the strapping black bouncers. This left Delilah and Andrea. Jeffrey—and everyone else on the dance floor—was mesmerized. They danced separately with their poles in a surprisingly erotic way (okay, Delilah had watched a lot of *Sopranos* episodes this winter, but where had Andrea learned to pole-dance?). Then they came together in a sensual, crowd-pleasing moment, and Jeffrey felt aroused, then disturbed. The only two women he'd ever made love to—well, it was powerful to see them together like that.

They kissed once, briefly but passionately, and Jeffrey's heart stopped, went into free-fall, then started again, pounding in sync with the bass. The Chief whistled, then pounded Jeffrey on the back.

"Look at our girls!" The Chief's tone of voice said it all: this was enough fantasy to last him the rest of his life!

As for Jeffrey, well, what was he to think? How to process this? The only two women he had ever loved had kissed each other. Jeffrey's past and his present, his present and his future . . . he wasn't sure what was going on inside him.

Addison said, "What just happened?"

He couldn't see. He'd missed it!

Jeffrey kept dancing. He spun around, he put his hands in the air. Those were his women, this was his entourage. They either fit in or stuck out, he was either not himself or more himself than he'd ever been before. He was hot and more than hot, he was warm, finally warm. This had been his idea. His idea! He was in heaven. They all were.

ADDISON

*Are you going to tell him? Are you going to tell him you love me?
I'm afraid.*

I'm afraid you won't get it.

The $9.2 million deal closed without a hitch, and Wheeler
Realty received a check for $368,000, half of which went into
Addison's pocket. Normally this would have been cause for cel-
ebration (corporate and personal), but Addison was distracted.

What to do with Tess's cell phone?

He had flat-out lied to the Chief. Addison was by no means
an honest person—he was a real estate agent, after all, prone to
stretching the truth, and he had for six months concealed his
affair with Tess. But something about looking Ed Kapenash in
the eye and flat-out lying about Tess's phone instilled fear and
shame.

Should Addison come clean? Tell Ed that yes, he had the phone?
Show Ed the text messages? Tess was afraid—of the water, of
Greg, of something more nebulous? There was no way to figure
out what had happened on the boat. The Chief had one idea;
Addison had another. Should Addison confess to the affair?
What would that help? It would help nothing, he decided. It
would only hurt.

Addison tucked Tess's iPhone in the top drawer of his desk,
which locked with a key. Addison had one key and Florabel had
a spare key swimming in the ashtray where she kept paper clips,
rubber bands, and safety pins. The Chief would never find Tess's
phone in Addison's top drawer, though it was the obvious first
place to look. Should Addison move it? Take it home or put it in
his car? The skin on the phone was traffic-light yellow, bright as
an alarm, impossible to miss. Would Phoebe find it?

He pulled the two pieces of the felt heart from his pocket.
He was not only emotionally feeble, but mentally feeble as well.

He believed that this heart had power, that it meant something. As he handled it, it ripped again. The heart was disintegrating. Was this a sign? Addison could not accept it as a sign.

Florabel loomed over his desk. She eyed the torn, misshapen pieces of heart on his desk.

"What is that?" She sounded disgusted, as if they were pieces of pig heart.

"Nothing," he said.

"You need to pull yourself together, Dealer," Florabel said. As ever, the woman was speaking the brutal truth. She slapped a whopper of a check down on his desk, covering the scraps of felt. "There's some money. Go get yourself a shrink."

DELILAH

Thoughts of escape occupied her at all times, the way some people, she supposed, fantasized about sex with Robert Downey Jr., or winning the lottery and buying a power yacht, or being selected for *American Idol.* Freedom had always been Delilah's drug of choice, and now, who could blame her? Tess and Greg were dead, everything was painful; even breathing hurt. Delilah dreamed about living alone in the South of France, riding a funny European bicycle down a path cut between fields of lavender toward a charming village where she would buy a baguette and runny Camembert and a bottle of wine that would aid her quest to block out everything that came before—her life on Nantucket, her friends, her husband, her children.

She used to love a crowd, she used to demand the company of others, but now she wanted only to be alone.

And even that wasn't quite true. She couldn't stand herself. She wanted to unzip her body and step out of it. She wanted to be attached to a machine that would erase her memory, obliterate her guilt, wipe her clean.

She had run away once before, in high school. There had been no reason for it other than boredom, a standard-issue teenage restlessness, and a desire to see what other possibilities the world contained. Delilah had had a pleasant childhood and a less-pleasant-but-still-okay adolescence, growing up in South Haven, on the shores of Lake Michigan. Delilah's father, Nico Ashby, was a real estate developer, responsible for the burgeoning suburban sprawl in the acreage just off the lake. He brought South Haven Taco Bell, Blockbuster, I Can't Believe It's Yogurt, Lucky Nail Salon, Subway, Stride Rite Shoes, and Mailboxes, Etc. He also had his hand in the bigger, uglier, more egregious development along Route 31 toward St. Joe's—the Wal-Mart with its attendant Big Boy Diner, the Staples, the eighteen-theater Cineplex, the Applebee's, the Borders. Nico Ashby and his wife and two daughters lived in a stunning Victorian house on the bluff that overlooked the town harbor and the South Haven Yacht Club (where Nico had been president for nine years). Nico was a local hero—a successful businessman, a philanthropist, a member of Rotary and the Lions Club, a model husband and father, a big, good-looking guy with a full head of dark hair, a bronze tan in three seasons, and a booming laugh. Nico Ashby—everyone knew him, everyone liked him.

Delilah's mother, Connie Ashby, née Albertson, was short, dark-haired, trim, pretty, and obsessed with the following things: her person (exercising, hair, skin, nails, and clothes, clothes, clothes), her daughters (bake sales, Girl Scouts, summer camp, decorating for school dances), and her husband. She met Nico at Michigan State; he was a starting linebacker, she was a cheerleader, petite enough to serve as the top of the human pyramid, the cherry on the ice-cream sundae. And yes, these people really got married. They were beautiful and blessed, they were successful, they had gorgeous, healthy daughters.

Delilah was loved and encouraged. She was brilliant in school, a fact that made her parents proud, but Delilah's precocity also allowed her the time and leeway to goof off. Delilah, as a teenager, was not beautiful. Her hair was too wild and curly; she wore braces for years. She had huge breasts and the rear end to counterbalance it. She was *voluptuous,* her mother said, but Connie Ashby weighed ninety pounds soaking wet (as did Delilah's sister, Caitlin), and it was clear that having a voluptuous daughter perplexed her.

Boys did not love Delilah, but they liked her. Her best friends were all boys, the best-looking boys in her class—the athletes, the dope smokers, the clowns. They liked her whip-smart sense of humor, her sense of freedom. Delilah Ashby was not afraid of anyone.

She ran away in early May, when the periphery of the lake was blooming with dogwoods and azaleas. The Ashby family had just gotten back from a week in Fort Lauderdale, where Delilah had looked upon the university students on spring break with envy. Freedom! She dreamed of a highway with no one on it, a deserted stretch of beach, an endless ribbon of blue sea, a grid of city blocks where no one knew her name and no one expected her to show up for lacrosse practice or memorize theorems or sit down to dinner at six and contribute to the conversation. Delilah itched, she could not sleep, the house was suffocating her. School and the kids in it—even Dean Markbury, whom she loved with the ferocity of a lion—were slowly killing her with their predictable sameness. She had to get out.

She needed money. She had saved seven hundred dollars from baby-sitting, and over the course of four days she stole. She stole from her father's wallet, from her mother's stash for tipping the manicurist, from petty cash in the kitchen drawer where the family grabbed five or ten dollars for the offering basket at church. She stockpiled a thousand dollars. She estimated it would last her three weeks.

She left in the middle of the night on her bike. In her backpack was the money, two bottles of water, an extra pair of jeans, a bra, five pairs of underwear, three tissue-thin T-shirts, her lacrosse workout clothes, sunglasses, flip-flops, and a box of Pop-Tarts. It was all she could ever imagine needing.

She had left a note on the kitchen table in the spot where members of her family normally left notes for one another. She had given the note careful thought. It said, *See ya!* Delilah wanted her parents to know that a) she had not been abducted, but rather was walking away from this nice life of her own volition, and b) she was not leaving in anger, but rather in the spirit of self-discovery. "See ya!" would also, hopefully, keep her mother from completely losing her mind, implying as it did that mother and daughter would set eyes on each other again. Delilah, although self-centered and self-absorbed, realized that what she was doing would destroy her parents as well as thirteen-year-old Caitlin, who worshipped her. (Delilah had peeked in on Caitlin before she left. Caitlin was breathing heavily through her orthodontic headgear. The sight of her and the knowledge of Caitlin's deep impending sorrow almost kept Delilah from going.) But Delilah was infected with the desire to be FREE, and once she was biking along the Blue Star Highway, her spirit soared. She was headed to Saugatuck, where she would catch a bus to Grand Rapids, and in Grand Rapids she would catch the bus to New York, where she would catch the Chinatown bus to Boston, and in Boston she would take the Plymouth & Brockton line to Hyannis. From Hyannis she would ride the ferry to Nantucket Island, a destination she had discovered in the pages of *National Geographic,* which she read in the high school library while she was supposed to be researching a paper on Blaise Pascal. She stumbled across the article about Nantucket by accident, but she was captivated by the way it looked—all quaint and historic and New Englandy. It looked like home.

And God, what a feeling when the bus pulled out of the depot, when the driver punched her ticket and said, "In Grand Rapids, head to bay nine. Bus to New York City." The sensation of miles of asphalt putting time and distance between Delilah and the life that held her down titillated her. She wasn't running from anything, she wasn't running toward anything—she was just running for running's sake, and it was a drug: the blurred landscape out the window was a soothing poultice for her itch. Go, go, go!

She transferred buses in Grand Rapids. Peed in the terminal, bought some peanut butter crackers because somewhere in her head was her mother's voice nagging her about protein. She had both seats to herself practically the whole way to New York. She stretched out and used her backpack as a pillow, she read seventeen of the *Complete Stories of John Cheever,* which had been assigned in her English class. She noted, with a certain satisfaction, the difference between reading a book because it was assigned and reading a book because she wanted to. Which led her to her next quasi-intellectual thought, which concerned Henry David Thoreau and his desire to live deliberately.

And that, Delilah decided, was why she had hopped on this bus. She was going to Nantucket Island because she wanted to live deliberately, she wanted to choose her path every second of her existence, she wanted to cultivate a heightened awareness. She was in charge of her well-being; she was her own person. Forget the edicts of home and school, the din of the hallways and the obligation she felt when Dean Markbury handed her a joint. (She had to take a toke to be socially acceptable.) She was free of that now.

Sing it: *Free!*

The bus stopped just before crossing the George Washington Bridge. Delilah had had a seatmate since they stopped in Williamsport, Pennsylvania—a brown-skinned man of indeterminate ethnicity (Salvadoran? Thai? Lebanese?). The man was about fifty and stunningly handsome. He had bulging arms, he wore a tight black T-shirt and jeans, he wore a diamond stud in his left ear and a pair of Ray-Ban Wayfarers. He had nice feathery black hair, and he wore what looked to be an expensive watch. But what was riveting about this man was that he held a pack of cigarettes in his hands the entire time he was on the bus. He opened the pack, inspected the filter ends, counted them perhaps, shut the pack. Opened the pack, pulled a cigarette halfway out, dreamed about lighting up right there on the bus, the inhale, the burn, the satisfaction, the high. The addiction met. Delilah was fascinated with watching his struggle. The want, the can't-have. The need, denied, minute after minute. It was almost sexual, watching this handsome, tough-seeming man, older perhaps than her father, want it want it want it. It was transferable. Delilah wanted a cigarette, too, and she wanted this man. The boys Delilah had known at school had wanted only one thing: to touch her breasts, to ogle them, bare. Would this man also want that? Did he notice her breasts? She breathed deeply, squared her shoulders, tried to edge her breasts into his field of vision. He wanted only the cigarettes.

The bus stopped; the mighty bridge loomed in the windshield. The man stood up, collected his backpack. Delilah was heartbroken. No! He could not leave! Was this even his stop, or was he getting off the bus solely so he could smoke? She wanted to follow him. Who was he, what was his name, where did he live, what country was he from, where was he going, what had he been doing in Williamsport, Pennsylvania ("Home of the Little League World Series," the sign said). There were a thousand stories contained within this man, a thousand stories in Delilah herself and everyone else on this bus, not to mention the thousand stories of the 8 million residents of the city on the other side of the bridge. Delilah watched this man's back—she would never see him again, of this she was sure—and then she eyed the cherry-red cover of the Cheever. It was a grain of sand. The stories that made up the world were infinite, like the stars.

New York to Boston, Boston to Hyannis. Out the window,

Delilah saw the ocean. On the ferry to Nantucket, she scanned the local paper and found several ads for rooms to rent. She craved a small space of her own, a hole in the wall, a hiding place like Anne Frank's where the Nazis wouldn't find her. She was very far away from home, and yet she felt exposed and obvious, as though she had a camera trained on her. She disembarked from the ferry. There were people waiting on the dock, but none of the people was waiting for her. She was a sixteen-year-old girl who had traveled twelve hundred miles to get here, to Nantucket Island, her newly discovered spiritual home.

The best thing about Nantucket was that it fulfilled its promises. It looked exactly as it did in the magazine. If anything, the air was more rarefied than Delilah expected—it was fresh, and filled with salt spray, evergreen scent, and fog. Delilah found a pay phone on the wharf and started dialing numbers from the ads in the newspaper. The first place she called had already filled the room, the second place ditto. The third place ditto, and this worried Delilah, because everyone knew the third time was a charm. At the fourth number, no one answered. Delilah filled with a hot, prickly panic. This was an island—she *had* to find a place to stay. It wasn't like she could just move a town over. The fifth place had to work (there were only five ads), but the man who answered the telephone asked Delilah how old she was (she said nineteen) and then what she looked like. Delilah had heard all the requisite warnings about people who didn't have her best interest at heart. She hung up. It was four-thirty in the afternoon. She was dangerously close to screaming out, *What have I done?*

Deep breath. She called the fourth place back, let the phone ring fifteen times, and after the sixteenth time someone answered. A little old lady. Yes, the room was still available. The room was free of charge. The woman—Tennie Gulliver, her name was—just wanted someone else in the house, someone to take out the trash, which she could no longer do, someone to be around in case the unthinkable happened. Delilah would be responsible for paying a quarter of the electric bill in addition to her phone charges. Okay?

"Okay," Delilah said.

Tennie Gulliver gave Delilah directions; she could walk from the wharf. Delilah slung her bag over her shoulder and walked through Nantucket town. The houses were dignified and old-fashioned; they had window boxes planted with geraniums and majestic front doors. There were lights coming on and cooking smells. Delilah crossed the cobblestones, she walked up brick sidewalks past galleries and restaurants and antique shops, an ice-cream parlor, a jewelry store.

Tennie Gulliver's house was on Pine Street, just off Main. It was an ancient among the elderly; the plaque on the front of the house said it had been built in 1704. The house stooped and sagged. The shingles were mildewed and the white paint of the trim was flaking away.

Delilah dropped the big brass knocker and waited a long time, long enough that she began to wonder if the unthinkable had happened to Tennie Gulliver between the time she had hung up the phone and now. But finally there was the sound of the lock being undone and the door swung open and there was Tennie Gulliver, all eighty-five pounds of her, with her white, cottony hair and her shrunken apple face and her cane. Tennie Gulliver looked exactly as Delilah had expected (a bit of a disappointment, since Delilah loved to be taken by surprise)—like the old woman who lived in a shoe.

It was as though Delilah had not only traveled twelve hundred miles across the country but also a hundred and twenty years back in time. Tennie Gulliver lit her main room with candles and the kitchen with a dim overhead bulb. ("I need proper light when I'm cooking!" Tennie said.) There was radio, but no TV. A rotary phone, but no answering machine. A gas stove, but no microwave. Delilah's room would be upstairs; there were in fact five bedrooms upstairs, and Delilah could have any one of them, Tennie said. Tennie's bedroom was on the first floor; it was the den, converted, because Tennie could no longer negotiate the stairs.

"Okay!" Delilah said. She liked the idea of having her choice of five bedrooms, of inhabiting all five on successive nights, like a girl who lived in a castle.

Actually, there was something about being here on Nantucket on her own, in this old, old house with this old, old woman, that made Delilah feel not like an adult but like a child.

As if reading her mind, Tennie said, "How old are you?"

Delilah lied. "Nineteen."

Tennie said, "Do you need a job?"

Delilah paused, thinking about her eight hundred and eighty-five remaining dollars. Despite her free rent, she would have to work. She had not thought about any particular job beyond her job of living deliberately. But she would have to make money deliberately.

She said, "I baby-sit."

Tennie stared. Could she hear? Her ears were like small white shells, but they were unencumbered by the beige hearing aids that Delilah's grandparents wore.

Delilah said, "Do you have grandchildren?"

Tennie said, "Vern's last name is Snow. He's the son I had with my first husband. The son I had with my second husband, Mr. Gulliver, Gully, lives in Sconset. He chops firewood for a living and should be avoided."

Delilah nodded. Everybody had a thousand stories.

"I'm going to heat up a lobster pie. You'll eat?"

"Yes," Delilah said. "Thank you." She lugged her backpack up the steep, narrow staircase. The five bedrooms upstairs were prim, spare, spinsterish, as appealing as five bedrooms in a convent or a nursing home. They were much alike, but Delilah claimed the only one with a double bed. The bed was about five feet off the ground; it was a bed for a giant. Delilah would need to stand on a chair just to climb up on top of its white chenille spread and lay her head on the stiff pillows. There was a nightstand with a dainty lamp made of milk glass wearing a fringed shade that looked like an old lady's church hat. There was a bureau that had twenty-seven drawers, and next to the bureau was a dressing table that supported a triptych mirror, open like a book. Delilah sat at the dressing table and looked at herself in the triptych mirror. She looked at herself deliberately.

She was safe here.

Delilah woke up the next morning in a fresh mood. It was the first day of her new life.

She could do whatever she wanted. So this, she thought, was freedom. What did she *want* to do? What did *she* want to do, really? Go for a walk? Spend money on a restaurant breakfast? Lie in bed for an hour and read Cheever? She descended the stairs to find Tennie making buttermilk biscuits and bacon and brewing some wicked-smelling coffee.

Tennie said, "You'll eat?"

Delilah breathed in, breathed out. It was amazing the obligation she felt, even to this woman whom she'd known only half a day. Did she *want* to eat breakfast with Tennie? She meant to stick to her guns, hold sacred her duty to herself. The bacon was crisp, the biscuits looked fluffy, and Tennie set out a pot of softened butter. There was cream for the coffee—real cream! Delilah's mother bought only fat-free lightener, and hence Delilah had never learned to like coffee. And Delilah's mother *never* cooked bacon. Full of nitrites, she said.

"Yes," Delilah said.

From now on Delilah's life would include bacon, and coffee with real cream and two teaspoons of sugar. And Delilah would get the biscuit recipe.

"You'll go see Vern about the job?" Tennie said.

Delilah was confused. What job?

"Where?" she said.

"Lobster restaurant," Tennie said. "In town. You can't miss it."

Delilah did not want to work in a restaurant. Dean Markbury waited tables at Denny's, plunking down Grand Slam breakfasts and club sandwiches for two dollars an hour. He had to wear polyester pants. But what if Delilah had no choice?

She pulled apart her biscuit; the flaky layers were like the pages of a book. She wanted to learn to cook. She wanted to meet the black sheep woodcutting son, who in Delilah's mind looked exactly like the man on the bus, and get married.

Or not. She would see.

Nantucket town on a mellow spring morning: no tourists to speak of, shopkeepers sweeping geranium petals off the brick sidewalk. They smiled at Delilah, and stared at her a few extra seconds, trying to place her. *Is that so-and-so's daughter? No, no, it's someone else, I don't know who that is.* It was liberating to be a stranger.

She found Vern's on her own. It was impossible to miss, at the base of Main Street. The sign in front said "Vern's" and another sign said "Lobster." Delilah wandered in. Well, it wasn't Denny's. There was a dark wood bar lined with tall stools, the seats of which were made from upside-down lobster pots. There were scarred wooden tables and hanging fishing nets and brass portholes fixed into the wall and green and red port and starboard lights. The door had been left wide open; a sweating glass of water and a bowl of lemons were on the bar. Delilah thought maybe the place was open for lunch, but it was empty.

"Hello?" she called out.

A muted TV was on over the bar—it was the midday news—and Delilah filled with dread. She did not want to think about the outside world, about Michigan or her weeping family. She watched the screen for a second—bad house fire in a place called Dedham. There were hundreds of millions of people in this country;

Delilah Ashby gone missing would not register beyond the limits of the South Haven School District. Right?

A man came out of the kitchen wearing brown rubber pants held up by suspenders.

"Hi," he said. "You're the girl living with Ma?"

This was Vern. He had thinning blond hair and a permanent sunburn and a thick New England accent. He said he would hire her even though she had no experience, because she could stay the whole season, right? She wasn't going to leave him in the lurch in the middle of August like Little Miss Smarty-Pants from Radcliffe, right? Right, Delilah said. He told her she could expect to make a hundred dollars in tips a night. The lobster dinner was $29.95 and included baked potato, corn on the cob, homemade coleslaw, and a dinner roll. Most people liked to start with a bowl of chowder or a plate of steamers, and most people liked a glass of chardonnay or an ice-cold beer, sometimes two or three of these, and then most people could not turn down the homemade pies, all in season—this week was lemon meringue—and hence the average bill was up there.

"Come Friday at three and I'll train you," Vern said. "Bring your working papers."

Working papers? Delilah fretted. She stood up to leave. What would she do about working papers?

"Before you go," Vern said. He nodded her back to the kitchen, and a warning bell went off in Delilah's head. Was this where he tried to have his way with her? And if he did try to have his way with her, might he forgive the fact that she didn't have working papers?

She followed Vern into the kitchen. It was immaculate—shiny countertops, sparkling stainless steel. In the sink was a wire bucket of clams. Vern took a shell out and pried it open with a short, dull knife.

"Cherrystones," he said. "Went out this morning myself and got 'em."

Delilah peered at the snotlike globule attached to its home shell.

"Mmmm-hmm," she said.

"Go ahead," Vern said.

Go ahead what? she thought. Touch it? Take it home? She smiled, sort of.

"Eat it," he said.

Eat it? She tried not to make a face. She breathed. If she ate this phlegmy-looking raw mollusk, would he forgive her the lack of working papers? She reached out two pincer fingers; he pried the clam loose with his knife. He was keen for her to taste it, not in a little-boy go-ahead-I-dare-you way, but in an avuncular, professorial way. She held the shell. Was she really going to eat it? She was from the Midwest, where there weren't even any sushi restaurants. Delilah was pretty sure, however, that Thoreau would have eaten the clam; he would have sucked it down for his own edification. Delilah would do the same.

At first it was foreign in her mouth. Slippery, chewy. Then it burst with sweetness. Sugar from saltwater. She swallowed.

Vern said, "Food doesn't get any fresher than that."

Delilah headed back to Tennie's at four o'clock. She chewed on the concrete problem of working papers; it was a relief, actually, to have a concrete problem rather than the abstract ones of whether she would be discovered and whether she was living deliberately or simply falling into another routine.

She opened the door to Tennie's house—she had been given her own key, which she kept clipped to her belt loop—and she heard a man inside. Her heart tripped up a second as she thought of the black sheep son, the woodcutter. She saw a man's head, black hair, visible even over the high-backed chair. A big man.

Tennie said, "Well, hello!" in a tone of voice Delilah had not heard her use before. A saved-for-company voice, or maybe an I'm-in-danger voice. Was Tennie being held captive?

"Hi," Delilah said. She stepped into the living room. The man turned.

It was her father.

One evening after a particularly difficult day, Delilah left the boys with Jeffrey and walked into town. She sat on the curb opposite Tennie Gulliver's house on Pine Street.

Had that story really been true?

Yes, every word, or approximately so, since that was what memory, or memoir, was: an approximation of the truth. Certain things were crystal-clear—eating the raw clam, seeing her father's face—but other things were hazy. Like what she and her father had said to each other on the way home. Or how Nico had actually found her. (When she'd asked him, he said, *I followed your breadcrumbs.*) Or what had made her give up her Thoreau dreams and do what was expected of her: finish high school, attend the University of Michigan, graduate in four years, pack up her room, kiss her parents, and then at the age of twenty-two return to Nantucket, where she was able to secure a job at Vern's as if no time had passed at all. And then she fell in love with the farmer who delivered Vern's corn on the cob and salad greens. She fell in love with Jeffrey Drake, even though he was not the black sheep woodcutter son, Gully, but rather a man just like her father.

Predictable.

Tennie Gulliver had been dead for years, and Vern had sold both Tennie's house and his restaurant, taken the money, and bought a place in Florida. Delilah pictured him now as an older man, eating Grand Slam breakfasts at Denny's. Was he happy?

She fantasized about running away again. Her anger at Andrea Kapenash was a tumor in her lung that was keeping her from breathing properly. Her secret knowledge of Greg's continuing affair with April Peck was an ulcer in her gut, and the guilt of her silence on that final morning was meningitis, inflaming her brain.

Her bones ached with regular old sad sadness. She felt strapped to this island like a crazy person to a bed. If she stayed, she was sure she would die.

Delilah stood up from the curb. A family by the name of Hebner had bought Tennie Gulliver's house, and it looked a lot better now. The Hebners had jacked up the house and squared the foundation; they had replaced windows and painted the trim and replaced the old door knocker with a brass clamshell. Still, it was Tennie's house, the very same house where Delilah had spent exactly one night the May she was sixteen. She had been so brave and so stupid. Delilah was older now by more than double; her own life's circumstances had been squared and given a new coat of paint. But really, nothing had changed.

PHOEBE

They had sent out seven hundred and fifty invitations to the cocktail party that would celebrate Island Conservation's purchase of the ninety-two-acre parcel in the savannah, and they had three hundred and ten people RSVP to say they were coming. Phoebe and Addison had bought benefactor tickets at a thousand dollars apiece, but Phoebe had not heard from Jeffrey and Delilah or the Chief and Andrea. Her own friends! She had sent them invitations with her name as cochair circled in red pen and festooned with stars as a kind of self-deprecating joke, but she hoped the message was clear: this was her thing, and they would be expected to come. Phoebe had a surprise planned, to boot, which they could not miss. Attendance was mandatory at a hundred and fifty bucks a ticket. It wasn't the ticket price that was holding them back, Phoebe knew; both couples could afford it. What was holding them back was their grief, their retreat from everyday normal, happy life. With the state Andrea and Delilah were in, they probably didn't even open their mail.

Phoebe would have to call them. Before, when faced with an unpleasant task, she would take a valium (three, four, six) and operate in a fog. But now she considered her pills poison. She had thrown every last prescription bottle into a shoe box and tucked the shoe box away. She wasn't hiding it from herself; now she was hiding it from Addison.

The necessary evil of the phone calls. Delilah first, because with Delilah things were slightly easier.

"Hello?" Delilah said aggressively. This could be good or bad.

"My benefit?" Phoebe said. "The Island Conservation thing next Friday? You and Jeffrey are coming."

"No."

"Yes, you are. There is no excuse that will work with me. You have to be there. It's the first thing I've chaired in a hundred years."

"I'm not going to anything this summer. This is the summer of no. This is the summer that wasn't."

Well, that was true. In previous summers the eight of them had been out all the time: at the celebrity softball game that benefited the kids' school, at the circus for the Atheneum, at cocktail parties, at the back table at the Company of the Cauldron, at the back bar of 21 Federal, at the summer concert for the Boys & Girls Club, at the Boston Pops benefit for the hospital. This year they had done exactly nothing.

"Understood," Phoebe said. Who was she to talk? She had been on a mental vacation for eight years. "But this you have to come to. This one thing. One night. Mark and Eithne are catering. Mark said he'd make the gougères with the melty cheese in the middle for you especially, okay, darling?"

"Not okay."

"Why not?"

"I won't be here."

"Where will you be?"

Silence. She was either bluffing or being dramatic. She never went away in the summer. Nantucket was Delilah's playground. Nobody enjoyed the island as much as Delilah. At ten o'clock at night you would find her at the turtle pond with her kids, dangling raw chicken from a string, waiting for the calm surface to break. Or grilling three-inch rib-eyes on her back deck, drizzling heirloom tomatoes with olive oil, jumping up and down if her croquet ball actually cleared the wicket. Or singing along as Greg sang "Hey Girl" at the Begonia.

"Where are you going?" Phoebe asked.

"To hell in a handbasket."

"Jesus, Delilah, you're coming to my event, that's all there is to it. Please? For me?"

"I can't."

"I have a surprise for you. A big, happy surprise."

"That's not going to work."

"Sure it is. I'm going to RSVP you for two people. Get a baby-sitter, okay?"

Silence.

"Okay?"

"Okay."

Phoebe could not bring herself to call Andrea. Some disturbing stories had reached Phoebe's ears. Andrea allowed the twins to roam town unsupervised, and she was acting out in other destructive ways. Phoebe could not call up with the frivolous business of a cocktail party. But Andrea and the Chief had to be there. Because of the surprise.

And so Phoebe called the Chief. The dispatcher, Molly, put her right through.

"Hey, Sunshine," the Chief said.

"Hey, Eddie."

"What's up?"

She told him: cocktail party for Island Conservation, her first flight in eight years, it was important to her that he and Andrea come.

"Okay, then, we'll come."

"You will?"

"Of course. I've been wanting to get out of the house. It will be good for Andrea, too. Real good."

Phoebe agreed with this. But wait—she felt funny. This was too easy; Phoebe had questions. Had they gotten the invitation when she sent it? If they had gotten it, why had they not responded? Phoebe had the strange feeling that Andrea had opened the invitation and had thrown it away, or, in her current state of mind, soaked it in gasoline, stuck it in a bottle, and turned it into a Molotov cocktail. Ed normally ran everything past Andrea first; he was the police chief, but everyone knew who the real chief was. It wasn't like him to make plans for both of them like this, without even asking.

"And I have a surprise," Phoebe said. "At the party."

"Is it legal?"

Phoebe laughed. "Yes."

"Well, okay, then. We'll see you next Friday, if not before."

Phoebe hung up. Mission accomplished. She should be happy. But . . . ?

Something felt weird, not quite right on either front. Or maybe what felt wrong was that there had been only two phone calls instead of three. No call to Greg and Tess. She couldn't let herself follow this train of thought, it would do her in, she would become just like the rest of them, singing a song out of tune. She would not think about it. She went out to the pool.

ADDISON

Florabel approached his desk with astonishing news. A couple named Legris Pouffet and Hank Drenmiller had made a full-price offer on the cottage in Quaise. Florabel looked like she was about to burst open like a piñata. Penny candy for everyone! Safe to say that Addison had never seen her this animated. Florabel was a lipstick lesbian, a stunning woman who despised everyone. She had managed the Wheeler Realty office for over a decade, but the first listing Addison had given Florabel to handle, with full commission, was the Quaise cottage, and this only recently, since Tess's death, since Addison could not bear to think about the cottage at all, much less deal with the business of selling it. The cottage was owned by an elderly couple from Princeton, New Jersey; the husband sat on the board of trustees at Lawrenceville, and this was how Addison had met him. The elderly couple had three cowboy children—they lived in places like Cody, Wyoming, and San Antonio, Texas—who had no interest in Nantucket and wanted their parents to sell the place. Sell it, yes, but the couple wanted three million dollars, not a penny less, for a four-hundred-square-foot summer cottage, and because of a three-hundred-year-old Wampanoag cemetery that abutted the property, a covenant was in place stating that the cottage could not be expanded. The cottage was essentially unsellable at that price with those restrictions; it had languished on the market for years.

Addison eyed Florabel suspiciously. "These Puffy Drenmillers know they can't add on, right? They can't tear it down and build something else. They can't touch it. They know this?"

"Yes!" Florabel said. She had told him once that she had been a cheerleader in high school, and as improbable as this had seemed at the time (she was an utter bitch, prone to sniffing at people, granting only her favorites a malicious smile), he now caught a glimpse of her game-day enthusiasm.

"And they still offered three million dollars?"

"Yes!" Florabel said. Her wide blue eyes were about to pop into bouquets of violets. She was genuinely happy. All it had taken was money, a 6 percent commission on three million dollars.

"Okay," Addison said. "Great. Good for you. Write it up." His voice was maudlin. He could not summon even a trace of perfunctory congratulation. He, Addison Wheeler, Wheeler Dealer, who loved nothing more than fresh ink on a purchase-and-sale agreement, who had been known to throw his hat in the air when a financing contingency was waived, who had been known to treat the entire office to a five-course lunch at the Wauwinet when a major property closed, could not even fake a smile in response to the news that an unsellable property had sold.

Florabel, thank God, could not have cared less about Addison's underwhelming response. She just wanted to be smug about her news with everyone in the office, and Addison was her first stop. He had given her the listing, but it had been something of a gag, a white elephant. Florabel had had beginner's luck—well, either that or she had true Realtor's skill, the ability to interface the right buyer with the right property.

She moved on to Arthur Dimmity's desk; Arthur could be counted on to scowl with undisguised envy, which Florabel would find gratifying. Addison should have given the listing to Arthur, he realized now; Arthur would have a hard time with a lemonade stand in the desert. He handled only rentals.

Addison wanted to run out of the office—but wait, he couldn't be too obvious. He counted to ten. The phone rang and no one answered it; it was Florabel's job, but she was too busy gloating. Addison should answer the phone, he knew, to show that answering the phone was not beneath him, and as a tiny concession to Florabel's good news. For all he knew, too, it could be the Puffy Drenmillers, calling to renege. But Addison was too upset to talk to anyone on the phone; he let the call go, so it would be picked up by the general voicemail box.

Behind him, he heard Arthur's strained congratulations. Arthur said, "How did you meet these people, the Drenmillers?"

And Florabel said, "Believe me, you don't want to know."

"Okay," Arthur said amiably (and this was why he wasn't a great salesman; he never pressed the issue). But this time Addison agreed—okay, who cared, nobody, not Arthur, not him, he was having a hard time holding steady. He had to get out of there! He surreptitiously unlocked his top drawer. Tess's iPhone was still there, hidden in the back of the drawer. He checked it every day, and every day it was cold and silent, though to him it hummed and glowed with radioactivity. Today, however, he was looking for keys, but the keys he wanted were not in his drawer—of course not, Florabel had them—but then he found a different set of keys and a thought came to him. Whoa. So many weeks since Tess had died, and he had not thought about the can of bug spray in her garage.

Addison found he could speak to Tess when he was driving because he was alone and moving forward, and the combination of these two things put him in a psychic state where he could communicate with the dead.

They're selling our cottage, he said. *It sold. It will belong to someone else at the end of August.*

His heart was dust. His spirit was the frilled brown edge of a badly fried egg. He was desiccated and dry; his body was filled with crumbly sand. He and Tess had loved that cottage. Addison had told her that he would buy it, he would pay the three million, she could leave Greg and he would leave Phoebe and they could live together in the cottage. Tess had laughed nervously. He was delusional, this wasn't real, it was a fantasy. No one could actually live in that cottage; she couldn't live there. What would she do with her kids?

She had never seen it the way he saw it. She had never been willing to give it all up, to give any of it up. Their affair had been . . . *what,* to her? A way to spend a few hours? A safety net, a security blanket, protection from the marital whiplash that Greg provided daily?

They had fought about it. Addison did not like to admit to himself that they had fought, but they had fought. He loved her insanely, he looked at her across the room when they were all together and couldn't believe she didn't belong to him. He had to endure watching her hold hands with Greg, and kiss him, and call him *Hon.* Addison told Tess that seeing her touch Greg made him want to set himself on fire. She said she tried not to touch Greg when Addison was around, but sometimes she forgot or couldn't avoid it. This made Addison boil over with jealousy and resentment: she tried not to touch Greg when Addison was around, but what about when Addison wasn't around? Did they make love? Did she make love to Addison in the cottage and then go home and make love to Greg? She said no, she was offended by the suggestion, but Addison was suspicious. Greg had animal magnetism; women threw themselves at him.

How often do you make love to him? Addison asked her.

Not very, she said.

I want you to leave him, Addison said.

I can't, she said. *The kids . . .*

The kids were her zone of immunity. Whenever Addison pressed her, she brought up her kids. She could betray Greg—God knows, he had betrayed her—but she could not betray her kids. She did not want her kids to have divorced parents, she did not want her kids to have a stepfather, and she, Tess, did not want a separation, a divorce lawyer, shared custody. She had left Greg for that one godforsaken week in November and she had said all those words out loud, she had chewed them up and eventually spit them out.

Addison pulled into Tess and Greg's driveway. He had shown their house only three times since it had gone on the market, all three times to visitors who did not know what had happened to the owners. No one had gone back to look a second time. Addison was thinking of lowering the asking price.

Tess had her own key to the Quaise cottage. Addison had not remembered this when he went through her house the first time weeks ago, but he remembered it now. He had asked her once where she kept the key—Tess was paranoid about getting caught; where would be safe enough?—and she had said, *I keep it hidden under the bug spray in the garage.*

He found it there. On one of the many shelves for house and garden necessities was an orange-capped can of Raid, and underneath it lay the key.

The day was sunny and dry after three days of showers, heavy fog, and thunderstorms. The Polpis Road looked scrubbed and squeaky-clean, like something that had just been removed from the box. The fields to the right side of the road were green and freshly cut; the view of the harbor to the left seemed polished.

Did you ever really love me? he asked.

Oh, God, she said. *Of course I did. But . . .*

But what?

It was complicated. Wasn't it?

She used to send him song lyrics (which he quasi-resented; it seemed so Greg-like). Her favorite line was from a U2 song: *You say in love there are no rules.* Tess liked to believe that her love for Addison was renegade, something beyond her control, something she could not be held accountable for, something that had happened to her, not that she had made happen. In this way, she was not responsible. Love had been visited on them from above at some point during their lunch together at Nous Deux. Sandrine had done it; Sandrine was a witch.

Addison pulled into the driveway of the Quaise cottage. Was he going to cry? It didn't matter if he did, he cried all the time now; he had stopped feeling embarrassed by it. He had not been to the cottage since, well, since the seventeenth of June, a Friday. Tess had met him while the twins were at camp. She had reminded him, on that day, of her impending anniversary; on that day, she had gently told him about the planned sail to the Vineyard.

Greg's idea, she said.

Tell him no.

I think that would be aggressive, she said. *It would send up red flags.*

He's trying to win you back, Addison said.

He can't win me back, Tess said. *I'm yours.*

So then why are you going? Addison asked.

And Tess said, *Please don't make this any harder than it already is.*

Meet me here on Sunday afternoon. Please—one last time before you go sailing. Addison went to the cottage every Sunday to change the sheets and do some basic housekeeping.

You know Sundays are impossible for me, she said.

The cottage was beautiful in the heart of the summer. The roof was draped with crimson climbing roses, like the back of the winning Kentucky Derby horse, and the woods beyond were full and lush. Paths between the trees were lined with hostas and jacks-in-the-pulpit. When Tess and Addison had been here the last time, the roses had not yet been in bloom.

In a few weeks, Addison had said, *we can walk to the water and go for a swim. No one will see us. This cove is completely deserted.*

I can't wait, Tess had replied.

Addison let himself in. He expected the place to be stuffy, but someone—Florabel? the caretaker?—had left the windows open, and the breeze moved through the screens, and the white, filmy curtains floated like ghosts.

They had made love that final time—Addison angrily, Tess apologetically—and when it was over, they lay in uncharacteristic silence. They never spent time in silence; the hallmark of their relationship was that they talked. Addison told her every detail of his day and she did the same. She knew the status of every one of his deals, and he knew the names and life stories of each of her students. The two of them talked and talked and talked; God, it was a relief, a pleasure, to have someone to talk to. At home, Addison could talk and Phoebe would listen, but it was weird. Sometimes she was cogent and understood him and came out with canny responses, but sometimes it was like firing a tennis ball into outer space. And Tess could talk to Greg about the kids or school, but he gave her the distinct impression that he was weary of both topics. She was forbidden from broaching the subjects of money, the house, his job singing at the Begonia, and anything related to the High Priorities (like April Peck). So what did that leave, exactly? Discussing the segments of *60 Minutes?* It would feel forced. Ditto conversations about books, painting, or sculpture. Tess could talk to Addison about these things, however, and never tire of it.

But Addison remembered that lying there, the final day in the cottage, he had struggled with the silence. He had had things to say, oh yes, things that would lead to other things.

He had promised himself he wouldn't do it, but he did it anyway (as he knew he would when he made himself the promise). He lay down on the bed.

Could he have stopped her from going sailing? Because God knows, he'd wanted to stop her. But everything he'd wanted to say was flawed, nothing was effective enough. He had vetted his thoughts carefully; he had taken a breath to speak, and then shut himself up.

I DO NOT WANT YOU TO GO SAILING WITH YOUR HUSBAND.

He could have shouted it in anger or repeated it a hundred times in a whisper-stream like a lunatic, but even that would not have conveyed the ardor of his feelings.

It was nothing but a parlor game to conjure now what he might have said if he had been brave enough to open his mouth. It wouldn't have mattered what he said, because she was going regardless.

Why?

Ah, the why. The why was the reason for their silence that final day; it was the reason for Addison's anger and her apology.

Why?

Not to go would be to send up a bunch of red flags, she said. But this was just her making excuses. She could easily have begged off. She hated the water and always had, she hated to leave the kids overnight. The last year of the marriage, thanks to the heinous event of April Peck, had been a shambles, and not worth celebrating. She was in love with someone else.

She could have said any of these things, but didn't. She was going sailing, therefore, because she wanted to. She wanted to celebrate the train wreck that had been their twelfth year of marriage, she wanted to hear the song Greg had written for her, she wanted to eat and drink and laugh and make love. She wanted to see the man *try*.

Right? Admit it!

Addison had not pressed her. He had strictly adhered to the tenet beloved of so many fourteen-year-old girls: *If you love something, set it free. If it was meant to be, it will come back to you.* But this, of course, was bullshit. If you loved something and let it go . . . it would (hello!) find something else to love.

It had never occurred to Addison to say, *I don't want you to go with Greg because what if something happens? What if you catch a gust the wrong way and the boat capsizes and you get caught underneath and you die?* Or, *What if your husband drugs you and throws you overboard?*

To which Tess would have said, *Oh, Addison, don't be silly.*

Addison moved to the window, where he could see the trees, the path, the ribbon of inviting blue water. They had made a pact to love each other the same amount, the maximum amount, an unimaginable, overflowing amount. He had loved her that much, but Tess had been misrepresenting herself. *I'm afraid you won't get it.*

The cottage had sold. Another couple would live here, would make love in the bed, would gaze out the window, would shower together or separately, would listen to Mozart or Mötley Crüe, would cook croque-monsieurs or goat cheese omelets, would sleep soundly or fitfully. And they would never know.

Addison took the felt heart, now in three pieces, out of his pants pocket. He scattered the pieces across the bed like sad rose petals. But then, because he couldn't stand to leave them, he shoved them back in his pocket, got up, and walked out the door.

ANDREA

Her time in the farm attic was coming to an end. The thought was hard to bear. She and Jeffrey had painstakingly detailed twenty of Tess's thirty-five years on earth, and Jeffrey had suffered through stories from Tess and Andrea's childhood in South Boston with the police department, the Mafia connections, the priests and nuns. Jeffrey had aired out a few stories of his own, stories Andrea had never heard (Jeffrey and Tess had discovered a mangy fox while hiking around Saranac Lake, and Tess had insisted that Jeffrey call a vet to try to save it. Did Andrea know that? No, she didn't, and the story delighted her.)

They were down to the wire now, though. They had talked, circumspectly, about the April Peck incident. Andrea had been very tense during this session. She waited for Jeffrey to reveal details she had never heard before, but no, he had been fed the same story as the rest of them. They had talked about the trip to Stowe, their last group trip. This brought them to within six months. And it was the last six months that troubled Andrea, because for the last six months of Tess's life, Tess had been different. She had been distant and unavailable; she had stopped going to mass with Andrea. She had told Andrea lies.

Lies! Andrea had not confronted Tess about the lies, because she had been baffled by them, embarrassed even. If Tess was lying to Andrea, then there must be something wrong with Andrea. Andrea was hesitant to discuss all this with Jeffrey, but maybe he could help her. This process they'd been through together had been painful and rough in places, but ultimately it was working. It was allowing Andrea to keep a tenuous grip on her sanity.

"So, let me ask you," she said. She was, as ever, at Jeffrey's desk, in his chair, overlooking charts and graphs of various crops' growth, piles of invoices to go out to restaurants, and bills. Jeffrey sat on a milk crate a few feet away. "Did you notice a change in Tess last winter?"

He narrowed his eyes. "Maybe," he said. "She seemed sadder to me, less gullible, less innocent. All of which you can chalk up to a woman who had been through what she had been through with Greg."

"Every Saturday night, five o'clock, rain or shine, we used to go to mass, right?"

"Right," Jeffrey said.

"So, at the beginning of February, the start of Lent, she quits church altogether. She cancels on mass for the first time, saying she has a PTA meeting. At five o'clock on Saturday? And there, at the church, I see both Karen and Lizzie, president and vice president of the PTA, and I *know* there's no meeting, I *know* she's lied to me. But the thing is that Karen and Lizzie were *always* at five o'clock mass and Tess knew it, so why would she hand me that particular story if she knew she was going to get caught?"

"Did you say anything to her?" Jeffrey asked.

"No. I let it go."

"And then?"

"Then she skipped Ash Wednesday. For the first time in thirty years, she did not go to get her ashes. When I asked her what was up, she said her day had been busy. She had a conference with a parent after school. Then she canceled on mass the following week, and then the *next* week she told me she would meet me at St. Mary's and she never showed. And when I called her, she said her car wouldn't start."

"The Kia?" Jeffrey said.

"The most reliable car in the history of automotives," Andrea said. "And there was other stuff . . ." It was all little stuff, stuff only Andrea would notice: Tess's tone of voice, her attitude. She was at times euphorically happy and at other times she burst into tears for no reason. She was uneven. But all women were uneven, weren't they? They suffered from PMS, hormonal ups and downs; Tess had had her share of reproductive chaos. Maybe her body chemistry was out of whack. But deep down, Andrea didn't buy it. Tess was not like other women. For starters, she was a kindergarten teacher: she was patient and kind, creative and organized. She loved children and she believed in the power of paint and crayons and glue and clay and storybooks. She had a class pet, a long-haired rabbit named Knickerbocker. She liked to play kick ball and push kids on the swings; she kept a drawer full of snacks and clean underwear and Band-Aids. Her room was always clean, she always wore a skirt or dress, she did not raise her voice. When she wanted quiet, she turned out the lights and held a finger to her lips. She was a saint. To see her moody and peevish . . . something was wrong.

Andrea had asked Ed more than once, "Do you think there's something wrong with Tess?" In response, Ed would shovel in mashed potatoes or grunt from behind the newspaper. If Andrea pressed him for an answer, he would say, "She seems fine to me." Andrea called this a typical male answer. To which Ed said, "When I give you a typical female answer, you can complain." Andrea brayed with disgust and Ed gave her some line

276 @ Elin Hilderbrand

about how women clearly felt things more deeply; they read subtext where men saw only white space.

"If you think there's something wrong," Ed said, "why don't you ask her?"

Right. Andrea found, however, that she was afraid. Afraid of her own best friend, her own younger cousin, whom she protected and worshipped. It took a night at Delilah's house and seven glasses of wine for Andrea to confront her. It was Oscar night. Every year Delilah served champagne and good caviar and she made Beef Wellington and they all dressed up (Addison always wore a tux and Phoebe her Valentino or Dior, and the rest of them did what they could). They filled out ballots, threw money into a pot, and the person with the most correct guesses won. This was usually Jeffrey, which was ironic, since he was constitutionally unable to stay awake through an entire movie. Oscar night usually saw them very drunk, and this past year had been no exception. Andrea stumbled across Tess sitting alone on the stairs in her black lace top and black silk pants, and Andrea, with chardonnay courage, decided that this was the time to confront her.

Is everything okay?

Tess looked up, unsurprised by the question. *Yeah.*

No, I mean it. Something's going on. What is it? You haven't been to mass in weeks.

I'm finished with the Lord.

What does that mean?

I don't want to talk about it.

Are you mad at me? This was Andrea's fear, a fear greater, perhaps, than she was willing to admit. Andrea knew she was tough, she knew she was prickly, aggressive, unforgiving, she knew there were women who disliked her and that even Phoebe and Delilah had their moments with her. But she had always saved her nicest, kindest, sweetest self for Tess.

Tess softened. *No. God, no, Andrea. I could never be mad at you.*

Andrea felt herself about to cry chardonnay tears. She had been racking her brain, trying to figure out if she had done something wrong, if she had made some kind of egregious misstep that had hurt Tess.

Is it . . . April Peck?

April Peck? Tess looked confused. Then she shook her head and her chin wobbled. *April Peck is such small potatoes.*

Such small potatoes. The phrase had stuck with Andrea because it was an odd turn of phrase, and because those were the final words on the topic. Addison had come bumbling into the conversation, interrupting them, pulling Tess to her feet, imploring her to come watch. They were about to announce best actress.

"Small potatoes?" Jeffrey said now.

Andrea looked at him. "What do you think that meant?"

Tess canceled lunch dates, she skipped her monthly book group, she claimed to be taking an intense Pilates class at the gym that met three afternoons a week. The Pilates class met from four to five on Mondays, Wednesdays, and Fridays, but one Wednesday, Andrea saw Tess in the ever-reliable Kia barreling down the Polpis Road at five minutes to five. She was driving like a bat out of hell, which was what caught Andrea's attention in the first place (this may have been a standard complaint from the police chief's wife, but in her opinion, people on this island drove way too fast). Then Andrea saw it was Tess and she nearly called her, though the last thing Tess should be doing was speeding and talking on the phone. Andrea checked her mental calendar, trying to figure out what would have put Tess on the Polpis Road at five minutes to five on a Wednesday. Didn't she have Pilates class? The health club was on the other side of the island. Andrea was the police chief's wife, not the police chief, but she decided to do some investigating herself. The detective work was elementary. Andrea called the health club to inquire about the Pilates class held at four o'clock on Mondays, Wednesdays, and Fridays. The man who answered the phone was flummoxed.

"Pilates? We offer Pilates Tuesday and Thursday at ten A.M. and Monday and Thursday at six A.M. and six P.M."

"Nothing on Monday, Wednesday, and Friday at four?"

"Spinning class Monday and Wednesday at three. Jazz dance Monday, Wednesday, and Friday at five-thirty. Do you want jazz dance?"

"Jazz dance?" Andrea said.

Later she called Tess at home. Tess was upbeat. "I'm making quesadillas," she said.

Andrea paused. "How was your Pilates class?"

"It was great!" Tess said. "I can feel it working. My abdomen is so much tighter."

Jeffrey was quiet. All Andrea could hear was the sound of the fans, which nicely mimicked the sound his spinning brain might make as it came up with myriad possibilities, then flung them away.

"Should I state the obvious?" he said.

"She was seeing someone?" Andrea said.

"She was seeing someone."

They sat with that a minute, Andrea shocked by the sound of the words. Well, hello, she wasn't an idiot. This possibility had shadowed each of Tess's mood swings, each lie, and particularly the phrases "finished with the Lord" and "small potatoes" when used in regard to April Peck.

If April Peck was small potatoes, what was big potatoes?

Seeing someone? But who?

"She would have told me," Andrea said.

"You're right," Jeffrey said.

"No, she wouldn't have," Andrea said.

"You're right," Jeffrey said.

"She thought of me as her mother."

"She wouldn't have wanted to disappoint you."

"I wouldn't have been disappointed in her," Andrea said. But even as she said them, the words felt false. Andrea had always had mixed feelings about Greg, but she believed in marriage. (She was Catholic! She grew up with a nun living in her basement!) When Tess and Greg had separated during that week in November, it was Andrea who had talked her into going back. It was Andrea who had made the picnic for the anniversary sail. She had broken the sacred rule of no gifts because she wanted Tess and Greg to be happy on their anniversary. She had sensed that Tess was getting ready to leave the marriage, and she had been saying, *Stay!*

She was seeing someone.

Andrea felt the firm clutches of certainty. Tess had been seeing someone. It explained everything.

She stood up to leave. She could handle only one revelation per day, and this was a biggie. But was it really as shocking as Andrea was making it out to be? Wasn't it like a pile of dirty laundry in the corner with a blanket thrown over it? Pull back the blanket and there it was, just as you knew it would be all along.

Jeffrey stood as well. He was looking at her intently, and she couldn't bear it, because this was goodbye. This was the end of the secret, strange journey the two of them had taken together. Andrea had entrusted her grief to Jeffrey, and he had been tender with it, he had spent hours and hours talking Tess's life through. It was a painstaking process that no one else would have donated the time to. Andrea had come here because she loved Jeffrey, and Jeffrey let her stay because he loved her, too. Now they had come to the end of the life story of Tess DiRosa MacAvoy, and this meant that Andrea would stop coming here, there would be no more stolen hours in the sweltering attic, and this was its own kind of heartbreak.

He came closer, and she knew he meant to kiss her. It was okay. He was a matter-of-fact man; she believed in his moral compass, in his sense of right and not-right. He took her chin and kissed her with the same deft skill that he did everything else—slip an egg out from underneath a hen, bruise a basil leaf and inhale its scent. He kissed her goodbye, a key turning in a lock.

"I don't want you to fret about this," he said.

But both of them knew she would.

THE CHIEF

The freezer at the Juice Bar went on the fritz. It was such a sophisticated machine that they needed a team of NASCAR mechanics to fix it, and so Kacy had the night free from work. She had volunteered to take the twins out to Tom Nevers for the carnival, a shabby slice of mainland American life visited upon their beloved island for ten days. The carnival meant neon lights, rickety rides, rigged games with rinky-dink prizes, and heart-stopping, teeth-rotting fare such as cotton candy, fried dough, corn dogs, and sausage grinders. The twins had been begging to be subjected to the depravity of the carnival for nearly a week (Drew and Barney had apparently already been *twice*), and the Chief was relieved when Kacy said she would take them. Andrea could not handle the manic chaos of the carnival, and the Chief felt he had put in enough carnival hours with his own kids. He gave Kacy eighty dollars, told her not to let the twins eat too much sugar, and wished her well.

He then called Andrea to see if she wanted to go out to dinner, just the two of them. Somewhere nice. The Straight Wharf?

She said no. She was exhausted. (From doing what?) She was going to take advantage of the peace and quiet by going to bed early.

The Chief was deflated. He was, if he could just say it, lonely.

There had always been the specter of his own grief floating around somewhere, and he acknowledged it now. He, like Andrea, missed Tess, but he also missed Greg. Greg, despite his faults, had been his friend. The friendship had been uneven, sure. The Chief was the police chief, and Greg had been a rock star. Morally, they were a heavyweight and a lightweight, a total mismatch. But the Chief had loved Greg anyway.

If they still lived in the Before and the Chief found himself stranded at work without options or obligations, he would have wandered over to the Begonia, taken a seat at the bar, hammed it up with Delilah, ordered a bleu burger with extra onions, and listened to Greg play a set. It was, in the Chief's opinion, a nearly perfect way to spend an evening.

He couldn't handle the Begonia now: no Greg, no Delilah, Faith with her smothering concern, the grating Irish trio onstage. He had a pile of backlogged work on his desk, the result of his preoccupation with the details of the accident, his distracted frame of mind, and the extra hours he had to devote to Andrea and the twins. He should stay and work. He would ask Freda, the evening dispatcher, to pick him up a burger from the Begonia, even though Freda was unfriendly, and especially so when she felt like she was being treated like a secretary or an errand girl. He would have to ask nicely.

At nine-thirty he was still at his desk, the burger, fries, and double dill pickles demolished. He had eaten three Rolaids and was two thirds of the way through his stack of paperwork. The attendant feeling of relief and accomplishment was keeping his melancholy at bay. He wouldn't even have realized it was as late as nine-thirty—his office was a concrete bunker, without windows—had Dickson not knocked on the door, making the Chief look up. Dickson had that goddamn look on his face.

"What is it?" the Chief asked.

282 ~ *Elin Hilderbrand*

"April Peck is here," Dickson said. "She got called in by the bouncer of the Rose and Crown for trying to pass off a fake ID."

The Chief fell back in his chair. "Jesus."

"I dealt with her. She said she got it somewhere online, couldn't remember the name of the site. I fined her three hundred bucks, took the ID, threatened to suspend her real driver's license. She said she wanted to talk to you."

"To me?"

"To you."

"Jesus," the Chief said.

"Normally I would have told her no. Normally I would have slapped her with a ninety-day suspension for trying to go over my head. But then I wondered if maybe you wanted to question her."

Question her. Dickson understood more than the Chief wanted him to. The Chief's stomach squelched. He'd eaten all that food and he hadn't moved a muscle. And he was nervous.

"Send her in."

Dickson opened the door and poked his head out into the hallway. "Hey, Dancing Queen," he said, "the Chief has agreed to see you."

April entered, resplendent in some kind of sparkly black-and-silver disco dress and silver stiletto heels. Her hair was up. She wore reddish black lipstick. She looked twenty-five, not eighteen.

"Miss Peck," the Chief said.

"You can call me April," she said. She offered her hand. "I feel like I know you."

"Do you?" the Chief said.

"Yes," April said. She sat demurely, thank God, with her legs angled to the side. "Greg used to talk about you all the time."

The Chief quietly burped up Roquefort and onions. "Greg?" he said.

"Greg MacAvoy."

The name reverberated against the concrete walls of the Chief's office. April's face was open; her eyes were wide and innocent. She did not look like a kid who had just been booked for identity fraud. Was she drunk? She had been steady on the stilettos. Was she a good actress? Or maybe the three-hundred-dollar fine and the fact that she might not be able to drive for the rest of the summer didn't bother her. Who was he kidding? If they took her license, she would drive anyway.

"Mr. MacAvoy was your singing teacher?" the Chief said.

"He was."

The Chief looked at April's shining blond hair and thought of how lost Greg must have been to let her lasso him. Had Greg been in that place men found themselves in when they needed bolstering? His sweet and pretty wife wasn't enough? His two healthy kids weren't enough? He needed more, he needed someone to worship him, someone to think he was a hero?

"And . . . ?"

"And he was my friend."

"Your friend?" the Chief said. Nerves jitterbugged across his chest and arms. April Peck should have been just another pretty girl in high school, not so different from the Chief's own daughter, but instead she was a repository of information, answers, the truth. Had Greg and April Peck been having a thing—one time, three times, every week, every day? Would Greg have a reason to want to drug Tess? The Chief understood that knowing the answers wouldn't bring Tess or Greg back, it wouldn't help the kids, but the Chief, as an enforcer of the law, wanted the truth.

He had to be careful. April Peck had been brought in for trying to pass off a fake ID. She was not here to answer questions about Greg. He could not make her answer. For all the Chief knew, April Peck would leave the office saying that the *Chief* had been inappropriate with her. Thinking this, the Chief felt the first true wash of sympathy for Greg. April Peck was a suicide bomber. The Chief should send her out right now with a ninety-day suspension. If Andrea knew April Peck was here, what would she say?

April said, "I know what people think."

"What do people think?"

"They think Greg and I were lovers."

The Chief burped again, and whispered, "Excuse me." He had to tread so carefully here. "Why would they think that?"

She shrugged.

The Chief said, "I'm a little confused, Miss Peck, about why you wanted to see me."

Her face transformed from a placid surface to a stormy one. She was going to cry, and immediately the Chief's guard went up.

She said, "This has been so hard."

The Chief nodded, though barely.

"I wanted to talk to you about Greg."

"What about him?"

"He was my friend. I miss him. I loved him. I mean, I *really* loved him. He listened to me. I have all this stuff going on—Derek, my ex-boyfriend, stalks me, my mother is dying of freaking breast cancer, and my dad and brother are in New York hell-bent on pretending my mother and I don't exist . . ." She snatched a tissue off the Chief's desk and noisily blew her nose. "And really, the only person I could talk to was Greg. He was so nice to me. He was kind. He was the kindest, because he could have gotten into so much trouble . . ."

"You accused him of sexual misconduct," the Chief said. "He was nearly fired."

"I know! I was confused. It was so completely fucked. I was jealous because it was clear he loved his wife and kids. I was never going to get the best part of him. They were."

"So did you lie to the administration?" the Chief asked.

April narrowed her eyes at him as if he were crazy. Crazy to think she lied or crazy to think she would now tell him the truth?

She blotted her eyes. "The amazing thing was that Greg forgave me. After all that, I mean. He forgave me, he listened, he was kind, and then . . ."

"And then what?" the Chief said.

"And then he died!" April said. She stood up and paced the back half of the Chief's office.

"You were in love with him?" the Chief said.

April threw up her hands.

"Was he . . . did he say he was in love with you?"

"I know what you're trying to do," April said. In the back corner of his office was a filing cabinet topped with a philodendron and some framed snapshots of Kacy and Eric when they were young. April picked up the pictures and studied them. The Chief did not like her touching pictures of his family.

"What am I trying to do?" he asked.

"You're trying to get me to admit to something," she said.

"Admit to what?"

"See? You're doing it again."

Were you lovers? Was he in love with you? Would Greg have a reason to drug his wife? The Chief could ask April these questions and she could lie or tell him the truth and he wouldn't know the difference. He cleared his throat. "Okay, Miss Peck, it's time for you to go. We are going to issue a sixty-day suspension of your driver's license."

April whipped around.

"That's a reduction of the maximum penalty, which is a ninety-day suspension," he said. He could have lowered the penalty to thirty days, but he would not do it. And if she gave him lip, he would up it to ninety.

"You're throwing me out?" she said.

"I'm not a therapist," the Chief said. "I am the chief of police. Since you don't have any new or pertinent information about Greg MacAvoy or your involvement with him, we have no further business. Should you ever decide there is something else I need to know, you are free to come in anytime and talk to me. Understood?"

April chewed her bottom lip. "Do you know what Greg said about you? Do you know what he told me?"

"Honestly, Miss Peck, I don't care."

She took a deep, resigned breath. "He said you were the greatest guy in all the world."

ANDREA

She didn't know what stage she was in anymore. She was in stage limbo. She missed Tess, she missed Greg, she missed Jeffrey, she missed Eddie and her kids, but mostly she missed herself.

She wondered, was she ever coming back?

There were certain things she could handle and certain things she could not. She could handle the fact that Tess had had a lover. Andrea was forty-four years old, old enough to realize that the heart wanted what the heart wanted whether it made sense, whether it was right or wrong. What Andrea could not handle was not knowing who Tess's lover was. She had to find out. She wanted to know him; she wanted to make sure that he had loved Tess enough. Had it been someone at the funeral? Who exactly had attended the funeral? Should Andrea pore over the guest book? Andrea couldn't recall anyone except their immediate group, the children, horrid April Peck and her mother, and Father Dominic. *Finished with the Lord.* Tess had stopped going to church altogether. Was Tess having an affair with Father Dominic? He was a young man, in his late thirties, and he was handsome as far as priests went. She could handle Tess having a lover, but not if it was Father Dominic. She struck his name off her mental list for her own sanity. She thought of other teachers at school, the principal, the superintendent. Flanders? Andrea stopped. Not Flanders. For a brief second, she smiled.

Andrea could handle small outings, but not big ones. Ed came home with two tickets to the Island Conservation benefit, a cocktail party on the savannah, that Phoebe was chairing.

"It's on Friday night," he said. "Kacy agreed to watch the kids. We're going."

"No," Andrea said.

"I bought the tickets," he said. "I told Phoebe we'd be there."

"No."

"She wants our support. The poor woman hasn't done anything since before—"

"I'm not going, Ed."

"She said she has a surprise for us."

"Now I'm really not going."

He put his hands on her shoulders. This was a gesture that nearly always worked. His face was inches from her face, his hazel eyes, his five o'clock shadow. She loved his face despite the fact that it only ever held one expression, one that conveyed steadfast dedication to the forces of righteousness. It was the proximity of his face that was meant to convey meaning, and the weight of his hands pressing down on her shoulders, telling her that he was present, he would not let her float away, but that he had needs and desires, too, and this was one of them. Going to this event for Phoebe was important to him. But she couldn't do it.

"You go," she said. "I just can't. I'll stay home."

He lifted his hands. "We'll talk about it later."

She could not handle a cocktail party, but she could handle a trip to the post office to mail a box to Esmeralda, Tess's adopted Brazilian orphan, who was, all of a sudden, sixteen years old. Andrea woke up suddenly in the middle of the night, realizing that she had forgotten all about Esmeralda. Tess still sent her care packages every three months. Andrea wrote a letter explaining that Tess had passed away, but that she had cared for Esmeralda very much; she had displayed Esmeralda's photo on her desk at school. Andrea wrote that she, Andrea, would be sending packages now. Along with the letter, Andrea packed brown rice, steel-cut oats, graham crackers, a copy of *To Kill a Mockingbird*, a new pair of flip-flops, a journal, and a framed picture of Tess.

Andrea struggled a bit with Tony at the post office about how to send the box and how to insure it, but they worked it out; all it took was paperwork and money. Tony flipped the box casually into the airmail bin and Andrea winced, thinking of the graham crackers, but she felt a sense of accomplishment nonetheless.

As she turned to leave, she saw a man in line and her knees buckled. She stopped and stared, and the woman coming up to the counter nudged her out of the way. Andrea stutter-stepped aside, still staring at the man unabashedly. He looked at her and smiled. It was the man from her dream, the Russian, Pyotr, who had made love to her in her old black Jeep, who had said, *It's your car, you can do what you want in it.* Who had been drowning until she saved him. It was him, not merely someone who resembled him.

Part of Andrea wanted to hurry out and not look back. But she had to know.

She said, "Do I know you from somewhere?"

The blue eyes narrowed. "Don't think so," he said. He had a broad accent. Australian? He stuck out his hand. "I'm Ian Bing. Teach Pilates at the health club. Do you belong to the health club, then?"

Andrea blinked. "No," she said. "I don't." Inside, she was fizzing and popping. He taught Pilates at the health club! This was the sign. This was the guy. Tess's lover. Andrea said, "But my cousin belonged to the health club. Tess MacAvoy? Did you know Tess?"

Ian's face was blank. He shook his head, the salt-and-pepper curls. "No. 'Fraid I don't."

Andrea scrutinized him. He looked sincere, but Andrea didn't

believe a soul anymore. She checked his ear—no earring. Still, it
was him. He had done all those things to her in her dreams. She
blushed, she couldn't help it, and then she said, "So you didn't
know Tess?"

"No," he said. "Did she take Pilates?"

"No," Andrea said.

Ian smiled at her as if to say . . . well, as if to say nothing. He
did not know Andrea, he did not know Tess. Andrea was making
a complete ass of herself, but it was *him,* Pyotr, the Russian.

Andrea hurried out to the parking lot.

Andrea could handle Kacy taking care of the twins, but she
could not handle Delilah taking care of them. Twice Delilah had
called to see if she could take the twins to the carnival with Drew
and Barney, and twice Andrea had said no on the basis that the
carnival was a ripoff and the rides were operated by heroin junk-
ies. Kacy then took them to the godforsaken thing and they ate
junk and rode the unsafe rides and came home with dirty feet, a
stuffed giraffe whose eye fell out during the car ride home, and a
pump-action toy gun for Finn, which Tess never would have toler-
ated, but how could Kacy protest when the Chief carried a gun?
Andrea huffed about the carnival, and Kacy said, as only a righ-
teous sixteen-year-old can, "If you don't like the way I'm taking
care of them, do it yourself."

Delilah had called Kacy about the movie. The movie was more
than a movie; it was a phenomenon. *Vunderkids 3* was premier-
ing on Friday. Delilah had flown all four kids off-island to see
Vunderkids and *Vunderkids 2* for the big movie-house premiere
experience the two previous summers, and she wanted to take
them again this year. It was now a tradition.

"So they're going with Delilah," Kacy said on Friday morning.

"What?" Andrea said. She tried to keep her voice level, because
the twins were right there at the breakfast table eating Cheerios,

wiggling with excitement about going to see *Vunderkids 3,* off-island, with Auntie Dee and Drew and Barney. In a real theater with Dolby surround sound and real popcorn with real butter—

"It's not real butter," Kacy said.

"—and big boxes of Milk Duds and Junior Mints. And huge cups of Sprite."

"Auntie Dee lets us get whatever we want," Chloe said.

Andrea pulled Kacy into the hallway. "What were you thinking?"

"Delilah said it was a tradition."

"How can anything be a tradition after only doing it twice before?"

Kacy huffed. She was lovely. Her brown hair was glossy, her face was golden with the sun, the acne across her forehead had cleared up. After thirty months of braces, her teeth were straight and pretty; she brushed with whitening toothpaste four times a day. She had been so, so helpful with the twins. She had essentially been their nanny all summer, and she hadn't asked for a penny. She looked at her mother and said, "If you don't want them to go, please call Delilah yourself. And then tell the twins yourself."

"You should have asked me," Andrea said.

"You leave me in charge to do everything except make decisions? Even you, Mom, can see that's unfair. It sounded fine to me. They're leaving after camp, and they'll be home on the last plane. I'll be here to wait for them because you and Dad are going out."

"No, we're not," Andrea said.

"Yes, we are," said Ed, emerging from the bedroom in his uniform. "The party starts at seven. And if you don't have anything to wear, I suggest you go out today and get something new." He was using his police chief voice. He was not suggesting anything at all; he was demanding it.

Andrea glared at her husband, then at her daughter. They

walked away, Ed out the door to work, Kacy into the kitchen to gather the kids for camp. Andrea retreated to her bedroom. She started to shake. She *could not handle this!* Everyone else was ready to pick up and move on—go to the movies, go to cocktail parties—but Andrea was not ready! She did not want to move forward a single step without Tess.

She picked up the first thing that caught her eye, the swimming trophy that she won in the city championships her senior year in high school. She had broken the record for the 200-meter butterfly. She threw the trophy against the wall, leaving a hole in the plaster the size of someone's head. Andrea collapsed on the bed. She had been doing so well.

DELILAH

It was just a movie, she told herself.

It had not even been her idea. Drew had seen the trailer for *Vunderkids 3* on TV and come charging into Delilah's bedroom while Delilah sat on her bed, staring out the window at the summer rain, staving off the demons in her mind, and said, "Mom! Mom! *Vunderkids 3!* We're going, right? You'll take us on Friday?"

"*Vunderkids?*" she said. News of this monumental event had slipped past her. She was full of holes. She asked Drew, mother to oldest son, if he would understand if they didn't go to the premiere this summer. Would it be okay if they went in a few weeks, when she was feeling up to it?

"But Mom," he said, "it's a tradition."

And then Barney skated in, wearing only boxers and socks, and contributed his two cents. "Yeah, Mom, tradition. We *have* to go."

Delilah eyed her two sweaty sons. Drew had defined biceps and Barney had lost the baby fat on his cheeks. They were growing, but they were still kids. They were vunderkids. They did not need to be dragged down into the pathologies of adulthood. They needed to be lifted up. It was true: flying to the mainland to see *Vunderkids* in a proper theater was a tradition. Delilah decided, on the spot, that they would go. On Friday. Friday night was Phoebe's event, Phoebe would never forgive Delilah if she missed it, and so Delilah would fly back with the kids at nine, drop them with a sitter, change her clothes, and then hightail it to the event. She would tell Phoebe that that was her plan, or she would have Jeffrey tell Phoebe so that Delilah wouldn't have to deal with the inevitable complaints.

Delilah set it all up. She bought the movie tickets online, she rented a car, she booked the plane. She called Kacy—Chloe and Finn had to come, it was part of the tradition—and she asked Kacy to baby-sit after they got home so Delilah could head out to Phoebe's event. Kacy agreed. They were all set.

It was just a movie. But Delilah's wheels started spinning. She did laundry, she called the cleaning ladies to come, and the carpet cleaner, and the landscapers to mow the lawn. On Thursday she grilled a rack of ribs and made her famous squash dish and her blue-cheese coleslaw and the four of them ate as a family for the first time in weeks in a clean house on a tended yard, with a little Crosby, Stills and Nash for background music. Delilah cleaned up and saved the leftovers in Tupperware while Jeffrey read to the boys. (Delilah had fallen into the habit of allowing the boys to watch the Red Sox until they fell asleep on the sofa. But Thursday night she said, "Up to read, boys. You're in serious need of some Dad time.") When Jeffrey came back downstairs, Delilah was in their bedroom with the candles lit; she had put on a camisole. They made love, and afterward Delilah went to the kitchen and brought back a piece of blackberry pie smothered with whipped cream. When the plate was devoured to a few purple smudges, Delilah fell back into her pillows and said, "I love you, Jeffrey Drake."

Jeffrey said, "Tonight was really nice."

She agreed. It had been really nice. But it wasn't quite real. "Don't forget, we're going to the movies tomorrow," she said. "You have to go to Phoebe's event by yourself, and then I'll meet you there, okay?"

"I'll just wait for you," he said. "We'll go together."

"No!" Delilah said. Her eyes flew open.

"Why are you shouting?'

"You have to go to Phoebe's event at seven. You have to go, no matter what. Promise me."

Silence. She punched his arm. "Promise me."

"Okay, I promise."

Her wheels were spinning! Friday morning she went to the store before anyone else was awake. While the kids were at camp, Delilah made chicken salad and a pan of her roasted asiago potatoes. She made cucumber-coconut soup and a bowl of corn and chive salad with pine nuts. Then she cleaned out the refrigerator; there were Ziplocs of old pizza and half-empty containers of eggplant parmesan from the farm market. In the very back she found a leaking container of strawberries covered with fuzzy green mold—the very same strawberries the kids had picked at the farm on the day Tess and Greg died.

Once the refrigerator sparkled, Delilah moved into her bedroom. She made her and Jeffrey's bed with clean sheets; she plumped the pillows. Then she cleaned off the top of her dresser. It was safe to say the top of her dresser had not been cleaned since Barney was born. Delilah liked messy surfaces. She liked leaving bits and pieces of her frantic life all over the place—*The New Yorker* opened to an Alice Munro story, an ad for Sergio Rossi shoes ripped out of *Vogue,* a recipe for gazpacho, a picture that Drew had painted, a pair of dangly earrings, an *Arrested Development* DVD, her hot pink thong, her birth control pills, a photograph of the boys dressed as pirates on the *Endeavor,* a gift certificate to the Languedoc, her gold pass to the Chicken Box. Delilah was proud to display these reminders of her personality; she was glad to be too busy to put everything back where it belonged. But now she swept up all the bits and pieces and hid them away. Then she dusted the top of her dresser and waxed it with Pledge. All that sat on the dresser's surface was a fresh white doily and her wooden jewelry box, closed.

She sat on the edge of her perfectly made bed. This room no longer looked like her bedroom. She pulled an overnight bag from the closet and packed a few things for her and a few things for each of the boys, just in case. Pajamas, toothbrush, change of clothes. It was just a movie, but what you learned when you lived on an island was, you never knew.

Her wheels were spinning!

She left a note for Jeffrey—at least, it was sort of a note—and went to get the kids from camp.

They took the 2:30 Island Air flight. Drew and Barney had flown on the eight-seater Cessnas dozens of times, but it was more fun with friends. The kids were slaphappy; Delilah probably should have told them to settle down for the sake of the other passengers, but she hadn't seen them this happy in a long time. It heartened her, and she would not squelch it.

She picked up the rental car, a Plymouth Voyager. A minivan. Delilah groaned inwardly, but the kids each claimed a captain's chair. They were happy.

They were in Hyannis and it was liberating. Thirty miles of water were separated Delilah and the kids from everyone else, and though it technically took only fifteen minutes to traverse the gap, it represented psychological freedom. Delilah cranked the AC and slipped in the kids' favorite disk of *High School Musical,*

Buckcherry, Smash Mouth, and good old Bob Seger. The kids had skipped lunch, they clamored, and so Delilah pulled into the drive-through at McDonald's and it was Happy Meals all around, and a huge Diet Coke for Delilah.

The Cineplex of their summertime *Vunderkids* tradition was in Pembroke, south of Boston. It was the very same Cineplex that Tess's brother used to manage before he moved to Attleboro to be closer to his kids. It was perfect. Delilah bought popcorn with extra butter, bucket-sized 7-Ups, nachos with melted cheese and shriveled jalapeños, a soft pretzel with mustard, a package of red Twizzlers, a package of Raisinets. This, she decided, would be dinner.

They munched and slurped. The kids were engrossed in the movie, their faces shiny with butter. They laughed; they cheered. Vunderkids! Delilah did not watch the movie; she watched the kids watching the movie. Delilah's wheels were spinning, but the kids were carefree. Delilah checked her watch. It was six-ten, six-twenty, six forty-nine. Phoebe's benefit started in ten minutes, and Delilah would not be there. Delilah was in an alternate universe, where she was set free from her usual circumstances. It felt good to be away; it felt *great*. She did not think about Tess, Greg, Andrea, the Chief, Jeffrey, April Peck, the Begonia, Thom and Faith, or her own horrible lack of discretion and judgment, her tragic mistake caused by love and attraction that were forbidden and profane, because she was living in the moment. She was at the movie with her children. She wanted to stay in the dark theater with her kids cheering forever.

When the credits rolled, Delilah filled with dread. She checked her watch. They had plenty of time to make it back to Hyannis for the last flight. Delilah made the kids use the bathroom and wash their hands and faces with soap. Then they piled into the car, humming the *Vunderkids* theme song.

"Well?" Delilah said, in her best gung-ho camp counselor voice. "What did you think?"

Yes, they had loved it. Yes she was the best mom-slash-auntie in the whole wide world!

"I can't believe it's over," Chloe lamented.

Delilah agreed. It had gone too fast. She had only begun to breathe like a normal person. The thought of going back to Nantucket and of having to attend a cocktail party weighed her down. She would skip the party, she decided, and incur Phoebe's wrath.

It was nearly dark outside. After Delilah had been on the highway for ten minutes, the chatter in the back quieted. Delilah did not want to go home yet. She racked her brain. How could they prolong this trip? What could they do? Delilah spied a billboard for a Friendly's ice-cream parlor at the next exit. Could she in good conscience buy the kids ice cream after plying them with so much grease and sugar at the theater?

"Hey," she said. "Does anyone want to stop for hot fudge sundaes?"

There was no answer. Delilah checked her mirror, then turned around to double-check. All four kids were asleep.

"Hey!" she said.

No one moved.

She did not think, and the not-thinking felt good. She turned herself around on the highway and headed west.

PHOEBE

She arrived back on the savannah at five o'clock. She had been there all day with her clipboard and her checklist and her skill at tying knots in the slick silver ribbon attached to the iridescent pearl-colored balloons. Was everything in order? Everything was in order. Flooring had been laid over the scrub grass and a tent was erected over the flooring. Once it was dusk and the tent was illuminated, it would indeed look like a party far out in the wilds of the African plains. The savannah was eerily beautiful, a 92-acre parcel of grassland with a few gnarled but majestic trees. Sankaty Head Lighthouse and a thin strip of ocean were visible beyond.

The caterers were setting up; the bartender polished glasses. Phoebe had her hair done in a twist. She was wearing a silver silk Anjali Kumar dress and a funky necklace of silver rope with silver and clear beads. She was wearing silver flats, out of respect for the savannah itself. Phoebe was nervous. She had actually held her prescription of valium in her palm and rattled it, wondering what to do. Take one? Last summer it would have been unthinkable to attend any social event without taking two valiums or preferably three, but last summer, and the six summers before, nothing had been expected of her. Tonight she had an announcement to make.

Fifteen minutes before the guests were to arrive, Jennifer handed Phoebe a glass of champagne. Just one sip, Phoebe thought. One sip would taste good.

Jennifer smiled at Phoebe. She was about to say something flattering. Jennifer, for whatever reason, thought Phoebe was fabulous—despite her eight-year hiatus in the netherworld—and Jennifer's faith in her gave her faith in herself. This night was going to be a watershed for Phoebe.

"First of all," Jennifer said, "thanks for helping. The party looks beautiful."

"It was nothing," Phoebe said. She meant this. Pulling the party together had been a layup. But Phoebe newly appreciated her gift for organizing this kind of thing. She had impeccable taste, and no detail escaped her.

"What you're doing for your friends is so amazing and generous," Jennifer said.

"Well . . ." Phoebe said. "I'm just sorry you didn't know them.

They were amazing and generous themselves." Tears welled up, and she blotted the corners of her eyes with a cocktail napkin. "Okay, this *cannot* happen when I'm making my speech."

"Amen," Jennifer said, and they clinked glasses.

The band started up. Phoebe had asked for Sinatra, Dean Martin, Bobby Darin, all the oldies. She wanted a real old-fashioned feel to this party; she wanted it to evoke an era gone by, the country club parties that her grandparents used to attend. The cocktail of the evening was the savannah sidecar. The caterers were passing devils on horseback, pimento cheese toasts, clams casino, classic shrimp cocktail, mini lamb chops with mint jelly, and gougères. People streamed in along a temporary walkway lined with luminarias. Phoebe and Jennifer stood at the entrance to the tent and greeted everybody. Phoebe talked with people she hadn't seen in years. She had studied the guest list; the trick was pinning the right names to the right people. She was listening to herself and was impressed. She was charming; she was funny! She wanted the party never to end. She would find something else to chair, she decided. She would follow in her grandmother's footsteps and be a philanthropist and hostess. It was her calling.

Suddenly Addison was upon her. She took stock: he was wearing khaki pants, white shirt, navy blazer, madras bow tie (Phoebe had insisted on the bow tie). He was wearing loafers with no socks. His hair, what there was of it, was combed. He smelled like aftershave and Jack Daniels. It was odd to see him this way— approaching her like any other party guest. It made him seem like a stranger. Phoebe remembered the spring she'd met Addison and how much she had adored him. He was balding, true, and he was divorced from a notorious socialite and had a baby daughter. He was not quite what she had imagined for herself (she had imagined someone like Reed). But Addison was rich and he was charismatic, he was seasoned, he had lived in other countries and done interesting things. He understood the way the world worked and he wanted to show Phoebe. She knew herself well enough to know that she needed someone older. This had ended up benefiting her. Addison had been strong enough for both of them. He was able to endure. That he had eventually fallen in love with Tess only showed that he was human after all. It also showed Phoebe how deeply she'd been buried. And despite Tess, Addison had not left her. She would thank him for that someday.

She wished she could greet Addison with the same enthusiasm and joie de vivre she greeted everyone else with, or she wished she could greet him with the kind of secret, quiet love that her grandmother always reserved for her grandfather (she had bloomed in his presence and wilted in his absence, even after sixty years of marriage). But what Phoebe felt when she saw Addison was concern, weariness, a dash of contempt, a dash of pride, a dash of hope.

How many drinks at home? she wondered.

He bent to kiss Jennifer first, out of courtesy, and then Phoebe. "Looks great," he said, of the tent, she supposed.

The contempt popped up, like a bottle Phoebe had been trying to hold underwater. "How many drinks have you had?" she whispered.

He smiled at her fondly, but it was an act. He held up one finger and moved into the tent.

One, she thought. Which meant two. Or, more likely, three.

The Chief and Andrea arrived a little while later. To Phoebe's delight, and her considerable surprise, they looked sensational. Normally when they went out on the town, they wore neutral colors. The Chief often wore a gray suit that he'd bought off the rack at Anderson-Little in 1989. Phoebe teased him mercilessly about that suit, but it didn't matter—she loved Eddie, bad suit and all. Andrea normally wore boring beige, or black. Tonight, however, Andrea had on a red silk halter dress and red sandals, and Ed wore navy pants, a white shirt, and a blue-and-white seersucker jacket. The Kapenashes might have raided Phoebe and

Addison's own closets, they looked so dashing. Phoebe did a little dance, waving her arms in the air. The champagne was going to her head.

"You look gorgeous!" Phoebe said to Andrea.

Andrea smiled, but Phoebe sensed impatience. She had to tone it down, or she was going to scare them away like two beautiful, exotic birds. "You look gorgeous, too, Eddie. Thank you for coming."

"Wouldn't have missed it," the Chief said.

"Where did you get the dress?" Phoebe asked Andrea.

"Hepburn."

"You're breathtaking."

"Well," Andrea said, rolling her eyes.

"I'm honored you're here," Phoebe said.

Andrea nodded matter-of-factly, as though to say, *You should be.* The Chief, however, squeezed Phoebe's arm and leaned in to kiss her cheek. "The tent looks great. I'm ready for a savannah sidecar. Where's Addison?"

"In there somewhere," Phoebe said, waving into the tent. "I have a really big surprise for later, okay? Try to stand near the front when I take the microphone."

"A surprise?" the Chief said.

"Big one," Phoebe said.

Andrea smiled again, but Phoebe could see the balloon over her head, and the words in the balloon said, *Whoop-dee-do.*

At eight o'clock Phoebe and Jennifer left their posts by the door and wandered inside to enjoy the party themselves. The band was playing "In the Mood," and the first guests had started dancing. Phoebe was offered a devil on horseback. What was it, exactly? A date stuffed with soft white cheese, wrapped in bacon, glazed with brown sugar and Worcestershire.

"Really?" Phoebe said. She had picked it off the catering menu because it had sounded old-fashioned. Phoebe ate it; it was delicious.

She was supposed to make her remarks at eight-thirty, but she didn't want to speak until everyone had arrived, and Jeffrey and Delilah were still at large—which went to show how backward everything was this summer. Delilah was normally the first one to arrive anywhere, and the last one to leave. She loved "to gather," whether it was a fancy event like this one or the kids' holiday sing or a sandwich picnic out at Smith's Point. Delilah thrived when she was being social, she loved good conversation, she sought gossip, she savored food and drink, she loved music; she always danced, dragging Jeffrey onto the floor against his wishes. She did not like to miss one single second of the action, and if she did, then she had to hear what she'd missed in excruciating detail so she felt like she'd been there.

But not this summer. This summer Delilah stayed home. There was no longer anything worth gossiping about. She ate Pop-Tarts and pizza and drank Diet Dr Pepper like a person who lived in a trailer park. Delilah reminded Phoebe of a doll she had had as a child. This doll—Annabel, her name was—had an off/on switch at the nape of her neck. When the doll was on, she giggled and cooed, she gulped her bottle and let out a healthy belch. When the doll was off, she lay there, blank and mute.

Delilah had been turned off.

At eight-thirty Jeffrey and Delilah still had not arrived. Phoebe, though she'd promised herself she wouldn't, called the house. Answering machine. Were they on their way? She would wait five more minutes. Ten minutes passed, and Jennifer touched Phoebe's back.

"You have to speak. People are getting ready to leave."

"Leave? Already?"

"The early birds. You have to do it now, while you have your audience."

But Phoebe didn't have her audience. She needed Jeffrey and Delilah. She checked the entrance to the tent. They wouldn't skip it, would they? They had bought tickets; Phoebe had spoken to

Delilah yesterday morning. Phoebe had said, "I'll see you tomorrow night?" And Delilah had responded affirmatively: "Tomorrow night." Were they blowing it off? It would be an infraction from which the friendship would never recover. But Phoebe herself had committed so many infractions.

Just then she saw Jeffrey enter the tent. His face was very brown. It was farmer brown. He wore Nantucket Reds, a white shirt with navy stripes, a double-breasted navy blazer. Jeffrey always looked good. It was Cornell, Phoebe thought. Jeffrey always looked like he was attending an Ivy League garden party.

She hurried over to him. "I'm so glad you're here," she said. "Where's Delilah?"

He frowned. He had a prominent brow, which knit itself into an expression Phoebe couldn't read. Exasperation? Fear?

"She didn't come?" Phoebe said.

"She'll be here," he said. "She's coming late."

"May I have your attention, please?" Jennifer had taken the microphone from the bandleader and was standing in the middle of the dance floor, waiting for the crowd to quiet down. Someone tapped a glass with a spoon. There were overlapping shushing noises. Shhhhhhh. Phoebe turned, panicked. Wait! Delilah wasn't here! She wasn't here yet, she was coming late, but not before Phoebe had to speak. Phoebe scanned the crowd for Addison, Andrea, and the Chief—where were they? She couldn't find them. When she had imagined this moment, she imagined the five of them lined up across the front. She imagined making her announcement and watching their faces pop open in private fireworks, happiness, surprise, joy. Maybe they would cry poignant, touching tears. Now this wouldn't happen. Would it still be okay? Phoebe had planned this party so thoroughly, every detail, down to the selection of the hors d'oeuvres, the choice of songs, the color of the balloons. And yet she hadn't been able to make things go the way she wanted them to.

"First of all, I'd like to thank everyone for coming. This is a very special night . . ."

Phoebe looked at Jeffrey. He lifted a cocktail off a passing tray and took a deep drink.

"There are so many people we'd like to thank. For the delicious food and wine, Mark and Eithne Yelle of the Nantucket Catering Company . . ."

Phoebe looked around. She saw a splash of red in the corner of the tent. Andrea? Was the Chief with her? Would they move forward when it was Phoebe's turn to speak? And where was Addison? Phoebe now rued her decision not to tell him what she'd done, but she had wanted him to be surprised, just like everyone else.

"I'd like to thank Sperry Tents, and the Perri Rossi Orchestra . . ."

Applause.

"But the real force behind tonight's festivities is our dedicated chairperson. This woman gave hours of her precious time, as well as donating her considerable talent, her keen eye for detail, and her unparalleled organizational skills . . ."

They had a rule in the group: no gifts. They'd had that rule from the beginning.

"Ladies and gentlemen, Mrs. Phoebe Wheeler!"

Applause.

As Phoebe made her way to the front, the people standing around her cleared a path. She would be okay; she'd had only one glass of champagne, and she hadn't succumbed to the lure of the valium. She would stay focused. Delilah wasn't there, but Phoebe couldn't worry about that now. Her heart was thudding, she had a case of the shakes. Deep breath! She took the microphone. It had been a long time since she had spoken in public, but she could do it. She had won a fifty-dollar savings bond in the Junior Miss pageant for poise and appearance. Poise! She had stood on her high school stage and announced Reed and Shelby Duncan as prom king and queen.

"Thank you," Phoebe said. She gazed out over the crowd. Faces, collars, necklaces, cleavage, hands holding drinks, legs, shoes, hairspray, perfume, cigarette smoke, Jack Daniels. They were just people, they all had hearts and lungs and tear ducts just like she did. She saw Andrea and the Chief in the back corner with Addison. Jeffrey approached them. No Delilah, but Phoebe couldn't let her mind wander. "As you know, one of the goals of Island Conservation is to create nature walks through our properties where such walks are appropriate, where families can best learn about the topography and the flora and fauna of the island without disturbing it. We have long wanted to create such a walk here on the savannah." She paused. She did not look at Andrea or Addison; she looked up front, at Jennifer beaming, at Jennifer's husband, Swede, at Hank who owned the sailboat and his glamorous French girlfriend, Legris. "In June, I lost two dear friends in a sailing accident. They were schoolteachers here on the island, who left behind seven-year-old twins." The crowd quieted. The tent was silent; three hundred people held their breath. "And I decided I would like to honor my friends by underwriting the cost of the savannah nature walk and naming it after them. So in September, work will begin on a three-mile loop that will be known as the Tess and Greg MacAvoy Nature Walk." Phoebe smiled. Had she said that correctly? She thought she had. There was thundering applause; someone whistled. Phoebe had an ending line: *I hope you and your families will treasure this walk in years to come.* But there wasn't going to be a chance to add this. The orchestra launched into Dionne Warwick's "Walk on By" (as Phoebe had requested), and Phoebe relinquished the microphone.

She stepped back into the crowd and Jennifer hugged her and handed her a fresh glass of champagne. "We are all so excited about this!" she said.

Phoebe felt like she was going to faint.

She said, "I have to find . . ." and she wandered away.

She meandered through the crowd, but these were her fifteen minutes of fame, she was the party's It girl, people wanted to talk to her.

A woman with butterscotch-colored hair in a beauty parlor do grabbed her arm and said, "My God, Phoebe, you're such an angel! Doing something like that in memory of your friends. And their children. Are the children still here? On island?"

"Yes," Phoebe said. "They live with their aunt and uncle now."

"God bless them," the woman said. "And God bless you!"

"Thank you," Phoebe said. She didn't want any congratulations and she did not want to be thought generous. Naming the trail had cost her $225,000. But she and Addison had money just sitting in the bank accruing interest, and they had nothing meaningful to spend it on. Phoebe wanted to give Greg and Tess a piece of Nantucket; she wanted the twins to be able to walk the savannah trail and see the beauty of the island and feel like Tess and Greg were still alive. Or if nothing that mystical happened, fine, at least the twins would feel like their parents had been remembered and honored. Phoebe had come up with the idea in her sleep. She had been thinking of Reed and the scholarship at Whitefish Bay High School and how happy it made her father, Phil, to hand a graduating senior a check for six thousand dollars each spring.

Phoebe shook hands with five eager-faced strangers standing in a semicircle. She bumped into Dr. Richard Flanders, the school superintendent, who enveloped her in the folds of his considerable person. She could smell his aftershave, and her right arm was cut off from the rest of her body, and she feared her missing arm was going to spill her champagne, or even drop it.

"That's a great thing you did," Flanders said.

Phoebe said, "Thank you."

This didn't feel right. She should have donated the money for the path anonymously, but that hadn't been possible because of the Tess and Greg connection. So now she was saddled with her good deed; it was making her uncomfortable in a way she hadn't predicted.

She saw her people, her dear friends and her husband, huddled together with their backs turned aggressively to everyone else, including the server, who was trying to offer the Chief a stuffed quail egg. They were talking among themselves in a serious, deliberate way that Phoebe had seen before. They had talked that way when Tess and Greg died; they had talked that way when Tess lost her baby; they had probably talked that way on September 11 when they realized Reed had died. They had closed ranks and were speaking in undertones.

Phoebe suddenly understood why they had the rule of no gifts. It was too complicated emotionally to give and receive things when there were so many tight, overlapping connections between the eight of them. They were too close, and gifts required fairness and reciprocity. *Here you go, this is for you. Oh, thank you, I love it.* A simple idea, but not simple with them. Gifts would inevitably cause a mess. Phoebe had caused a mess. They found her gift offensive. They were offended that Phoebe had thought of this tribute and then executed it without their input. Andrea—of course!—would never allow Tess's and Greg's names to be attached to something without her approval. Addison would be pissed because Phoebe had spent nearly a quarter of a million dollars without asking him. (But she was prepared for this; some of that money was money that she'd earned herself, and then invested wisely with Reed.) Still, Tess had been Addison's lover, he was the executor of the will; Tess and Greg belonged to him. And they belonged to Andrea. But that, in a way, was why Phoebe had done this secretly. Tess and Greg had been Phoebe's friends, too, and she wanted to honor them *her* way, without input from the people whose connections to them were believed to be more important.

Phoebe broke into the circle, ready for her flogging. Sure enough, Andrea was crying.

"I'm sorry," Phoebe said.

Andrea swiped at her nose. "It was beautiful," she said. "A beautiful gesture."

Jeffrey said, "Delilah is going to kick herself for missing it."

Addison pulled Phoebe in close and kissed her temple. "You're a genius," he said.

ANDREA

By nine o'clock she felt she had done her duty. She had drunk two glasses of chardonnay, she had eaten six hors d'oeuvres, she had listened to Phoebe's speech, which honored Tess and Greg in a way that Andrea herself should have thought of had she not been so pathetically inward-looking, and she had wept a few tears without breaking down. She had even danced with Eddie to their favorite Sinatra tune. In Andrea's mind, she deserved a bronze star for outstanding courage.

But now she was ready to go.

"Already?" Ed said. "It's only five minutes to nine. The band is playing until midnight."

The thought of having to hold herself together for three more hours nearly brought Andrea to her knees. "I want to go home," she said.

"Another hour," Ed said.

"Now," Andrea said. "Poor Kacy—"

"Delilah's not even here yet, so poor Kacy nothing. And when the twins do get home, she'll put them to bed and make fifteen dollars an hour for watching TV."

"Ed," Andrea said, "I can't stay."

Addison approached them, holding a drink. He was glassy-eyed.

"Are you drunk?" Andrea said.

"Exhausted," he said. "I haven't been sleeping."

"Something on your mind?" the Chief asked.

Addison said, "If I thought I could sneak out of here without Phoebe's beheading me, I would."

"My savior," Andrea said. "Will you take me home?"

The Chief's eyes lit up. "Would you mind?"

"Not at all," Addison said.

"You're okay to drive?" the Chief asked.

"I'm okay."

"I'll drive," Andrea said.

"Are you coming back?" the Chief asked Addison.

"Not if I can help it," Addison said. "Phoebe has her own car. She came early, she has to stay late."

"I'll stay with Phoebe," the Chief said. "And Jeffrey. And Delilah is coming."

"She better be," Andrea said. "She doesn't get a free pass to miss this if I don't."

"We'll cover for you," the Chief said. He kissed Andrea goodbye.

Andrea took off her shoes and walked barefoot with Addison to his car. Addison was whistling, as happy as she was to be sprung free. They climbed into his Mercedes, which had deep, soft seats and the intoxicating smell of expensive leather. There was an empty highball glass in the console.

"You drank on the way out here?" she asked.

He said, "Don't tell the Chief."

She said, "Well, please don't kill us on the way home."

He said, "Would it really matter if I did?"

She looked out the window, at the moors rushing by. It was a beautiful night, there was a moon, the party had been nice,

Phoebe's gift was inspired—and yet Andrea had a hard time feeling anything. Would it matter if she died tonight?

She said, "Tess had a lover." Her breath put a mist on the car window.

Addison said, "Do you want to come to my house and have a glass of wine?"

"Okay," she said.

JEFFREY

Phoebe was the star of the evening, and it was good to see. She was glowing like her old self. She caught Jeffrey's eye, pulled away from a group of people he didn't know, and glided over to him. Her dress was silver, and her eyes picked up some of the sparkle.

"Where is your wife?" she said.

Jeffrey checked his watch. "Her plane gets in at nine-fifteen."

"Her plane?" Phoebe said.

"She took the kids to the movies," Jeffrey said.

"The *movies?*" Phoebe said. "Why tonight?"

Jeffrey shrugged. It was hard to explain to someone who didn't have kids. "Tonight was the night. Anyway, I'm going to get her at the airport. I'll be back with her in half an hour."

"You'd better be," Phoebe said. "The band is playing until midnight."

Jeffrey got to the airport at ten minutes past nine. It was a Friday night in August and the place was abuzz—planeloads of businessmen from New York, Boston, Washington, walked into the terminal and were greeted by pretty wives, shouting children, frenzied golden retrievers on leashes. Jeffrey had had two cocktails at the party, which had affected him oddly. He was unaccountably anxious. He wanted to see his wife come off the plane with the four kids. There had been moments today when he had questioned his own good judgment about letting Delilah go in the first place. Was she mentally stable enough to travel with four kids? She had seemed better the night before. She had cooked, they had made love, eaten the pie. It had been fine, it would be fine; Jeffrey had no reason to worry, but he wished he'd stuck to beer.

He sat and sat. The stream of businessmen slowed to a trickle, then stopped. Jeffrey looked at the clock; it was quarter to ten. He checked at both airlines. Any more planes coming?

No, sir, that was the last section.

Jeffrey called Delilah's cell phone. The call went straight to voicemail.

He called their house. No answer. Then, he called the Kapenash house. Kacy answered the phone.

"Kacy?" Jeffrey said. "Is Delilah there? Are the kids there?"

"No," she said. "They're not home yet."

"Has Delilah called you?"

"No," Kacy said. "She said they'd be on the nine o'clock flight."

"I'm at the airport," Jeffrey said. "I've been here forty minutes. They weren't on any of the planes."

"And you called Delilah?"

"Got her voicemail," Jeffrey said. He hadn't talked to her since that morning. "Okay, let me try to find her."

Jeffrey called Delilah's phone again and again was shuttled to voicemail. "Goddamn it, Delilah, call me!" he said.

He couldn't go back to the party without her—Phoebe would be angry, the lovely balance she'd achieved would, possibly, collapse in a lopsided heap of unnecessary worry and upset—and so he went home. He hated drama; that was the farmer in him. He liked things that were steady and reliable: the seasons, weather that fell into patterns that could be predicted, cycles of the earth. Plant a seed, watch it grow and bear fruit, harvest the fruit, allow the plant to wither, die, and nourish the soil for the next planted seed.

Of course, there would be a reasonable explanation: they had missed the showing of the movie they were supposed to see so they had to wait for the next showing; Delilah got stuck in traffic on the way home, or they got sidetracked by a Chuck E. Cheese or a roadside fair and missed the last flight. And Delilah, as usual, did not make sure her cell phone was charged and it ran out of power. Fine.

But he did not feel fine. What he felt was a gnawing sense of unrest. Since Tess and Greg had died, their home life had been a brewing storm. Jeffrey knew this, but he was busy at the farm. It was August. Jeffrey had always maintained that there was no difference between July and August other than that July was corn and August was tomatoes, but every day the farm market proved him wrong. The place was packed. The line at the deli was a dozen people long, Joanna, the baker, was making five dozen triple-berry pies a day, and the corn bin was filled with three hundred fresh-picked ears one minute and empty an hour later. Jeffrey couldn't focus on anything but survival. Pick the corn, the herbs, the flowers, the beets and cucumbers and summer squash and zucchini and carrots, the lettuce and kale and turnips. Tend to the gourds and the pumpkins, the dahlias and chrysanthemums. Water, reap, sow. Pray that Delilah would hang in there until January, when Jeffrey took four weeks off and could give proper attention to her emotional crisis. But he wasn't an idiot. He had sensed that things were about to break. He was watching out of the corner of his eye. Delilah was a pendulum. Manic and hyperalert one minute, weepy and despondent the next. Why on earth had he let her take the kids off the island?

At home the house was quiet. He opened the fridge and found it clean and stacked with food. Was Delilah planning a party?

312   Elin Hilderbrand

Had she meant to have people over here, after the event? There was a case of cold Heineken lined up like green glass soldiers in the bottom drawer, and Jeffrey grabbed one.

There was a note on the kitchen counter, which he hadn't seen when he'd rushed in at six-thirty to get dressed. A note? It was a regular white index card. Written in black Sharpie, it said, *This does not mean I don't love you, I do, that's forever. Yes and for always.* He read the index card again. It was a lyric from "Suite: Judy Blue Eyes." Greg used to sing the song all the damn time and Delilah sang along in harmony. The first third of the suite was, in Delilah's estimation, the most perfect song ever written.

Was this note meant for him? It was in Delilah's handwriting. Was it old, or had she meant for him to find it tonight? He tried her cell phone again.

You have to go, no matter what. Promise me.

The back of his throat ached. He went upstairs to the boys' rooms. In both rooms, the beds looked like they had been made up by chambermaids at the Ritz-Carlton. The dressers were tidy, drawers pushed all the way closed. He opened the drawers. Were there clothes missing? The drawers did look emptyish, as they tended to when Delilah let the laundry slide.

Jeffrey took a deep breath.

He did not like drama, nor did he like to jump to conclusions. But he didn't like the way things were stacking up: a fridge full of food, the clean house, pretty beds, neat dressers, the note. He had thought things were getting *better.* He had congratulated himself; he had waited out Delilah's instability and the storm had cleared. Delilah was correcting. But no.

ADDISON

The house was impeccably clean, but Addison straightened up anyway. He wiped dust out of a wineglass. Andrea drank chardonnay. Addison had a whole wine cooler full of whites, and there, on the bottom shelf, were two bottles of his favorite Mersault, the wine he and Tess had drunk at lunch at Nous Deux, the wine Addison swore he would never drink again. He opened the bottle.

Tess had a lover.

He looked in the pantry for snacks. Mixed nuts, a box of Bremner Wafers. Did they have any cheese? He checked the fridge. No cheese.

He tasted the Mersault, poured a glass for Andrea, then decided he would pour a glass for himself even though he had vowed never to drink it again. He handed Andrea her glass and put the nuts in a bowl. Andrea said nothing. He should put on music.

He said, "Where should we sit?"

She said, "Oh, Jesus, Add, I don't give a shit."

This was somehow exactly the right answer. It struck the right tone: they were going to be frank with each other. Addison was going to suggest they sit out by the pool, but that seemed too pleasant. There were two barstools at the counter. Addison sat, then Andrea sat, and Addison set the bowl of nuts equidistant between them.

"So," he said.

"Let's not talk," Andrea said. "Let's just drink for a while."

Addison nodded. Fair enough, he thought. The effects of six Jack Daniels had hit him; he was now officially drunk. Andrea probably needed ten more drinks before she was ready to hear what he had to tell her. But Addison couldn't wait. He said, "I was having an affair with Tess. I was in love with her."

Andrea drank her wine. She said nothing.

She drank the whole glass in three minutes; Addison was timing her. He refilled her glass; his hand was shaking. He wanted her to say something, but he was afraid of what she would say.

I'm sorry, he said to Tess.

He felt a hundred pounds lighter. He felt like he could take the back stairs two at a time and leap across the swimming pool.

Andrea was staring into space; her face was halfway between contempt and what he thought might be relief. Andrea was tough, and always had been. Addison tried to remember when the two of them had ever been alone together like this for any length of time. In Vegas they had sought out the slot machines together. Andrea had been feeding the machine next to his when he hit for seventeen hundred dollars. She had been the first person to hug him and jump up and down as the machine blinked his good fortune. On September 11, she had come to the hospital where the doctor was examining Phoebe after her miscarriage. She had hugged Addison and moaned with him. She had checked in every day for weeks, stopping by with homemade soup and doughnuts from the Downyflake. Addison remembered wandering with Andrea through the National Gallery in London. They had stopped in front of Renoir's painting *Les Parapluies.* And then there was the time Addison and Andrea had taken the surfing lesson in Sayulita, Mexico, with a grungy expat named Kelso.

Addison broke the silence by saying, "Do you remember that surfing lesson we took?"

She did not respond. Addison had been the most unlikely surfing partner in existence, but the Chief and Jeffrey in their stoic, stony way had flat-out refused, and Greg was such a good surfer already that he didn't want or need to take a beginner lesson. Phoebe was too prissy, Delilah was too uncoordinated, and Tess was afraid of the water. Which left Addison. Andrea pleaded. *Come on. I've never asked you for anything.*

He gave in because she was correct, she had never asked him for anything. Together they donned wetsuits and paddled out on their boards to chest-high water, where Kelso, the goateed, tat-tooed, pierced, stoned surf instructor, pushed them into waves. Andrea stood first, then, a hundred tries later, Addison stood. It had been a revelation, riding the water like that, even for a few seconds before the inevitable crash. He and Andrea had talked about it with Kelso over beers at the cantina later.

As they were finishing their bottle of wine (it had taken them thirty-two minutes), the phone rang. Addison checked: it was Jeffrey.

He said, "Should I answer it?"

Andrea said, "Do you think now's really the time?"

He said, "Would you like me to open another bottle of wine?"

She said, "Please."

He opened the wine. The house was dark. Too dark to see the elephant in the room?

He said, "Are we going to talk about it?"

She said, "I'm curious. Why bring up the surfing lesson?"

"I don't know. It just came to mind. It was something you and I did together."

She said, "You went with me when no one else would."

"It was no big deal. I had fun."

She said, "Why didn't you tell me about Tess earlier?"

Addison said, "Is that not obvious?"

"Tess . . ." Andrea said, but she couldn't go on. The name hung there in the dark house. The name was nothing more than a breath. "I knew there was someone. I figured it out, finally. While she was alive, I thought there was something wrong. I thought it was me."

"You?"

"She stopped going to church with me. Said she was finished with the Lord. Then I caught her lying about where she'd been and what she'd been doing, and my feelings were hurt. I didn't understand."

Addison reached for matches. He lit a few candles on the bar.

Andrea said, "Just recently I figured out it wasn't me. I figured out it was somebody else."

"It was me."

"It was you." Andrea shook her head. "Jesus, Add, what were you thinking?"

"I was thinking I loved her."

"You loved her?" Andrea said.

"Loved her, adored her, worshipped her."

Andrea nodded. Her eyes were blazing in the candlelight. She reminded him of a lynx or a panther. "I would thank you for that, if it weren't so *wrong*. What were your plans?"

"I wanted her to leave Greg. I wanted to live with her. Marry her."

"Did she want that?"

"No," he said. "If I were to be very honest with myself, I would have to say . . . I don't think she did."

Andrea nodded, nose in her wineglass.

Addison felt a shadow covering his head and shoulders, like a big, scary presence lurking behind him. He had never meant to disclose everything, but he saw now that it would be pointless to tell some but not all. "I wanted her to tell Greg about us on the sail. I asked her to tell him."

"To tell him on their *anniversary?*"

"I thought it would be a good time. They were going to be alone, without the kids."

"Do you think she did it?" Andrea asked.

"I have this feeling . . ." Addison said. God, he had waited so long to say this, just *say it*. "That she told him and he killed her."

Silence in the house. The candles flickered.

"And that would make it my fault," Addison said.

DELILAH

She drove and drove. She crossed the state line into New York. Now, she was officially kidnapping. At every exit she thought, *I should turn around.* But it felt too good to be headed away from Nantucket. It felt good to be putting miles between her and the site of her agony. After she drove through Albany, she had to decide if she wanted to cross the state on the throughway or via the southern tier. Which would be safer? She suspected the throughway would have more troopers. She chose the southern route. Leatherstocking land, the stomping grounds of James Fenimore Cooper. It was literary, the path they were taking. Literary? She was crazy. As long as she knew she was crazy, she was sane, right?

Delilah was monitoring herself for signs of exhaustion. She had awoken that morning at five when Jeffrey left for the farm; she had gotten out of bed at six to go to the grocery store. It seemed impossible that this was still the same day. Ten-thirty, eleven-fifteen. Her heartbeat was irregular. By now Jeffrey would realize she was gone. Her cell phone was in her purse, but she had shut it off, and she decided she would not check it to see what it contained. She was both giddy and profoundly terrified. Her actions were irresponsible, criminal even, but what could not be explained were the dual monsters of her grief and her guilt. She had to try to outrun them.

She had no idea where they were headed. She wanted to start over; she wanted another life. The life she'd been given, she had ruined. Where could she get a new life? The first place that popped into her head was Sayulita, Mexico. She would put the kids in school, they would learn to speak Español, they would learn to surf, they would become as brown as the natives. Four sophisticated expat children. Delilah would open a fish taco stand.

She would not take the kids to Mexico.

She would take them to . . . South Haven, Michigan, the town where she had grown up, the house where her parents still lived. Was that where she was headed? Could Delilah show up on the Victorian porch of the Ashby homestead with four kids, two of them not her own? Would her mother let them in? Would she bake cookies and show the kids the path down to the lake? Lake Michigan was as big as the ocean. They could pick blueberries, take day trips to Saugatuck and Holland. Delilah could sleep in her childhood bed with Chloe next to her and the boys on air mattresses on the floor, and Delilah would finally be safe to think.

Ironic that the place she had run away from as a teenager was the place she was now running to. But it made sense, right? In a circular kind of way?

There was a stirring in the back. Barney, of course. "Mom?" he said.

She would have to come up with a way to explain this. *We're going to visit your grandparents. We're going on a road trip. It's an American summertime tradition!* She couldn't frighten them. She had to pick her words so, so carefully.

"Yes?" Delilah said. "I'm right here, babe."

There was a noise. A yelp, a bark, a splutter, a splash. A stink. A strangled cry. Delilah inhaled sharply. Oh no! No! Yes—again a retching sound, a spewing forth. Barney was sick. He was vomiting. He had thrown up all over the back of the car, all over his legs, all over Chloe's legs. Oh God, the stench. He was gagging or choking—half a gallon of 7-Up or whatever toxic green elixir he'd ordered, two pounds of popcorn floating in coconut oil, chunks of red licorice. Delilah had long suspected that Twizzlers were made out of plastic and were therefore indigestible.

"Mom!" he cried out.

"I'm right here," she said. "We're stopping." She pulled off at the next exit, where there was a Holiday Inn. They were in the town of Cobleskill. Delilah told herself this was okay. She would not panic.

She parked the car and turned around. Puke everywhere. Oh God, the minivan. It would never be the same. Barney was covered with radioactive goo; he was crying. She wanted to hug him, hold him, wash him, throw his clothes away, tuck him into a clean bed. But he had to wait. But he was only six. Could he wait?

"I have to leave you here. I'll be right back. I am going in that door right there to get us a hotel room and then I'll be back, okay?"

"No!" he howled. He was sobbing. Her baby. Her darling. She could not leave him even for the ten minutes it would take to check into the hotel.

Drew opened his eyes. He said, "Go ahead, Mom. You get us a room. I'll stay here with Barn."

Delilah did not wait to see if this offer was satisfactory to Barney. She hopped out of the car and hightailed it inside. She seemed to have brought the funky, underbelly-of-the-movie-house smell with her. Barney had puked in her hair.

It would be Murphy's Law that during the times when you most needed a capable front-desk person to expedite your hotel check-in—at midnight, say, when you had a barfing child in the car—what you ended up with was an incompetent moron. The dude moved in slow motion, exactly like the fake-out trick the Vunderkids used against the villains. Delilah was so fatigued that for a second she became confused. Was this actually part of the movie she had just not-watched? The guy was lanky and had the wispy, flyaway hair of a mad professor. He was a sallow yellow color with even yellower teeth, and his nose was as big as a wedge of cheese. His name tag said "Lonnie," a sad, outdated name that fit him.

Lonnie slid a form across the desk that Delilah was supposed to fill out. She had to get the kids in a room. Hurry!

After God knows what further processing, moving so slowly

it was like going backward, Lonnie slid her key cards across the desk.

"Room 432, fourth floor, all the way in the back. The easiest way to access it is to—"

Yes, yes, she said. She could find it. Of course it sounded like Lonnie had just assigned her the room that was the farthest point away from the parking lot.

She hurried back out to the car (she had visions of some demented personality driving away with the kids while she was inside, kidnapping them from the kidnapper). She scooped up Barney, sacrificing her own clothes. She woke the other kids, and they trailed her like sheep. They marched the chilly halls of the Holiday Inn, which was sinister in its lack of character. Barney had his legs wrapped around Delilah's waist and his hot, foul-smelling mouth agape against her neck. She had not had a spare hand for the overnight bag; she would have to retrace her steps the mile and a half back to the car. She would strip Barney first, put him in the shower (a nightmarish thought—the kid *hated* the shower), and pile him into bed with his brother.

She found Room 432, the last godforsaken room, but blessedly right across the hall from the ice machine and vending, and she tried to negotiate the key into its slot without being able to see her hands. Somehow she got the door open and stepped inside. There was a bathroom to the immediate left, a short hallway with an open closet, shelves for an iron and a dry cleaning bag, two double beds, a TV on the dresser, a desk, a table, two chairs, a pastel painting of a windmill and a couple of hounds, a window with long, heavy brocade curtains, and an air conditioner turned up full blast. The room was about thirty-five degrees.

"Okay!" Delilah said. Here was shelter.

"Auntie Dee?"

It was Finn. She turned around to address what sounded like panic in his voice, just in time to see him spew a great green wave of vomit in the vicinity of the brown plastic trash can, but really it splattered all over the dresser.

"Bathroom!" Delilah barked. She sounded unsympathetic, she knew. But Jesus, what was happening here? She laid Barney down and wheeled Finn into the bathroom, lifting the toilet seat and pushing his head down just in time for the next pulsing gush to splash into the bowl.

Chloe moved to the far bed, unaware or unimpressed, took off her shoes, and climbed in.

Teeth! Delilah thought. Chloe needed to brush her teeth, but Delilah had to deal with first things first, and besides that, the toothbrushes were in the overnight bag. Drew stood next to Delilah and said, "Mom?"

"Are you going to puke, too?" she asked.

"No," he said.

"Okay, good." She knew he wanted direction; he wanted to help. Eight years old and already a troubleshooter. Did she need to say it? He was just like his father.

Delilah said, "Are you capable of getting your brother out of his clothes?"

Drew nodded like a good soldier. "You bet."

Delilah bent down to stroke Finn's back. This was her fault. She could not take kids who were used to just-picked corn and organic free-range chickens and expect their systems to handle near-poisonous quantities of sugar and tallow.

If Jeffrey were watching this . . .

She tried to push this thought from her head.

. . . he would say she was getting what she deserved.

The minivan was covered with puke; the hotel room had been desecrated and they'd only been there ninety seconds. She, Delilah, was streaked with vomit; she had vomit in her hair. She heard a familiar tussling in the room, and she knew that although Barney was parched and dehydrated, or possibly brewing another bubbling batch of barf, he was also actively resisting his older brother's stripping him down.

Drew insisted. "Mom said!"

Barney said, "Get off of me!"

Delilah left Finn moaning and groaning and separated her boys. She whipped off Barney's clothes with no mercy while Drew complained.

"You said I could help!"

She threw the fouled clothes into a pile in the corner. What she needed was the overnight bag from the car. Could she in good conscience send Drew to go get it? He was strapping and athletic, he could deal with the car keys and the hotel key card, he could get the bag and trek all the way back here. But could he do it in the middle of the night, when—Delilah was sure—there were abductors and pedophiles lurking in the fields beyond the hotel parking lot?

No.

"I have to go get the overnight bag," Delilah said. She wanted her toothbrush and the kids needed a change of clothes.

Delilah waited until Finn was strong enough to stand up, then she walked him to the bed where his sister was fast asleep, stripped him to his boxers, and got him under the covers. She adjusted the air conditioner. The room was starting to smell. Delilah threw a few of the thin hotel towels over the obvious places where Finn had vomited.

"I'll be right back," Delilah said to Drew. Barney was huddled under the covers.

"Can I watch TV?" Drew asked.

"No," Delilah said. It was one in the morning. What would be on the hotel TV but pornography?

"Please?"

"No, Drew. Everyone else is asleep."

He gave her a face. "This place sucks. I hate it here."

Well, that made two of them, but Delilah couldn't articulate this because the kids would take their cues from her. She had to be upbeat, no matter what. "I only pulled over because your brother was sick. This isn't anyplace we're staying."

"Where are we staying?" Drew asked. "Where are we going?"

Michigan, she thought. The idea had taken root in her. The kids splashing in the lake, the kids picking blueberries.

"Someplace else," she said.

She hiked down to the parking lot for the bag. She was exhausted. Really fucking tired. She just wanted to sleep.

When she got back to the room, she heard a noise she did not like. The door to the bathroom was shut. She pushed it open.

Drew was on his knees, puking into the bathtub.

PHOEBE

Everyone had left her except for the Chief and the hundred other people who were dancing. Phoebe had no shortage of dance partners. She danced with Swede, she danced with Hank Drenmiller, she danced with the executive director of Island Conservation. They all told her how wonderful she was, how generous and kindhearted. Phoebe felt like the belle of the ball, the way she used to feel on special nights before Reed died, like she was pretty and charming and so, so lucky to have been born into her life.

But something was eating at her, an impostor feeling, a feeling that she did not deserve any of this. She had been drinking champagne all night to combat this feeling, but as was always the case with alcohol, her underlying feelings became stronger rather than weaker. Pretense peeled away, exposing . . .

The band finished "These Boots Were Made for Walking," and Phoebe and the executive director separated and politely clapped. Phoebe scanned the crowd. Everyone was having a *lot* of fun; she could feel good about that. She saw Eddie on the fringes of the room, holding a savannah sidecar. He wasn't dancing and he wasn't talking to anyone, but he looked happy.

Phoebe was rafting down a champagne river. The band launched into "Love Potion Number Nine." Phoebe grabbed the Chief's hand. "Come on, Eddie. Let's dance."

"I don't dance," the Chief said. "You know that. Not with my wife, not with the Queen of England."

Phoebe pulled him onto the dance floor. "But with me, tonight, yes."

"No," he said, but he was trying not to smile.

"It's my party," Phoebe said, "and you'll dance if I want to."

And guess what? The Chief could dance. He was as strong and solid and surefooted as Phoebe's father. He led, she followed. She was seventeen again, at the Whitefish Bay Pool Club at her homecoming dance. She had been runner-up as queen to Shelby Duncan, Reed's girlfriend. Reed and Shelby had looked silly but sweet in their foil crowns.

Phoebe became confused. The Chief twirled her, then gathered her up in his arms. He was her father. He was a safe place. She looked him square in the eye. He stopped, held her out at arm's length.

"That was a great thing you did," he said.

Phoebe said, "There's something I have to tell you."

The Chief did not move. The song ended, people clapped. Phoebe was falling. Falling! She let go of her pole and toppled into the champagne river. She was drowning. Would anyone save her?

Phoebe told the Chief as they sat on folding chairs in the dark night outside the bright oval of the tent.

"I gave Tess a pill," she said. "Only one. But it was a doozy."

Phoebe tried to explain, but her words were jumbled. Tess

and Addison having an affair, in love, discovered by Phoebe in the cruel, cold days of early April. She saw them together at the Quaise cottage, but she said nothing. What could she say? She understood. In a weird, drug-addled way, she approved. But not really, of course. Not wholly or completely. She had her moments of clarity, her flare-ups of jealousy. Addison was in love with Tess. But Phoebe said nothing, did nothing. She hid beneath a shroud of drugs. She waited. Days, weeks, months. She watched the affair; she took its temperature. Addison was in deeper than Tess. Tess wanted to pull away; Addison wouldn't let her. He wanted her to leave Greg. How did Tess feel about this? Phoebe couldn't tell.

Tess came to Phoebe two days before her anniversary. The sail was going to happen; they had checked the forecast. There would be plenty of wind. Greg was gung-ho about the sail, about the anniversary celebration; they needed it, they deserved it. He had a surprise. He had written her a song. Andrea was making a picnic. Delilah was taking the kids overnight.

Tess had not needed to ask. Phoebe anticipated her. She knew Tess was nervous about the sail (all that open water, the wind, the waves), and there was additional anxiety on top of it, something else, something Tess was going to do or say, something she was either going to confess or suppress.

Phoebe said, "I'd like to give you something."

Tess looked like she might protest. No gifts! Delilah went to Phoebe for drugs, as did Andrea and Greg when they had a pulled shoulder muscle or a headache. But never Tess.

"That would be great," Tess said.

Phoebe could have taken it easy on her. Ativan, Xanax, even a valium or two would have been enough to take the edge off. But in the back of her mind, Phoebe held the vision she had seen through the cottage window. Addison in bed, holding Tess in his arms, Tess's eyes closed, Addison gazing at the ceiling.

Phoebe gave her one of the precious Number Nines, the contraband pills that came from Reed's college roommate Brandon, off the big drug company black market. She would send Tess straight to the heroin stratosphere.

"Be sure to take it with food," Phoebe directed. She put the pill in Tess's palm and folded her fingers over it.

"She took it," the Chief said.

Phoebe nodded. Tess had taken the pill, and she had drunk the champagne that Andrea had packed. Then the boat caught a gust and Tess had lurched or been thrown overboard. She was not a great swimmer under the best of circumstances, and with the drug coursing through her, she hadn't stood a chance.

Greg most likely had died trying to save her.

Finally Phoebe cried. Not the breathless, hysterical sobs that she had released in the shock of first finding out, but rather, she cried deeply. She was a bottomless well of sorrow, guilt, and regret. She cried like a woman who had done the unthinkable. She had killed her best friend, leaving two children motherless.

"I didn't mean to kill her," Phoebe said. "I just wanted to . . . I don't know . . . give her a shove. But what else can I think now, but that I . . ."

Even with ten savannah sidecars in him, the Chief was a man of reason. He touched her back and said, "You didn't kill her. You gave her the pill to calm her nerves. You were trying to help her."

Phoebe wanted to be tried for murder. She wanted death row.

"I could have given her Ativan," Phoebe said. "But I gave her the Number Nine."

"The pill wasn't what killed her. She drowned. She fell off the boat, which would make it an accident. Or . . ."

"Or she was pushed," Phoebe said.

"Or she was pushed." The Chief sighed. "But here's the thing—I'm glad you told me. The drug showed up on the tox report, and that tox report has been eating at me since . . . I didn't know what to think. Well, what I thought was that Greg shot her full of smack, then dumped her overboard so he could be with April Peck."

Phoebe said, "What I did was no better. I gave her a pill I knew she couldn't handle. I wanted to ruin her anniversary. Tess was having an affair with my husband and I wanted to turn her into a zombie. And then she *died,* Eddie. She is dead and Greg is dead, and it is *my fault.*"

"All you did was give her the pill," the Chief said. "You didn't make her take it."

Phoebe would not be comforted. "It's the strongest opiate out there. It's not even legal, Ed. I would take one, you know, in the darkest days, and I would be in outer space. I couldn't drive or make a sandwich. I couldn't wash my hair. I was so out of it." She looked at him. "I'm a monster."

The Chief took her hand. The tent blazed before them like a big white birthday cake. Phoebe felt exhausted, weak, full of heartache. The fact of the matter was, she missed Tess. The absolute truth was that Tess and Addison could have gotten married and left Phoebe homeless and destitute, and it still would have been better than this, because Tess and Greg would be alive. They would all be together. Still.

JEFFREY

Where, where, where?

He was the woman's husband. He should know the inner workings of Delilah's mind. And he did, didn't he? It was Delilah's belief that people were predictable. They always acted like themselves; no one was truly capable of change. Presumably she applied this theory to herself. In their first, torrid week of dating, she had described herself as a bird that was unable to be captured or caged. She told him the story of how she'd run away in high school. Every time he and Delilah argued, she threatened to leave. Her presence in his life, she'd always maintained, was temporary. This had felt like an empty threat, because Delilah had a deep dedication to house and home. Their house was a finely feathered nest; it was a haven for their children and their friends and their friends' children. Would Delilah have expended so much energy building and nurturing a home only to abandon it? She assured him she would. And look, she had.

Jeffrey had called Addison and Phoebe at home, but no one answered; he didn't want to bother them on their cell phones if they were still at the party and ruin their good time. He didn't call the Chief or Andrea because he didn't want either of them to panic—to put out an APB or call Delilah a kidnapper.

He told himself he was overreacting. Delilah had gotten stuck off-island and for some reason had not been able to find a way to contact him.

But he was a smart man and he knew his wife. This had to do with Tess and Greg. It had, Jeffrey believed, to do with Delilah and Greg. Delilah and Greg had worked at the Begonia together for years; they had spent God knows how many late nights together drinking, smoking dope, singing, and keeping each other's secrets. Delilah always took Greg's side; she was his champion. She was his closest friend in a circle where they were all close friends. Jeffrey was too proud to admit it, but their friendship had always gotten under his skin. He blamed it for certain deficiencies in his own relationship with Delilah. Greg got to be her boyfriend, leaving Jeffrey to be her . . . what? Her father. Here was Jeffrey now, another version of Nico Ashby, chasing down his daughter who was on the lam.

He took another beer out of the fridge and sat down in a chair, to wait until morning.

ADDISON

There was only an inch or so left in the second bottle of Mersault. Both Addison and Andrea were quite drunk, but despite the raw and emotionally treacherous nature of their discussion, they were having a good time. Or maybe it was just Addison having a good time. He and Andrea had stopped talking, but they were listening to jazz, bobbing their heads, and Andrea, while not exactly smiling, had softened her exasperated expression.

She said, "Tell me why you got kicked out of Princeton."

"Ah," Addison said. "The Princeton story."

"Ed says it's a great story."

"But it's just that—a story. I didn't actually get kicked out of Princeton. I just didn't graduate with my class because I was short on math credits."

"Tell the story anyway."

And so he obliged. The week before graduation, Addison and his buddy Blake Croft crashed a garden party that the dean was throwing for donors to the annual fund. Addison and Blake wore straw boaters and pastel dinner jackets. They drank Mount Gay and tonics and ate oysters from the raw bar to improve their virility. The dean, recently divorced, was at the party with an extremely beautiful and extremely young woman named Nadine. Nadine targeted Addison, engaged him in a private, racy conversation, and then led him by the hand to the powder room, where they . . . Here Addison wiggled his eyebrows, but Andrea did not crack a smile. Addison, in his defense, did ask Nadine about the dean, and she said, "Oh, he's an old fuddy-duddy." Addison happened to agree.

When Nadine and Addison emerged from the powder room, disheveled and glowing, the dean was standing there, waiting in line.

"But that wasn't the bad part," Addison said.

"What was the bad part?" Andrea deadpanned.

"Nadine wasn't the dean's date," Addison said. "It was his daughter."

"Oh," Andrea said, nonplussed.

Addison shook his head. He was very drunk. Perhaps he'd told it wrong.

Andrea said, "Did that story teach you anything?"

"Yeah," Addison said. "It taught me to be careful about women."

"But not really," Andrea said.

"But not really," Addison said.

There was a clatter at the door. Phoebe and the Chief swung in.

"We're home!" Phoebe sang out. She looked at the Chief. "Your wife is here."

Andrea stood up and straightened the skirt of her red dress. "Nightcap," she said. "And a little bonding. Addison just told me what happened at Princeton."

"What happened at Princeton?" Phoebe said.

"I'm exhausted," Andrea said. "I need my pillow."

"God, me too," Phoebe said.

The Chief took Andrea's hand. "I missed you," he said.

"And I missed you," she said.

"And I missed you," Phoebe said to Addison. She crossed the room and fell into his lap. She was quite drunk. She might have been drunker than he was. "Did you miss me?"

"I missed you," he said.

In the chilly, dark depth of their middle-of-the-night bedroom, Addison and Phoebe made love for the first time in over nine months.

Addison felt Phoebe climb on top of him; he felt her shift her hips and breasts, he felt her mouth on his neck and her hands rubbing up and down his sides, and before he knew it, he was responding. He could not believe what was happening; he could not believe this hot, sweet, hungry person was his wife. She had been this way once, but that was a long time ago. This, right now, did not feel like a rediscovery, not just like riding a bike; it was as though another woman had sneaked into his room to entice him.

"Phoebe?" he said, just to be sure.

"Please?" she said. She thought he would turn her down. He had turned her down earlier in the summer. But tonight it was okay.

Why? He would wonder this only later, once he lay breathless and spent and Phoebe drifted off to her contented dreams. It had to do with the obvious: he had told the truth to Andrea. He had shared the burden, he felt lighter, and this was, he realized, the first step in letting Tess go and getting on with his life. Phoebe was his life. Then there was the other part of the night to account for. Phoebe's benefit, a gorgeous, elegant affair, and her incredibly generous, surprisingly appropriate and touching announcement: a nature walk named after Tess and Greg. It was a magnificent gesture. The naming of the trail was a great, good thing that Phoebe had done. It accepted Tess and Greg's deaths instead of trying to escape the reality.

So on a night that included accepting and honoring, letting go and moving on, Addison and Phoebe found each other, again.

DELILAH

It was two o'clock in the morning. The kids were asleep; the room smelled. Delilah was exhausted. She was scared. Her imagination was threatening guerrilla warfare. She had no defenses. She was about to surrender. *Take me.* Thoughts led to other, darker thoughts. This was awful. She had been so vigilant for so many long nights, but now she had nothing left. Her head fell forward on the limp stem of her neck. She rested her face on the cool tabletop.

Okay.

Here came Tess with the kids. The Kia pulled into the driveway as it had hundreds of times before, and as ever, Delilah checked to make sure the house was clean enough, orderly enough, a decent environment for raising children. TV turned off; dishes out of the sink. Her own kids had to be either outside playing or inside doing a creative project. These things mattered to Tess. Today Drew and Barney were out back, beating the hell out of the croquet balls.

Tess emerged from the car, looking adorable—the red polka-dot sunglasses, the jean shorts, the cute flip-flops. But Tess looked worried. Delilah had known the woman a long time, she recognized every expression, and something was wrong. Something was wrong with Delilah, too. Her head was heavy and aching, her teeth gritty. April Peck in the Scarlet Begonia. Greg singing "Tiny Dancer." Greg and April Peck, pulled up at the beach. They had mended the fence. Greg had been lying, perhaps this whole time. Betraying Tess. Betraying Delilah. Supposedly he told her everything.

He would not get away with it.

Tess kissed the kids a hundred times. She hugged them, then hugged them again. She said, *Please be good. I love you. You know I love you.* The kids nodded, kissed her back, then tried to pull away. She held them fast until they twisted out of her grasp and ran out to the backyard to claim their favorite croquet mallets.

Delilah walked Tess back to her car. Was she going to do it? She was furious beyond fury, she was finished, she didn't care if Greg ever spoke to her again. All she wanted was for him to pay. Her teeth tingled with a metallic residue. She had vomited; she had fought with her husband, who had done nothing wrong. She was not going to let Greg have a lovely anniversary.

She said to Tess sotto voce, *How are you? Are you okay?*

And Tess said, too quickly, *Yes. Fine.*

Delilah took a deep breath. Jump?

Tess said, *I'm just worried about the kids.*

Delilah bristled. Worried about leaving the kids with Delilah? *They'll be fine,* she said. *We're going to pick strawberries this afternoon.*

Tess said, *I have a funny feeling.*

Jump.

Delilah said, *Listen, I don't know how to say this so I'm just going to say it. Okay?*

Tess nodded mutely. One last chance to back out! Delilah heard the kids laughing in the backyard. Tess and Greg were her friends, they were the closest thing to family she had on this island—but as Jeffrey liked to remind Delilah, she did not belong in the middle of their private affairs.

She did not belong in the middle. The truth was in her cupped hands, but it was not Delilah's job to set it free.

I know things have been hard for you and Greg, Delilah said. *Jeffrey and I are rooting for you guys. Have a nice anniversary, okay?*

Tess looked puzzled, as if to say, *That's it?*

Okay, Tess said. *Thank you.*

Delilah said, *You don't have to thank me. Give a call when you get back.*

Will do! Tess said. Suddenly she smiled. *God, I'm nervous. I actually have butterflies about spending time with my own husband. I guess that's a good sign, huh?*

You know it is, Delilah said. She waved as Tess backed out of the driveway and drove away.

*   *   *

Delilah lay with her face on the table in the gloomy hotel room. There was a blue glow from the digital clock: 2:58.

Delilah had not told her. She had not said the words that would have kept Tess from getting on that boat. She had kept her mouth shut, the truth trapped. She had not wanted to get in the middle of Tess and Greg's private affairs. Less generously, she had wanted to be the only person who knew Greg's secrets. Always she had wanted to be the one who knew the most about him.

And . . .

And what?

Tess and Greg died. Greg's mind was elsewhere, the wind got the best of him, he lost control, the boat went over, they got caught underneath. He tried to save Tess but couldn't? He had pushed Tess off the boat on purpose, then had second thoughts and gone after her? He told Tess about April Peck himself and Tess had jumped? No one would ever know what happened, but Delilah knew one thing. Whatever happened, it had been within her power to stop it, and she had not.

Delilah woke up stiff-necked to the sound of Barney breathing through his nose.

She lifted her head off the table. Barney was sitting across from her.

"Mom," he whispered. "I'm thirsty."

He was pale and sweaty, his hair in cowlicks, his eyes sunken but alert. Delilah stood up. Her whole body ached from sleeping at the table like some overworked paralegal. She felt Barney's forehead. Cool and moist. Drew lay in bed, stirring, but Chloe and Finn were still asleep and unmoving, with the covers pulled over their heads. Delilah went out to the hallway for a bucket of ice, and then, from the bathroom tap, she poured glasses of water.

She brought Barney water, which he inhaled, then she checked Drew's forehead. Cool to the touch.

Delilah brought Barney a second glass of water. "I'm going downstairs to pay the bill," she said. "I'll be right back. Will you get dressed?"

"What about breakfast?" Barney said. "I'm hungry."

"We'll eat on the road," Delilah said. "We'll find a Bob Evans."

"Awesome," Drew said.

Delilah smiled. The kids felt better; they could be made happy with breakfast at Bob Evans and other things they didn't have on Nantucket. The rest of the wide world was a cornucopia for them.

She went down to the desk to pay the bill. Lonnie was still working.

"Where are you headed today?" he asked her.

"I don't know," she admitted.

He cocked his head, confused.

She thought back to the Delilah who had been determined to live deliberately. She would deliberately get the kids breakfast. Then, she would decide what to do. Her neck hurt. Her soul hurt.

Tess! Greg!

She was to blame for their deaths. This wasn't something she could run away from.

When she got back to the room, the kids were gone. Delilah blinked. She checked the room number on the door: 432. She studied the room: it was empty. The TV was shut off. The overnight bag sat agape on the floor; the vomity clothes were in a pile. Where were the kids? Were they hiding? Delilah checked the closet, behind the brocade curtains, under the beds. Then she ran out into the hallway, shouting names. Shouting! She would wake up every other guest on the fourth floor, but she didn't care.

"Drew! Barney! Barney DRAKE!"

Nothing.

Delilah couldn't wait for the elevator. She dashed down the stairs to the lobby and called out to Lonnie. The kids, three boys, one girl. *Where are they?*

Lonnie stammered.

"You didn't see them? Hear them? They didn't run past here?"

No.

Where should she look? Were they at the pool? In the game room? She would check there first: yes, okay, the indoor pool, then the adjacent game room, the modest amusements of this crap hotel. Or they had decided they couldn't wait for Bob Evans and had gone for breakfast at the rinky-dink restaurant. They were hungry, they wanted pancakes and bacon, a wedge of pale melon, a thin disk of out-of-season orange.

Delilah concentrated on breathing. She had not used Lamaze during the births of either of her children, but she was using it now. In deep, out in short puffs. She ran down the hall to the pool. The indoor pool was a sad turquoise rectangle in a disintegrating tile room that smelled strongly of mildew and chlorine. The plastic resin lifeguard chair was deserted, and a stack of scratchy white towels stood untouched. No one had been in here for days.

The adjacent game room held two old-fashioned pinball machines that flashed their lights and made distorted groaning noises, a defunct Ms Pacman game, and a foosball table with half the players amputated from the waist down. No Drew, no Barney, no Chloe, no Finn. She had managed to lose four children. Not only her own children, but other people's children. She touched her face; her cheeks were burning.

The restaurant held a little more promise. It was hopping! Nearly all of the tables held families with small children eating pancakes meant to look like Mickey Mouse swimming in ponds of syrup and topped with butter meant to look like whipped cream. Delilah weaved through the tables. Had the kids been lured down here by the smell of bacon and sausage?

The kids were not in the restaurant. Delilah hurried back to the front desk. Lonnie was still there, looking as morose as ever.

"Did they come past?" Delilah asked.

Lonnie shook his droopy head.

Delilah walked through the automatic sliding door. She stood beneath the portico and surveyed the parking lot. Beyond this hotel was highway. Would they have walked? There was just no way.

"Drew!" she screamed. "Barney!"

Somewhere in the parking lot, a car alarm sounded. Had she set it off?

She raced through the parking lot. Lamaze breathing—but there wasn't time! She had to find them! Delilah was not religious; she did not pray. This was a flaw, she saw now, a hole, a void. Tess and Andrea were Catholic, and Greg and the Chief, however reluctantly, had gone along with that strict and structured faith. Addison was Episcopalian, Phoebe had been Episcopalian but since 9/11 had developed her own religion, a cross between Buddhism and drug-induced hallucinogenic voodoo mysticism. Jeffrey was Presbyterian, a staunch farmer, pitchfork-wielding, *American Gothic* Protestant. He took the boys to the Congregational church on Sundays at 10:30 twice a month; he donated to the offertory basket, belted out the doxology, spent a month of weekends doing odd jobs around the antiquated, drafty interior. Delilah had been raised an unwieldy combination of Lutheran and Greek Orthodox but had dropped both. She went to church with Jeffrey on Christmas Eve because she liked the carols. But the rest of the time she was spiritually adrift.

Delilah circled the hotel, inspecting it from the outside. There were nooks and crannies, places to hide—service entrances, housekeeping headquarters, a separate, canopied entrance for the families who took their kids to the Holiday Inn for breakfast on the weekends as a treat.

"Barney!" she screamed. "Drew! Andrew DRAKE!"

"Mom!" someone shouted.

And then she saw them. She almost choked on her relief. It was a palpable thing, a thick chemical vapor that filled her up and made her wheeze as she tried to cry out. The relief nearly stopped her heart.

Behind the hotel, in what might have been called the back courtyard, was a playground. The skeleton of a swing set, two scabby seesaws, and the rusted disk of a merry-go-round on which spun Chloe, Finn, and Barney. Drew was pushing.

"Jesus!" she said. She was crying now. "I was so scared. I thought I'd lost you."

They did not speak. They observed Delilah as if she were an alien just stepped off a flying saucer, as if she were some unidentifiable wildlife emerging from the bush.

"I was so worried!" she said. "Thank God you're safe!" Thank God, thank God. She realized that this angst, this panic, this frantic hair-raising fucking *worry* was, of course, what Jeffrey, Andrea, the Chief, Phoebe, and Addison would be feeling once they realized Delilah was gone with the kids. Delilah couldn't stand to think of anyone else feeling this way. Somewhere inside her guilty and broken self, there was a beating heart.

Delilah waited until the merry-go-round slowed, then she sat down between Finn and Barney. She gathered Drew and Chloe into her lap, and although they were way too old for this, they allowed her to hold them anyway.

"Are we going home now?" Barney asked.

She kissed the top of his head.

"Yep," she said, like the unflappable mom she was. "We're going home now."

THE CHIEF

He was tired in the morning and suffering from something of a hangover. He'd considered taking a sick day from work, which he did once a year, but a call had come to the house from Dickson, asking the Chief to get down there as soon as possible.

The Chief did not like the sound of Dickson's voice. "Why?" he said.

"April Peck is here to see you," Dickson said.

"Oh, Jesus," the Chief said. He was glad Andrea was still asleep. He hung up the phone. Kacy was buttering an English muffin at the counter. "What time are the twins due home?"

"Um," she said. "I'm not sure." She sounded funny. Or maybe that was because of the ringing in the Chief's ears. He and Phoebe had danced awfully close to the band's brass section.

"Okay, I have to go in to work. Please don't wake your mother. Will you be around when the twins get home?"

"Um," Kacy said. "I guess?"

April Peck, the Chief thought. Sweet Jesus. "I have to go," he said.

He was unwashed, unshaven, in his street clothes, and he had to make do with the truly atrocious coffee that Molly made for the station. These were all bad omens. And somehow he had to make room in his mind for Phoebe's confession of the night before. Greg had not drugged Tess. Phoebe had given her a black market pill. Addison and Tess had been having an affair. So now he knew where the opiates in Tess's blood had come from, and the phone calls to and from Addison could be explained, but was the picture any clearer?

Dickson was standing at the threshold of the Chief's office.

"She's in there?" the Chief said.

Dickson nodded once. "Wants to talk to you and you only."

"It's okay." The Chief opened the door to his office, and Dickson reluctantly returned to work.

She was wearing a gray T-shirt and running shorts. She wore no makeup, and her blond hair was in a ponytail. She was staring into her lap. The Chief set his coffee down and collapsed in his chair. He felt like crap.

"What can I do for you, Miss Peck?"

She raised her face. It was red and splotchy from crying. The Chief tried not to react. He couldn't do this. Did the girl understand? He was not a therapist. He could not just sit here and "listen" while she talked about Greg.

"Miss Peck—"

"I was with him the night before he died," she said.

The Chief did not move. Jeffrey had told him this, but was there more?

"What happened?" the Chief asked. "You say you were 'with him,' but what does that mean? What happened between the two of you?"

"It's not what we did or didn't do that's important," April said.

And the Chief thought, *The girl is so misguided.*

"It's what he *said*. It's what he *told* me."

The Chief allowed himself to breathe; then he took a sip of the mouth-puckering coffee. "Okay," he said. "What did Greg tell you?"

"He told me he loved his wife. He told me he would never in a million years leave her or his kids. He made me repeat it. *You love your wife.* He said he did not love me. He said he couldn't be my friend anymore." She sniffled. "He said he loved his wife."

The Chief nodded. "Anything else?"

"He said he'd written her a song, for their anniversary. It had a really strange name."

"What was it?" the Chief asked. His voice was husky.

"Beyond Beyond."

"Beyond Beyond?"

"Yeah, as in beyond . . . beyond."

The Chief wrote the word twice on his desk blotter. "Okay," he said. "Is there anything else?"

"No," she said, and stood up. "Does that help?"

"Yes," he said. "It helps."

When she got to the door, the Chief said, "Miss Peck? What made you decide to come in?"

April chewed her lower lip. She said, "My mother died yesterday afternoon. At the hospital."

He was momentarily speechless. Then he said, "I'm sorry."

April said, "I have to straighten out my act if I'm ever going to amount to anything."

And with that, she left.

ADDISON

In a matter of hours, the world was different. He had confessed to Andrea about his affair, he had made love to his wife for the first time in months. And yet life beckoned. Phoebe rose early to get back out to the savannah to help clean up, and Addison went into the office.

It was very early, but Florabel was there, at her desk, drinking the devil's coffee—black, strong, steaming hot.

"How was the party?" she asked.

The party? It took Addison a minute to figure out what party Florabel was talking about. "It was great!" he said. "The food was delicious!"

"You met my clients? Hank and Legris?"

Addison scratched his nose. Did those names ring a bell?

Addison was a professional bullshitter; he was very good at feeling his way through the dark until someone turned on the lights.

"Hank," he said.

"And his girlfriend, Legris. They're friends of Phoebe's? They have that huge sailboat?"

"Oh, right, right, right," Addison said. The guy with the sailboat, Hank. Friend of Swede and Jennifer's. Addison had actually been on that boat twice, ten or so years earlier. There had been no Legris then that Addison knew of. Back then, Hank had been newly divorced and had a quartet of young women hanging off him. "Which clients?" he asked.

Florabel gave him a look. "I only have two clients, Dealer. Hank and Legris are buying the Quaise cottage."

Addison smiled and nodded to mask his sinking heart. Hank the sailboat guy was buying the Quaise cottage. Hank and Legris, friends of Phoebe's?

"I'm a little confused," Addison admitted.

"Phoebe is friends with my clients, Hank and Legris, who are buying the Quaise cottage. Phoebe was the one who told them about the cottage in the first place, actually."

"She was?" Addison's whole face was itching now. This was not right. Phoebe didn't know anything about any of his listings, much less his most confidential listing, which was the Quaise cottage.

"Yeah! The reason they bought such a small place is because they have that enormous boat."

Well, that made sense. But not the other part.

"Phoebe wasn't the one who told them about the Quaise cottage," Addison said.

"Yes, she was."

"She didn't know about it. She doesn't know a thing about any of the properties."

"Well, she knew about the Quaise cottage. I told her about it. She came in here looking for you one day this past spring and I told her you were probably out at the cottage. Remember how much time you spent over the winter fixing it up?"

Fixing it up. Addison scanned his desk for something to grab. Was Florabel making this up to torture him? He was afraid to look at her. He stared at the phone, willing it to ring so that Florabel would answer it and he would have a chance to breathe.

"Phoebe's never seen the cottage," he said.

"Sure she has," Florabel said. "I told her exactly where it was and she went up there. And later she called to thank me. She said she found you, no problem."

"Found me?" he said.

Florabel nodded, her lips a smug line.

"When was this?"

"This past spring. March, April."

Addison narrowed his eyes at Florabel. She was such an unpleasant bitch. Was she trying to blackmail him? Was she thinking he would increase her commission, or give her a chunk of cash from the company's operating budget?"

"What are you after, Florabel?" he asked.

"I'm not after anything, Dealer. I wanted to know if you met Hank and Legris. If Phoebe introduced you. If you made a connection with them, our clients, the buyers of the Quaise cottage."

"I did not speak to them at the party," Addison said. "Phoebe did not introduce us."

"What is wrong with you?" Florabel said. "I was only *asking!*"

He immediately wanted a drink. What time did they start serving at the Begonia? Could he go over there and get one? He decided he could not. If he got all muddled and messy right now, he would not be able to sort through this and make everything come out okay. Florabel was wrong. Phoebe did not know about the Quaise cottage. The phone rang and Florabel answered it. This gave Addison a chance to think, slowly and calmly, about what

Florabel had said. Florabel said the buyers of the Quaise cottage, Hank (last name?) and his girlfriend Legris (What kind of name was this? It sounded like a name from the bayou), were friends of Phoebe's. This was true. Although who knew what kind of friends they were. Phoebe had known Hank a long time ago, back when she was actively chairing events and attending events that other people chaired, back when she was hanging out with Jennifer and Swede. Phoebe had reconnected with Jennifer and Swede this summer at Caroline Nieve Masters's Fourth of July party, and she had, to Addison's knowledge, been out on Hank's sailboat twice since then. Okay, let's say that made them friends. Did Phoebe mention the Quaise cottage to Hank and Legris? No, because Phoebe did not know about the Quaise cottage. Here Addison took a moment to reflect. He did not like the way Florabel called him Dealer to his face. He knew this was his nickname around town, but to call him Dealer to his face was blatantly disrespectful. Addison had never asked Florabel to stop, because he knew she wouldn't. She was that disobedient, that awful. Why had he not fired her years ago? Whywhywhy? Well, she was one hell of an administrator, more organized than Martha Stewart; she kept the office in order, she overlooked no detail, and . . . she was honest. She would not cheat him and she would not lie.

And since Florabel did not lie, then what she said was true: Phoebe had showed up at the office one random afternoon in the spring, looking for Addison. Addison was at the Quaise cottage, "fixing it up." Florabel, because she did not lie, told Phoebe that Addison was at the Quaise cottage. She gave Phoebe directions; she may even have drawn a map to the cottage on a piece of Wheeler Realty notepaper. Phoebe drove out to the Quaise cottage. Then, this summer, she mentioned the cottage to Hank and Legris when they said they were in the market for "a little place."

All this was fine. But Addison still had questions.

One: Did Florabel know Addison had been meeting someone

out at the Quaise cottage? (Another reason that Addison had never fired Florabel was that she was the smartest person Addison knew. She was clinically smart; she belonged to Mensa.) So yes, safe to say she knew exactly what was going on. She sent Phoebe out to the Quaise cottage on purpose, she probably *insisted* that Phoebe journey out to Quaise to find Addison, because . . . that was the kind of evil bitch that Florabel was.

The bigger, more crucial question was . . . when Phoebe drove out to the Quaise cottage, what did she find?

Should he call Phoebe?

What was the point? Phoebe knew.

Florabel was trying to get his attention. "Dealer!" she said. She was in front of her desk, snapping her fingers in his face. "God, what is *wrong* with you today? Your wife is on the phone."

Phoebe? Now Addison was scared. "Take a message," he told Florabel. "I'm busy."

"Busy?" Florabel said. "Jesus, Dealer, if you were my employee, I'd fire you." She got back on the phone and hung up seconds later. "She wants help out on the savannah. She said there are hundreds of cocktail napkins scattered across the grass."

"Okay," Addison said absently.

Phoebe knew about Tess. She found out at some point in the spring when she went looking for Addison, but she found Florabel instead, and Florabel directed Phoebe to the Quaise cottage. Phoebe saw Addison's car and Tess's car. She either figured it out from just that, or she peeked in the window (which was too awful to imagine, so scratch that part). She didn't tell anyone. She didn't tell Delilah, she didn't confront Tess or Addison. She had spent the spring under a blanket of heavy medication; possibly the reality hadn't registered.

Or she didn't care.

Or she saw things for what they were. She, Phoebe, had become a pharmaceutical wasteland. She had been incapable of any real emotional connection with Addison for eight years. After

Reed died on 9/11, she had disappeared. And for those eight years Addison had stood by her. He supported her and worried about her; he flushed pills and went with her to see Dr. Field. He kept her comfortable; he relieved her of all responsibility. He paid the house cleaners double, he learned to like takeout food, he took her on vacations where they stayed at the finest hotels, he kept their social life alive, he made excuses for her when she passed out in her soup or when she blanked out in the middle of a conversation. He kept her safe; he carried her up mountains and across rivers. He gave a hundred thousand dollars to Reed's scholarship fund and put another hundred thousand into trust for Domino. He went to hours and hours of grief counseling, where Phoebe either cried uncontrollably or sat in a stupor. He gave up all dreams of having a baby. The miscarriage, which also occurred on 9/11, was an accident, caused by extreme stress. Phoebe could get pregnant again, with ease. But no, she wouldn't, she didn't want to. She wouldn't let Addison touch her.

And he had lived with that, for years and years.

And then Tess came to him, or he went to Tess, it was a mutual discovery, they were in love.

Maybe Phoebe understood this. Maybe—God, was it possible?—she approved.

Addison remembered back to when he met Phoebe. She was lying on a towel in Bryant Park. She had been wearing a short, flowered sundress, eating salad out of a plastic container. Addison felt like he had found a diamond bracelet lying in the grass. He remembered his astonishment. You mean something this beautiful doesn't belong to anyone?

He'd snapped her up. All these years later, he'd held on.

Oh, Phoebe.

He unlocked his top desk drawer, where he had stashed Tess's iPhone. It was time to stop hiding things; he would give the phone to the Chief. And there, in his top drawer, was an envelope with his name on it. In Tess's handwriting. Holy hell! Tess's handwriting? It sure looked like it. Addison looked around. Florabel was on the phone again, whispering with one of her girlfriends.

Addison opened the envelope, and there was a note inside. It said: *I am going back to Greg and my kids. I will explain my reasons when I get home. Please know you will always have a piece of my heart. Tess.*

He folded the note back up, slid it into the envelope, and put it in the drawer.

He sat in a bubble for . . . well, he wasn't sure how long.

Florabel was snapping at him again. "Dealer! What about helping Phoebe pick up the cocktail napkins? Are you going?"

He looked at Florabel, who was the only person with a key to his desk drawer. He opened the drawer and pulled out the envelope. "Did you put this here?"

She sighed in a way that seemed almost sympathetic. "I did."

"Where did you get it?"

"I found it weeks ago," Florabel said. Now her voice contained an uncharacteristic element: guilt. "I found it in the Quaise cottage, back when you first gave me the listing. And then, swear to God, Addison, I *completely* forgot about it. I just found it again last night when I was cleaning my desk. Is it important?"

Addison shrugged. The phone rang, and Florabel seemed eager to answer it. Well, either she was lying, which she never did, or she was telling the truth and had "forgotten" it, which she would never do, and had "found" it when she was "cleaning her desk," which she never did because her desk was always immaculate. Florabel had been holding on to the letter until she sensed Addison could handle it. She must have guessed who it was from and what it said. Possibly she'd even opened it and sealed it back up without a sign of tampering. Possibly Florabel had been not only a cheerleader but a CIA operative.

I'm afraid you won't get it. The note. She had left it there for him to find on Sunday, when he normally went to the Quaise cottage to change the sheets and straighten up. But he hadn't gone on that Sunday because the $9.2 million Polpis Harbor deal had come through, and then the next day Tess died. So Florabel had found the note instead.

Was it important? *Please know you will always have a piece of my heart.* He pulled out the three pieces of frayed red felt and laid them on his desk blotter. Which piece?

He gathered the pieces up, stuffed them deep in his pocket, and headed out to the savannah to help his wife.

JEFFREY

As he stood on the wharf waiting for the ferry to dock, he could have had any number of thoughts, but for whatever reason, he found himself remembering the afternoon he had been shot.

It had been seventeen years earlier, in the frantic but emotionally dry period of his life after Andrea left him but before he met Delilah. He was a one-man show at the farm at that point; he did everything himself.

In the late fall he was turning over the land where he had harvested pumpkins. The furrows were scattered with busted-open pumpkins like split skulls, spilling out seeds and pulp. The pumpkin patch was in the southwestern corner of the farm, bordering the thick pines along Hummock Pond Road. Jeffrey was on the plow, watching as the pumpkin remains were turned over, back into the soil to nurture it. He heard a noise and thought the plow had encountered a rock—and the next thing he knew, he was falling off the plow into the dirt. He groaned. There was an incredible searing pain in his side; he felt as though his shirt had caught fire. What the hell? He felt like his mind was being sucked through a tunnel at warp speed. He touched his side where the pain was and lifted his hand. Blood. His shirt was soaked with it. What the hell? He had no idea. He blacked out.

A passerby called 911 and Jeffrey woke up to a couple of female EMTs lifting him onto a stretcher and sliding him, like a loaf of bread into an oven, into the back of an ambulance.

"You've been shot," one of the EMTs said. She had cut away his flannel work shirt and was inspecting his wound. "Someone was after a deer."

He tried to lift his head but found he could not.

He stayed at the hospital for three days. Three days that he couldn't afford to lose, but what could he do? He'd been shot, as surely as if he'd served in the Gulf War or been caught in the crossfire in Morningside Heights.

The day after he'd been shot, a policeman walked into his hospital room. This seemed unremarkable at first; someone had mentioned that the police wanted to talk to him. What ended up being remarkable was that the policeman was Edward Kapenash, the new chief. They were short-staffed at the station, so the Chief was handling this himself.

"Besides," the Chief said to Jeffrey, "it's not every day that someone on Nantucket gets shot."

Jeffrey took an instant dislike to the guy, not only because of that comment but because he realized that this guy, Ed Kapenash, was Andrea's boyfriend.

Jeffrey said, "You're Andrea's boyfriend?"

"Fiancé," he said. "I asked her to marry me two weeks ago." He took a small notebook out of his breast pocket, eager to get down to business. "Do you know Andrea?"

"I'm Jeffrey Drake," Jeffrey said, though he would have figured the Chief already knew his name.

The Chief lowered his notebook and said in a tone of voice that could only be described as warily interested, "Oh, I see."

The two men took stock of each other in the deadly silent moment that followed. Jeffrey lamented how unfair it was that he was lying prostrate in bed with a gunshot wound while the Chief stood by the bed in his starched uniform with his gleaming badge.

"Well, anyway, congratulations. Andrea is a wonderful girl."

"Yes," the Chief said. "She sure is."

Another moment of silence followed, during which Jeffrey thought, *You'd better take good care of her.*

The Chief said, "So! Tell me what happened."

The ferry sluiced through the green water of Nantucket Harbor. It was a beautiful, bright, still afternoon and Jeffrey had to squint, but he picked out Delilah and the kids on the foredeck. His heart settled. Thank God.

When Delilah had called from her cell phone at eight-thirty that morning, Jeffrey had barely been able to contain his rage. "Where *are* you?" he said.

"Cobleskill, New York."

He ground his back molars together to keep from shouting. He said, "What are you doing in Cobleskill, New York?"

She said, "We took a little detour. But don't worry, we're coming home."

This does not mean I don't love you, I do, that's forever.

He said, "When?"

She said, "We'll be on the three o'clock ferry."

"The ferry?" he said. "Why don't you just fly home?"

She proceeded to tell him about the time she ran away in high school. It was a story he'd heard numerous times before—she realized this, right?—and he was about to interrupt her when she said, "The one thing I think about, even now, is how I wished back then that someone were standing on the dock waiting for me."

Delilah and the kids waved from the bow of the boat. Jeffrey waved back. Delilah always said that people were predictable, that they could be counted on to act exactly like themselves. She wanted someone standing on the dock waiting for her.

And here he was.

THE CHIEF

He waited a few weeks to let the dust settle, and then he called a meeting.

Everyone agreed: they had things to talk through. Strange, difficult, secret things.

Where to meet? The Chief wanted them all to meet in the conference room at the station, but Andrea said, "Good God, Ed, no."

Addison suggested the opposite end of the spectrum—the Begonia—but that was shot down immediately.

Delilah offered to have everyone over to her house after the kids were asleep. They agreed on ten o'clock. Delilah lit candles and set out hummus and olives and Marcona almonds and fresh figs and soft cheese. All of them sat around the table as they would have to play Scrabble. The house was silent except for the sound of their breathing.

The Chief said, "Okay, then."

And it all came out, like stuffing from a pillow.

Addison in love with Tess. *Are you going to tell him? Are you going to tell him you love me?*

Greg's continuing relationship with April Peck. *I was with him the night before he died.*

Delilah seeing Greg parked at Cisco Beach with April Peck but not telling Tess.

Phoebe giving Tess a black market opiate.

Andrea and Jeffrey meeting in the farm attic.

Tess leaving a letter for Addison. *I'm going back to Greg and the kids.*

The Chief meeting with April Peck. *He said he loved his wife. He wrote her a song.*

"Beyond Beyond." The song's title was taken from a poem, apparently.

And then, seemingly apropos of nothing, Andrea said, "And I didn't become a nun."

The Chief covered her hand with his own. "Thank God," he said.

"We all blame ourselves," the Chief said. Even he, the chief of police, held himself accountable; he could have confronted the Greg and April Peck situation back in February but had chosen to turn a blind eye. "If you look at what we know, it went like this. Greg was going back to Tess, Tess was going back to Greg. Greg had written her a song, Tess had agreed to a sail. They drank champagne, they ate their picnic lunch, and Tess took the pill—because it was windy on the water that afternoon, the seas were rough, and she was scared. The Coast Guard report, corroborated by evidence from the medical examiner, is calling this an accident. Tess and Greg were drinking, Tess was loopy from the pill, Greg was not a good enough sailor to be out on the water under those conditions, the boat capsized, and they drowned. From the injuries sustained, it looks like they were trying to save each other."

The candlelight flickered. Delilah placed her index fingers along the sides of her nose. "They were trying to save each other," she said.

"They were trying to save each other," Addison said.

"It was an accident," the Chief said. "It was nobody's fault."

"It was *nobody's* fault," Andrea said.

"Forgiveness is a powerful thing," the Chief said. "I forgive myself, and I forgive each of you. I forgive Tess and Greg. But we have a job ahead of us. We have two kids to raise. Chloe and Finn are going to live with Andrea and me, but it's going to take all of us to help turn them into healthy, productive adults. It's going to take all of us to love them the way their parents would have. Okay?"

"Okay," the table echoed.

Jeffrey said, "I think we should have a moment of silence."

"Agreed," the Chief said. And for a long time they were quiet. Andrea and Phoebe had their heads bowed; Delilah stared out the dark window. Addison took off his glasses and pressed his eyes.

Then Jeffrey cleared his throat. "Thank you," he said.

The Chief nodded, and reached for a chip. Delilah turned on music: Stevie Wonder singing "I Believe." Andrea said, "Can I please have a glass of chardonnay?"

And then Phoebe stood up. "Wait a minute," she said. "Wait a *minute!*"

They all stopped.

Phoebe said, "Addison and I have something to tell you."

EPILOGUE

PHOEBE

She paid the money, she okayed the landscape architect and the signage, she monitored the progress, tramping out to the savannah even on brutally cold winter days, and she picked the day of the ribbon-cutting. June 20: the one-year anniversary of Greg and Tess's death, the anniversary of their anniversary.

Chloe and Finn were going to cut the ribbon, and all of them—the Chief, Andrea, Kacy and Eric, Jeffrey, Delilah, Drew and Barney, Addison, Phoebe, and their baby, Reed Gregory Wheeler, age four weeks, two days, confined to a Baby Bjorn—were going to walk the trail for a ceremonial first time.

It happened exactly as Phoebe had imagined it. Chloe and Finn cut a yellow satin ribbon at the head of the trail (which meant that Chloe cut and Finn stretched out his hand to make it look like he was cutting), and the forty-seven Nantucket citizens present clapped politely (and yes, some cried).

Phoebe stood with baby Reed asleep against her chest and watched as Andrea, the Chief, Addison, Jeffrey, and Delilah read the sign.

**The Gregory MacAvoy and
Tess DiRosa MacAvoy Memorial Trail
Donated with love by the Castaways**

The Chief turned and smiled. Drew and Barney and Finn raced ahead on the trail, yelping like Indians. Chloe asked if she could pick wildflowers, and Phoebe said, "This is conservation land. Do you know what that means?"

Chloe said, "Does it mean no flowers?"

"Well, maybe just one," Phoebe said. "Since it is your mom and dad's trail."

Chloe smiled and bounded ahead to catch the boys.

Just as Phoebe had imagined it, it was a beautiful day.

DELILAH

You didn't expect her to let Phoebe have the last word, did you?

There was one last story to tell. And really, it wasn't the *last* story, at least not chronologically. But it might have been the most important story, in some elusive way.

In one of the middle years, they took a trip to Sayulita, Mexico. Sayulita was on the west coast, north of Puerto Vallarta. It was unspoiled paradise—sugar-sand beaches, great rolling waves, lush green cliffs towering above. The town was a cross between

Spanish colonial architecture and a funky expat enclave. There were coffeeshops and taco stands and chickens in the street. They had rented a four-bedroom house built into the side of one of the lush green cliffs. There was a stone path that led from town to their house; it was a steep walk that left them all winded, but then astounded by the view from their upper deck. The house was a study in simplicity; it had arched doorways and outdoor showers and was kept cool by lazy ceiling fans and thick walls of stucco. There was a brick patio and an oval saltwater pool. There was a hibiscus bush in the yard, which delighted Tess no end; she had a peachy-pink blossom tucked in her hair all week, and as a joke, the rest of them walked around with hibiscus blossoms protruding from one of their nostrils or their cleavage or their fly.

The trip to Sayulita had been their best trip, Delilah saw now, because it wasn't about the flash and cash of Vegas, or the important sights of London, or the hipster scene of South Beach. It had been barefoot and carefree; they were eight individuals allowing one another to be individuals, and yet coming together as a whole that was greater than the sum of its parts. Delilah's memories of Sayulita glowed. She remembered strolling in town with Andrea, Tess, and Phoebe, each of them buying a pareo from a wizened woman with tobacco-stained teeth. They wore the pareos all week over their bathing suits. They bought fish tacos from a twelve-year-old boy and his mother. These tacos remained the best thing Delilah had ever eaten. The fish was snapper, caught in the early morning by the husband/father and marinated in oil, lime juice, garlic, and chiles, and then grilled on a hibachi that was attached to the cart. The grilled fish was wrapped in a handmade tortilla with fresh tomato, chopped iceberg, chunks of creamy avocado, crumbled white cheese that had no name other than *queso,* and the whole thing was drizzled with a tangy lime crema. The tacos were ten bites of nirvana, a mouthful so delicious that Delilah would shake at night with cravings, and the taco cost seventy-five cents.

Phoebe was partial to banana shakes. Andrea and the Chief adored the carne asada from a cart a block away. Greg bought a bottle of *tequila especiale* from a man who loitered outside the grocery. Everyone was certain that the tequila would kill them, but the man had brainwashed Greg that it was indeed *mucho especiale,* even though the bottle cost only two dollars. "The guy said it can cure *cancer!*" They made margaritas from the tequila, using limes from the tree in their yard, and they all acquired a buzz that moved from silver to gold. It was magic tequila! In the morning they felt happy and light, healthier than they had the day before. Could they import the stuff and make a fortune?

They lay around the pool in a human chain, sharing books; Andrea ripped her paperback in half and gave Delilah the beginning while she finished the end. The Chief got up early every morning and spotted whales offshore with his binoculars. Andrea wanted to learn to surf, and she convinced Addison to go with her. The other six watched the surf lesson from the beach. They felt proud of Andrea; she was such a gifted swimmer, a natural on the board. They cheered Addison on; the dude was not gifted, but he was a good sport. When he finally stood up and rode a wave, they gave him a standing ovation.

There was one night that stood out in Delilah's mind, though she couldn't remember if it was their third night or their fifth night or their seventh. They were drinking the bewitching margaritas, they were watching the sun sink into the water, Greg was strumming his guitar, Tess had a hibiscus in her hair. Jeffrey was sunburned, Addison was sore from his surfing lesson. Phoebe had wrapped her pareo in a way that made it a fetching dress. The Chief had been on a secret errand in town. He'd cut a deal with the fisherman and came back with a bag full of marinating snapper and all of the other fixings for the fish tacos. Delilah would make them!

Margaritas, fish tacos, tiki torches, the eight of them sitting around the outdoor table in their usual order. They played

Scrabble using only Spanish words, then it got too dark to see the tiles and none of them properly spoke Spanish anyway, so they switched to cards, but they were so high from the magic tequila that all they could handle was Go Fish. They abandoned the cards and Greg played his guitar and they sang Peter, Paul & Mary songs—"If I Had a Hammer," "Leavin' on a Jet Plane," "Blowin' in the Wind"—until they all agreed it was time for bed. Tomorrow was another day.

The couples floated into the house, holding hands.

Jeffrey and Delilah.

Phoebe and Addison.

Eddie and Andrea.

Tess and Greg.

They headed to their own rooms.

Closed the door.

Climbed into bed.

And turned off the light.

Good night.

ACKNOWLEDGMENTS

My deepest thanks to Christine Smith, for saving my life.

Reading Group Guide

The Castaways

A Novel

by

Elin Hilderbrand

A CONVERSATION WITH
ELIN HILDERBRAND

Was there anything in particular that sparked the story for The Castaways *in your mind?*

It kind of came to me whole: What if there were four close-knit couples and one of those couples died? The rest of the novel unfolded from there. The most interesting thing was starting the novel with all of my characters finding out that Tess and Greg were dead. It was a very dramatic way to begin. This is probably also the place where I should say: My husband, Chip, and I do have very close friends here on Nantucket, and we do count them not only as friends but as family. We have even been to Las Vegas with some of them! However, no real people are represented in my books—ever.

Did you have the characters' relationships completely laid out when you started the novel, or did you let some of the stories develop as you wrote?

My characters always develop as I write. Once I get into their heads, they take over. Most always, I don't know what's going to happen until I sit down that day to write.

The Castaways *is written in six distinct voices. Is it difficult to write the story from the point of view of so many different characters? What are some challenges and benefits of telling the story in this manner?*

Well, obviously, it allows the story to be told in six ways, from six perspectives, so that the reader gleans information he wouldn't have with a single narrator. I loved all eight of my characters and relished the opportunity to "be" all of them. They were all so different that I had no problem channeling them in distinct ways. When I was the Chief, I was not confusing him with Phoebe.

Who is your favorite character in the novel, and why?

I think I identified the most with Delilah ... she and I share many characteristics. (For example, I cook all the time, and I am very active with my children. I also have something of a tempestuous and dramatic nature. I feel things very deeply.)

However, really, in my gut, my favorite character was Addison. He was just so charmingly flawed. He is the perfect example of a man who has every material thing a person could want, but who yearns for something more meaningful. And he tries so hard. He is filled with love and good intentions, even though he really can't get out of his own way.

My other favorite character was his receptionist, Florabel. She was a hoot to write, and every time I went in to revise, I kept giving her more air time because she was just so funny.

You have a twin brother, Eric, to whom the book is dedicated. Was your relationship with Eric the basis for the relationship between either set of twins in The Castaways?

Both and neither. My relationship with Eric is very close. Most days we're normal siblings. But then there are times when I feel more connected to him than anyone else in the world because he has, quite literally, been with me from the beginning. That sense of connectedness comes through in Finn and Chloe's relationship (and, yes, when we were seven years old, I was very much the dominant twin).

The relationship between Phoebe and Reed is idealized a bit for the sake of the novel. I will say that I got the idea of Reed dying in 9/11 from a true-life experience. On September 11, 2001, my own twin, Eric, was working at Salomon Smith Barney in downtown New York. His secretary called him from the Staten Island ferry to say that a plane had hit the World Trade Center. Eric and his coworkers ran down to the street and they watched the second plane hit. Eric called me at 9:10 (I saved the phone bill) and he was screaming into his phone that the world was going to end. And, in retrospect, he had reason. On that day, the world as we knew it ended. After Eric had walked uptown to safety, I urged him to write down his experience of that day. Because he had been there, he had seen it—and I knew it was going to be a critical moment in history.

There's a paragraph in the book that summarizes how each of your eight main characters came to live on Nantucket. What first brought you to the island, and what made you decide to make it your home?

I came to Nantucket in the summer of 1993 after breaking up with my boyfriend, whom I lived with in Manhattan. I wanted to go someplace completely different—the beach! So I got a room in a house on Nantucket. That summer, I met my husband-to-be, Chip, and we decided to make Nantucket our seasonal home. In 1994 I let my New York apartment go, I quit my job teaching at Dobbs Ferry Middle School, and I moved to Nantucket. For the first few winters, we traveled the world—Asia, Australia, South America. Then I went to the Writers' Workshop at the University of Iowa. And it was while I was in Iowa that I realized I couldn't live without the sand and the water. In 1998 we bought a house and moved to Nantucket for good.

On what project are you currently working? Do you ever struggle to come up with new story lines?

I am working on my new novel, entitled *Silver Girl*, which is based on a fictional character not unlike Ruth Madoff. My main character's name is Meredith Delinn. She is a Catholic who grew up on the Main Line in Philadelphia, and she marries a boy she met at Princeton named Freddy Delinn, who has just been arrested for running a $50 billion Ponzi scheme that left thirteen thousand people destitute. Because it is *my* novel, Meredith is a lovely, sympathetic, deeply wounded woman, and she has a best friend from childhood who calls her and rescues her by bringing her to a secluded beach house on Nantucket. It's fascinating for me to take a real story and turn it into my own fictional work. I do have a string of ideas for novels, but the Ruth Madoff thing grabbed me because I believe it's likely that her situation is nuanced and complicated beyond anyone's understanding.

What books are you currently reading? In what ways do your favorite authors influence your writing?

My list of favorite authors never changes: Jane Smiley, Lorrie Moore, Richard Russo, Tim Winton, the late great J. D. Salinger, Toni Morrison. Recently, I have enjoyed the work of both Stewart O'Nan and Ward Just. But the best book I've read in the past twelve months is *Appointment in Samarra* by John O'Hara. A forgotten classic! I am a voracious reader; I consider reading to be as much a part of my job as writing, because I get inspired by other people's stories and their use of language. It makes me excited to sit down and write myself.

QUESTIONS AND TOPICS
FOR DISCUSSION

1. The novel opens with the tragic death of Tess and Greg MacAvoy; as it develops, we see how the lives of their six best friends are forever altered. How do you think the relationships of each couple within the group would have developed if Tess and Greg had not died on their sailing trip?

2. The heart of the novel explores the dynamics of a close-knit group of four couples, the complexities of their friendships, and how they get along with each other. What are the dynamics like in your circle of friends? Have you faced similar struggles?

3. *The Castaways* is set mainly on the island of Nantucket. How does this setting contribute to the story's insular nature as the novel portrays a tight-knit group of four couples?

4. The novel occasionally leaves the Nantucket setting to travel back in time to the group vacations taken by the Castaways. Discuss the importance of the setting for each of these trips and how it plays a part in the development of the characters and the plot.

5. Hilderbrand describes how each of her eight main characters came to live on Nantucket. Which characters seem the most at home on the island? Discuss the factors that brought you to settle where you live now.

6. *The Castaways* is told from multiple points of view. With which character did you feel the most connected, and why? Did that change in the course of the story?

7. The surviving members of the Castaways are all grieving in their own way after losing two of their best friends. Discuss how grief manifests itself in each character and how each handles that grief. How have you handled grief in your own life?

8. Delilah says at one point that honesty should be met with honesty, yet then she makes an important decision not to share the truth. Discuss the role of honesty and dishonesty in the novel and the ways in which moral ambiguity creates conflict for the characters.

9. By the end of *The Castaways*, grieving has led many of the characters to reach an acceptance of the tragedy and an absolution in their lives. Discuss how each character achieves this absolution and learns to move forward.

10. What do you think the future holds for the three surviving couples and their children?

THE CASTAWAYS COCKTAIL:
THE SURFSIDER

Named after the town in Nantucket that is also home to Surfside Beach, this cocktail is a spin on the classic Southside cocktail (2 oz. gin, 1 oz. lemon, ½ oz. simple syrup, fresh mint), which is a requisite cooler for any beachside vacation.

    4 lemon verbena leaves
    4 cucumber slices
    ½ oz. lemon juice
    ½ oz. simple syrup
    1.5 oz. G'Vine "Floraison" gin
    ice
    club soda
    3 dashes A. B. Smeby "Summer Verbena" bitters

Quickly muddle the verbena and cucumber with the lemon juice and simple syrup. Add the gin and ice and shake. Pour contents into a highball glass and top with soda. Finish with 3 dashes lemon verbena bitters.
Garnish with cucumber wheel.

A Note on G'Vine Gin

G'Vine is a French gin based out of Cognac. Most gin products are, at their core, distilled from grain. The unique thing about G'Vine gin is that it is made from neutral grape spirit, from the wine of Ugni Blanc grapes. Ugni Blanc is also known as a Trebbiano and is used in the brandies of Cognac and Armagnac. In addition, the gin is infused with the flowering Ugni Blanc blossoms, which are picked before they turn into grape berries. This period is called "Floraison," hence the name. Nine botanicals are distilled separately (ginger root, licorice, green cardamom, cassia bark, coriander, juniper berries, cubeb berries, nutmeg, and lime) and then blended with the base and distilled one final time. The result is a unique gin that is quite smooth due to the grape distillate and floral in a similar vein as Hendrick's.

Created at The Modern by Ehren Ashkenazi. For more delicious cocktails, see *Mix Shake Stir: Recipes from Danny Meyer's Acclaimed New York City Restaurants.*

ABOUT THE AUTHOR

Elin Hilderbrand lives year-round on Nantucket, where she enjoys going to the beach, cooking for her young adult children, and occasionally dancing in the front row at the Chicken Box. You can listen to her podcast, *Books, Beach & Beyond,* at booksbeachandbeyond.com.

. . . AND HER MOST RECENT NOVEL

Elin Hilderbrand revisits some of the characters from *The Castaways* in her new novel, *Swan Song.* Following is an excerpt from the novel's opening pages.

PROLOGUE

Thursday, August 22, 6:00 p.m.

Rumors about Nantucket Police chief Ed Kapenash's retirement have been swirling around for the past two years, though when asked directly, the Chief said, "I'm far too busy to contemplate retirement." However, three days after the Big Scare in February, Ed told his wife, Andrea (from his hospital bed at Mass General), "That's it, I'm finished, I'll just stay on through the summer while we find someone to replace me."

"Another *summer*, Ed?" Andrea cried out. She was shaken — and for good reason.

Ed had been giving a safety talk in the gymnasium of Nantucket Elementary when his left arm started to tingle. He felt short of breath, his vision splotched — and the next thing he knew, he was being loaded onto a medevac chopper and flown to MGH for emergency bypass surgery.

"You had the kind of heart attack we call the widow-maker," Dr. Very Important said. "A full blockage of your LAD artery. You were lucky the paramedics were right there. Otherwise this could have ended differently."

Yes, the fire chief — Stu Vick — and EMTs from his department had been in the school gym as well, waiting for their turn to speak, when Ed hit the floor.

As Dr. Big Shot gave Ed a lecture about exercise, diet, and, above all, *stress,* Ed gauged Andrea's reaction to the term *widow-maker.*

Not good.

"You should retire *now,*" Andrea said. "You might not survive another summer." She looked at Dr. Master of the Universe because she needed him to hear the backstory. "Ed has been admitted to the Nantucket hospital three times in the past two years for chest pain. They wanted to send him up here for testing but he *refused.*"

Ed sighed. He'd married a tattletale. But also, Ed felt guilty. Had he played fast and loose with his health? Yes. Could he just give two weeks' notice and leave the public safety of the island up for grabs? He could not.

He would retire in the fall.

Now here it is, August 22, and the Chief is celebrating: His last official day of duty is Monday, August 26. His replacement, Zara Washington, was the deputy chief in Oak Bluffs on Martha's Vineyard, so she understands island life as well as Ed does. Zara has moved into her housing, and after two weeks of shadowing Ed, she is eager to take over. Andrea has planned a big retirement party for Ed at the Oystercatcher in a couple of weeks and there will be some official hoopla arranged by Governor Healey. But for now, the Chief is enjoying a night out with his people: Andrea; his son, Eric; Eric's girlfriend, Avalon; his and Andrea's best friends, Addison and Phoebe Wheeler and Jeffrey and Delilah Drake; and Ed's daughter, Kacy, a NICU nurse who moved back from California this summer. Kacy had intended to bring her friend Coco as her plus-one but... Coco works as the "personal concierge" for the Richardsons, a couple whom Ed and Andrea (and the Wheelers and the Drakes) became acquainted with this summer, and when Ed opted not to include the Richardsons in tonight's dinner, the Richardsons turned around and threw a sunset sail on their yacht, *Hedonism*—and so Coco has to work.

"I guess everyone has abandoned the Richardsons," Kacy said. "Coco didn't recognize the names on the guest list—they're mostly strangers."

Strangers who evidently hadn't been warned about the Richardsons, Ed thought. Some weird things had happened this summer.

Back in June, the Richardsons were a hot commodity; they'd nearly become part of "the Castaways," which is what the Kapenashes and the Wheelers and the Drakes call their friend group (because they all "washed ashore" on Nantucket decades earlier). Part of the appeal of the Richardsons was that they were younger, still in their forties. The Castaways, Ed in particular, had been feeling their middle age.

For tonight's dinner, Ed chose Ventuno, a restaurant housed in one of the historic residences downtown, and Andrea reserved the entire upstairs for them.

They ascend a narrow wooden staircase and find their table draped with white linen and lit by candles near the windows that overlook the charming brick sidewalks of Federal Street. All their guests have already arrived.

Ed takes his seat at the oval table and reminds himself to appreciate the things that Andrea accuses him of missing: the crystal wineglasses, the low centerpiece of dahlias and roses, the fact that Eric has worn a tie without being asked. The air smells of garlic and herbs; Tony Bennett croons in the background. This is exactly the evening Ed wanted—and yet he can't help but feel melancholy. The summer is ending, and so is his career.

After Addison assesses the wine list—it's long been his job to serve as their sommelier—he catches Ed's eye over the top of the menu.

"There's no time to get in your feelings, Ed," he says. "A bold yet subtle Barolo awaits."

The wine, Ed has to admit, tastes divine even to his unsophisticated palate (left to his own devices, he's a beer drinker), though he holds himself to half a glass. What he's really interested in tonight is food. Andrea is seated next to him but she's whispering with Phoebe and Delilah about the Richardsons. *They couldn't leave it alone; they had to one-up us!*

The Chief is going to use his wife's obsession with the Richardsons to his advantage. He does some ordering for the table—two fritto mistos, the farfalle with crab and local corn (sourced from Jeffrey and Delilah's farm), the strozzapreti with sausage and broccoli rabe, the ricotta crostini, the stuffed clams.

"Ed," Andrea says in a warning tone. Andrea is the police chief now, at least where Ed's diet is concerned.

Ed throws in an order of the giardiniera and a Caesar salad. He waits until Andrea turns away, then says to the server, "For the main course, the Fiorentina." This is the finest steak on the island; Ed dreams about it the way some men dream about Margot Robbie. It's a thirty-three-ounce porterhouse served with roasted rosemary potatoes. Ed pushes away thoughts of the salt, the fat, his heart. At home, it's been chicken, fish, and vegetables for the past six months.

When the steak arrives sizzling on the platter—the scent is enough to bring Ed to his knees—he helps himself to two rosy-pink pieces. This might be what kills him, but what a way to go.

Andrea notices the fried shrimp and squid, the helpings of pasta, and the rare steak, but she zips her lip. She's proud of Ed—he's lost thirty-five pounds, started jogging three mornings a week, switched to decaf coffee, stopped going to the Nickel four times a week for lunch (the shrimp po'boy is his kryptonite), and he's at least pretending to meditate ten minutes each day. Andrea is also relieved that they made it to the end of the summer without any major incidents. That's not to say the summer was boring—*au contraire*! The moment Phoebe introduced them to Addison's new clients the Richardsons, their summer became a blur of lunches at the Field and Oar Club, pickleball, sailing excursions, and parties, parties, parties. Andrea hasn't had a summer like this since before her kids were born. For most of the summer, the Richardsons seemed like a gift sent from the heavens to remind them that they weren't too old to have fun.

But when Andrea thinks about the Richardsons now, she...no, she won't let them live rent-free in her head. She'll just feel happy that Ed is enjoying his steak.

Addison makes a toast. "To our fearless leader!" Everyone raises a glass; Ed is honored but also a little embarrassed. He drinks his red wine—he thinks Addison might have refilled his glass without his noticing—and suddenly, he grows reflective.

He moved to Nantucket from Swampscott thirty-five years earlier when the chief of police position opened. People had warned him that policing on an island would be different than on the mainland. It was like a small town except that it was thirty miles out to sea, so there was no getting away. This has been tricky enough to navigate even in the off-season, and during Ed's tenure, the year-round population has doubled. But come June, the island explodes with summer residents, short-term renters, and day-trippers, some of whom feel inclined to rent mopeds despite not having a clue how to operate them. There's traffic to deal with, scores of parking tickets on the daily, kids from the cities and fancy suburbs with their designer drugs and entitled attitudes giving his officers lip.

Beyond that, there's real trouble—domestics, vandalism, drunk driving, overdoses, accidental deaths. Ed worked a case out in Monomoy half a dozen years earlier that he still believes was murder, though they never quite figured it out.

Their server shows up with a dessert sampler for the table—an apple crostata with cinnamon gelato, baba au rhum, and cannoli.

Phoebe takes a bite of the crostata and says, "This tastes like fall."

"Blasphemy," Delilah says. "There's still an entire month of summer left."

Ed is considering a cannoli, but he's afraid he's pushed the limits of his diet far enough. Andrea is the one who places a cannoli on his plate, her cheeks flushed from the wine. She leans over and kisses him on the lips, a good kiss, one that promises more later. "It's your special night."

Ed gazes around the table, and his eyes land on Kacy. She looks wistful, maybe even lonesome; she keeps checking her phone. *It's funny,* the Chief thinks. *No matter how old your kids get, you still worry about them.* Kacy and Coco were close all summer, a Millennial Laverne and Shirley, but things between them seem to have cooled. When the Chief asked Andrea if Kacy and Coco had a falling-out, Andrea said, "They're grown women, Ed." Whatever *that* meant.

After coffee is served, there's another surprise. Their server turns up the music — Harry Connick Jr. singing "It Had to Be You" — and moves the other tables so they have room to dance. Andrea takes Ed's hand. "Come on, Chief, let's show them how it's done."

Phoebe and Addison join them on the improvised dance floor, then Jeffrey and Delilah. In that moment, the word *retirement,* a term that previously evoked only dread for the Chief, seems filled with promise. The weight of the island's problems will be lifted from his shoulders. He and Andrea can travel; he'll be able to go out fishing on Eric's charter boat whenever he wants — maybe he'll even take a job as Eric's first mate. They'll enjoy other nights like this when the Chief can have more than half a glass of wine.

He'll be free.

"Are you sure you won't get sick of me hanging around all the time?" he asks Andrea. Before she can answer, Ed's phone buzzes in his pocket.

Andrea groans. "Please just let it go."

He checks the screen. It's the station, line four, which means it's an emergency.

"I'm sorry," Ed says. "I have to—"

He steps off the dance floor, lifts the phone to one ear, and plugs his other ear with two fingers. It's his dispatcher, the aptly named Jennifer Speed, whom they just call Speed. The woman defines *efficiency*. "Do you want the bad news or the bad news?" she asks.

The Chief doesn't want any news and Speed knows it. He has one hundred hours left as Nantucket's police chief. "What is it?"

"There's a fire out in Pocomo," Speed says. "The NFD is on the scene. I talked to Stu, who says it's a total loss. Burned to the ground."

"Pocomo?" the Chief says. "It's not..."

"The Richardsons' house, yes, it is," Speed says. She pauses. "Was."

The Chief closes his eyes. He feels Andrea's hand on his back. "What else?" he says.

"Their assistant, woman by the name of Colleen Coyle?"

"Coco, yes," the Chief says. "I know her. She's a friend of Kacy's."

"Apparently the Richardsons were having a party on their yacht when someone called them about the smoke at their house, and they hightailed it back. The girl, Coco, was on the boat, but when they got back to the mooring, she was gone. As in, no longer on the boat."

"No longer on the boat?" the Chief says. "Where did she go?"

"Nobody knows," Speed says. "She's missing."

"Is she the only one?"

"As far as I know, everyone else on the boat is accounted for, and Captain..."

"Lamont?" the Chief says.

"Yes, Lamont Oakley called the harbormaster. The harbormaster called us."

The Chief turns back to the table. Kacy's face is bathed in blue light from her phone; she gasps and looks up at him. The *Nantucket Current* must have just broken the story.

"Thank you, Speed," he says. The Richardsons' house burned down, and Coco is missing? The Chief wants to believe this is a prank, a gotcha for his final days. But he knows it's real. If he's honest, he would admit he feared something awful like this would happen with the Richardsons. "Tell them I'm on my way."

1. THE COBBLESTONE TELEGRAPH

Most towns have a rumor mill. We here on Nantucket have what's known as the cobblestone telegraph—and Blond Sharon has long been the switchboard operator. *Everything* goes through her.

But this summer, a twist: Blond Sharon is now the topic of gossip. Everyone on the island is talking about how Blond Sharon's husband, Walker, left her for his physical therapist, a woman who is less than half Walker's age. Walker tore his ACL skiing over the holidays, and in March, he announced that he'd fallen in love with "Bailey from PT." He was leaving Sharon; he wanted a divorce.

Ouch, we thought. It's hardly a new story, a middle-aged man leaving his wife for a younger woman, but we thought Blond Sharon's family was bulletproof. Sharon is an exemplary mother. She secured her sixteen-year-old twin girls, Sterling and Colby, coveted internships at the Nantucket Historical Association (unpaid, but so good for their college applications). Sharon's thirteen-year-old son, Robert, has type 1 diabetes, and Sharon monitors his blood sugar using an app on her phone. We feel bad that Sharon has been dropped like a hot potato at the age of fifty-four, but none of us feel guilty talking about it. When we think of how many hours Blond Sharon has spent blabbing about other people's business, we can't help but see this moment as a kind of poetic justice.

The good news, we all think, is that Sharon has her sister, Heather, to lean on. Sharon and Heather are polar opposites: Sharon is blond and Heather is brunette; Sharon is a stay-at-home mom, Heather is an attorney with the corporate finance division of the SEC in Washington. Blond Sharon is like the flight attendant who overshares about the pilot's hemorrhoids and the famous talk-show host seated in 3C; Heather is the black box. The only thing Heather has ever done with a secret is keep it.

Heather is also the voice of reason. When Sharon admits that what bothers her most about Walker leaving her is being a cliché, Heather says, "Just promise not to wear statement necklaces and fake eyelashes and take cruises in the Mediterranean looking for a rich replacement husband."

Sharon blinks. That had been her plan exactly.

"This is your chance to reinvent yourself," Heather says. "Do you remember the quote you taped to your bedroom mirror when we were young?"

It wasn't a quote, Sharon thinks. It was the last two lines of the Mary Oliver poem "The Summer Day": *Tell me, what is it you plan to do / with your one wild and precious life?* Sharon discovered the poem one summer when she worked shelving books at the New Canaan Public Library. The lines, which Sharon typed out on her father's electric Smith Corona and taped to her bedroom mirror, had always seemed like a challenge—but when she thinks about it now, it feels like one she has failed to meet. She has spent her one wild and precious life selecting wallpaper and scheduling the pool cleaners; she has spent it reading *People* magazine in line at the market and fruitlessly trying to improve her backhand. She has spent it scrolling through her phone.

But there is something that Sharon has dreamed of doing, something we never would have guessed.

It has been Blond Sharon's secret lifelong desire to become an author.

Well, we think, she's certainly demonstrated her keen interest in other people's stories, the seedier and more salacious, the better. Since beloved local novelist Vivian Howe died a few years ago, there has been no one to write about the dramas that occur every summer on Nantucket. Could Blond Sharon take her place? Does she know the first thing about writing fiction?

Summer is a prime time to embark on a self-improvement project, Sharon thinks—and she signs up for a virtual creative-writing workshop. The instructor's name is Lucky Zambrano, which makes it sound like he's a Mob boss, but in fact, he's a recently retired Florida Atlantic University English professor. He tells his students that he's teaching this online class to keep busy because his wife passed away last year.

So Lucky is a widower, Sharon thinks. She sits up straighter and yanks at the bottom of her blouse to show a bit more cleavage. There are two other students in the Zoom class, both of them women and both about Sharon's age, though neither quite as well preserved as she is. One is named Willow, the other Nancy.

"Oh," Lucky says. "Nancy was my wife's name."

Does this give Nancy an advantage with Lucky? Sharon wonders. Nancy has one of those short, no-nonsense haircuts that means she's probably already married. Willow is wearing long feather earrings and has never seen a Botox needle.

"Let's get to your first assignment," Lucky says. "Character. What I'd like you to do is venture out into the world somewhere, could be your local farmers' market, your office building—Nancy, I see you work at the DMV, that's a fertile environment—and choose two individuals to observe. Then I'd like you to dramatize a scene between the two with an eye toward developing this scene into a story. The late great novelist John Gardner famously said that there are only two plots: One, a person goes on a journey, and two, a stranger comes to town." Lucky pauses and Sharon furiously scribbles on her legal pad. Sharon is hopelessly old-school; both Nancy and Willow type on their laptops. "Go forth and observe, then, my friends. We'll meet again next week and you can share what you've written with the group."

When Sharon clicks Leave Meeting, she's energized and, dare she say, inspired. She won't be one of those orange divorcées on a cruise ship; she's going to create a dazzling second act for herself as a published author. She snatches up her legal pad, ready to venture out into the world to observe. In a way, this has always been Sharon's mission—to find out what's really going on. But now she has a more noble mission. Now she's going to write about it.

Sharon plops herself down on a bench at the Steamship Authority ferry terminal. Where better to observe a person going on a journey or a stranger coming to town? Sharon wears her enormous Celine sunglasses and a white tennis visor, though those of us who are waiting for the ferry to arrive—notably Bob from Old Salt Taxi and Romeo, who works for the Steamship Authority—notice Sharon right away.

Why, Romeo wonders, does Blond Sharon have a notebook and pen at the ready? He can't think of a single reason, but Romeo loves a mystery...especially one that involves a beautiful woman.

As soon as Sharon gets settled, the boat pulls in. She scans the people coming down the ramp. Does anyone look promising? No, no, no; it's all day-trippers, the women in roomy sundresses, the men in cargo shorts, everyone in ugly sensible shoes. Fanny packs, backpacks. Why is the casual traveler in America so decidedly unstylish?

Her eyes latch onto a young woman over by the luggage cart. She has a look not seen often on Nantucket—she's like a human piece of art. Her black hair is short and cut in angles and spikes. She's wearing a tight black tank that leaves an inch of her midriff bare. She has a tattoo of a flamingo on her left shoulder and another that looks like a gecko just above her ankle. Sharon sees a gemstone sparkling in the girl's nose as she lifts a lumpy army-green duffel off the luggage cart. This person is more than a casual tourist; this is someone arriving for the summer.

A stranger comes to town! Sharon thinks. She abandons her spot on the bench and creeps over to get a closer look. Should she offer this girl a ride to wherever she's going? Sharon is about to tap the girl on the shoulder when a second young woman appears. This young woman has honey-colored hair cut in a neat, sassy bob and she's wearing slim white jeans and a fitted navy blazer. She hoists a brightly patterned Vera Bradley bag off the cart. Sharon has the exact same bag at home.

"Here, take my number, Coco," the second woman says. "Keep in touch, okay? Let me know where you end up staying."

"I'll figure it out," Coco says. "I always do. And hey, Kacy, thanks for the chowder—it meant a lot."

The second woman, Kacy, waves a hand as if to say *It was nothing.* She walks into the snarl of traffic in the parking lot. Coco's shoulders sag as she pulls out her phone. The poor girl has come to Nantucket with a giant duffel bag and doesn't have a place to stay? Sharon is about to offer to walk her over to Visitor Services to see about available hotel rooms—but then a couple of things happen in rapid succession. One is that a black Suburban pulls up, and Romeo from the Steamship opens the tailgate door and slides Kacy's suitcases into the back. It isn't Romeo's job to help with luggage, so Kacy must be some kind of VIP. A second later, Sharon realizes the person driving the Suburban is the chief of police, Ed Kapenash. The young woman must be his daughter. Yes! Kacy Kapenash! Last Sharon heard, she was working as a nurse out in San Francisco. She must be back for a visit.

The second thing that happens is that Sharon's phone rings. Inwardly, she groans. Before Walker left, Sharon's phone was attached to her ear; this had been one of Walker's major complaints (but how was Sharon supposed to get any news if she didn't chat?). In a few short months, Sharon has turned into a full-blown Millennial when it comes to talking on the phone—she'll do anything to avoid it.

The display says Fast Eddie. Eddie Pancik is Nantucket real estate royalty and Sharon's male counterpart in the gossip department. He's one of six people she'll answer her phone for.

"Edward," Sharon says.

"Hey there, beautiful," Eddie says. Eddie has, of course, heard the news about Walker trading Blond Sharon in for a younger model but he won't mention it. "I just closed on Triple Eight Pocomo Road. A couple appeared out of nowhere and offered the full asking price. Twenty-two mil."

What? Sharon thinks. The house at 888 Pocomo Road has been something of an albatross for Eddie. It's famous for its octagonal decks, and Jennifer Quinn recently gave the interior a complete cosmetic refresh (it was the last project she took on before *Real-Life Rehab,* her HGTV show, took off). But... Triple Eight sits right on the water, and, thanks to climate change, harbor levels have been rising each year, eating away at the property's small private beach. The forensic geologist reported that the first floor of the house would be underwater in eighty to a hundred years. Unfortunately, there's not enough land behind the house to move it back, and neighborhood bylaws prohibit lifting it up.

Who pays twenty-two million for a doomed house? Sharon wonders. Someone either stupid or crazy.

"I want to introduce you to the wife," Eddie says. "She's a self-described 'party animal.'"

Sharon cringes. *Party animal* brings to mind someone like Keith Richards in the 1970s, Rob Lowe in the 1980s. But Sharon could use a new friend, even a shortsighted one. *A stranger comes to town, part deux!* she thinks. "Great, feel free to give her my number."

"Already did," Eddie says. "She wants to join the Field and Oar Club."

There's no chance of that happening, as Eddie well knows, but instead of reminding him about the lengthy wait list and the nominating and seconding letters, Sharon says, "Proud of you, honey."

"Thanks, bae," Eddie says and he hangs up because he needs to get to the bank with his commission check. He's glad he called Sharon with this news before going. If Blond Sharon doesn't know about it, has it even happened?

During the short time that Sharon was on the phone, Kacy Kapenash has reappeared at the luggage cart; it seems she isn't finished with Coco. "I just talked to my dad, and he says it's fine if you stay in our guest room for a few days."

"You're kidding!" Coco says. "That's amazing—thank you, you're *such* a lifesaver." Coco follows Kacy to the waiting Suburban.

Sharon returns to her spot on the bench and scribbles down all the details she can remember, including the flamingo tattoo, the army-green duffel, the "I Love Rock 'n' Roll" haircut.

As she's describing the heartwarming scene between the two women, Romeo approaches; his large form casts a shadow on her page. "Hey, Sharon, what's up?"

Sharon glances at him. *Is Romeo single?* she wonders. "I'm writing a short story."

Romeo grins. How has Sharon never noticed how attractive he is? "Cool, can I be in it?"

"I'll have to think about that," Sharon says. "It's going to be pretty scandalous."

"*Scandalous* is my middle name," Romeo says.

Sharon writes in her notebook: *Romantic hero—Romeo Scandalous Steamship Guy?* It feels a little unlikely, but then she reminds herself that it's fiction—anything can happen.

LOOK FOR THE WINTER STREET SERIES BY
ELIN HILDERBRAND

Winter Street

"Open this diverting tale of family dysfunction, and you'll find a
holiday package filled with humor, romance, and realism."
— Jocelyn McClurg, *USA Today*

Winter Stroll

"Addictively readable…A slice of holiday life from a master of
domestic fiction."   — Susan Maguire, *Booklist*

Winter Storms

"A perfect mix of love, tears, and joy."
— Kathleen Gerard, *Shelf Awareness*

Winter Solstice

"Hilderbrand is a quality storyteller who keeps the reader riveted,
and her characters come alive on the page."   — *Publishers Weekly*

Back Bay Books • Available wherever paperbacks are sold